JAN BURKE

NINE

a novel of suspense

simon & schuster

new york london toronto sydney singapore

SIMON & SCHUSTER
Rockefeller Center
1230 Avenue of the Americas
New York, NY 10020

SIMON & SCHUSTER and colophon are registered trademarks of Simon & Schuster, Inc.

For information about special discounts for bulk purchases,
please contact Simon & Schuster Special Sales:
1-800-456-6798 or business@simonandschuster.com

Designed by Karolina Harris

Manufactured in the United States of America

10 9 8 7 6 5 4 3 2 1

Library of Congress Cataloging-in-Publication Data
Burke, Jan.
  Nine : a novel of suspense / Jan Burke.
    p. cm.
  1. Police—California—Los Angeles—Fiction.   2. Fugitives from justice—Fiction.
3. Los Angeles (Calif.)—Fiction.   4. Serial murders—Fiction.   5. Vigilantes—Fiction.
I. Title.
PS3552.U72326 N56 2002
813'.54—dc21   2002030212
ISBN 0-7432-2389-6

For my admired friends
John F. Mullins
and Barry A. J. Fisher
who fight the good fight
and, remarkably, still have a sense a humor.

NINE

prologue

His boss wanted to kill him.

Julio Santos let that thought run through his mind over and over again as he watched Bernardo Adrianos finish his meal. These last few days had been challenging for Julio, trying to behave naturally, to pretend that he was unaware that Adrianos wanted two of his bodyguards dead—Julio and Julio's partner, Ricky Calaban. Ricky was even worse at hiding his feelings. Julio had sent him outside a little while ago, afraid that he'd blow everything.

Adrianos leaned back from the table and belched. He was built like a bull. He wore his shoulder-length black hair in a ponytail. Ricky had once said that both of Adrianos's grandfathers were bald, and that Adrianos was just trying to grow out enough hair to make wigs for himself. Julio didn't know if that was true.

Adrianos was covered in tattoos, and you could see a big difference in the ones he got on the streets when he was a kid and the elaborate ones acquired after he had become wealthy—thanks to trading in drugs, whores, and similar business ventures. None of that bothered Julio. That was just giving the people what they wanted. But Adrianos had broken faith with Julio, and that was unforgivable.

Adrianos eyed Julio for a moment, and reading the look, Julio felt more certain than ever that Adrianos was wishing him dead. Maybe Adrianos had decided to kill him tonight. The irony of it made Julio smile. Adrianos narrowed his eyes, then reached into the pocket of his big, loose pants. Julio tensed, then saw that Adrianos was sticking to routine—the boss was holding a little pearl-handled knife. Adrianos opened the knife and used the tip of the blade to clean his fingernails.

Julio thought Adrianos's after-dinner manicure was a disgusting habit, but took some pleasure in knowing he would not have to witness it again. He forced himself to hide that pleasure.

Adrianos sighed. "It's not really all that great, with no one around."

No one here to kiss your ass, Julio thought, but he said, "At least you were able to get out for an evening, Mr. Adrianos."

"Fucking cops. I need to get out of L.A."

Julio made no reply.

Three days ago, when the two strangers had played the tape for him, Julio had seriously considered killing Adrianos—just blowing him away without worrying about what Adrianos's friends and business associates would do about it. The tape had been made from an illegal wiretap, the strangers told him. On it, Adrianos's voice was clearly identifiable. He bad-mouthed Julio and Ricky, and said that he was unhappy about the number of close calls he had experienced lately.

Julio's pride had been wounded. Adrianos had a temper that led him to behave recklessly, and he tended to get involved in matters that should have been left to others to handle—that sort of thing was exactly the kind of trouble that had put Adrianos on the FBI's Most Wanted list. If there had been close calls, the close calls were his own damned fault. Typically, though, Adrianos was shifting the blame.

The caller, whose voice Julio hadn't recognized, had asked Adrianos if he wanted the bodyguards to work for him in some other capacity, but Adrianos turned that idea down flat. "They'd be unhappy," Adrianos said. "And they know too much. You know what will happen if the FBI gets one of those two to testify against me? They have to disappear."

The more he had heard, the angrier Julio had become. Here he had risked his damned life twenty times over for the son of a bitch, and Adrianos was talking about putting a fucking contract out on him. Ricky felt the same.

But the strangers—who spoke fluent Spanish and had cautiously approached Ricky and Julio through their families—convinced them to calm down and listen to a proposition.

An extremely generous one.

The strangers would take care of Adrianos, and privately. Julio and Ricky weren't required to do much of anything—supply a small amount of information, such as the name of this restaurant, Adrianos's favorite. Tell them the name of the wine the boss usually drank. Subtly convince Adrianos that he could enjoy a meal at the restaurant on a night when it was usually closed. It had been easy.

They didn't let him in on all their plans for Adrianos or tell him why they were going to all this trouble. They were rich—Julio knew that much. And there were more than just the two involved in it. Maybe one of them had lost a kid brother or sister to drugs, or something like that. He didn't think they were connected to the Colombians or the Russians or any part of the mob. They called themselves some stupid-ass thing—Project Nine. Yeah. Whatever the hell that meant. Some vengeance deal, he was sure.

Julio didn't care about any of it, because they were helping him to get a step ahead of Adrianos. They had already shown their good faith by buying his mother a beautiful home in Mexico, in a place where she would be safe from retribution if things went wrong. But nothing had gone wrong yet. Julio thought there was something about these guys that said they were used to getting their way, and he had confidence in them.

Julio figured they were giving Adrianos some poison in the wine tonight or something in the food. As Adrianos cleaned his nails, Julio thought he saw the first signs that the poison might be kicking in. Adrianos's movements seemed slower than usual. He wondered if it really did take his boss longer than usual to work over all ten fingers, or if his own eagerness for the poison to take effect only made it seem so.

"I gotta drain the dragon," Adrianos said, lumbering to his feet. He swayed. "Had too much to drink." He slowly looked around the empty restaurant and said, "Where is everybody?"

"You have the place to yourself tonight, Mr. Adrianos, remember?"

"Oh . . . yeah. That's right." Slightly slurred. He frowned, then said, "I mean, where's Ricky and—"

"Ricky's watching the alley. Everybody else is in the kitchen, having a little dinner. You told them to, remember?"

"Oh, yeah." He faltered as he took a step forward. He gave Julio a hard look. "You didn't slip something into my wine, now, did you, Julio?"

"No, sir," Julio answered truthfully. "I've been sitting here, right across from you all evening, Mr. Adrianos. And you saw the waiter open the bottle. Your other team has been in the kitchen, keeping an eye on things there."

Adrianos seemed satisfied. He walked back to the bathroom, let Julio look around in it first, and then went in. Adrianos, the fucking weirdo, always wanted someone in the bathroom with him when he was taking a leak. "Wouldn't want to be caught with my pants down, now would I?" he was fond of saying. "Any public place, one of my bodyguards comes in with me. Always."

Julio hated this duty, but he never let Adrianos see any hint of that. Adrianos wasn't as stupid as he acted, and Julio had never met anyone who was as cruel as Adrianos could be when angered. The list of things that could make Julio feel queasy was short. There hadn't been anything on that list before he met Adrianos.

"Who was that waiter?" Adrianos asked as he opened his fly.

Julio prepared to out-and-out lie to his boss for the first time in the ten years he had worked for him. "The regular staff knows you, sir. We didn't want anyone to say they had seen you here. So—"

But he didn't have to finish the lie after all. Adrianos staggered, then fell face forward into the urinal, his jaw and forehead striking the chrome and porcelain with a loud crack. He didn't move.

Julio didn't either. Even though Adrianos had betrayed *his* trust, Julio didn't feel good about betraying Adrianos's in return. Julio considered himself to be a man of honor. He kind of thought of himself as a knight who had taken an oath to protect Adrianos, and here was his liege lord—lying facedown in the piss pan. Julio was surprised to find that his stomach was a little upset.

He heard a sound and whirled, his .45 out and aimed as the restroom door opened. A young man stepped in, his black boots loud on the tiled floor. He seemed oblivious to the weapon. Julio had seen him before, although he didn't know his name. Part of their agreement was that Julio would not learn his name. Julio reholstered the gun, one of two he wore during almost any waking hour. He had other means of attacking or defending as need be. This was no time to start being careless.

The young man had changed out of the clothes he had worn when pretending to be Adrianos's waiter this evening. The athletic shoes had been replaced by the boots, which made him seem even taller—Julio thought he might be six five or so in his stocking feet. The apron and white dress shirt had given way to a finely tailored black sports coat, long-sleeved silk turtleneck, and a pair of jeans. Easier now to see how muscular he was—playing the role of waiter, he had slouched and behaved subserviently, while now there was nothing of the servant in him, either in looks or posture.

Julio believed that under other circumstances, he would have been able to spot this man as a threat. How had Adrianos failed to notice that the hands of his waiter were so large and powerful? He was probably about five years younger than Julio, so was somewhere in his mid-twenties. Julio assessed him with a certain professional detachment, wondering if he could take him. He told himself he could but acknowledged that it would be experience that made the difference.

The kid had dark hair and a handsome, almost angelic face—until you looked into his eyes. How had Adrianos failed to noticed those eyes? Unless Julio missed his guess, this guy enjoyed his work.

He started thinking of the man as "the mechanic." It didn't help his stomach to settle.

The mechanic studied Adrianos. He said, "Thank you," without looking up at Julio.

"No problem," Julio said.

The mechanic pulled Adrianos away from the urinal and rolled him over onto his back. Adrianos was a big man, weighing about two hundred and fifty pounds, but the mechanic didn't seem to have any trouble moving him. He didn't ask for help and Julio didn't offer it.

"We've taken care of Mr. Adrianos's other friends," he said. "Except Ricky, of course. He left half an hour ago. One of my team members is waiting in the van in the alley outside. He'll drive you to your next job."

"Ricky's gone?"

The mechanic looked up at him. "Is that a problem?"

"No, sir." There really wasn't any problem. Julio didn't care what happened to the other bodyguard. Adrianos was dead, and Julio was rich. That was all that mattered. He let out a long breath. "Okay if I wash my hands?"

"Of course."

As he washed up, Julio kept an eye on the other man, who seemed faintly amused by something. A phrase kept going through Julio's head: *Better the devil you know . . .*

But that was bullshit. Adrianos wasn't a better devil. Even if this was a double-cross, Julio now had a chance to survive. He was good at survival. There was no future with Adrianos. That was for damned sure. Julio looked at his former boss again and thought about how easily this had all gone down. These new guys were planners. What were their real plans for him? A thought struck him. "The owner of the restaurant—"

"He's fine, but he's no longer the owner. You ask a lot of questions."

"Sorry." Julio dried his hands and adjusted his coat, making sure he'd be able to reach his weapons, and started to leave. He heard Adrianos groan and turned in surprise.

"No, he's not dead yet," said the mechanic. He was taking something out of his jacket.

Julio moved his hand back to the .45, then relaxed as he saw that the mechanic had removed a little leather pouch with a syringe and a small vial in it.

The mechanic filled the syringe, then stabbed it into Adrianos's neck. He removed the needle without putting pressure on the plunger, and stabbed it in again.

When he did this a third time, Julio said, "Trouble finding a vein?"

He looked up at Julio and smiled. "You're right, of course. Better to wait until he can feel it."

1

A black-winged bird swooped past Kit's left shoulder, and he shied away from it, crouching down low, half losing his balance. The heavy bundle he carried fell from his arms, landing on the leaf-strewn path with a soft thud. This seemed to him another ill omen, and he quickly and silently apologized to the canvas-wrapped form. He cowered there for a moment, cringing as the raven circled back—but the bird flew higher this time and soon was gone from sight. He waited in vain for his fear to follow it.

What did it mean, a raven coming so close to him?

Make sense, he warned himself. *Don't think crazy thoughts about birds.*

But fear proved tenacious, and his mind caromed through a maze of remembered terrors. He began shaking.

He made a determined effort to steer his thoughts toward the logical. The raven was a bird, not a supernatural creature. The raven had been attracted to the burden Kit carried into the woods.

You are not a boy, he told himself. *You are a twenty-six-year-old man. Don't act like a child.*

He told himself it was the chill of the autumn air that made him feel cold—not his dread, not his superstition. Not that he had dreamed the digging dream just last night.

A beetle moved over the canvas, and he brushed it away, then gently lifted the bundle again. "I'm sorry," he said once more and continued into the woods.

When he was first deciding on a place for the burial, Kit had thought of one with a view. But no one knew better than he did that killers often buried their victims in such places, and so he had searched for a location only he could find again, where the markers would not be so obvious to anyone else.

When he came to the chosen site, he carefully set the bundle aside and steeled himself for the next chore.

The digging.

The ground was not as hard here as in other places in the woods, but he found this task so difficult to begin, he nearly decided to choose some other way. A glance at the canvas bundle brought back his resolve—the other choices were not fitting.

Inside his leather gloves, his hands were slick with perspiration. He took hold of the small spade. The grating ring of its first stab into the earth made him dizzy, but again he took himself to task. He looked at the hard muscles of his arms, his large hands, his booted feet. He fitted his strength into a harness of remembered movement—thrust and step and lift and swing, thrust and step and lift and swing—settling into a rhythm divorced from thought, a familiar cadence that lulled him into the mindless completion of his work.

Still, he was weeping by the time he settled the small body into its resting place, and wept as he covered it. He placed a layer of stones within the grave when it was half-filled, to discourage scavengers. This he covered with soil. When he finished, he gathered leaves and spread them over the surface, so that it blended in with its surroundings. He stood back and looked at the grave from several different angles. When he felt confident that it was unlikely to be found, even by someone who was looking for it, he packed the spade away.

He had a kind of expertise in burial.

As he reached the ridge, he saw smoke coming from the cabin's chimney. He began running.

Spooky had found the matches.

2

Lakewood, California
Sunday, May 18, 9:45 P.M.

Homicide Detective Ciara Morton grinned at the nude male body hanging upside down over the bathtub. "I love it when somebody else does my work for me," she said.

Alex Brandon took his gaze from the dangling carcass and glanced at his partner. Here was Morton, standing in this hot, fetid, crowded bathroom, smiling over the dead man, while the sheriff's department rookie who had found the corpse was getting sick on the front lawn. He shook his head. "Wrong, Ciara. Somebody else just made more work for us."

"Taking Bernardo Adrianos out of commission?" she said. "You're right. Should have called the pound for a dead animal pickup, not us."

He ignored the laugh that brought from the coroner's assistant, who was standing in the hallway, and went back to contemplating the scene before him, wishing he could hold his breath longer. The acrid, sour smell of aging blood thickened the air.

The vacant house, on a street lined with similar small 1950s-era homes, was located in Lakewood, one of several area cities policed by the Los Angeles County Sheriff's Department. Neighbors had called the LASD to complain about the stench.

Alex rubbed a hand along the back of his neck, trying to loosen the tension there. Unlike Ciara, he found nothing to celebrate in the scene before them. Alex had spent weeks hungering for the chance to bring Adrianos to justice, but he felt no satisfaction in discovering that Adrianos's other enemies had caught up with the drug trafficker first. In fact, it was a letdown.

For a brief moment, he allowed himself to imagine what it might have been like to be working this case not with brusque Ciara Morton, but with his previous partner, J. D. Dodson. After more than a decade of working together, J.D. and Alex would have gone about this work totally attuned to one another, without stepping on each other's toes — or those of anyone else working on the case. He knew nothing good would come of such thoughts, though, and he focused again on the scene before him.

Alex looked up at the small sliding glass window above the tub. Didn't seem as if much air was coming in through it. At least it was open now. Those who had arrived earlier at the scene had been forced to wait until the crime lab and coroner got the information they needed on the temperature of the body and the room — and for the window latch to be dusted for prints — before opening it. The heat and stench must have been nearly unbearable.

He heard the rumble of the gasoline generator the crime lab had brought with them — the only source of power. The hot, bright, portable lights reflected off the white tiles of the bathroom, casting harsh shadows over the macabre stage before him.

The average human body holds just over a gallon of blood, and Alex figured most of Bernardo Adrianos's gallon lay in the cloudy, putrefying layer in the bottom of the tub. Adrianos's long ponytail rose from it like a wick to his head. His face was battered and nearly unrecognizable. All along his heavily tattooed body, dried rivulets of blood from a multitude of small cuts overlay the artwork on Adrianos's skin. Some of the black lines on his skin were moving. Ants, Alex realized. The flies weren't dining alone.

Enrique Marquez, one of the homicide detectives who had originally caught the call, stood on the other side of Alex. Marquez had noticed that the tattoos on the victim's arms matched ones he had seen in a department bulletin. "He's the one who murdered your witness, about three months ago, right?" he said.

"Yes, he's the one," Alex said, trying not to think of that other scene, trying to concentrate on this one.

Ciara wasn't going to let it go, though. "Our witness? No, Marquez, he killed our witness, the witness's wife, the witness's two-year-old son, and the witness's four-year-old daughter. Adrianos didn't go easy on any of them. I mean, he could have beaten the murder rap and kept the heroin coming in over the border without touching those kids, right? Two and four. That was the first case Alex and I worked together. You're lucky you didn't walk in on that one, Marquez. Alex here hasn't been sleeping well since."

Marquez shifted uncomfortably and glanced at Alex.

"That's true," Alex said calmly, hiding his irritation. His anger at the loss of the witness, his sense of defeat, were nothing compared to what he had felt when he found the children. Alex had followed a trail of blood outside the witness's house to a metal garbage can. Adrianos had crammed the small bodies of the children into it.

"You saw the mirror?" Marquez asked.

Alex turned to look again at the mirror over the sink. Mixed with his own reflection, he saw the large numeral painted in blood:

9

The single curving stroke was neat and even.

"Any idea what that's about?" Marquez asked.

"Not offhand. You find what it was painted with?" Alex asked. "A brush? A cloth? A glove?"

"No, not yet. Looks like a brush, though. The lab's going to take a sample to see if it's the victim's blood."

"Don't call him a victim, Marquez," Ciara said.

"The owners of the house moved out of here over a year ago?" Alex asked quickly, hoping to head off an argument. He turned back toward the body.

"Yes," Marquez said, "but the coroner doesn't think the vic— uh, the body's been here more than a couple of days. Not enough insect progress, and after a while, the body would have pulled apart. It's already stretched out a little."

"Blood in the tub is still liquid, though," Alex said. "After two hot days, wouldn't it be more congealed?"

"Coroner wondered about that, too. He found a puncture wound here." Marquez carefully leaned over and pointed with gloved finger to a bruised place on Adrianos's left arm. "He thinks the killer used an IV anticoagulant."

Alex grimaced. "Injected something into Adrianos so that he'd bleed to death faster?"

"All guesswork right now, but the coroner says these wounds don't seem to be all that deep or in vital places. No spray from arterial wounds, for example. But none of these little wounds ever clotted, like they normally would have."

"So if this drug was used on him, it made him into something like a hemophiliac?" Ciara asked.

"I think so," Marquez said. "No definite answers until toxicology does some tests."

"Great," she said. "Judging by their current backlog, we won't have a report in my lifetime."

"It might take weeks," Alex agreed. "But I think we'll be able to move this one to the front of the line."

"Dream on—they'll know this one is an AVA, and no one will be in a rush."

AVA—asshole versus asshole. Alex didn't think she had that right, though. That type of killing wouldn't have been staged so elaborately—and there could be no doubt that this was a dramatic production. But who was the intended audience?

"You find his clothes anywhere around here?" he asked Marquez.

"No sign of them."

"You checked the whole house?" Ciara said.

Seeing Marquez bristle at the insult, Alex said, "Don't jump to conclusions, Ciara—Adrianos could have arrived here in his birthday suit. Maybe we couldn't find him because he's been hiding out at a nudist colony."

"Talk about nothing to hide," she said, staring pointedly at the dead man's genitals.

Adrianos had been stripped and bound. The thick rag stuffed in his mouth further distorted his face. His arms were securely tied behind him, and a taut line of black rope extended from there to his ankles, which were also tied together. From there the rope looped from between his ankles into two cleanly cut holes in the ceiling above the tub.

"It's a rappelling rope," Alex said as he briefly studied the uppermost knot, a figure eight.

"You think a rock climber did this?" Ciara asked.

Alex hesitated. "Could be."

"Maybe a sailor," Marquez said.

"Alex is a climber," Ciara said. "He knows a rappelling rope when he sees one."

Marquez looked at Alex, but Alex was looking up at the place where the rope disappeared into the ceiling. "Rope goes up over a beam," Marquez said. "Wraps around it a few times. The access to the attic is just outside this room, in the hall. I took a look, thinking there might be prints in the dust, but the attic has been vacuumed between here and the access."

"Vacuumed?" Ciara said in disbelief.

"Yes, vacuumed," Marquez said. "This wasn't a spur-of-the-moment killing."

"No shit," she said. "Brilliant observation."

Marquez sighed in exasperation, then turned to Brandon and said, "I'll be out front if you need me, Alex."

"Nice going, Ciara," Alex said when Marquez was out of earshot.

"Fuck him if he can't take a joke."

"Let's go outside," he said. "I could use some air."

3

He walked toward the back of the house, wondering if she would follow him. He figured he had a fifty-fifty chance of being ignored. But he heard her footsteps behind him. The back door was open, and he went out without touching it, even though the lab had already dusted for prints. This had been the point of entry, they had been told. A piece of cake for anyone with even the most basic burglary skills.

He saw that no one was in the yard, stepped out into the center of it, and took a deep breath. It would take a while to stop smelling the sour blood smell, but he was glad to be out of the close quarters of the bathroom. And although the evening was warm, it felt twenty degrees cooler outside.

He thought for a moment about killers who tortured their victims, who swept up—no, *vacuumed*—and generally left crime scenes too clean. He didn't like any of it, hated what his experience told him—this wasn't a one-time foray into murder. This was the work of a planner. What else had been planned? Already completed?

The climbing rope. That especially disturbed him. He wondered if it disturbed him because he had a climber's regard for such a rope, or if he was not paying enough attention to his gut instinct. This scene had immediately reminded him of another, long-ago series of murders.

He cut off that line of thinking. Impossible that it was the same killer.

He turned to look at Ciara. She held her chin up, and in the wash of moonlight on her face, he could see the defiant set of her mouth. Her arms were crossed over her chest. She was tall and dark-haired, in her mid-forties—six or seven years older than he, but with less time in the department.

He thought again of J.D., who had been dead for almost a year now. What a contrast this new partner made to that old man.

Then again, he supposed, by appearance Alex and J.D. themselves could hardly have been more different. When they had first teamed up twelve years ago, Alex—with only seven years in the department—had been the youngest of the one hundred and ten detectives in the LASD Homicide Bureau. J.D. was one of the oldest.

J.D. was an overweight, chain-smoking, hard-drinking black man who had grown up in Compton. His nose had been broken at least twice, and a thick scar gave an odd bend to the end of his left eyebrow. He had been the first person in his family to go to college. He hated heights.

Alex was muscular and athletic, blue-eyed and white. He worked out almost daily, had never smoked, and drank little. He was the first person in the Brandon family to attend what his brother called "a mere state university"—rather than an Ivy League school, or USC, or Stanford. He had spent most of his childhood in Malibu and Bel Air, and loved rock climbing. For a brief time, some of the other detectives had referred to the team as "J.D. and G.Q." Somehow J.D. had put a stop to that. Probably, Alex thought, with a single look.

Whatever their apparent differences, they were a solid team. Alex's uncle, a longtime member of the department—his inspiration for joining it—had taught him a great deal about law enforcement, but J.D. took that education to another level.

J.D.'s coolheaded, deceptively easygoing approach appealed to Alex. Walking into the midst of a horrific crime scene, J.D. would light up a cigarette and say, "Let's not get excited." Calmly, he'd put the pieces together as only he could. He would sit down in an interrogation room with the most hardened killer, look him straight in the eye, and say, with seeming sincerity, "I understand completely why you did it. Let's talk." He had obtained more confessions than anyone else in the department, and never by using anything but his presence, his mind—and something he called "the knack."

He was brilliant in almost every way except in his care of himself. He had died of a massive coronary. Alex had wept more at J.D.'s funeral than he had at his own father's. And gone back to work with a vengeance.

Ciara was the only detective in Homicide who had a clearance rate anywhere near Alex's own. About sixty-eight percent of her cases had been cleared to the point of highly probable suspects named or in custody. For someone as new to Detectives as she was, that was incredible.

He had to admit being impressed by that—he had been in the homicide bureau much longer than Ciara, but she obviously had the knack, too.

Three months ago, his captain had asked him to take her on as a partner, and he had agreed. Every now and then, he saw how much it bothered her to answer to someone younger, but even though they had their ups and downs, for the most part, they got along fine. He just wished she'd learn the proverb about catching more flies with honey than vinegar. He was her last chance, after all—Alex was the only person in Homicide who was willing to be her partner. Behind her back, most of the others referred to her as B.B. Queen. The B.B. stood for Ball Buster.

The few other women in the homicide bureau liked her less than the men did.

Watching her now, he thought dispassionately that she was the kind of woman more likely to be described as handsome than pretty. She worked hard to keep in shape, and even her worst enemies among the males in the homicide bureau eyed her with appreciation when she walked down the halls. Thinking of them, he said, "You tired of working with me?"

"How can you even ask such a stupid question?"

"Marquez goes back and tells the captain what you said in there within earshot of a coroner's assistant and a lab tech, what do you think is going to happen?"

"The captain's not going to transfer me out of Homicide. My clearance rate is too high," she said, but her voice betrayed her lack of certainty.

He stayed silent. She knew as well as he did that success in closing cases might not be enough to keep her from being transferred.

"Aw, come on, Alex. I'll go out and apologize to Marquez on the front lawn at the top of my lungs if you want me to."

"No, let him cool off. And aim for something less dramatic and more sincere."

"You could be right. Maybe after he hangs out there with that puking kid for a while, I won't look so bad."

"I feel sorry for that rookie. Lab tech really chewed him out."

"Serves him right. Maybe next time he'll go outside to hurl. The stupid bastard used the crapper *and* flushed it. God knows what evidence is out in the sewer lines now."

"I don't think these guys were careless enough to leave evidence in the toilet."

"No . . ." She unfolded her arms, and he watched her expression change from annoyance to concentration. "You said 'guys'—plural. More than one killer?"

"Probably. Wouldn't be easy for one man to get past Adrianos's bodyguards and subdue a guy like him. Adrianos never had fewer than two men guarding him. And it's unlikely one man could hoist someone of Adrianos's size up over the tub. If there had been a pulley or other device—"

"We should ask Marquez if there was one in the attic."

Alex didn't say anything.

She sighed. "I'll go out there and apologize to him."

He shrugged. "Like I said, give him a minute to cool off. You've been riding his ass since we got here."

"He'll live," she said absently. Her brows were drawn together. "So, which of Bernardo Adrianos's competitors took care of him before we could?"

"Maybe it wasn't his competition."

"Come on, Alex. Guys like Adrianos are never safe. I'm betting someone wanted a piece of his lucrative import business."

"Another drug dealer? I don't know. Dealers at his level have hit men at their beck and call. A pro probably would have downed him with one shot and left him where we never would have found him. Whoever killed Adrianos wanted him to be found."

Alex saw the beam of a flashlight at the back door, and a slender young woman stepped onto the porch. She was wearing a crime lab jacket. She nodded toward them, then crouched down to take photographs of the doorframe.

"What are you doing?" Ciara called to her.

The tech explained that there were tool marks on it that might be useful. "Unless this place has been robbed before," she said.

Ciara turned back to Alex. "So if this isn't drug lord warfare, what other possibilities are there?"

"I don't know." He hesitated, then said, "It reminds me a little of the way Jerome Naughton used to work."

"Who?"

"About a dozen years ago. One of my first cases in Detectives. I was looking for him because J.D. and I were fairly sure he'd murdered his wife. Later, we learned we were right, although we never found her body."

"Before my time, I guess," she said, a little stiffly.

"Before you were in Detectives, anyway. Thing that makes me think about Naughton is that he'd hang his victims upside down like this—kind of like a hunter hangs a deer—over a hook above a bathtub. He usually chose abandoned properties or ones that had been vacant for a while."

"You said his name was Naughton?"

"Yes—but this is not as much like his work as it sounds. For one thing, his victims were always women, and he wasn't so neat about the blood. In fact, his scenes always had blood all over the place. Supposedly, that was part of the thrill for him. So that doesn't fit. And I don't think he used that trick of drilling holes and tying the rope over the beam."

"Starting to sound like there's not so much in common after all. But we should check this Naughton guy out. Any idea where he is now?"

"Dead. His fourteen-year-old stepson killed him. Long story, but some people thought the kid might have been Naughton's accomplice. I'm not sure I agree with them, but no one ever had a chance to really question him at length." An image of the boy came into his mind—a handsome face beneath old bruises; thin, but strong, with jet-black hair and large, haunted gray eyes. He didn't think he'd ever forget that kid's eyes.

"Why not?" Ciara was saying. "No—let me guess—he's dead, too?"

"No, not as far as I know. He wasn't questioned, because his grandmother was Elizabeth Logan. She had been looking for him for years."

Ciara gave him a blank look.

"Logan Cosmetics?" he said.

"Oh. Big money."

"That's an understatement. Elizabeth Logan made money and married money. Probably aren't fifty people in Los Angeles that have as much money as the Logans—if there are that many."

"You'd know more about that than I do, Mr. Silver Spoon."

Alex had long ago learned that there were those who would never forgive him for growing up among the wealthy—no matter what had changed since then or how little he regretted the loss of that world. It was a prejudice that wasn't worth complaining about—but one he'd prefer not to find in a partner.

"Ah, shit, Alex, don't take offense."

He stayed silent.

"I'm sorry, all right?" she said.

"Sure." He watched as the lab tech began to remove the strike plate from the door.

"So Elizabeth Logan took care of her grandson?" Ciara asked, drawing his attention back to her.

"Yes—listen, there really isn't much in common with the Naughton cases. His victims were always women, and there was never any evidence that the kid participated in the killings."

"But he murdered his stepfather," Ciara said.

"Self-defense, or damned close to it. In all likelihood, it was exactly the way the D.A. decided it was—Naughton terrorized the boy, made his life a living hell—even killed the boy's mother right in front of him. The kid killed Naughton because he believed that was the only way he'd ever get away from him. The sad thing is, he was probably right. Nothing more to it. Otherwise, he would have been brought to trial—money or no money. And as far as I know, the boy has never been in any trouble since."

"But you're going to try to find out what he's been up to lately."

He smiled. "I might."

"Personally, I think it's way too big a stretch. You haven't heard anything about this kid for a decade, and if this was his sort of gig, he'd have been in trouble before now, right?"

"Most likely."

"Face it, Alex, this is probably a job done by a pro, a guy who picked his killing spot carefully and was not impulsive. Adrianos pissed off the wrong people, and that's all there is to it. As for the method—maybe his enemies hired someone new to the trade who enjoys his work."

"Christ, I hope not."

"What do you think that nine on the mirror is all about?" she asked.

"Hell if I know. But that's another thing that doesn't seem to fit if this is just drug dealer versus drug dealer. What kind of message is the number nine? And who's supposed to get the message?"

"His business associates. Someone is using this to say they're all working for new management. Which reminds me, Alex—I wonder where his body-guards are?"

"Probably welcoming Bernardo to hell."

"Shit. I guess that means we'll get called out to some other spoiled meat scene one of these days. Probably closer to Adrianos's home ground than Lakewood. With any luck, maybe the LAPD will catch it instead of Sheriff's."

"Might be on television then," Alex said, and she laughed.

The sheriff's department seldom got the media attention given to the Los Angeles Police Department. Alex didn't think that was necessarily a bad thing.

"Well," she said, "even if the bodyguards do drop dead inside L.A. city limits instead of somewhere within our jurisdiction, we've got the big news here."

"Something tells me I'll soon wish he had been found in L.A., too."

He watched as the tech began to put away her camera and tools.

"I don't suppose we can hope for latent prints?" Alex asked.

The tech shook her head. "Nothing that will be of use. Because this place has been on the real estate market, we've got all kinds of prints everywhere in the house except the bathroom, the back doorknob, and the attic. Those are wiped clean. Same with footprints." She glanced at Ciara, then added, "De-tective Marquez was good about preserving the scene—he let us check the hallway and bathroom floor before anyone other than the first officer on the scene stepped in there. Looks as if his are the only shoeprints on the bathroom floor. There are some others in the hall. They're odd—I think the killer wore plastic booties or something else that left an indistinct, uniform flat sole mark. Big enough to be a man's, but don't try to take that to court—that's just a SWAG—a scientific wild-assed guess."

"Any SWAG about the rope?" Ciara asked, and Alex wondered if she was setting the tech up.

"That may be our best lead yet. Sailing supply. Again, a guess. Maybe even for some other special outdoor use—rock climbing? But I don't think it's something from a hardware store."

"Unless I miss my guess," Alex said, "it's a common brand of static rope—a rope that's designed not to stretch. That type of rope is used for rappelling. You can buy them at outdoor equipment and sporting goods stores."

"You're a climber?" the tech asked, looking at him with new interest.

"Yes," Ciara said, "he's crazy. But he knows rock climbing equipment."

They were interrupted by Marquez, who came rushing out, nearly knock-ing the tech down. "Man, when it rains it pours. You've got a lieutenant, the FBI, and the *L.A. Times* on the front lawn."

"God damn it all to hell," Ciara said, hurrying past him. "I'm going to close the blinds on the bathroom window. The *Times* will make it a photo op."

"Did you say the FBI?" the lab tech asked. "Why would they be here?"

"Bernardo Adrianos was on their Ten Most Wanted list," Alex said.

He was distracted by the sound of an approaching helicopter and looked up. "Shit. Not one of ours, Enrique. Television. You suppose the neighbors called them, or that knucklehead with the Feds?"

Marquez had other things on his mind. "You'd better not let B.B. Queen get anywhere near a reporter, Alex, or all our asses will be in a sling."

4

Everett Corey finished working out in his private gymnasium at the back of his property. He poured Fiji water into a Baccarat crystal glass and eased his thirst. He was alone in his large hillside home this evening, as he most often chose to be. Solitude allowed him to be free of the inadequacies of others. No need to make the effort to ignore their failings, large and small.

He was a handsome man, the product of good-looking parents. He had no memories of his mother. When he was not quite two, she had agreed—as a condition of an otherwise generous divorce settlement—never to make contact with her only child by the marriage. His father had no photos of her and never mentioned her. When he was fifteen, he learned that she had been dead for some years. He felt nothing in the way of grief and no desire to locate any of his maternal relations. Relations, he had learned from those on his father's side, were a damned nuisance to any person of substance.

Everett Corey was unmistakably his father's child. He had his father's green eyes, and his build, height, and athletic grace. His hair was golden blond, rather than the paler shade of his father's, but in other respects he closely resembled him.

Other men, Everett knew, were easily persuaded by his father. Women were charmed by him. And because of the power he held over them, his father generally held other people in contempt. Everett understood that perfectly.

Everett and his father had never been affectionate with each other, but until he reached the age of fourteen, Everett had faith that his father could and would use his charisma and wealth to shield his son from any unpleasant consequences. Everett often got into trouble as a child. He knew his father found this irritating, but to those outside their home, he never failed to present anything but the staunchest support for his boy.

Then the world changed. During the ninth grade, Everett had been expelled from school and arrested for viciously assaulting a younger boy—a boy who, in Everett's opinion, totally deserved to be beaten nearly to death—and things had not gone as smoothly as they usually did. To Everett's shock, his father had failed to get the better of Alex Brandon, the sheriff's department detective who had taken Everett into custody. His father had immediately posted bail and Everett had not served time in a common juvenile detention facility, but in retrospect, he often thought that might have been preferable to the punishment he did receive.

The compromise his father's lawyers had arranged instead was that Everett was sent away from home to live at Sedgewick, an exclusive private school in Malibu. The wealthiest families in the Los Angeles area—families in Brentwood, Malibu, Bel Air, Beverly Hills, the Pacific Palisades, and other exclusive enclaves—sent their sons there. But only—as Everett knew—if they were misfits. If you were kicked out of other schools, if you had behavior problems, if you abused drugs or were violent, you went to Sedgewick. If your parents believed you were out of control, they sent you to Sedgewick. If your family no longer wanted you under its roof, you went to Sedgewick.

He disliked the faculty and staff. He disliked the dormitory and food. He disliked the discipline.

He wrote letters home, pleading with his father to make some other arrangement. His letters went unanswered.

He was an intelligent boy who wasn't challenged by the curriculum at Sedgewick. With little else to occupy him, he began to test his own power to influence others and learned that he could exercise a remarkable amount of control over certain of the other boys. He began to be less homesick.

By the time he came home on a summer break, the rift between Everett and his father was complete. If his father was pleased, at first, to find his son's manners and behavior impeccable, he was also made aware of an unmistakable coolness beneath the civility. Invitations to play tennis or chess were courteously refused; gifts politely accepted and immediately ignored; conversational gambits deftly turned aside. If his father insisted that Everett join him, Everett complied, but his father found him a distant and distracted companion. Dinners at home became tense, silent affairs. After that first summer, Everett did not return to his father's Malibu mansion until after graduation.

His father was dying of what the world was told was cancer, but which Everett knew to be AIDS. A few weeks after graduation, the same man who had arrested Everett when he was fourteen—Alex Brandon—questioned Everett and his friend Cameron Burgess, wanting to know their whereabouts on the night Cameron's father met with violent death.

To Everett's surprise, his own father shielded him, just as he had in earlier years. His father had sworn to Detective Brandon that the young men had been with him, constantly keeping him company at his bedside.

That autumn, while playing tennis on the estate's private court, Everett was informed that his father had died. He continued to play out the set with Cameron.

The inheritance was held in trust for three years, during which its value increased steadily. On his twenty-first birthday, a little more than four years ago, Everett became a man of enormous personal wealth.

He was not as stupid as his father, he thought now, admiring the way his body looked after his evening workout. He took care of his body. He might have multiple sexual partners, but he chose them carefully and never had unprotected sex. He wondered if he might call someone for sex tonight.

He had no sooner thought this than the phone rang. He checked the caller ID display. Reluctantly, he answered.

"For your sake, Frederick, I hope this is important," he said.

"Are you watching television?"

"No. I have better things to do with my time."

"Not tonight! It's on—finally! Turn on CNN or MSNBC. Or both of them! And it's on the local news, too!"

"Do try to stay calm," Everett said lazily, and had nearly hung up when he heard the other voice say—

"Are you still leaving tonight?"

He brought the receiver back to his ear. "Is there any reason why I shouldn't?"

"No, I guess not. I just thought you'd like to see how things develop, you know—how they're covered by the media."

"I already know that they will be covered inaccurately."

"But still—you're famous now!"

"No, I'm not. And I have no desire to be. I doubt I'll ever desire something so crass," he said.

"Yes, well—*bon voyage* then," Frederick murmured.

"Thank you." In a more tender voice, he added, "You know I don't begrudge you your enjoyment of this, don't you?"

"Oh, no, I know you don't. But you're right—it's—it's so *bourgeois,* isn't it? I'm going to turn it off right now."

Everett smiled to himself and said, "No, please. Watch it. No harm in that, really. I may watch it for a moment or two myself."

They said their good-byes and hung up. He decided he couldn't fault Frederick, who was an excellent gatherer of information, for being aware of news reports.

He turned on the nearest set and stood motionless as the screen flashed the helicopter camera shots from above the house in Lakewood.

"Repeating our top story this hour, a fugitive on the FBI's Most Wanted list was found dead in this Lakewood home earlier this evening. The L.A. County Sheriff's Department and the FBI report that Bernardo Adrianos, a suspected drug trafficker who reputedly murdered a family of four . . ."

He hit the mute button on the remote control. "Suspected. Reputedly. Bullshit."

He pressed the record button and videotaped the segment, smiling to himself as a petite redheaded reporter approached a tall, lean, dark-haired detective. Alex Brandon. The television cameras showed that his eyes were light blue, but Corey knew they failed to capture the startling color. Until he had observed other members of the detective's family, Corey had thought the color of Alex Brandon's eyes might have been achieved with tinted contact lenses.

He wondered why Detective Ciara Morton wasn't with Brandon. Corey watched his movements with interest. A shame, really, that he was in law enforcement. The man had an air of self-possession, a presence that was wasted in this line of work.

Brandon stayed calm as the reporter shouted a question and thrust a microphone at him, but it didn't require lipreading skills to see the answer was a firm "no comment." Corey watched until Brandon was out of the frame, then switched among the channels, glad he did not have to listen to the inane comments of the newscasters.

Finally, all of the stations had moved on to other stories or were merely showing the same footage they had shown earlier. He turned the television off. He glanced at his Omega watch, placed the videotape in a hidden safe, and walked across the darkened lawn to the mansion.

Upstairs, he showered and changed into a set of clothes he had bought in

Berlin last year. He changed his shoes as well, and put on a pair of dark-rimmed glasses with lenses that did nothing to change his excellent vision. He opened a drawer that contained Tag Heuer, Rolex, Raymond Weil, and other fine timepieces, including a few vintage Hamilton railroad pocket watches. He took off the Omega and replaced it with an inexpensive watch with a plastic band, which he had purchased at a shop near a German university.

He practiced a few key German phrases, not because he doubted his ability to speak the language fluently, but because it helped him to get into the role he would be playing, that of a young German student traveling before starting college. It was the identity he had created with the phony passport that was now tucked into a backpack. The backpack contained nothing that would alarm airport security personnel. The weapons he needed would be awaiting him at his destination.

He was ahead of schedule, so he went down the hallway to his favorite room in the house and unlocked the specially constructed door. Even before he was through the second door of this room-within-a-room, he felt anticipation as he heard familiar sounds from the other side of the door.

Clicking and whirring. Snapping and chiming. Buzzing and ticking. Mechanical sounds.

A motion detector turned on the lights as he entered his kingdom of mechanical devices. Many were playthings collected by his father and grandfather. The most valuable of these was an eighteenth-century automaton. The lifelike mechanical boy's intricate design included a mechanism in his chest that made him appear to breathe, and gears that moved his hand, arm, and eyes as he wrote his school lessons. Everett ignored him, as he ignored clockwork tin figures, jack-in-the-boxes, an antique electric train. He barely glanced at the mechanical banks—a girl skipping rope, a lion chasing a monkey up a tree, a dentist pulling a tooth. He walked past the clocks with elaborate mechanisms that marked the hours with waltzing couples, marching soldiers, and hounds chasing foxes. These objects had been built by others, long ago.

He moved to a workbench at the far end of the room. Here were projects that revealed his own ability to create mechanical things. Until recently, the most prized among these had been a large clock that worked by feeding steel balls through a series of chutes and levers and balances. There were others, devices that completed sophisticated movements at the flip of a switch.

Everett considered his mood, then pressed a series of buttons. From a pair of overhead speakers, he heard the energetic *Turkish March* from Beethoven's Ninth Symphony. He pressed a lever, then watched the workings of the initial model of an invention of his. The full-scale version of the invention was now in place at another location, awaiting its single, glorious use.

It was not an especially complex mechanism, but he enjoyed watching it work all the same. In appearance, it seemed to be a clock attached to a closed tube containing shiny steel balls. Like a clock, it marked time. But as predetermined increments passed, it released the heavy balls one at a time. Each then rolled along a wooden pathway, toward nine wooden channels. Eight of the nine had gates across them. When the ball rolled into the open channel, copper tabs at the channel's end came into contact with it, and the metal ball acted as a bridge for an electrical current. The current would close a gate at the top of the channel, and open the gate for the next. When all nine balls were in place, they lit a small bulb.

Of course, electrical timers could do more than light bulbs.

He switched off the current on the timer, turned off the music, and smiled.

He finished locking the room and made his way toward the curving marble staircase that led to the mansion's entry hall. As he passed a small Louis XVI marquetry table, the phone on it rang. Again he checked the caller ID display. He recognized the cell phone number. He picked up the receiver and said, "I sincerely hope you aren't going to tell me anything that will displease me."

There was a pause before the voice on the other end said, "Kit has a young boy living with him."

"A child, Cameron? Living with that lunatic? Be serious."

"It's true. Not his own. Ten years old or so, I think. I didn't get close enough to see."

"You didn't harm the child?"

There was another silence. "I did only what you asked me to do. Molly's dead. He's already found her."

"And he caught a glimpse of you?"

"I made sure he did."

Everett smiled in satisfaction. "Perfect, then. As always, you are perfect. The rest will unfold as it should, boy or no boy. I'll see you at Kennedy. You'll be able to get to Denver International in time?"

"I'm almost there now."

"Excellent. In a few hours, then. And remember, we're strangers."

"Yes."

He carefully replaced the receiver and made his way to the curving marble staircase which led to the mansion's entry hall.

He checked his airline tickets. All in order, of course.

He heard the Maserati coming up the drive.

He looked at his cheap watch. Morgan was right on time.

Project Nine was in motion again.

As he set the alarm system, he thought of the clockwork boy, alone in the dark.

Nothing, he decided, could take the place of reliable friends.

5

Fort Collins, Colorado
Monday, May 19, 1:08 A.M.

Kit pulled his jacket closed against the chill of the night air as he stepped out of the Suburban's heated interior. A big thermometer near the gas station door said it was forty. He looked up at the sky just as thick clouds obscured the moon.

Not an omen, he told himself. A sign of rain on its way, nothing more.

He paid for the gas and bought two Cokes at the station's convenience market. When he tried to hand the can of soda to Spooky, she refused to take it. He placed it in the cup holder, opened his own can, and took a long sip, wondering if he should have bought Jolt or Mountain Dew or something with more caffeine in it. Only about an hour or so to Denver, but he was tired.

He started the truck.

"I don't want to go to California," Spooky said. "I want to stay here."

It was a refrain he had heard over the past few hours. "In Fort Collins?" he asked, as if hearing it for the first time.

"No, not Fort Collins. You know what I mean."

He pulled out of the station and headed toward Highway 87. He had stayed away from the biggest highways until now, taking Highway 14 after Rabbit Ears Pass outside of Steamboat Springs, although U.S. 40 would have been the faster way into Denver. But he was sure that the attacker would have taken the faster road, and this was not the time to engage his enemies.

Besides, traveling with Spooky in his Suburban, they were two, and two into fourteen was seven, which was lucky. So Highway 14 was the better choice all the way around.

He hadn't been able to do much with a number like eighty-seven. He tried not to let that bother him, but it did.

"I can't take you back to the cabin," he said now. "It's not safe there."

"Molly was old. Old dogs die. We should stay in Colorado."

He pulled to the side of the road, stopped, and turned to face her.

"We've been over this. Molly did not die of old age."

"You don't know for sure!"

"Yes, I do!" He saw the alarm come into her face. He rarely raised his voice—he felt instant remorse when he saw that he had startled her. "I know for sure," he said quietly.

Spooky stared back at him in defiance, but he knew she was scared. After three years with her, he was adept at gauging her moods. When he had first met her, she was ten years old. He had made the mistake most people made when first observing her—he thought she was a boy. She was small for her age and thin; her dark hair was cropped short, her brows thick over large brown eyes, her face grubby, her clothing male. And she happened to be near the sink in a men's room.

That winter day, three years ago, he was on one of his frequent trips between his homes in L.A. and Denver. Just over the Colorado state line, he had stopped at a gas station that had a good-sized convenience market attached to it.

Kit walked into the washroom and saw a man drying his hands. The man was unaware that a skinny urchin was relieving him of his wallet. Kit prevented the theft by the simple expedient of leaning against the door so that the child, whom he now realized was female, couldn't make her escape. Her eyes widened. He snatched the wallet from her grasp, then held it out to the other man.

The man, who had a beefy build and was a couple of inches taller than Kit, wanted both his wallet and retribution. Kit saw her look of abject terror, remembered all the times in his own childhood when he had longed for an adult who would protect him, and intervened. "I saw her take it, and now you've got it back. No real harm done, is there?"

"Stay out of this," the man said.

Spooky, looking quickly between them, stood closer to Kit. "He's my brother!" she told the other man.

He looked between them in disbelief.

"Think of me as her guardian," Kit said. "Check your wallet. Is anything missing?"

The man looked, admitted nothing was missing, but his rage didn't lessen. He started to reach for the girl.

"Leave her alone," Kit said, stepping forward to block the move.

The man saw something in Kit's eyes, perhaps, because he faltered and moved back. "I ought to call the police," he said.

"You can, of course, but I'll have to report that you had taken a female minor into a men's room for God knows what purpose."

Behind him, he heard the bathroom door open and close.

"She's no more your sister than I am," the man complained.

"I said I'll protect her. Do you doubt that?"

Kit saw the man think this through, saw the moment he decided not to fight, then stepped outside and looked around, but the girl dressed as a boy was gone. When he went in to pay for the gas, he realized his wallet was gone, too.

Almost all of his cash was in an inner pocket of his jacket, so he was able to pay what he owed. He found his wallet—minus cash and credit cards—in a trash can just outside the store. He got into the Suburban, spent a few moments vividly remembering what it was like to want to run away, and thought like a ten-year-old. He drove slowly past a small park and a convenience store, watching for a shorthaired urchin wearing torn jeans, a white T-shirt, and a loose-fitting jacket that wouldn't have provided much protection against the elements on a cold Colorado day. She wasn't in either place, but he found her fairly soon. As he passed a fast food restaurant, he saw her standing in line to place an order, and he doubled back.

Before he had managed to get out of the Suburban, she was in trouble again. The man who had been standing in front of her in line had discovered that his own wallet was missing, and was chasing her. She ran toward Kit, and he saw her eyes widen the moment she recognized him. He thought she might hare off in another direction, but instead she ran to him. "Give me his wallet and get in the green Suburban," he told her. "I won't harm you."

Later, it scared him that she believed him. He wouldn't have harmed her, but she had no way of knowing that. He managed to convince yet another irate victim of her thievery not to call the police.

Kit got back into the Suburban. She reached into one of her jacket pockets and handed him his credit cards and cash without saying anything. Her fingers, as they briefly touched his hand, were ice cold.

"Have you eaten yet?" he asked, turning the heater up a little.

She shook her head. He pulled the SUV into the line for drive-through ordering.

"Are you going to take me to the cops?" she asked.

"No. I'm going to take you home."

"I don't have one."

"Look—"

"It's true. My mom died last summer. Bonnie and me, we live in a car. We did, anyway."

"Bonnie—is that who takes care of you?"

"Do I look like someone is taking care of me?" she asked angrily. "I take care of myself."

When he simply looked at her, as if waiting for more information, she finally added, "Bonnie's my older sister—she was supposed to take care of me. But she took the car and left me. Is that guy back at the gas station going to call the cops?"

"No. What about your dad? Where's he?"

She shrugged. "I don't know who he is. Never have."

"Do you have some other family I can take you to?"

"No."

"No? What about your grandparents?"

"Dead."

"Aunts or uncles?"

"No."

They reached the display board for the fast food, and he asked her what she wanted. She told him. As he finished giving an order large enough for three kids her size, she crossed her arms and glared defiantly at him, then said—in a voice loud enough to carry over the ordering microphone—"I won't give you a blow job for it."

Over the speaker, there was the sound of laughter coming from within the restaurant, then a voice said, "That's okay. We can only accept cash."

Mortified, for a few seconds Kit wished he was not boxed in between two other cars, or he would have driven away without the food. Then he stopped thinking about his own embarrassment and considered what it might mean that she felt it necessary to say such a thing at her age.

"Well," she said, seeing his embarrassment, "that's what Bonnie's boyfriends made her do before they'd give us money." She shuddered. "Bonnie said I'd have to do it sooner or later, but I don't want to."

Kit thought of the years of terror spent under his stepfather's control and said, "If I have anything to say about it, no one is ever going to make you do anything that's—anything sexual without your permission, and they're not going to even ask for your permission before you're an adult."

She studied him for a moment, then said, "Where are you going?"

"To Denver, and then to my home in the mountains."

They moved up a car length.

"Will I like it?"

"Will you—? Wait a minute. I don't think you should be living with me. I'll help you all I can, but I'm no parent."

"You could do better than Bonnie."

He didn't doubt it, but said, "Let's think about other options. Tell me the truth—you don't have any other family you can go to?"

She shook her head. "Just Bonnie."

"We'll look for Bonnie, then. You sure there are no aunts or uncles?"

"I don't think so, or Bonnie would have made them take me a long time ago."

He paid for the food. He ignored the cashier's grin.

He turned on the radio as they drove away. It was tuned to an oldies station. She didn't object to this.

"I'm Kit. What's your name?" he asked her.

She shook her head.

"Not going to tell me?"

"No. If I change my mind about you, I don't want you to know who I am."

"Okay. Make one up, then. I've got to call you something."

She smiled, obviously enjoying the power this gave her. The song on the radio was a Classics IV tune from the sixties—"Spooky." As it reached the refrain, she said, "That's my name. Spooky!"

He smiled and said, "All right, Spooky." He thought that would last about five minutes. He would learn how stubborn she could be. It had helped her survive.

Eventually, she told him enough about her recent life to allow him to be thankful for her hardheadedness. She had started dressing and acting like a boy to make herself unattractive to one of Bonnie's "boyfriends."

Kit put Moriarty, a longtime friend of his family—who on most days would tell people that he was a private security specialist—on the job of learning Bonnie's whereabouts. Moriarty had been both devoted friend and employee to Kit's grandmother, and he had continued to work for Kit after her death. Kit trusted no one more than Moriarty.

Moriarty learned that Spooky's real name was Emily, but Kit didn't let on that he had been given this information for almost two years. He never called her Emily except when they had to pass muster with the court system. Away from judges, lawyers, and social workers, they pretended he had never heard her real name.

Bonnie was a Jane Doe in a Tucson morgue when Moriarty located her. She hadn't survived a month after she had abandoned Spooky. She had sold the car, and had been living with a group of runaways in a tunnel near Fifteenth and Kino there, sneaking in through a break in the chain link fence that sealed it off. A sudden downpour had rapidly filled the tunnel, and Bonnie, who probably would not have survived even had she known how to swim, drowned.

When Kit told Spooky her sister was dead, Spooky didn't cry. But she demanded that Kit teach her how to swim. She was now a strong and avid swimmer.

She had also learned how to defend herself.

She was intelligent, and when Kit realized that she wasn't ready to cope with school, or schools to cope with her, he hired a private tutor to home school her—a retired teacher who knew just how to handle Spooky's rebelliousness. Through the tutor Spooky also met some of the kids who lived nearby, but Spooky preferred the company of Kit or Moriarty. He noticed that she seemed better able to form friendships with those who were her own age than she had been three years ago, but she was at her best when she felt safe, with Kit.

Although the legal aspects of becoming Spooky's guardian were complex, the court proceedings were not as difficult as he had feared they would be. Moriarty did locate an aunt, but the aunt did not want a pickpocket runaway who started the occasional fire living under her roof.

Over the next three years, Spooky gradually set aside most of her thievery and arson. Only in times of high stress would Kit feel the need to hide matches from her.

He looked over at her now and figured that soon no one would mistake her for a male. Her brown hair was still cut short, in a boy's style, but her face was losing its childishness—those brows now only accented her brown eyes, her cheekbones were becoming more prominent—although the pout she wore at the moment was pure kid. She crossed her arms over her denim jacket. He looked away then. She was small for thirteen and didn't really have breasts yet, but they were on their way.

He hated himself for even considering this fact. He felt no attraction to her, but he did not trust himself where women—and she soon would be one— were concerned. These days, he saw less and less of the tomboy child he had taken under his protection. She was acting more and more like a teenaged

girl. He pulled back onto the highway, thinking that thirteen was an unlucky number. He decided that the first person who said thirteen was an
unlucky number was raising a female child.

Rain began to fall, and he turned on the wipers.

She stayed silent for five minutes—so far, a record on this trip.

When she finally spoke, she asked in a low voice, "Did she—you know—
suffer?"

He swallowed hard but was glad to be able to tell the truth. "No."

"She was a good dog."

"Yes."

"Are you going to get another dog?"

"Not right away."

"Good." She opened the can of Coke. "Will we see movie stars in California?"

The child again. He would have smiled, but he knew she would have resented it. "Maybe. Some live near the house."

"Where is it again? I keep forgetting the name."

"Malibu," he said.

"How far is it?"

"Far."

"Can I drive some of the way?"

"No."

"You never let me drive."

"So why do you keep asking?"

She smiled and shrugged. "Nothing wrong with trying, is there?"

"No. But save yourself some trouble and wait a couple of years to ask
again."

She rolled her eyes.

"How far to Denver?"

"Not much farther."

"How long can we stay there?"

"Not long. Just tonight."

She put the Coke back in the holder. Within a few minutes, she was asleep.

He watched the rain and wondered if he should leave her with someone,
someone who might keep her safer than she would be with him or his staff in
Malibu. He knew of one or two people he could trust to be good to her, to be
patient with her, who could even cope with her tendency to start fires and her
practice of picking pockets. But they could not keep her as safe as he could,
because he knew his enemies.

He passed Denver International Airport and found his grip tightening on the steering wheel. He forced himself to relax his hands, and kept driving.

The one who had killed Molly was long gone by now, he was sure.

He felt grief for the dog swell within him and fought it off.

Drive, he told himself. *Just drive.*

So he drove and turned his thoughts to the problem of how his enemies had found the cabin.

6

Manhattan Beach, California
Monday, May 19, 2:25 A.M.

The night air was warm, heated up by desert winds, so Alex rolled the windows down on the Plymouth as he made the trip from Lakewood to Manhattan Beach. The fourteen-mile journey would have been a quick trip up the San Diego Freeway at this time of night, but Caltrans had closed off most of the lanes for repairs, so he took Lakewood Boulevard south to the Long Beach traffic circle, and from there took Pacific Coast Highway. Despite its name, at this point the highway cut inland most of the way, and wasn't an especially scenic drive. It got him where he wanted to go.

He lived in a small two-bedroom home that was one of a legion of similar World War II–era stucco boxes that had once helped to meet the demand for housing for aircraft factory workers. He never put much work into the place, always thought of it as temporary housing. In another two years, he'd have put his twenty in with the department, and he'd leave the L.A. area for good. That was the plan. Retire young and away from L.A. So far, that was all there was to the plan. He spent almost every day of his life studying the problems of people whose futures had come to an end in L.A. County—they kept him too busy to make elaborate plans for his own future, but he knew he didn't want to be buried anywhere near them.

As he pulled into the driveway, he saw lights on. His uncle, John O'Brien, must still be awake. He wondered if John was having a rough night.

John was staying with Alex for a few weeks while he recovered from knee surgery—a classic cop ailment, brought on by years of stepping in and out of patrol cars. He was able to move around the house now but was forbidden to drive. Alex was glad he had talked John into recuperating at his place—it made him feel as if he had paid back a small portion of a large debt. Alex believed he owed more to John O'Brien than to any man on earth.

John was his mother's younger brother. Alex was eight years old and Miles, his older brother, was ten when they first met John. John had joined the army in 1966, just after college, and because he wasn't fond of his wealthy brother-in-law, he didn't see much of his sister after her marriage. He served most of his time in the military with Special Forces, mostly on an A team working with the Montagnard in the central highlands of Vietnam. He returned to the States in 1972 with the rank of captain, a Purple Heart, and a Bronze Star. (Alex learned of the medals a year later, in an unauthorized search of a foot-locker—that had earned him the only whipping he had ever received from his uncle.) John stopped by for what was supposed to be a brief visit to his sister in California, and for reasons Alex was unaware of then, decided to leave the military and stay in the Los Angeles area.

Although he had received more lucrative offers, when John left the military he joined the sheriff's department. Over the next three decades, he worked mostly in LASD field operations, and as part of the department's specialized teams for hostage rescue and other emergency operations. Except for periods of time as a tactical operations and weapons trainer, he passed up any promotion that would have taken him away from working on the streets, or teaching those who did.

As an adult, Alex came to realize that John's decision to live near his sister's family had probably been the result of the soldier's taking the measure of his brother-in-law. He was also undoubtedly able to see that his sister was unhappy and that her troubles weren't just a matter of typical marital discord.

Alex's father was a handsome, athletic man, capable of great charm, who had never held a job or felt the need to get one. If asked what he did for a living, he would have said he was an investor. Managing his substantial inheritance did take up some of his time. Spending it took up more.

While Alex's grandmother was alive, she kept her volatile son somewhat in check. Despite occasional rebellion (most notably, eloping with Alex's mother), he wanted to please the old woman, and lived for those rare moments when he did. When she died, he gradually began to enjoy the lack of restraint.

He wanted the best in life, not because he enjoyed the luxuries for which he paid so dearly, but because he was competitive. If his friends owned an Italian villa, he had to have a larger one, in a better location. If they threw a lavish party on a yacht, he had to host a more extravagant one on a bigger yacht. The Brandon millions, wealth that had been in the family for five generations, dwindled. All so that an insecure man would be admired by friends who were, if not wishing him ill, hoping to best him.

By the time John came to California, Alex had already learned when to steer clear of his increasingly moody father. At times exuberant and playful, his father could just as easily fall into despair. The affable man who saw him off to school in the morning might become the angry one by the time he returned home.

As one risky venture after another failed to bring the change of luck his father believed was bound to come his way, his parents began to argue. The Brandons were forced to sell their Malibu home when Alex was twelve. Alex remembered his mother protesting—uselessly—that a twenty-room house in Bel Air was more than was needed.

Visits from John were the only relief in the growing tension at home. John spent time with both nephews, but Alex was more eager to join him than Miles. Miles didn't care for the discomforts of camping, fishing, or hiking, while Alex would have been happy to live in the woods. When John took his nephews to basketball, football, hockey, and baseball games, Miles didn't want to sit in less than the best season ticket holder's box seats—possible, because their father's unused tickets were often available to them—but Alex was equally pleased to sit next to John on a hard bleacher in the nosebleed section.

Sometimes, they met other sheriff's deputies, and Alex liked that, too—their teasing, rough humor, the camaraderie that seemed so much more genuine than his parents' friendships. Once, at home, Miles referred to the officers as boorish. John hadn't been there to hear it, but Alex noticed that shortly after that, Miles never happened to be invited on the days they went to those gatherings. Miles started referring to John's home in Long Beach as "Uncle John's little place" and seldom ended up going with them there, either.

Alex didn't care who was with them or where they went. What mattered was a chance to be with John, who, in contrast to his father, was calm and steady. Alex felt safe with him.

Early one evening, Alex returned to the house in Bel Air after a day of hiking in the Santa Monica Mountains with John. Only a few lights were on, and as always, John insisted on making sure an adult was home before leaving him. Alex explained that his mother and Miles were at the symphony, that his father was probably upstairs. "Besides, I'm fourteen," Alex said. "I'm not some little kid. I can be home by myself."

"I'll be waiting right here while you get your dad," John replied.

"It's a big house. Twenty rooms." He blushed the moment he said it.

"Much bigger than my *little place?*" John said with a smile. "Better get started, then."

Embarrassed to be caught acting snobby like Miles, and chafing at John's refusal to acknowledge his advanced age, Alex stomped upstairs, impatiently calling for his father, throwing open doors and snapping on the lights of those darkened rooms—while John looked on serenely from the foyer below.

Later, John said that Alex had fallen utterly silent, that it was the way Alex reeled back from the study doorway, his stumbling gait and his wide-eyed, white-faced look of shock that made John run upstairs toward him. Alex found it hard to believe; in his mind, he could clearly hear the piercing sound of his own scream, just as he could clearly recall the sight of his father's body, the shotgun, the spatter on the wall—the damage to the face and skull that had brought one man mercy and left none for his son.

The last of his father's debts were paid with the sale of their home and its furnishings.

John took them in. From Bel Air, they moved to his small three-bedroom home in Long Beach. For the first time in their lives, Miles and Alex shared a room. For the first time in their lives, they attended public schools. Miles, who was then sixteen, resented these changes more than Alex did, but both did well in school. Their mother accepted it all with calm grace, taking a job as a receptionist, focusing her life on the needs of her sons. She died when Alex was twenty, but she had, he thought, been happier during those few years in Long Beach than at any earlier time he could remember.

Miles won a scholarship to USC, but John covered the many expenses the scholarship did not. While Alex paid his own tuition to Cal State Long Beach, John also helped him in innumerable ways. Although he had never received any pressure from John to work in law enforcement, it was his admiration for his uncle that led Alex to join the sheriff's department.

Alex thought it was likely that John was being kept awake by curiosity rather than pain—he had probably caught the story about Adrianos on the news, and was awaiting details. As he approached the porch, the front door opened, and John limped out, a mug of coffee in his hand.

"Damn it, John, you're supposed to be staying off your feet," he said in a low voice, trying not to wake his neighbors. "And what are you doing drinking coffee at this time of night?"

John pulled the door closed and said, "If I want to hear an old woman bitch at me, I'll marry that widow across the street who keeps hitting on me. And this coffee's not for me, it's for you." He held the mug toward Alex.

He took it but said, "If she's been hitting on you, I guess I'll offer to drive her to the eye doctor. But it will have to wait until morning, because I'm whipped. So I'm not staying up all night shooting the breeze with you, or having any coffee, so—"

"Yes, you are. You have a little drive ahead of you."

Alex stared at him.

"Some friends of ours were by a little while ago."

"What friends?" Alex asked warily.

"Kell and O'Neill. From the Malibu Station."

Alex felt a chill of apprehension and something else he couldn't quite name, a hollowness in his gut. Uniforms coming to the house from Malibu. His brother Miles lived in Malibu. But John wouldn't be offering him coffee if Miles or any member of his family was injured or dead.

He saw that John was watching him closely, and silently cursed.

"Friends of yours, then," he said aloud. "What brought a couple of uniforms all the way down here from Malibu in the middle of the night?"

"They were bringing my grandnephew to me."

"Chase?"

"I'm surprised you remember his name."

Alex frowned. "You talk about him often enough. What the hell is he doing here?"

"Waiting for a ride home."

He looked around in frustration, as if hoping to find someone who would talk sense. It occurred to him that he still hadn't made it past his own front door. "Let's discuss this inside."

"No, the kid's asleep, and I don't want to have him overhear nasty remarks from his loving uncle—shit like 'What the hell is he doing here?' "

"Forget I asked. I don't care why he's here. I just want to get some sleep. This is another attempt on your part to get me to talk to Miles, and it won't work. So call my less than beloved brother and tell him to come and get his kid."

"Miles is out of town."

"According to you, Miles is always out of town."

John nodded. "That's a big part of the problem. Probably why his kid is getting picked up for taking little joyrides in other people's vehicles."

"Christ—he's here in lieu of being arrested? What next? And I still don't see why this should be my problem."

"Maybe that's the attitude I should have taken when you were about his age."

Alex looked away. He thought of John taking in their damaged family under his roof. John was six years younger then than Alex was now. How had he managed it? Even before that, he'd done what he could for his family, left a promising military career to be a presence in the lives of nephews who were strangers to him.

"If I shamed you by that remark," John said, "then I'm making progress."

"John . . . you know why this is different."

"Because I wasn't cuckolded by my brother?"

Alex didn't reply, but John dropped his gaze.

"Well, shit," John said. "Now I'm ashamed."

"Don't be. Look, I've been called all kinds of things, heard all kinds of words attached to what happened between me and Clarissa and Miles, and it all lost the power to bother me a long time ago."

John shook his head. "Like hell."

Alex laughed softly. "You see me pining away?"

"I'm not saying you don't have women in your life—that's always been a little too easy for you. No, don't get fired up—I'm not saying you're unkind to any of them. But for all that, you haven't exactly rushed back to the altar."

"How many alimony checks are you paying a month?"

"Two—as you well know—and we are not talking about me."

"Okay, so I'm married to the job. Here I am, coming home after two o'clock in the morning—and that's not the worst of it by any means. I don't have to tell you what the job does to relationships."

"Don't try to take the easy way out with me, Alex. What happened with Miles and Clarissa—" He paused, and Alex could hear his frustration when he said, "You know what really bothers me? You and I talk about everything under the sun, boy—except that."

"You were there, John," Alex said, his voice still low. "You were there the night I found my brother and my wife going at it on my living room floor. Did I need to talk to you about it? Was there some part of that you failed to understand? It was all perfectly clear to me."

"Don't be a wiseass."

A silence stretched between them, then Alex said, "Look, Clarissa and Miles made their choices years ago. I didn't try to stop her leaving me, and I didn't try to stop him from marrying her afterward. I've never interfered with them in any way."

"Alex—"

"I married her before I was old enough to legally buy a beer, John. Didn't last two years. This isn't a matter of heartbreak—it's a matter of not wanting to have anything to do with people I can't trust. The only thing I've asked is that they stay the hell away from me. Now you tell me you want me to play taxi driver—come to think of it, they've got enough bucks to buy a cab company, so maybe you should call Clarissa and suggest that to her."

"You call her and suggest it. Be an asshole. Make her congratulate herself on her choices."

"Oh no. You're the one who'll make contact. Since Chase is here instead of jail only because he dropped your name—what the hell are you laughing about?"

"Your name," John said, still grinning.

"What?"

"He had a phony driver's license on him and gave them a false last name but told them he was Detective Alex Brandon's nephew. Think about it, Alex. If they had called my house, they would have heard an answering machine."

"He dropped my name? Jesus, what nerve this kid must have!"

"You ought to meet him and find out for yourself."

Alex shook his head, then took a sip of coffee.

"All that bullshit that happened with you and Miles and Clarissa," John said, "none of that was Chase's fault."

Alex frowned. He kept drinking the coffee.

"You agree with me?"

"I'm not blaming him."

"So you'll give him a ride home?"

"I'm loading up on caffeine, aren't I?"

"So you think you might want to try to develop some kind of relationship with your only nephew?"

"No, you old geezer, I don't. But I finally realized that you were going to sit out here blowing more hot air than the damned Santa Ana, and if I have any hope of getting even an hour's sleep, I'd better take Miles's juvenile delinquent home. So wake the little bastard up and get his criminal ass out here before I change my mind."

John laughed. "Caught on, did you?" he said and hobbled back inside.

Fifteen minutes later, a sleep-tousled but wary young man came out of the house. He was tall and thin, blond and blue-eyed—the "Brandon blue" as John called it—and had his father's good looks. Alex had seen photographs of Chase before now—John made sure of that. But beholding the flesh-and-blood version of Miles's son was another matter altogether. For starters, he looked a lot like Miles did at his age, and Alex found himself thinking of those difficult years, of how hard Miles had taken their father's death, how afraid he had been. "What's going to happen to us?" he had asked again and again.

And now, at fifteen, his son Chase was scared, too.

The thought struck Alex suddenly, as he watched the boy approach, and he wondered what the hell this kid had to be afraid of. Chase's eyes looked so much like Miles's at nearly that age, held that same uncertainty—it was as if all Miles's DNA had passed his fear along with all his other traits.

But Miles had lost that old fear before he turned eighteen. Alex didn't much like what had replaced it—a level of ambition that would have been admirable if it hadn't been so damned ruthless. Was that hidden somewhere in this kid, too?

Alex couldn't see much of Clarissa in Chase's features, and he was grateful for that.

Chase took one look at Alex, then nervously glanced back at John. John hobbled forward and put a hand on Chase's shoulder. "Alex, allow me to present your nephew, Chase."

Like they were at a damned cotillion, Alex thought.

Chase put out a hand.

Alex, not even bothering to look at what he knew would be a commanding stare from John, shook hands with the boy.

Chase glanced down at the rough and abraded hand that grasped his own. Not his father's smooth and manicured paw, Alex thought. The boy said nothing.

"You two better get going," John said, not hiding his pleasure. "Chase, your uncle Alex has had a long night already, so behave yourself."

"Yes, sir," Chase said. He paused and added, "Thank you, Uncle John."

Nothing rebellious.

"You're welcome. You call me anytime you need help."

"Yes, sir." He got into the car.

Alex handed the empty mug back to John and said, "What'd you tell him that's got him so scared of me?"

"What makes you think you're the center of the universe? He's not scared of you."

"Then what?"

"Not your problem, Alex, remember?"

"You're an evil old man," Alex said, and got into the car.

Chase was studying the interior of the Taurus with the look of someone who finds himself in a cheap foreign hotel bathroom, unsure of how to operate the toilet. Alex figured the department-issued sedan was probably the least expensive vehicle the kid had ever been in. If he had any derisive comments in mind, though, Chase didn't say them aloud.

They didn't, in fact, say a word to each other until Alex hit traffic. At three in the morning, when the worst thing about traffic should have been dodging the occasional drunk, he had come across another Caltrans repair crew.

"Shit," he said. Why did this kid have to pick this, of all nights, to show up on his doorstep?

"Sorry," Chase said.

"Not your fault," Alex said, in spite of what he had just been thinking.

"Can't you—you know, like, put on a siren or something?"

"No."

"Oh."

They were stopped near a lamppost a moment later. Chase, looking at Alex's hands on the wheel, said with no little awe, "Were you in a fight?"

Alex saw what the boy saw in the yellowish lamplight. Skinned and swollen knuckles, broken nails, abrasions here and there. "No. I went climbing on Sunday."

For a moment, Alex was sure that Chase would pursue the topic, but they moved again into darkness, and he fell silent. Alex saw the Sepulveda off-ramp and took it.

"Uh—Uncle Alex?"

Uncle Alex. It sounded strange to hear it.

"You don't mind if I call you that, do you?" Chase asked anxiously.

"No, I don't mind."

"Well, anyway, this isn't the way to my house."

"You still live off a little private road in Rameriz Canyon?"

"Yeah."

"I grew up in that house. I know how to get there."

"You grew up in our house?"

"Your dad didn't tell you that?"

"No, but he doesn't talk to me much about . . ."

"About me?"

"No."

They rode in silence for a few more minutes, then Alex said, "We lived there until I was twelve. Your grandfather lost a lot of money, and we moved to another house, in Bel Air. Your dad tell you about that?"

"Is that where my grandfather killed himself?"

Alex saw it as clearly as if he had just stepped through the door — the room, the body, the unholy mess of it. "Yes," he said.

"My dad said you were the one who found him — Grandfather Brandon, I mean."

"Yes. And after that we went to live with John," he quickly added, heading off further inquiry about suicide by shotgun.

Chase seemed to pick up on his discomfort, though, and said, "So you lived in our house? That's so crazy. What room was your room?"

Alex described it.

"No way!" Chase said, laughing. "That's my room!"

Alex was a little surprised by this. He would have suspected that Miles would have given his own former room to his heir. But he only said, "What do you know."

And he began to wonder what the kid did know.

He considered his options, made a decision, and turned onto Sunset and headed west. He ignored the voice of reason, the one that told him there were shorter routes to the Coast Highway. He ignored some other impulse that said there were longer ones.

"Your dad ever tell you why . . . why we aren't close?"

Chase shrugged. "He said you just didn't get along so well now. That sometimes that happens."

"Yeah, sometimes it does."

"Well, isn't that kind of stupid? Like, I mean, I never had a brother — but, you know, if I had one, I don't think I'd act like you guys do."

"Maybe you wouldn't."

Chase heard the rebuke in it and stayed silent.

The road began to wind, curving its way toward Pacific Palisades. The sky was darker here; the homes larger and farther apart. Concentration on the road was not distraction enough, though, and Alex found himself not liking the silence.

"What school are you in?"

"School's out for the summer," Chase said. Alex heard a return of anxiousness in his voice.

"When it's not out for the summer, where do you go?"

He took so long to answer, Alex thought he wasn't going to reply. "My dad says they're going to send me to Sedgewick."

"Sedgewick!"

"You know it?"

Every member of the sheriff's department who had ever worked in the Malibu area knew about Sedgewick—the brats of billionaires, the Hollywood hell-born. "Aren't most of the kids who end up there kind of troubled?"

Chase laughed. "Yeah, troubled. That's one way to say it. It's where fucked-up rich kids go to fuck each other up even more."

Alex wasn't so sure he was wrong, but he said, "You talk that way around Uncle John?"

Chase looked away from him. "No, sir. Sorry, sir."

"One extreme or the other, I see."

Chase didn't answer.

"I take it you'd rather not go to Sedgewick."

"Hell—heck, no. I hate the kids who go there. They're meaner than—they're really mean."

"What about your mom?" he made himself ask. "Does she want you to go there?"

"That—"

Whatever word it was going to be, he bit it off. "I take that to be a yes," Alex said.

"It was her idea. She knows the owner of the school. *Really well.*"

Alex let it pass. The last thing he could afford to do was to get into some conversation with this kid about his mother's virtue. He made the turn onto Pacific Coast Highway, heading north. "You tell John about this plan to send you to Sedgewick?"

"No. I don't want him to be—you know, ashamed of me."

"So you steal cars?"

Chase went back to brooding in silence.

"Talk to John about it. He has more influence with your father than I do."

As they came nearer to the house, Alex felt a mixture of anticipation and trepidation. He hadn't seen the place in years—from the day he heard that Miles had bought their childhood home, he had avoided this road. Chase gave him the code for the new security gate. He punched it into the keypad, and the gate swung open. At the end of the long private drive, the mansion loomed before him, many of the lights on. He felt some sense of recognition, but not of homecoming. Miles had changed it.

The front door opened, and a woman peered out.

"Looks as if your mother waited up for you," Alex said.

Chase wasn't looking at her, though.

"Uncle Alex? Thanks. I'm—I'm almost glad I got in trouble. I've been wanting to meet you for a long time."

Stay safe or leap into the abyss? He leapt. After all, the kid had jumped first. "I'm glad I met you, too, Chase. But next time, just call. It will be easier on all of us."

"I don't have your number."

Alex pulled out a card and gave it to him. "Pager number's on there, too."

Chase quickly tucked it away, now watching his mother coming down the steps.

One leap was enough for an evening, though. "Do me a favor, Chase," Alex said, as the moonlight caught Clarissa's features. "Don't force me to make small talk with your mom."

"Sure." He quickly got out of the car and waved.

Alex waved back and turned the car around.

He looked in the rearview mirror and saw Clarissa staring after the car.

Miles had changed her, too, Alex thought. Time and Miles.

Just not enough.

7

Manhattan Beach, California
Monday, May 19, 7:02 A.M.

He answered the phone with the practiced motions of a man who is more often awakened by it than an alarm clock. Half-roused from a brief, deep sleep, he mumbled, "Brandon."

"Alex? It's Dan. We've got trouble."

He rubbed a hand over his eyes and looked at the clock. "Trouble?"

"I need for you to get in touch with Morton and head on over to Avalon as soon as possible," Lieutenant Dan Hogan said. "I've got a helicopter waiting for you at the Aero Bureau."

"Avalon?" he repeated, still not fully awake. "On Catalina?"

"Yes. I know you got in late, but we've got two more bodies in connection with the case you worked on last night."

The sense of dread he had felt the night before returned. "Someone found Adrianos's bodyguards on the island?"

"Maybe you can tell me that. Did he have any female bodyguards?"

"No. The victims are females this time?"

"One male, one female."

"So maybe a bodyguard and his companion."

"All I know is that we've got two more bodies hanging upside down over a bathtub, and I want to make sure nobody calls me up to say there are three more of them somewhere else in this county before the day is out. Get there before the media gets wind of this, Alex. Murder cases are rare on Catalina, so you know the press will make the most of a double homicide."

The sense of urgency that Alex felt with any new case increased tenfold. It wasn't a matter of the potential for negative publicity—handling that was Hogan's problem. What bothered him more was the knowledge that the killers were setting the pace, and a fast one. They had also chosen two sites within LASD jurisdiction to display bodies in a way that was bound to grab attention. He wondered, uneasily, whose attention they wanted and why.

Forty-five minutes later, Alex and Ciara were on a sheriff's department helicopter, taking off from the department's Aero Bureau at the Long Beach Airport.

"You don't know anything more than that?" Ciara asked him.

"No," he said. "Just that we're supposed to meet a Deputy Black there."

She made a sound that was almost a growl. She didn't look as if she'd had much sleep, either.

Soon they were flying over the Long Beach Harbor, above the *Queen Mary*. From this perspective, the size of the ship was more evident than from the nearby dock—the *Queen Mary* dwarfed every other vessel in the harbor. He watched the white sails of pleasure boats, the larger ferries, the barges and freighters making their way past the breakwater.

The winds of the past few days had died down but not before they had managed to clear away the smog and haze. It would build up again, but for now, the view from the helicopter was breathtaking.

The journey to Santa Catalina Island would take about fifteen minutes. Alex decided that it might be the last pleasant fifteen minutes of the day and became determined to enjoy it. He had already seen the skylines of Long Beach and Los Angeles, the backdrop of the mountains with the last of their winter snow, and now the harbor and curving coastline. If he could have stayed up here, with this sort of visibility, he might have thought about loving the L.A. area again. But he knew days like these were a come-on for a different bargain, and he didn't let himself be taken in.

The island, its green and brown peaks rising above the sea, was only twenty-two miles from the mainland. Far too soon, the helicopter was landing.

Due to local laws, most of the vehicles used on Catalina were golf carts. The sheriff's department carts were painted to look like cruisers, with department insignia. For the short drive from the Avalon Substation to the crime scene, Alex and Ciara rode in the back of one of the carts. He kept waiting for Ciara to make a crack, but she was quiet.

They soon rolled up to the front of a small vacation rental home. The smell hit them before the cart came to a stop.

The day's best fifteen minutes were definitely over.

Deputy Evan Black met them outside. He was a tall man with short blond hair, and green eyes that held a look of lingering amusement, as if he were a man who had just heard a good joke. His skin was deeply tanned. Alex guessed him to be in his early thirties.

The deputy who had driven them over introduced them to Black but made the common error with Ciara's name. "It's pronounced 'Keer-ah,' not Sarah," she corrected. "But you can pronounce it 'Detective Morton.' "

"I'm sure no one will forget that now," said Black, smiling. Ciara gave him a hard look, but he didn't seem to see it. "You made good time. Crime lab folks haven't arrived yet."

"How many of you have been inside to have a gander while you waited?" Ciara asked.

Black remained unperturbed. "Just me. Before that, only ones in were the couple that discovered the body."

"The couple?" Alex asked.

"Yes, sir. The bodies were discovered by a couple that cleans the place every Wednesday. But the next-door neighbors called the owner—guy lives on the mainland—to complain about the smell. He called the cleaning people, so they showed up this morning to check on the place."

"About what time?" Alex asked.

"A little after six."

"Kind of early for housecleaning, wasn't it?" Ciara asked.

"They were planning to take a quick look inside and then go fishing. They saw the bodies, hurried over to the station, and we've asked them to stay there so that you can talk to them, if you'd like."

"Thanks," Alex said. "A little later, we probably will. When did you get here?"

Black glanced at some notes. "At six-seventeen. Dale Howell—the deputy who's back there making sure no one tries to enter through the back door—he was with me, but I'm the only one who went inside. It was obvious that there was no chance of the victims being alive, so I backed out. We secured the scene and called the station. I mentioned that this was similar to the scene in Lakewood, so—"

"Just how in the hell did you know that, Deputy Black?" Ciara asked. "We managed to keep most information about the scene off the evening news."

He gave her a rueful grin. "I don't want to get him in trouble, but . . . well, I know the guy who sang into the porcelain amphitheater."

"The rookie who got sick?"

"Yes."

Ciara seemed ready to say something, but Alex spoke first. "That turns out to be lucky for us, then. Any sign of forced entry?"

"No, sir, nothing obvious—but, as I said, I haven't looked around in there much."

Alex thanked him. Ciara and Alex put on latex gloves and entered the small house. The deputy remained outside.

It was typical of a vacation rental property: mismatched sturdy furniture, the few items of décor firmly nailed down or too heavy to lift. Nothing seemed disturbed. No sign of a struggle, just the overpowering scent of decay. As they walked toward the back, the smell became worse.

The scene in the bathroom was nearly a duplicate of the one in Lakewood, with two bodies instead of one. But here, the air was thick and close—no one had been there before them, opening windows. Alex began to feel more sympathy for the Lakewood rookie.

The bodies faced away this time, toward the wall behind the tub. Alex glanced at the mirror and saw two numbers painted in what appeared to be blood.

"Seven and eight," he read aloud. "Hell."

He glanced at Ciara, who was looking a little queasy. "Let's hope that's what it means," she said, "and not seventy-eight."

"Trust you to find the bright side," he said, and she laughed.

The female victim had been strong and wiry. Her long brown hair was streaked with gray and dipped into the blood beneath her. The male was thin, his blond hair cropped close to his head. Two letters had been amateurishly tattooed on his neck: AD.

"You know of any local gangs that go by the initials 'AD'?" he asked.

"No," she said. "Wait—isn't that one of those El Monte groups? One of those white supremacist outfits—Aryan something or other?"

"Aryan Destiny," he said, and frowned. He carefully positioned himself so that he could lean over the tub without disturbing the bodies.

"What are you doing?" Ciara asked. He noticed that she had moved nearer the door. *Probably trying to get some air,* he thought.

"I want to look at their faces."

"Cripes, Alex—don't fall in."

But he wasn't listening to her. He was staring at the faces of the victims, then back at the mirror. He closed his eyes for a moment, hoping against hope that somehow what he was seeing would change, that when he opened them again, the scene before him would be transformed. But when he opened them again, the same two lifeless faces stared back. Two faces he recognized, even in this state.

"Oh God," he said quietly.

"What is it? What's wrong?" Ciara asked anxiously.

"We've got trouble," he said, and moved back from the tub. "If we've ever had bigger trouble, I don't know what it was."

"What are you talking about? Who are they?"

"Valerie Perry and Harold Denihan."

"What?" She stared at the bodies, then at him. She scowled and said, "You're shitting me. Very funny, Alex."

"I'm totally serious."

"You're telling me that we've got two more fugitives on the FBI's Most Wanted list dead in our jurisdiction? That two criminals who committed crimes in completely different parts of the country, who have nothing to do with each other, who committed totally different crimes—that they're both hanging over that tub?"

"Yes. We'd better call Hogan. Hell, we'd better call the captain."

"Alex—maybe seeing Adrianos last night—"

"Take a look," he invited, stepping past her to allow her to move into the small room.

She hesitated. "Perry and Denihan have nothing to do with each other!"

He glanced back over his shoulder. "They've got at least one thing in common now."

8

Hogan had a show going.

Brandon never ceased to be amazed at how quickly the lieutenant could put a presentation together. It was his forte—the ability to use computers had been no small part of Hogan's rise within the department. Didn't know shit about detective work, but that didn't make him any different from most lieutenants, in Alex's estimation.

In the time since he had received Alex's first calls from Catalina, Hogan had managed to put together a computer "slide show." Hogan had also loaded in photos Ciara had taken with a digital camera at the scene.

The conference room at the homicide bureau was crowded. Alex counted twenty-three people, among them Homicide Bureau Captain Bill Nelson, all of the other lieutenants, the head of the crime lab, Enrique Marquez and other detectives, as well as a public information officer, or PIO. Alex watched their faces. They were tense and serious, aware that the department was about to become the focus of a tremendous amount of attention, most of it unwanted.

Hogan had just finished going over the Adrianos case, and now a blurry photo of a smiling, narrow-faced woman appeared on the screen. Her long gray and brown hair was parted in the middle, her skin was tanned and creased. She had the look of a woman who had once been pretty but had not aged well. Nothing in her brown eyes reflected what she was capable of, which had probably been the key to her success as a killer.

"Valerie Perry was a white female, aged forty-seven," Hogan said. Everyone had seen this one—it had probably been posted in every law enforcement department in the country, on the FBI's Ten Most Wanted Fugitives flyer. Still, they stared at her face as if seeing it for the first time. "Until recently, she spent most of her time in the Phoenix area. She ran a boardinghouse and only accepted clients over sixty-five years of age, although for the past five years, most were in their eighties, and none were younger than seventy-eight. She carefully screened her tenants, making sure they were unlikely to have family members who'd be looking for them." The next few slides were of elderly men and women. "She didn't charge much to provide room and board, and although residents didn't seem to stay there long, there was never a shortage of renters.

"Ms. Perry took nicer vacations than most people who do that for a living," Hogan continued, "but her neighbors weren't aware of that, among other things." The image on the screen changed to excavations made in a large sandy yard. "Remains of ten men and three women whose Social Security checks were still being cashed were found behind Valerie Perry's boardinghouse."

The slide changed to the face of a young man with dark eyes and a weak chin. "The remains of a twenty-seven-year-old male were also found—apparently those of her accomplice and boyfriend. Perry and her boyfriend had a falling-out—he had found a new girlfriend, and apparently Ms. Perry wasn't pleased about that. When the new girlfriend hadn't seen him for a few days, she reported him missing. That led police to investigate, and it was discovered that Ms. Perry had already fled, taking a large amount of cash with her. That was in February of last year. Until this morning, she had not been seen since March of this year—that was when a national television program aired information about the case, and callers from locations in Colorado, New Mexico, and Nevada indicated that they had seen her over the intervening months. It was clear to investigators that she had indeed been in some of these places, but they failed to locate her. The trail went cold after that."

"Which program?" Alex asked.

Hogan seemed a little put out by the interruption, but consulted his notes and said, "*Crimesolvers USA.*"

"Based in Santa Monica?"

"I believe so, yes. One of those shows that wants to be the next *America's Most Wanted.* To continue—"

But this time the captain interrupted. "Why do you ask, Alex?"

Alex saw Ciara smile. Focusing his attention on the captain, he said, "Whoever is doing this is getting his information from somewhere. He has leads even we don't have. If he's not getting information from the FBI itself, or other law enforcement agencies, maybe this show is the answer. Have the other fugitives on the FBI list been featured on it?"

The captain looked to Hogan.

"Not exactly *featured*," the lieutenant said carefully. "Not all of them. But at the end of the program, they do go over the FBI list, show the photographs of all ten."

"Worth talking to the staff, then," the captain said.

"Was she number seven or number eight?" the public information officer asked, not looking up from his notes.

There was a stunned silence. The PIO looked up anxiously, only to be met with the captain's scowl.

"The FBI doesn't rank the criminals within its top ten list," Alex said. "There is no number one, two, three, and so on. A fugitive is either one of the ten or not."

"Oh."

"Lieutenant Hogan," the captain said, "I believe you have some information about the other victim?"

It didn't take Hogan long to find his stride again. He clicked something on his computer keyboard, and the projector showed a new image, that of a slender man with close-cropped blond hair. "You're probably already aware that Harold Denihan was a member of Aryan Destiny, a white supremacist organization. The nearest branch office of this group is in El Monte, but Denihan was part of a Kentucky unit. He's wanted in connection with the bombing last January of a Louisville, Kentucky, church two years ago. He was identified as the purchaser of components, and diagrams of the church and bomb-making equipment were found in his home. The bomb killed seven, but if things had gone as he had hoped, it would have been a much higher number. He appears to have been able to elude capture because he's been aided by his knuckle-headed brethren." He paused, looked at his notes, and said, "He's also been featured on the *Crimesolvers* program."

"Any chance the victims have some connection to one another other than being on the FBI list?" Captain Nelson asked.

"Not that we know of at this time, sir," Alex answered. "We'll check further."

"It seems highly unlikely, sir," Hogan said.

Captain Nelson took over the meeting. "You have probably noticed that we do not have a member of the Federal Bureau of Investigation present at this meeting. Undoubtedly, they will want to claim jurisdiction over these two cases, especially because others will have reason to believe that these individuals were brought here from other states against their will. None of that is proved, however, so—you may expect some delays before we are working with the FBI. These are homicides in our jurisdiction, no matter who the victims are, or where they came from. Sheriff Dwyer fully intends to cooperate with authorities in the jurisdictions where the victims allegedly committed their crimes, but as you know there have been recent difficulties between our department and the Bureau."

Brandon exchanged a glance with Ciara. She rolled her eyes. "Difficulties" hardly began to describe the level of animosity between the leaders of the FBI and the LASD at the moment. The two agencies had worked together to bring charges against a number of Los Angeles County politicians accused of accepting payoffs from organized crime. The sheriff's department had cooperated fully, knowing that federal charges would carry higher penalties on conviction. The FBI had not shared the information it gathered—nothing new there—and insisted on using its own lab, and only its own lab, to process evidence in a major sting operation. The cases were high profile, and Sheriff James Dwyer—who held an elected position—had enjoyed the positive press, even though he allowed the FBI to take more credit than many of his employees thought they deserved. But when the cases went to court, defense experts successfully attacked the FBI's handling and testing of the evidence, and what had promised to be a source of pride in interagency cooperation became a fiasco.

For the last six months, department cooperation with the Bureau had been minimal. Brandon wasn't surprised that the department was delaying working with the FBI, but wondered how long the sheriff would be able to ignore the inevitable pressure to involve the Bureau in the murders of three fugitives on its Most Wanted list. He figured it wouldn't be long, but that wouldn't be his fight, anyway. Politics were everywhere, and the LASD was no exception. His uncle's sage advice and his own years with the department had taught him more than a few things about the delicate business of not becoming ensnared in them.

"What do you have to go on, Detectives?" Captain Nelson asked, snapping Brandon's attention back to the meeting.

"At present, not much, sir. Detective Morton and I have questioned neighbors in the area of both scenes, and none of them saw anything. We suspect the victims were drugged, brought to these locations, and killed at the scene.

We suspect the use of an anticoagulant, and we're checking with area hospitals to determine if any thefts of such substances have been reported lately. We still have some checking to do in connection with the Catalina house—that scene had to be arranged by someone who knew the housekeeper's schedule and something about the rental itself—so we're looking into the rental history. Unfortunately, there are problems in connection with the rental company."

"What problems?"

"They had a computer crash and tell us they won't be able to retrieve the records."

"Convenient, isn't it?" Ciara said.

"I'm inclined to agree," Captain Nelson said.

"They've got a good reputation on the island," Alex said. "We're going to see what we can put together from the paper records, and we'll have someone check out the computer's hard drive to see if the data can be recovered."

"And the owner of the property?" Nelson asked.

"We've hit a couple of snags there," Ciara said. "But we've confirmed that he's been running a conference this past week, and it's unlikely that he's managed to do that and hunt these two fugitives down, kill them, and hoist them up in his own house."

"Hmm. You have any other leads?"

Alex said, "The rope appears to be of a kind used by climbers, so we'll be looking at sources for that as well."

He saw the looks on the faces of the others in the room and knew what they were thinking. That he didn't have shit to go on.

A man from the crime lab asked, "Do you think number ten—or whoever the killer is ranking as number ten—on the list is out there rotting upside down over a tub full of blood somewhere?"

"Could be. But for all we know, these three are the only ones that we'll find here. We have no way of knowing unless we locate the other seven fugitives."

"Or their bodies," Ciara said.

The comment irritated Alex. Not once in his years with J.D. had he ever found himself wishing his partner would just shut the hell up. He had always watched J.D., taken his cues from the more experienced detective. He wondered if what really rankled was that Ciara didn't defer to him as he had to J.D.

"Do we have anyone working up a psychological profile of the type of individual who might commit these murders?" Nelson asked.

"Not yet, sir," Hogan answered. "But we're going to try to get Shay Wilder to take a look."

"Wilder?" one of the others asked. "Isn't he retired?"

"Yes," the captain said. "But Lieutenant Hogan is right—he's the best person we could turn to for help with this. Let's hope he'll give us a hand." He paused, then added, "Hard to figure out what's going on with this one, other than who his targets are."

"Detective Brandon," the man from the lab said, "one of our techs said you know of a similar set of cases?"

Alex felt his spine stiffen. He glanced at Ciara, who quickly said, "That's not exactly true. Your tech was eavesdropping on a conversation between my partner and me. The tech jumped to a conclusion—"

But the captain interrupted. "Not exactly?" he asked Alex.

"The tech apparently didn't hear me say that the man who committed those murders is dead." Seeing that wasn't going to be enough, he told them about Jerome Naughton. "Eight victims that we know of. With the exception of Serenity Logan—his wife—none of them were from the Los Angeles area."

"And you're sure he acted alone?"

"Fairly sure, at least as far as the killings went. His stepson—Kit Logan—was undoubtedly traveling with Naughton during that time. From what he told us—and the evidence supported this—Naughton would find a victim, hang her upside down over a bathtub, and torture and kill her. Getting sprayed by arterial blood was apparently a turn-on for him. At various points in the process, he posed the boy with the victim, or had the boy photograph him posing with her." Alex hesitated, then decided to leave it at that.

The room was tense, quiet. Nelson broke the silence by saying, "How old was the boy?"

"When he killed Naughton?"

"No. When this started."

"About eleven."

"God almighty," Marquez said.

"He was able to tell us where the victims had been killed, and knew the exact locations of their burials," Alex said. "Prosecutors in each of the cases didn't believe there was any reason to suspect the boy was anything other than a captive himself. He was fourteen at the time he killed his stepfather. As far as I know, that's the only murder he ever committed."

"How did he kill Naughton?"

"Bashed his head in with a shovel. And undoubtedly saved a ninth victim's life. She was tied up, starting to go through the same treatment."

"Is that why he killed Naughton?" Ciara asked. "To rescue her?"

Alex hesitated, then said, "No."

The others waited.

"He left her tied up in the house. We didn't talk to Kit immediately after he killed Naughton, but he claimed that Naughton had kicked his dog, and that was what had set him off."

A ripple of laughter went through the room. Ciara frowned. Alex had seen this sort of disapproval from her before.

"Go on," Nelson said.

"He killed Naughton, took the dog, and ran away. He got to a pay phone and called his grandmother collect. His grandmother was Elizabeth Logan, and she had lawyers on the way before anyone in law enforcement talked to him. She claimed he was nearly incoherent when he called her, but she did get the information about the ninth victim from him, and she called authorities."

"Ninth, right?" Marquez said. "That was the number on the mirror—nine."

Alex shrugged. "Maybe there's a connection, but why now?"

"Maybe somebody else kicked his dog," one of the others said, and again there was laughter.

"Any idea where he is?" the captain asked.

"No, sir. I plan to try to find out, but—"

"But all hell has been breaking loose. I understand." He paused, then said, "I'm forming a task force for these cases as of now. Detective Brandon will be in charge of this task force, and if—God forbid—any other cases bearing any resemblance to these three come in, they are to be referred to him immediately. Is that understood?"

Heads nodded all around.

"Whether or not the victims are on the FBI list," Captain Nelson said, "similar crime scenes or staging should be reported to him at once. And any murder of a fugitive on that list, even if in a different manner, will be referred to him. Let me know what resources we can put at your disposal, Alex, and you'll have them."

Alex thanked him, although he wasn't sure he was grateful. Nelson didn't seem to hear him anyway—Alex realized that the captain was watching the reactions of Ciara Morton and Dan Hogan. Neither of them looked happy.

"Alex," Nelson said, turning back to him, "I've arranged for a meeting with Sheriff Dwyer. He'd like to have us brief him before a press conference he's scheduled, so we should head over there now."

9

"Guten Abend."

Everett smiled sleepily and returned the greeting to Cameron Burgess, wishing him a good evening. They would speak only in German while in this country. This was not a burden to either of them. In addition to their native English, Everett's closest associates in Project Nine were required to speak French, German, Italian, and Spanish fluently, and to be conversant in at least one other language.

In high school, as he had considered plans to make life at Sedgewick more interesting, he had studied books on the training of Special Forces units. He had no desire to serve in the military, but he found certain aspects of the model useful for developing his own elite unit. The language training appealed to him. They would be an international force to be reckoned with.

At Sedgewick, among his fellow students, he looked for recruits. They must be boys who were not simply unhappy at home, but truly disconnected from their parents. They must be boys who were physically fit and intelligent, but whose intelligence was seldom recognized by others. It was essential that they lacked self-confidence. Any sense of worth, they would receive from him alone.

He began to learn what would draw such young men closer to him, what would give him increasing levels of influence over them, and acted accordingly. He envisioned using that influence to create an ultimate, unstoppable force, a team that could be put into action to achieve any purpose of his choosing, to settle any grievance on his behalf, to demonstrate its power in any way he asked.

He looked for boys who would be followers by nature, and chose three of them from a group of slightly younger boys.

Cameron Burgess was quiet and withdrawn, friendless before he met Everett.

Morgan Addison, who had instituted a reign of terror at home and in his previous school, now found the tables turned—at Sedgewick, he was picked on by bigger and more violent students. Prior to receiving Everett's protection, he lived in fear of them.

Frederick Whitfield IV was eager to please, to be appreciated for his talents. Everett was the first to recognize that Frederick's love of snooping could be useful.

They became the inner circle that helped him to maintain control over many other students at Sedgewick. He gave them focus and purpose, fed their need for excitement, and provided the mixture of sternness and affection they longed for. He taught them to look at the world as he did, to believe in his ideas about justice and being effective. He would choose missions; they would carry them out. They became more physically fit, took on tasks that were more and more daring, and became more dependent on him in the process.

As they all grew older, he had come to recognize that he would need other holds over them, and devised new plans. He now had enough incriminating evidence to send any of them to prison. He was pleased that he had not yet needed to consider using it.

They were now at an age, however, when he thought he might begin losing them. Morgan had recently become obsessed with surfing. Frederick had always been easily distracted, and Cameron unpredictable. Bigger and more stimulating challenges were needed. Project Nine was the perfect answer. Among his reasons for devising it, the continued loyalty of his followers was by no means the least important.

He sat up in the bed and looked at his watch. He calculated the time difference between Los Angeles and Frankfurt. Again he spoke in German to Cameron. "No wonder it feels as if it's just time to get up. I wonder what our friend Alex Brandon is up to today?"

"Probably sleeping in after a long night in—" Cameron stopped himself before saying Lakewood. "*Mit nummer neun,*" he finished.

"Yes, fitting. And I said number nine would be the first, didn't I?"

"Yes. And seven and eight next."

"You have a perfect memory."

Everett was pleased to see him blush at the praise. He studied Cameron, and decided something was bothering him. Cameron's tall, broad-shouldered frame would have appeared relaxed to anyone else. He sat crosswise in a large leather recliner, his long legs dangling over one of its arms. He rubbed the palm of his hand over his short, dark brown hair, and kept his intense gaze on Everett. For a moment, Everett was distracted, wondering whether he had ever met anyone whose eyes were as dark as Cameron's. Did the long lashes make them seem darker than they were? No, he decided. One could hardly tell where iris left off and pupil began. Large, gorgeous dark brown eyes.

It was the movement of one of Cameron's hands, a stroking movement, back and forth through his hair, that Everett saw as a signal of Cameron's anxiousness. He had learned to read him long ago, at first using this habit with the hair and even more subtle "tells" to defeat him in high school poker games. Later he used them to convince Cameron that he knew and understood him better than anyone else, which was undoubtedly true.

"*Hast du nicht geschlafen?*" he asked.

"No, I didn't sleep," Cameron admitted. "I wanted to make sure our prey was still here."

"And he's not."

Cameron's brows drew together. "No."

"Any idea where he is now?"

"Mexico. He took the bait for Oaxaca."

"That's excellent."

"But his watcher told us he was here."

Everett didn't bother to hide a bemused look. "Is P.T. still alive?"

The hand came down. Cameron smiled. "I told him not to worry."

Everett laughed. "You were kind to do so."

"I am the soul of kindness. I'm even kind to animals. I put that poor old mutt of Kit's out of its misery."

They both laughed at that.

"So," Everett said, "give me a few details. Herr Majors—he is still calling himself Majors?"

"Yes."

"Herr Majors received an invitation from one of his creepy friends to visit Castillo del Chapulínes Resort."

"Right. Slick wrote to tell him that he found a safe haven there, free of harassment. Too bad Slick's kid never found a safe haven."

Everett's smile faded. "Will this one be more difficult for you?"

Cameron went very still for a moment, then relaxed. "No. It will be easier. I'll enjoy it more."

Everett wondered if this were true. Catching Majors was an unsavory business, but perhaps Cameron was right. Ultimately, it might be more rewarding than most of the others. A trip down memory lane. The first man they had killed together was a child molester.

He was Cameron's father.

In order to trap the man who now called himself Majors, they had made use of two sex offenders, men who used the chat room names "Slick" and "P.T." on Internet sites that were popular with male children. Slick and P.T. pretended to be boys and invited potential victims to other, more private sites. These sites required the victims to give out identifying information, including addresses. From there, they would arrange meetings.

Everett and Cameron had unearthed Slick's and P.T.'s real identities when researching a customer list their team had hacked into. The customer list belonged to the man who now called himself Majors. After careful study, they became certain that Majors had been in touch with them. Majors, they knew, sought assistance through the help of others of his kind—assistance he sometimes acquired by blackmailing his own customers. It wasn't difficult to get them to extend such help. Few people wanted others to know they had purchased snuff films featuring children.

Everett and his friends offered relief from the blackmail. Relief that guaranteed privacy and a total absence of law enforcement involvement. For men who knew that Majors was on the FBI's Most Wanted list, the chance to escape him was too good to pass up—as were the generous cash payments they received for betraying him.

One of the customers being blackmailed, P.T., was here in Frankfurt. Because he was frightened of Majors, P.T. was nervous about working with them. They had an easier time buying the help of the man who lured Majors to Oaxaca—Slick, an American just out of prison.

"Majors is still using the credit card?" Everett asked.

"Oh yes," Cameron said, "the one we arranged for him to receive. The one for which he's the only real customer, credit supplied by us. Which means the records are entirely accessible to us. He's booked a room at the resort for two weeks."

"Excellent. We become jet-setting German tourists in Mexico. What's worrying you?"

"I don't want this one to get away."

"Cameron—"

"I know he won't. I know we won't fail."

"Exactly."

"It's just—I don't want him to have time to hurt anyone in Mexico."

"He's being watched, remember? You need sleep. Do you want to rest here or on the jet?"

"The jet."

He stood up and began to gather his gear, items stored here in preparation for any work they might need to do here. Everett watched as Cameron paused to run his fingers along the strap of a daypack. The strap concealed a garroting wire. When he turned back to Everett, his eyes were bright with anticipation. "P.T.?"

Everett considered his friend. Tease him or indulge him? It was always a delicate balance with Cameron. He judged Cameron's mood and smiled. "Have him meet us at the airport."

1 0

Kit was watching Spooky swim laps in the indoor pool of his Denver home when one of his two cellular phones chirped. He knew immediately that it was a business call. The other phone was set to vibrate silently when a call came in, and only one person had that phone number. Until last November, about once or twice every month, he had received a call on it. But over the last six months, it hadn't rung at all. Nevertheless, he kept it with him at all times, even sleeping with it, and was especially cautious about having fresh batteries available for it.

It was the business phone that rang now, and he answered it.

"Mr. Logan?"

"Yes."

"We've located the jet. It left Frankfurt several hours ago."

"The passengers?"

"Two German businessmen. Young men. No names yet."

"The names don't matter. They won't be using their real names. And the flight plans won't be real, either—they'll be changed at the last moment."

"Yes, sir. As before."

"Exactly. But it will be easier to keep track of a private jet than two men."

"As soon as we have further information, we'll let you know. Anything else we can do for you now?"

He put a hand in his windbreaker and touched the rabbit's foot there.

"Check the German newspapers for any reports of homicides over the next few days. Especially strangulations."

"But they aren't there now—"

"It's unlikely that any bodies will be found immediately. They aren't stupid."

"No, sir."

"Neither is my staff. Thank you for the information." He took a deep breath and asked about the caller's children. He was not someone who found social interaction easy and had to remind himself to ask such questions, to make small talk. His grandmother had taught him how to proceed in these matters, but he did so as an anthropologist might, a man trying to fit into an alien culture, and never with any real ease. So it was with some relief that he reached the point in the conversation where he felt it would be all right to end the call.

Spooky came out of the water then and wrapped herself in a beach towel. "Was that your girlfriend?"

"I don't have a girlfriend, and I don't want one. You know that."

"So, are you gay?"

"I don't have or want a boyfriend, either." He told himself not to let her nettle him.

"So—what, you're like, what? A nothing?"

"Right, a nothing."

She bit one corner of the towel, twisted it as she chewed. "Sorry," she said after a moment. "That wasn't very nice of me."

"No, but don't worry about it. Get dressed."

"Are we going out for dinner?"

"If you'd like. What do you want?"

"McDonald's."

He winced. Spooky saw travel as an opportunity to eat french fries and cheeseburgers. Not to his own tastes, but he said, "Okay."

Spooky laughed and hurried off to change.

He sat watching the water, letting it soothe him.

He had been worried all day, because he had dreamed the digging dream again last night. Usually, he thought of it as one of his least disturbing memory-dreams, but the last time he had dreamed it was the night before Molly was killed.

He made an effort, not entirely successful, to consider the matter of the killing of the dog dispassionately. He knew that by making sure he was seen, Cameron had left a warning—no, not a warning, he decided, but a challenge—an invitation to strike back. He wasn't exactly sure what Everett wanted from him, although he could make some guesses. It would be Everett's plan. Wherever Cameron was, Everett was behind the scenes, manipulating. Were others involved? He would go to Malibu to learn what he could. And he could keep Spooky safer there.

He felt the other phone vibrate then and forced himself to be calm, to let it ring twice before answering. Could be a wrong number. Probably was a wrong number. He flipped it open.

"Hello, Kit? It's Meghan Taggert."

Meghan. Not a wrong number after all. He felt elated, but hid that, as well as his mild annoyance that she gave her full name. He would have recognized her voice. It was low and rough, a voice of whiskey and smoke, although he had never seen her drink or light up a cigarette. Still, he was so pleased that she had finally called again, so relieved that she was safe, he wasn't going to quibble. "Hello, Meghan," he said, not letting his voice betray his feelings.

"Do you have a minute? Am I bothering you?"

"No—I mean, I have time, and you aren't bothering me. It's good to hear from you."

"I wondered—I'm calling—it's about Gabe."

It was always about Gabe. He hid his annoyance at that, too. "Have you heard from him?"

"No, nothing since . . . not since . . ."

"Before he became a fugitive," he said.

"Right. Listen, I shouldn't have called. I'm sorry, I guess it's just an old habit. I feel worried about Gabe, so I call you. I shouldn't. It's not fair to you."

"I like that you call me. I'll do whatever I can. You know that. I'm . . ." He searched for a word. "I'm honored that you call me." That didn't sound right, but he hurried on, afraid she'd hang up on him for saying such a dumb thing. "I'll do whatever I can, but I can't help out if you don't tell me what's troubling you."

She hesitated, then said, "It's nothing, really. Just—has he contacted you lately?"

"No, I haven't talked to him since last summer. Just before . . . before the news."

"Before the murders."

"Yes."

"Do you believe he did it?" she asked quietly, as if asking softly might soften his answer. "Do you think he could kill a family?"

He thought of her trouble-prone brother, who had been his closest friend at

Sedgewick. Gabe, who did his best to welcome the new kid to the school, while others whispered uneasily that Kit had murdered his stepfather because of a dog. Sedgewick was a school of truants, misfits, and bullies, but even among them, Kit's history was extreme and caused the other boys to think of him as a hard case. Most were wary of him, stepping away from him as he walked down the halls. Not Gabe. Beneath Gabe's party-boy, man-on-the-edge façade, Kit learned, he was acutely aware of the feelings of others.

Gabe was at times heedless but rarely intentionally unkind. And he wasn't violent. Even after Kit convinced him to learn to defend himself (on the grounds that he needed to be able to look after Meghan), Gabe would rather run from a fight than throw a punch. Yes, his addictions had led him to become a thief, and his attitude about taking material things was wrong—Kit doubted even Gabe believed the rationalization that the theft of heavily insured goods really didn't do much harm. Even so, taking a diamond ring wasn't the same as taking a life.

"No," he said. "I'll never believe that of Gabe. But . . ."

"But he was there, with the people who were breaking into the house, and so the law will say he's as guilty of murder as the guy who did the shooting. Just for being with them!"

"Meghan," he said gently, "he probably wasn't just with them, he was probably there to do some breaking and entering."

"Yes, you're right. That's his history, after all."

The guilt came washing over him then. "I knew he had done things like that before. And I knew he was broke. He'd asked me for money."

She must have guessed the direction of his thoughts, though, because she said, "You couldn't have stopped him, Kit. Even if you had given him the money he asked for—and I don't blame you for turning him down, either. He just would have used it to get drunk or high."

"I guess I can't help but believe . . . maybe if he'd had money, Gabe and his friends wouldn't have been there, and those people would be alive."

"I didn't give him money, either. Does that make me guilty, too?"

"No, of course not."

"Maybe not, but I think about it every day, Kit. Every single day. I ask myself if I could have prevented it from happening. Even though I know he would have spent everything I gave him or you gave him—it would have been gone in no time. Just like his inheritance. You've always stood by him, and he's been nothing but a pain in the ass. But this—it's so awful, Kit. Worse than anything he's ever been involved in before. I guess I've been ashamed to call you because of it."

"No, Meghan. Don't say that. Please. He's always been in one kind of trouble or another. It's not your fault. It's just—just the way he is. He doesn't like killing. He would have hated that. He just got mixed up with the wrong people."

"Is that really all it takes? I don't know."

What could he tell her? That no effort on her part would have made a difference? That her brother would have to save himself? No, she wouldn't be able to hear that, not now. Besides, he knew that he'd do anything he could to help Gabe, if Gabe ever sought his help again.

Would Gabe contact him? It had been almost a year since he had talked to him.

Now he wondered if he had been too certain of Gabe's ability to stay concealed. What if someone other than the FBI was looking for Gabe?

He thought of the private jet that had flown to Germany.

"Kit?"

Her voice brought his thoughts back to her. Cautiously, he said, "Meghan, you can always call me. Always. I'm not just Gabe's friend. I'm your friend, too."

There was another long silence. He agonized over what he had just said to her. Had he been too eager? Did he say something offensive to her? Would she ever call again?

And then, to his shock, he heard her crying.

"Meghan, please—please don't cry."

"God, Kit. I'm sorry. I should have called you a long time ago."

He was silent, unsure of how to proceed.

He heard her sniff. "Man, can you believe it? Me, crying. In a hotel lobby no less. Where the last thing I want to do is make a scene."

"Why are you at a hotel?"

She laughed. "Like my brother, I'm a fugitive from the FBI."

"What?"

"No, not because I've broken any laws. But they're watching the house, probably thinking Gabe will try to contact me, or that I'm hiding him or— God knows. I just couldn't take it anymore. I'm sure my phone has been tapped. So I took off. I'm in Albuquerque, trying to unwind a little. Not that it's working—I keep having this sensation of being watched, so I guess I'm still too uptight. I'm using one of those prepaid calling cards from a pay phone. Ridiculously paranoid, right?"

"No, smart. Did you use a credit card to pay for your hotel room?"

"Yes. Oh—I guess they do know where I am now," she said in dismay.

"Maybe not yet, but they probably will soon. You said Gabe hasn't contacted you since the robberies?"

"Not a word. To be honest, I almost hope he won't contact me. No, that's not true, either. I don't know what I want anymore. Sometimes I want him to be caught before he does anything else so stupid, so wrong. But when I think of him facing the death penalty, I go crazy. I can't think of letting that happen to him. I think I'd rather help him get to another country, or—I don't know. I don't know."

He screwed up his courage. "I could come there. I could come and get you, help you get away for a few days. I'm on my way back to L.A. from Denver. I'm taking Spooky to Malibu."

"I thought you said she usually stays home when you travel, that someone stays at home with her then."

"Usually her tutor or one of my employees stays with her. But I decided to bring her with me this time." He hesitated and decided he would tell her the rest when they were face-to-face. "I have some business to take care of in L.A.—I don't think I'll be there for long."

"It would be so good to see you, but I don't want to put you to even more trouble."

"No trouble. In fact, I'd be putting you to trouble. You haven't met Spooky yet."

"Maybe I could help keep her entertained while you go to meetings or whatever it is you have to do."

"That would be great," he said, even as he began to question the wisdom of his plan. This was no time for behaving impulsively. But to see Meghan . . . to make sure she was safe . . .

"I'm staying at the Sandia Towers," she said. "Can you pick me up here tomorrow?"

He could hear his own pulse. He forced himself to think, to calm down. "Just to be on the safe side, let's meet away from the hotel. It will make life a little more difficult for anyone who is following you. Do you have much luggage?"

"Just a small overnight bag. I can get anything else I need in L.A."

"Are you afraid of heights?"

"No, not at all."

"Then tomorrow afternoon at about four, take a cab to the Sandia Tramway and take the tram to the top of the mountain. From the hotel to the peak, it's probably a trip of about thirty minutes. There's a restaurant there called the Peak Experience. We'll meet you there, okay?"

"Great."

"Bring a warm jacket and wear shoes you can walk in—I won't be able to park closer than a mile from the restaurant."

"Okay. And—thanks, Kit."

"See you soon."

Spooky came back out just as he ended the call. "Who was that?"

"A friend. Are you ready to go?"

"Yeah, I'm starving. What friend?"

"Someone you'll meet soon. Let's go."

"A woman?"

He sighed. "Yes."

"Who is she?"

"An old friend."

"Your girlfriend?"

"We've just had this conversation, haven't we?"

She shrugged and looked away. They walked out to the Suburban in silence. He kept a hand on the phone, still warm from being held during the conversation. His fingertips touched the rabbit's foot. He thought of how much he liked the sound of Meghan's voice.

And now he would see her in person for the first time since he graduated from high school.

The rabbit's foot did not prevent him from being assailed by doubts.

"I wish you were gay," Spooky said.

1 1

Alex watched as Sheriff James Dwyer, a consummate politician, deftly avoided directly answering questions about FBI involvement in the cases, managing to turn every inquiry into an opportunity to talk about the capabilities of his own department. Tall, silver-haired, sharp-eyed, and smooth-spoken, he was in his element, while Alex felt distinctly out of his own.

Before today, the only time Alex had done more than shake hands with Dwyer was at J.D.'s funeral, when Dwyer had offered brief condolences. Alex had never expected more. Over sixteen thousand people worked for the L.A. County Sheriff's Department, and almost ten thousand of those were sworn officers. Between its detectives and the man at the top, there were several levels of command. Contrary to the image of the lone cowboy with a tin star that the word "sheriff" sometimes evoked, the L.A. County Sheriff was the chief administrator of a law enforcement agency that was the principal police force in forty-one cities, staffed nine county jails, provided security for the courts, and much more. Dwyer didn't have time to shoot the breeze with one homicide detective.

On Alex's few previous high-profile cases, J.D. had been the one to go to headquarters with Nelson to brief the sheriff. Dwyer spent a few minutes talking about J.D. today, making an effort to put Alex at ease. Some of that might have been the irrepressible campaigner at work, but Alex had also been struck by how quickly the sheriff absorbed the basic facts of the cases, how many details he had wanted to know.

"I understand you're trying to get Shay Wilder to take a look at these cases," Dwyer had said.

"Yes, sir."

Dwyer had smiled. "Good luck. If the stubborn old cuss will let you in his front door, give him my regards."

Now, at the end of the press conference, Alex realized how well Sheriff Dwyer and Captain Nelson had anticipated what the sheriff would be asked by the press. Just before the follow-up questions became too probing, Dwyer said, "That's all we have for you now, ladies and gentlemen."

Alex heard but ignored the repeated cries of his name from members of the press.

"Detective Brandon! The FBI must surely have more background on these cases—when will they be called in to investigate?"

"Detective Brandon! Can you tell us if the couple who found the bodies on Catalina are suspects at this point in time?"

Picturing the mild-mannered, elderly couple, who had been thoroughly unnerved by their discovery, Alex wanted to laugh at that one. But he kept his face straight and his mouth closed.

Nelson, no fool, had already made his way off the platform and out of the room. Alex tried to follow.

"Detective Brandon!" Diana Ontora, from Channel Three News, moved in front of him as he descended the platform steps. "Whoever's doing this—aren't they really heroes?"

She thrust the microphone so fiercely into his face, he thought she might have been trying to give him a bloody nose.

"No, they're not heroes," he answered, then tried to move by.

She blocked him again and said, "But they've stopped three killers—killers the country's top cops couldn't catch—right?"

"They've committed three murders."

"Technically, yes," she said, still not budging. "But really, they've rid the country of three of its worst criminals, and all without costing taxpayers a dime. Aren't they making this department and every other law enforcement organization in America look bad? Aren't you a little afraid of the competition?"

"This isn't a game," he said and moved around her.

"They killed a man who brutally murdered a family of four, including one of your witnesses," she shouted after him. "Don't you wish they had killed him sooner?"

He kept walking.

Alex was due over at the studios where *Crimesolvers USA* was taped. The producer, Ty Serault, had a reputation of going out of his way to be cooperative with law enforcement—not surprising, given the nature of his program—and had agreed to talk about the staff who had worked on the show on the nights when the segments about Valerie Perry and Harold Denihan aired. When Ciara, who was already headed back to Catalina, heard this, she had asked Alex if he had promised to take the guy for a ride with the sirens on.

"He's not a wannabe, if that's what you're thinking. He's just trying to help out—and you have to admit, the show helps."

She shrugged. "I'm sure hanging out with Hollywood types is more interesting than going over rental receipts on Catalina."

"Not necessarily," he said, and she laughed.

Now, as he drove to Santa Monica in his department-issued Taurus, he wondered if a new vigilantism was about to rear its ugly head. A show like *Crimesolvers USA* did its best to encourage the public to leave the actual apprehension of criminals to professionals, to stay clear of suspects and simply call the police with information. But he didn't expect that sort of wisdom to prevail as word of these cases spread.

From the outside, the studio where *Crimesolvers USA* was produced looked like any other industrial building. A set of large satellite dishes perched on the roof was the only indication that it might be something other than a warehouse. No sign indicated that this was the home of Serault Productions. He pulled up to the wrought-iron fence that surrounded it and pushed a button on the intercom. He identified himself and said, "I'm here to meet Mr. Serault."

A young woman's voice said, "Okay, park in any space marked 'visitor.' " The gate opened. Alex looked around but didn't see a camera. For a guy who produced a show about criminals, Alex thought, Ty Serault didn't seem to have spent much on security. He parked and looked around the lot. There was a new silver Lexus in the space marked T. Serault. The other cars in employee spaces included four Japanese compacts, four American-made SUVs, and a lime-green VW Bug as the tiebreaker.

Serault was a block of a man, big and square-shouldered, with a square head to match, dark hair buzzed down to a shadow over his skull. He had a prize-fighter's face, and a low voice that held traces of his native Louisiana. His dark brown eyes had a spark of humor in them, and Alex knew from talking to others in the department that Serault had brains to match his brawn.

He ushered Alex into an office lined with commendations from law enforcement agencies. "Quite a press conference you just came out of, there. Ontora ended up looking worse than you did, but she'll want to even the score in the next round."

"With any luck, the PIO will handle that one."

Serault smiled. "If he doesn't, at least you've learned you ought to leave the platform in the middle of the herd. Stragglers get cut out."

"I'll keep that in mind. In the past I've found reporters waiting at my car, though, so I'm not sure I'm going to be able to escape."

"For a while now, probably not. You've got a hell of a mess on your hands, don't you?"

"Not many people will understand that, I'm afraid. They won't mind hearing that someone has killed these three."

"No, probably not. You think someone on my staff might be helping your vigilantes?"

"Just following every lead I can."

"Hmm." Serault pulled a desk drawer open and removed a small stack of files. "I hope you're wrong, but I can see that it's a possibility. Whoever captured these three criminals had information about them that no law enforcement agency in the country was able to turn up. I don't mean to imply any lack of effort on the part of law enforcement—we both know that you can't be focusing on the FBI's list all of the time. How many murders a year do you—the sheriff's department—investigate?"

"Last year, a little under three hundred. So far, this year has seen a slight increase, but not by much."

"Almost one a day—provided no gang wars break out."

"Gang violence is a factor, yes."

"My, my. No wonder. And except for the cities like L.A. that have their own departments, y'all have the whole county to cover, right? Calabasas to San Dimas, Catalina to Palmdale—what is that, about four thousand square miles?"

Alex smiled. "Sheriff's department Web site?"

Serault laughed. "That was kind of clumsy of me, wasn't it? Should have made you wait and come around tomorrow, when I'd have my act worked out."

"You didn't need to go to the trouble, Mr. Serault."

"I want you to know that I'm on your side, Detective Brandon. That's all. But actions speak louder than words." He handed the folders over to Alex. "The shows including the segments on Valerie Perry and Harold Denihan aired at different times, and the staff on the phones varied a little. What you have is a list of employees, and if they no longer work here, I've given you the most recent contact information we have for them. We don't have much turnover in our production staff, but answering phones is entry level, sort of an intern's job, although we screen them better than most places would."

"Are they students, then?"

"Some are. They're mostly young people. They aren't looking to make a career out of answering phones. They just like being connected with a television show. Once the novelty of that wears off . . ."

"I understand." Alex glanced at the files and noticed they included not only former staff members' names, addresses, and phone numbers, but also their hire dates and dates of employment. There were even copies of applications and employee ID photos. "Thanks. I appreciate the effort that went into this."

He laughed. "Oh, one of my assistants did that. I was screwing around on the Internet, remember?"

"Nevertheless, I know your staff is busy, and it was good of you to have someone take the time to put this together."

"All I ask is that you keep this information confidential—I value your work, but my staff values its privacy."

"Of course."

Alex looked at the lists again and said, "You have the Maricopa County Sheriff's Department and the Phoenix police on here . . ."

"When we air a show, basically, it's a tape, but we have a live studio segment, when we ask people to call. When that's going on, we have law enforcement officers from concerned agencies in the studio. So we had officers from Arizona on Perry's night, and Kentucky for Denihan's night. When reruns air, we don't usually have as many people taking calls." He glanced at his watch. "I have to get to a meeting, so I'm going to hand you over to Nola. She'll meet you in the reception area. She hires and trains all the phone staff, so I figured she'd be the most help to you."

Alex thanked him again and stood. He was nearly at the door when Serault said, "One other thing, Detective Brandon."

What was it going to be? Alex wondered, as he turned back toward Serault, who was suddenly looking uneasy. Alex had not forgotten that Serault was, when all was said and done, a member of the media, and half-expected some request to be involved in the investigation, or special access to information, or coverage of the investigation when it was over.

"I don't want you to take this wrong," Serault said.

Alex waited.

"This program, it's all about law and order—real law and order. In the last five years, we've covered all kinds of investigations and helped in any way we could to bring criminals to justice. So—so perhaps you can see that I'd hate to have any damage done to our reputation. I'm trying to cooperate here, and I hope you can appreciate the fact that I really didn't have to give you any information."

"I'm not so sure that's true, Mr. Serault, but—"

"All right, let's just say, I'm giving you information without making you waste the time it would take to get a court order or making you fool with my attorneys."

Mildly annoyed that Serault might be trying to bargain with him, he said, "You've certainly been helpful so far. But—"

Serault held up his oversized hands, meaty fingers spread. "I'm not going to get in your way, believe me. But I don't want this program to have any association with vigilantism or—or downright murder and kidnapping. Not if I can help it. If we let someone like that in here, then no one is more sorry than I am for it. I'm just asking you to let the public know that if somehow we did make a mistake, that you'll let them know *Crimesolvers* did all it could to help you catch that person."

"I'm sure the department wouldn't hesitate to acknowledge your help."

Serault gave a sigh of relief and slumped back in his chair. Alex left him sitting there and went out to the reception area.

While he waited for Nola Phillips, Alex looked over the files. He noted that only three people who no longer worked for the company had worked on both segments, only four more had worked on both segments and still worked there.

"Detective Brandon?"

He looked up from the paperwork to see a petite blonde approaching him. Her short hair was styled into spiky tufts and peaks; her pale complexion was enlivened by a slash of bright pink lipstick and a small silver nose ring; her large blue eyes were slightly magnified by the black-rimmed rectangular lenses of her glasses. He wondered if the glasses were supposed to be a somber note. She wore a skintight lime-green blouse, black leather pants, and black Charles David stiletto heels.

"The Volkswagen," he said, and she laughed.

"How'd you guess?"

"The blouse," he lied, and liked the impish, doubting look she returned.

"I'm Nola." She glanced at the receptionist and added, "Let's talk in my office."

Her office was a windowless cubicle at the end of a hallway, past the closed metal doors of the studio. The room would have been completely dark, but she had plastered most of its surfaces with glow-in-the-dark stickers shaped as stars, planets, dinosaurs, and insects. "They keep me from bumping into the furniture while I find the switch," she said as she made her way across the room to the desk. She snapped on a desk lamp, and the room was made only slightly more officelike. She gestured toward a pair of beanbag chairs, but knowing they weren't made for the comfort of those who wore weapons, he opted for a more traditional office chair. She seemed disappointed but took the chair behind the desk, then propped her feet up on it. She held out her hand and said, "Gimme."

"I wish I didn't know you meant the folders," he said, handing them to her, and she laughed again. He liked the laugh, too—a laugh with meat on its bones. Watching her look of intense concentration as she studied the files, he doubted Nola Phillips had giggled since she was five. Which, he reminded himself, was probably not all that long ago.

"I saw the press conference," she said. "You're looking for someone in these files who could be a killer?"

"Not necessarily. Could be someone who accepted a payment for information. And your staff person might not have known the real reason the other party wanted the information."

He moved closer to the desk and pointed out the names of the seven who had worked on both shows. He started with the ones who were still employed by the company, then moved to the ones that had left. As he went through the list, she offered reactions: "No, not in a million years. Wouldn't catch him jaywalking. . . . No, she's one of those people who would confess immediately if she did. . . . Doesn't have the nerve. . . . Doesn't have the imagination."

A former employee, Dwight Neuly, was working on a "creepy student film." Alex made a note to talk to him. She had moved on to the next name.

"Eric? Hmm. Really sophisticated one moment, goofy kid the next. He worked really hard, but he was also a clown. But he seemed, like, I don't know, really harmless."

"Harmless?" Alex took the folders back and stood. "Maybe he just didn't know what he was up against."

She smiled. "Is your day just starting?"

"Oh no. But the hours are hard to predict. What about you?"

"I've only been in since two o'clock, so I'm around for a while. Ty is easy-going about hours, so long as you're here when he needs you during the production season and you get your work done in other times. One of the reasons I like working here."

"Any of the people in this file going to be here this evening?"

"No, sorry. They only come in on the night the show airs—Thursday. Want to come back then?"

"If I need to, yes. Will that be okay with your boss?"

"Sure. He loves having real cops around here."

"Tell him to open an all-night coffee shop."

"Not a doughnut shop?"

"And here I thought you'd avoid the stereotype."

"Sorry." She openly assessed him. "I take it back. You have definitely not been sitting around eating doughnuts."

"Maybe I work out so that I can. But that reminds me—any of these seven people involved in sports of any kind?"

"I don't know. Eric was in good shape, so was Dwight."

"Okay. Thanks for the help. I'll start by seeing if I can run down Creepy Dwight and Harmless Eric."

"Don't tell them I said that!"

"Wouldn't dream of it."

"What do you dream of?"

"Pardon?"

"Your dreams. Dreams interest me. I do dream interpretation."

Not being a believer in such things, he found himself wishing he had left five minutes earlier, before she said this, but he could see the earnestness with which she asked, so he decided to play along. His dreams of the last few nights had been unpleasant surreal versions of crime scenes, and he wasn't going to speak of them to her. So he thought back to the most recent pleasant dream. "I dream of cliffs."

"Oh! Fear and vulnerability."

He smiled. "Not for everyone. So long, Nola."

He left her staring after him, the desk lamp light reflecting stars and dinosaurs on her glasses.

1 2

Frederick Whitfield IV was in stealth mode. And enjoying himself immensely.

He was seated at the hotel bar, wearing dark sunglasses, drinking a club soda. He was dressed in a cheap suit and inexpensive men's dress shoes. He didn't like wearing the clothes, hated them only a little less than the midsize rental car he was driving. For a guy who was used to wearing Armani and Ferragamo, and driving a Lamborghini, it was a lot to put up with all at one time. More than the clothes and the rental car, he hated the haircut and hair color he had adopted: short and light brown. But he was playing a part, and he was willing to make sacrifices.

Frederick was pretending to be an FBI agent. No one had asked him to do this. He had no false identification or weapon with him, and he hadn't told anyone that he was with the FBI. But he believed himself, in this moment, to be a perfect imitation of an agent. He was fairly sure that if a real FBI agent walked into this bar, right now, he would feel a sense of recognition, of brotherhood, if not an out-and-out conviction that here was a fellow member of the agency.

Morgan Addison had followed Meghan Taggert here. Morgan, a surfer, had found the oceanless Land of Enchantment less than enchanting. Frederick had quickly volunteered to take over the watch.

Morgan had been mistrusting at first. "I don't get it, man. Most of the time, you kiss Everett's ass."

This was true. Frederick readily admitted it. "He's like a magnet. When he's near, I can't resist doing whatever he wants me to do. When he's away . . ."

"I don't know," Morgan said warily. "Ev's gonna be pissed at me anyway, because I think Meghan knows she's being watched. I think that's why she came here."

"Perfect," Frederick told him. "This covers you with Ev. If he complains about your handing this over to me, you just tell him she made you."

"You want Ev to think I fucked his dream woman?" Morgan asked in disbelief.

Frederick held back a sigh of impatience. "First, she is *not* his dream woman."

"Yeah, right. Whatever you say, Freddy."

"Second, do not call me Freddy."

"I'm crapping my pants in fear here, Freddy."

"Fine. Stay there. I'm going to bone that little surfer girl you're so hot for."

There was a silence.

Interpreting it correctly, Frederick said, "Yes, I know all about her. Did you think that was a secret you could keep from me, Morgan? I know her better than you'd think. We had a drink together this afternoon."

"God damn it—"

"Just a drink, that's all."

"You're lying."

"Oh no, we definitely had drinks."

"If you've so much as held her hand—"

"I'm crapping my pants in fear here, Morgan."

Morgan fell silent again.

"I can get the next flight out," Frederick went on. "You can be on your way home in three hours. You can find out what the lovely—what's her name? Sherry. Yes, Sherry—what your little hottie refused me. So far, anyway. Spoke of no one but you, Morgan, truly. But, you know, a girl gets lonely . . ."

"You are such a prick!"

"I see. All right, I'll say good-bye and see what progress I can make on the beach."

"No, forget it. Come on out here. But if I get back there and find out that you've put some move on her, you might as well not come back to L.A."

Sitting at the bar now, recalling the conversation, Frederick started to smile to himself. Would an agent smile? Yes, he decided, especially if it was a knowing smile. He allowed it.

He had come here straight from the airport. He had rented the car using one of four stolen California driver's licenses he kept on hand, and charged it to the matching credit card Everett had issued to him. He had credit cards for all the names on the licenses. Everett and Cameron had control of the bank that issued them.

Project Nine had resources that extended far beyond these, of course. At the moment, out of necessity, he wasn't making much use of them. He was, as he liked to think of it, working solo.

This had been emphasized from the moment he arrived at the hotel. At the entrance booth to the parking structure, he paid cash for a magnetic striped ticket that would allow him to go in and out of the structure all day. Morgan waited until Frederick saw Meghan Taggert's BMW, and drove off, which meant Frederick was on his own to procure a weapon. Frederick had been a little pissed about that.

But in the next moment, over the rental car radio, he heard something that lifted his spirits. A newscaster announced that reports just in from Los Angeles indicated that three criminals on the FBI's Ten Most Wanted list had been found dead there. A press conference had been scheduled for five-thirty Los Angeles time.

Frederick could hardly contain his glee. He hurriedly checked to make sure his tinted contact lenses were in place and smiled at the brown-eyed stranger in the mirror. He put the sunglasses on. Cool.

He spent the next few minutes calming himself, going through a set of breathing exercises designed to help him focus. "Special Agent Frederick Whitfield IV," he said aloud, with as much baritone as he could manage.

He got out of the car, and despite the warmth of the day, donned the suit coat. He moved with purpose as he made his way to the lobby of the luxurious hotel.

Once there, he suffered a slight shock. A slender young woman with straight, dark hair reaching to her shoulders, silvery-blue eyes, and—although she was neither speaking nor looking at them—the undivided attention of every male in the lobby, was waiting for an elevator. His quarry, Meghan Taggert—and she was only a few yards away from him. He quickly realized that she seemed to be lost in thought—distressing thought.

Of course. Meghan had always had one big worry to contend with, and his name was Gabriel Taggert. She was thinking of her brother. She had suddenly left her home and traveled here without warning.

She had to be planning to meet Gabe.

And Special Agent Frederick Whitfield IV was going to be on hand for that moment. That asswipe Morgan was going to be missing out on all the glory.

Frederick watched her get into the elevator, watched the lights on the lobby panel, saw that the elevator stopped on the seventh floor.

He glanced at his watch. Fourteen minutes to go before the press conference. He smiled. Easy work for an agent of the fucking FBI, now, wasn't it? He caught another elevator car, rode it up to the seventh floor, exited cautiously, and, hearing a door close in the hallway to his right, turned in that direction. He opened his cell phone. He dialed the hotel's number.

"Ms. Meghan Taggert's room, please," he said.

He walked along the hallway, listening to the sound of the ringing phone. He was trying to decide whether it was 716 or 718, when the ringing stopped.

"Hello?" she said a little breathlessly. Softly.

God, he loved her voice.

Which door? Just say hello again, he willed her silently. He waited, listening, but she hung up.

He moved a little farther away from the doors, called again, and said to the operator, "I'm sorry, I was just talking to one of your guests on my cell phone when I must have hit a dead zone and lost the signal. Could you reconnect us? Her name is Meghan Taggert."

As the operator made the connection, he moved back to the doors. This time, the phone rang several times before she picked it up.

"Hello?" she said again, almost angrily.

Room 718, then. He hung up and went back down to the lobby. If he hurried, he'd be just in time to watch the press conference.

In her room, Meghan hung up the phone after the second call. She stood up and paced, hugging her arms across her stomach, looking at the phone as if it were a weapon left behind by an invader.

Kit was the only other person who knew she was here.

Be sensible, she told herself.

She called the hotel operator.

"Oh, that was a young gentleman. He didn't give a name, but he did mention that he was having trouble with his cell phone."

"Thank you," Meghan said, feeling relieved.

She turned on the television set. She watched the evening news every night now, expecting an announcement of Gabriel's capture. Or worse.

The newscaster smiled and said, "Three of the FBI's Ten Most Wanted fugitives have been found murdered in the Los Angeles area. We'll take you to a live press conference at the Los Angeles Sheriff's Department. We'll have this and other stories when we return."

She sat down hard on the bed. *Not Gabe*, she begged silently. *Not Gabe*.

She thought of the phone calls. Kit must have learned something and called to warn her, to tell her what had happened.

Frederick Whitfield IV finished his club soda slowly. The bar was buzzing with talk of what they had done. He eavesdropped with all the pleasure of a man who is hearing his work praised by strangers.

"Ask me, couldn't have happened to a nicer bunch of folks," a woman next to him said, and laughed harshly. She was a big blonde and bore all the marks of a heavy drinker. She raised her glass. "Here's to seven more of them kicking off as soon as possible."

Frederick obligingly clinked his glass with hers, as did the man on her right. The man was leathery and thin. "Amen to that," he said in a flat Midwestern accent. "It's about time the government realized that if they just sit around and coddle these criminals, worrying about their rights, people are going to take matters into their own hands."

"Jesus, yes," said another man, two seats down. He had abruptly ended a discussion of baseball with the bartender when the news came on. "It's not just that. It's their damned incompetence. People are tired of shivering in their beds, waiting for the cops to figure out how to catch these guys."

"That's what I'm saying," said the leathery man. "The cops catch them, and they have to let them go."

"Because the ACLU and the courts and all of them are all screwed up," said the blonde, leaning into him.

"Exactly right, darlin'," said the baseball fan, and got a wink for being agreeable.

"That one guy killed a family—witnesses," Frederick said, thinking it was time to add his mite.

The blonde slewed around on her chair to smile at him. "Who needs a son of a bitch like that walking around, right?"

"Right," said the leathery one, and she slewed back.

"I think they ought to find whoever's killing them," the baseball fan said seriously, causing everyone to stare. "And then make him the director of the FBI!" he finished, causing laughter all around.

Frederick laughed harder than any of them.

She could only take so much, Meghan decided. She hated to call Kit again, but after all, he had just tried to reach her. She didn't bother going down to the lobby. She used her cell phone. He answered on the first ring.

"Meghan? Are you okay?"

"You heard the press conference?"

"Press conference?" he repeated blankly.

"Oh—I thought that was what you were trying to talk to me about, the last time you called."

She heard the pause before he asked, "When?"

"About twenty minutes ago," she said, her voice sounding small, even to her.

There was a silence, then he said, "I haven't called, Meghan. Someone else knows you're there."

She let out a low moan. "Never mind me! They're going to kill Gabe."

"Meghan, no—they'll try to bring him to trial."

"No! You don't understand." She told him about the vigilantes. "I'm here in New Mexico, and those sick bastards are looking for Gabe! They may already have him."

"Meghan—we've got to try to learn more. We can do that in L.A. Until then, there really isn't much we can do for him."

Panic started rising. "But if Gabe—"

"Are you forwarding calls from your home phone to your cell?"

It was a practical question. She felt the panic ebb. "No, but I can set that up from here."

"Good. Do that right away, so Gabe can reach you more easily. Now—we need to think about your safety."

"I can defend myself."

"I'd like to believe that, but no one is a one-person fortress," he said.

"And why be foolish, right?"

"Right. Given these news reports, I think you have to take every sign of danger seriously. You need to make sure no one tries to use you to get to Gabe."

"Maybe the FBI's already followed me here."

"Maybe. If it is the FBI, you'll be okay. But if it isn't—" He stopped. "Call hotel security and tell them someone has been trying to break into your room—sticking a card in the key slot, banging on the door. Tell them you are afraid to stay in the room, that you want a new room, and you want an escort from this one to the new one on another floor. Make the hotel security office describe the person who is coming up and don't open the door to anyone who doesn't have ID and exactly match that description."

"Should I just go to another hotel?"

"I already considered that. I think you'd be followed. The Sandia Towers will take care of you, just let them know you want their help. Tell them you got a couple of crank calls just before the problem started. Tell them you don't want any incoming calls. When you get to your new room, call me, okay?"

"Okay."

"I'm going to see if I can arrange some additional private security for you until I can get there. In the meantime, you don't open the door for anyone, and you only answer the cell phone. All right?"

"Yes, all right. Thanks, Kit."

"Meghan—"

"Yes?"

There was a long pause. "Don't talk yourself out of doing what I've asked you to do. You'll hang up, you'll ask yourself if it was all your imagination, or maybe even wonder if you're causing too much trouble. You won't be. Promise me—"

"I'll do everything you asked me to do, Kit."

"Thanks."

She called the hotel security office. She found that without any effort at all, she could sound as if she'd been scared out of her wits.

They responded immediately.

Frederick lingered a little longer, unable to tear himself away from the congratulations and good wishes he was receiving—undercover, on behalf of the project—in the bar.

But soon his new comrades were distracted by the sports news, and he bid them adieu. He strolled over to the front desk and waited patiently in line. Normally, he would have been able to use the privileges of those with membership in the frequent guest program. He found himself in the rather novel position of not being catered to, but he felt proud that he had remembered to stand in the not-so-special line.

He smiled at the registration clerk. She was a young African-American woman. He thought she was quite attractive. He glanced at her name tag and said, "I'm embarrassed to admit this, Rashida, but I'm a little superstitious. I need to stay on the seventh floor. I need two sevens and a one in the room number. Ideally, you'll give me room seven-seventeen, if it's available."

She seemed taken aback for a brief moment, then said, "Let me check."

He worried a little at that hesitation, but he decided that it was, after all, an odd request. And she wasn't behaving as if she felt suspicious—just dealing with a crazy white guy. That was okay. She typed something into the computer, then said, "It's already reserved, but let me check with my supervisor. I'm sure we can get you into that room."

He removed his sunglasses. "Thanks. It's silly, I know."

She smiled, and he was pleased to hear her give a shy little laugh. "It's not a problem at all—you just wait right here, and I'll take care of this right now."

She went through a door behind the front counter, into an office. There was a two-way mirror on the wall between the registration desk and the office.

Reflected in the two-way mirror, he saw for the first time that he had one brown eye, one blue.

He quickly put his sunglasses back on and considered bolting away from the desk. Undoubtedly Rashida had noticed and had laughed at him. He felt a sudden surge of anger.

But—wait a minute, he thought. David Bowie's eyes were like that, weren't they? Maybe she liked the idea of a man with features that were a little unusual. It wasn't as if they were strange enough to land him in a circus, for God's sake.

Rashida returned, smiling, with an older woman in tow. The older woman was Hispanic. Her name tag identified her as Consuela Ramon. Managers, he noticed, got to have last names on their tags. She wore a walkie-talkie that crackled at her hip. She was smiling, too. "Mr. Grady?"

He nearly didn't respond. "Oh yes," he said, remembering which credit card he had given Rashida. "I'm Mr. Grady."

"We'll be happy to give you that room. We're just waiting for housekeeping to check to make sure it's clean and ready for you."

"Thank you," he said.

Rashida flirted with him while processing his registration. Consuela didn't seem to mind. In fact, she helped the next two people in line while Rashida concentrated on him. Rashida was obviously so dazzled by him, she could hardly keep her mind on what she was doing. She nearly didn't return his credit card. He had to ask for it. He wondered about that for a moment, but she gave it right back, apologizing.

He was putting the card back in his wallet when he heard a male voice on Consuela Ramon's radio. "Consuela, we'll be right there."

And she glanced at him and smiled.

He turned and walked away.

"Mr. Grady?" Rashida called. "Mr. Grady, your room key!"

He walked faster, not looking back. Once outside the hotel doors, he ran to where the lame-ass car was parked. He hurried into it and, tires squealing all the way down the ramps of the structure, made it to the exit gate. He jammed

his prepaid ticket into the slot with some anxiety. The gate seemed to take forever to lift, but at last his car could fit beneath it, and he peeled out of the
structure just as a beefy security guard ran toward him, shouting. He saw the
parking booth guard step out into the street and take note of the car's license
plate — reading its actual plate number, not the phony one he had written on
his registration card at the front desk.

"Damn!" he shouted, as he pounded the steering wheel. "Damn, damn,
damn!"

Now he'd have to ditch this car and steal another one. A big pain in the ass
all the way around.

He thought of Everett learning about this misadventure, and shouted,
"Fuck me!"

He saw an old man in the car next to him looking on in disapproval. He was
about to flip him the bird, then started admiring the old dude's wheels. Not
bad, he decided, and discreetly followed him home.

13

Blue Jay, California
Monday, May 19, 6:21 P.M.

Gabriel Taggert was alone and sober when he saw the newscast.

He would have preferred to be neither.

At no time since he had first arrived at this cabin had he felt more compelled to seek the comfort that could be found in a bottle or a pill or—for him, the most sweetly beckoning of them all—a line of white powder.

Even more alluring, though, was the thought of contact with either of the only two people who had ever really given a damn about him: his sister Meghan or Kit Logan.

He fought all these temptations.

Throughout the vast majority of his twenty-three years, Gabe Taggert had been a herd animal. Never leading it, never bringing up the rear, always finding a comfortable place in the middle.

After things had gone so horribly wrong up north, his ability to blend anonymously into the middle of the herd had allowed him to hide for a time in several cities. That ability probably prevented him from being arrested on federal felony charges. Charges, he was well aware, that could lead to the death penalty.

So for several months, he stayed in cities. But this time, unlike every other time he had been in trouble, he felt vulnerable in the herd. He could not simply become an easygoing joker, a party boy looking for a little fun. The raves he went to—looking for oblivion, for instant friends—only intensified his awareness of harsh realities, his new mistrust, his sense of isolation. He could lie easily enough about who he was, and he might find a place to crash for a few nights, and he might even find someone to pretend to laugh with, but his nerves were raw, and the press of humanity in the cities had grated against the ends of those nerves.

One night last January, a pretty girl with beautiful red hair had invited him to come home with her. He could appreciate her looks, knew in some part of his mind that she was exactly the sort of woman who appealed to him. He hadn't been able to get it up.

This had happened to him before, when he had been drunk, or loaded on downers. Nothing took the edge off a night of snorting cocaine like booze or tranquilizers, and more than once his sexual drive had been blunted in the process. But that night, he was neither drunk nor loaded. No excuses. Only a sense of separateness. Of being too contaminated by his own sins to touch her.

Later, sitting in a bar, looking down into an empty glass, he had thought of how kind she had been about it, and how that had almost made it worse. He had left her and started drinking.

He wondered about Kit—who had killed—and if that killing bothered him. But even as he thought this, he knew their cases weren't the same. Although Gabe hadn't done any actual killing, in many ways, he felt that his hands had more blood on them than Kit's. Even the police knew that Kit had acted out of desperation—he had never been arrested for killing his stepfather.

Gabe wondered if he had finally put himself beyond Kit's forgiveness. He thought he might have placed himself beyond his own.

He wasn't sure he could withstand escape much longer—he could manage to stay free, but why should he? He thought of Meghan and wondered what it would do to her if he chose one of the two options ultimately open to him— surrender or suicide.

As he leaned against the table in the bar, he felt the press of a pair of keys against his chest, keys he wore on a chain around his neck. One fitted the door to Meghan's guest house. The other, he had never used.

Kit had given him that one, and the chain, almost five years ago. Kit had taken him to the large, relatively isolated cabin in the forest, a place then owned by his grandmother. He had invited Gabe to come to the cabin any- time he'd like, on two conditions. The first was that he not tell anyone else of its existence.

"My grandmother," Kit said, "doesn't come up here. She lets me use this place because she knows that sometimes I need . . . privacy." In a wry voice he had added, "I'm so used to being in a fine and private place."

Gabe hadn't caught the allusion at the time.

The second condition for receiving the key was that whenever he made use of the cabin, he must not bring anyone with him.

"If I can't tell anyone about it, I'm not likely to bring anyone," Gabe had said impatiently.

"What I'm saying is, that's why you should come here. You need to get away from other people. You need to learn how to be alone. One of the reasons you get in trouble is because you don't know where others end and you begin."

Gabe hadn't liked hearing that, but he took the key, telling himself that Kit could go fuck himself, and that he'd plan a big fucking party up here, and tell everyone about the place, and to hell with all of that privacy shit.

But he never did any of those things, and he never took the key from around his neck. He had called Kit from time to time, usually to ask for money. They would catch up on each other's news but didn't speak of Kit's offer to use the cabin or the key. In times of trouble, Gabe found himself fingering the chain.

Later, he added Meghan's key to it. When women asked him to take the chain off, he'd smile and say he was a latchkey child and needed to be able to get back home again.

So on that January night in the bar, he had paid his tab and hitched rides until he reached Lake Arrowhead, and then, with nothing more than a light coat to protect him from the evening's bitter cold, made his way to Blue Jay and then on to the cabin, a walk of several miles. He struggled through the snow on the front walk and fumbled with numb hands to use the key for the first time, smiling to himself at the thought that he hoped Kit had tested the damned thing before giving it to him.

The door opened easily. He flipped a switch. Lights came on. The place was dusty, but there was wood for a fire and dry clothing in the closet that fit him a little snugly but would do.

That was five months ago.

He thought Kit had probably forgotten by now that he had ever offered the use of the place. Gabe decided that he'd take advantage of this refuge until he figured out what to do next, or until Kit showed up and demanded that he leave.

The water had been turned off and drained from the pipes to keep them from breaking, but he found—to his surprise—a note addressed to him on yellowing paper, telling him how to turn the water supply on and off again, along with other information that would be helpful to him.

Gabe smiled to himself—he should have realized that Kit, always a move ahead of anyone else on the board, would have been prepared for any possibility, even that Gabe might return here one day.

Reading down the list, he discovered there were cupboards full of canned goods and other staples, including coffee. The second to the last line of the note was, "Try this sober, if you can. But if you can't, you're still welcome to stay as long as you need to." The last one was, "So glad you made it here."

He had looked outside just then and saw a deer standing in the moonlight. It stayed still for a long time, then moved off. He heard a soft creaking sound that unnerved him, until he remembered his earlier visit here, when Kit had taught him to listen to the snow.

"You wouldn't think it makes noise," he had said, "but it only looks quiet and still. It's changing all the time."

Aloud, to the empty cabin, Gabe had asked, "Is it too late for me, Kit?"

The snow made a sighing sound. Or maybe he did. He wasn't sure.

For five months, he had been sober. It had been hell at first, and most days, only by occupying himself with shoveling snow and other exhausting activities did he wear himself down enough to cope with it.

He had grown thinner. The clothes Kit had left here fit Gabe loosely now.

He shaved his hair off and grew a beard. He hiked to the store if he needed anything perishable.

He hadn't turned the television on much, but he started watching the news, in part to see if Kevin Delacourt had been caught.

Kevin had been the leader. There had been four of them involved in the crime that November day. It was supposed to have been a burglary, no violence. It wouldn't have been Gabe's first burglary, and not his first one with Kevin. Kevin, as always, had come up with the idea. It seemed so easy. An isolated home in the wine country, an estate owned by a retired movie mogul who fancied himself a vintner. An old man in his fifties who had married some hottie starlet who was thirty years his junior and had three kids with her. They lived away from Los Angeles because the old man didn't want to keep meeting friends who would ask him what he was working on these days.

Kevin said the owners of the home were away on vacation.

He had been wrong.

All of Gabe's nightmares were about just how wrong Kevin had been. Most of what he thought about during any given day was the same.

None of the family had survived. Of the four robbers, one had been killed by the old man, one had been captured by police, and Gabe and Kevin had escaped. Farrell, the man who was caught, had apparently named Gabe as both the planner and the shooter, although Gabe hadn't even carried a gun that day. Farrell never mentioned Kevin. Gabe ended up on the FBI's Most Wanted list. Farrell was undoubtedly too afraid of what Kevin might do to him if he ratted him out. That night, Kevin had surprised them all with what he might do.

Until he had seen the press conference, Gabe had remained somewhat philosophic about the possibility of his own capture. He had decided that he wouldn't offer resistance, but he probably wouldn't surrender. He'd let fate decide the issue and hope that Kevin was caught and linked to the killings. If Farrell knew that Kevin was locked up, maybe he'd tell the truth about what happened.

But Kevin wasn't on the FBI's list. His face wasn't on the newscast that followed the L.A. County Sheriff's press conference, like Gabe's was. The three victims of the vigilantes were shown with big *X*'s across their faces. Like they were items on a "to do" list, rather than human beings. How long before someone put an *X* over his face?

He listened to the newscaster, a woman named Diana Ontora, talk about the other criminals. He cringed to see himself ranked as one of them, to hear himself described in terms of what happened on one awful night.

He wondered if these vigilantes, who seemed to know more than the best law enforcement agencies, had some way of finding him.

He tried to turn his thoughts away from his fear.

He thought a lot about Meghan, as he often did, and—as always—with a deep sense of shame over what this must all be doing to her.

He also thought about Kit. Among the many books in the cabin, he had found a volume of English poetry. He picked it up again now, and opened it to a page that Kit apparently bookmarked long ago. Andrew Marvell's "To His Coy Mistress." Two lines especially caught his attention, because he remembered what Kit had said, so long ago—

> *The grave's a fine and private place,*
> *But none, I think, do there embrace.*

"I'm so used to being in a fine and private place," Kit had said. But what could he have meant?

No matter how hard he thought about it, Gabe couldn't understand the reference. It occurred to him that he knew little or nothing at all about Kit Logan's past, other than the fact that Kit had killed his stepfather, that Kit's stepfather had killed some women, and one of those women had been Kit's mom.

Over all the years, it had been Gabe coming to Kit with his problems, never the other way around. Kit had protected him. Kit was protecting him now, though he doubted Kit knew that.

And even Kit's protection could go only so far.

The news that someone was killing off the FBI's ten most wanted had scared him. Now, thinking about it, he couldn't see that it was any different than worrying about a shoot-out with police or fearing that his former partner in crime would catch up with him. Maybe these vigilante guys, whoever they were, were heroes.

Meghan would be worried, though. He wondered if he should call her. He hoped she would call Kit—he knew she often talked to him about her wayward brother.

But none, I think, do there embrace.

The line kept running through his head.

1 4

Alex felt the drag brought on by a lack of sleep, the urge to call it a day, but decided not to delay talking to Ty Serault's former employees. Other than looking for matches to the climbing rope, and the work Ciara was doing on Catalina, they had too little to go on to ignore this possible link.

He tried calling the former *Crimesolvers USA* employees. Dwight Neuly was in and willing to talk to him if he could make it soon—at eight-thirty, Neuly needed to meet with the editor of the student film he had directed. Alex looked at Eric Grady's address. It was closer, but Neuly was available now, so he made the drive to USC, where Neuly had agreed to meet him. He called ahead to the campus police, and after meeting with them briefly, parked off Jefferson, near the halls that *Star Wars* built.

Neuly was as cooperative as any student at the end of a term was likely to be. After talking to him, Alex was fairly sure he had no connection to the murders. He would check further into his financial health, but to all appearances, he was not in need of money. Neuly claimed that he had spent the last week trying to finish a project for a film class. He had pulled out a Palm PDA and beamed the names and phone numbers of five members of his postproduction crew to Alex's own Palm—telling him that any time they couldn't vouch for, his roommate could.

When he got back to his car, Alex called in and checked his messages. A reporter from the *Los Angeles Times* wanted to know if he would verify that anticoagulants were injected into the three victims discussed at the press conference today. Alex swore. On top of everything else, they'd have to figure out who was leaking information to the press.

He looked through the files again, resisting the idea of driving back to the Santa Monica area, where Eric Grady lived. He studied Grady's employee ID photo. Grady had mugged for it—Nola had said he was a clown, and apparently he took the role on from the beginning. Most of the other employees had posed with serious expressions bordering on grim, but Grady's face was close to the lens and grinning.

He called the phone number in the file and learned that the number was no longer in service. He started to thumb back through the file to see if another contact was listed on Grady's application. He paused as he came to the copy of Grady's driver's license photo, attached to his Immigration and Naturalization Service I-9 form, which required proof of citizenship.

The man in the photo on the license was not Grady.

Or, more probably, the man on the employee ID badge wasn't.

There was some resemblance—thin faces, dark hair cut in an identical style, dark eyes—but Alex immediately noticed that even in the employee photo, taken at its odd angle, the differences were readily apparent—the jawline, the shape of the earlobes, the noses.

He cussed himself out for wasting time talking to Neuly, then ran a DMV check on the driver's license for Grady.

The answer came back quickly. Eric Grady was deceased.

He asked for a date of death.

"Last year. July fifth. That's a presumed DOD."

He looked at the application. "Eric Grady" had applied for a job two days after he was dead. The employee who used his name and driver's license had been hired by Ty Serault on July 7.

He called the homicide bureau and got one of the detectives on duty to run a computer check for him, to look up all the information available on Grady's death.

The call came back within minutes. "He was a John Doe for over half a year. One of our cases—in fact, you should talk to Ciara. It was hers."

"I will. Tell me what you have, though."

"He was twenty-two, hadn't been seen since a Fourth of July party last year in Malibu. At first, no one missed him. His body was found in Carbon Canyon in February of this year. Didn't identify him immediately, but Ciara brought a forensic anthropologist in on it. Got the age and sex, and from there, Ciara put it all together. Theory was that he wandered off drunk from the party sometime after midnight on July fifth—he was found not all that far from the party house—stumbled in the dark and fell to his death."

He thanked the detective and hung up. For a few moments, he sat in the car, resting his forehead on his fists on the steering wheel. Angry at himself for not seeing the differences in the photos earlier, Alex also wondered what kind of background checks Serault was doing.

So the phony Eric Grady was in a position to take calls—or hear of other calls—from people who thought they were seeing FBI fugitives in various parts of the country. He had joined the *Crimesolvers USA* staff just after the real Eric Grady died, used his ID and probably his references to get the job. He left the staff not long after the body was found, perhaps fearing publicity about the case would expose him.

But the identification of John Does didn't make the news as often as the public supposed. For that matter, murders didn't always get attention from the media. Alex just happened to be working on three cases that had the full attention of the country at the moment.

He looked at the goofy photo of the young man on the ID badge. The clown. Some clown. He'd sure as shit brought the circus into L.A. County.

Alex got back on the freeway, heading toward the last known address for the phony Eric Grady. He tried calling Ciara but only got her cell phone's voice mail. She might be on her way back from Catalina, out of cell phone range. He left a message for her.

He called Serault Productions and asked for Nola Phillips.

"Nola? I'm hoping you can help me out here. Who takes the photos for the employee ID badges? Is that done there at the studio, or off-site?"

"We do it here. One of my jobs. I take the photos and then laminate them onto a badge."

"Do you keep the negatives?"

"I take them with a digital camera, but yes, I keep the files. Why?"

"Eric Grady. His photo was a little—"

"Dumb? Yeah, I thought so, too. But that's the one he wanted on his badge."

"Do you have any others of him?"

"I'll look."

"He worked for you for eight or nine months and left about two months ago, right?"

"Yes, I think so. It's in the files we made for you."

"Anyone else worked at his desk since he left?"

"No, I don't think so. We haven't filled that position yet. Ty wanted to wait until summer. We start taping new segments in August, so we hire in June and July."

"How late will you be there tonight?"

"Until eleven or so."

"Mind if I come by again?"

"Not at all."

"I've got another stop to make, but I have a feeling it won't take long. I'll call when I'm on my way from there."

Eric Grady's "apartment" turned out to be a rented private mailbox. The store in which it was rented was closed for the night. Alex turned around without getting out of the car and called Nola to say he was ten minutes away.

Ciara called back before he reached the studio. She hadn't had any luck on Catalina, but she was bringing several boxes of papers back to the office, to continue following up on the next day. He told her what he had learned about the *Crimesolvers* employee.

"Eric Grady? God damn, this means we'll have to reopen that one. This is going to be so hard on the family." She was silent for a moment then said, "I can see how perfectly his identity would work for someone else, though. He was from Missouri, a good student, well-liked, but a little restless. He had decided to take a few months off from school, and his family disapproved. So, they weren't communicating much. He worked as an extra in some films and made friends here, too, mostly in the Topanga Canyon crowd. He ran out of money, but he was one of those guys who could always find someone to stay with. I think that was losing its charm, though—he told some people at the party that he was thinking of going back home."

"So everyone here thought he went back to Missouri, and everyone in Missouri thought he was still out here."

"Right. So it was autumn before a missing persons report was filed by his family, and months before anyone even knew that the party was the last time he was seen. No progress was being made on it. I got called out to a scene that was just John Doe's bones in a canyon, and we didn't make the connection at first."

"The remains were skeletonized?"

"Completely. In fact, we never recovered the complete skeleton—predators had made off with the smaller bones. We didn't know it was Grady until the dental came in."

Alex glanced down at the open folder on the seat next to him, open to the copy of Eric Grady's driver's license. He saw the young, hopeful face in the photo, and closed the folder.

"Well," he said, "now we know what happened to his wallet."

Nola was waiting in the reception area, standing very still and looking even a little more pale, ignoring the banter of the security guard who now sat at the receptionist's desk. Her blue eyes were fixed on Alex's face as he came in, and he tried to smile for her. She didn't smile back.

You know, he thought. *You looked at his employee records and now you know.*

The guard slid a sign-in sheet toward him, and he filled it in and then silently followed her down the hallway, this time not to the glowing kingdom of dinosaurs and stars, but to a larger room on the opposite side of the hall. She flipped a switch and fluorescent ceiling lights hummed to life.

Four metal desks. Three were decorated with framed photos and plants. One was cleared off. She pointed to the empty desk as if accusing it and said, "That one was—" She had started to say, "Eric's," but caught herself. She dropped her hand. "That one was his."

"Thanks." He started toward it.

"He wasn't Eric Grady."

He turned toward her and said quietly, "No. Eric Grady is dead."

She clenched her fists. "Did that asshole—who is he, anyway? The guy who worked here for almost a year, pretending he was Eric."

"I don't know. Not yet."

"Did he kill the real Eric?"

"I don't know that either."

"Probably yes."

"Maybe. At the very least, he didn't report Eric Grady's death."

"Oh, right, and then he went around hanging people upside down over bathtubs!"

He didn't reply.

She splayed her hands out in front of her and said, "Sorry, sorry. I just— I'll be okay. I will. Really."

He asked if she had called Ty Serault.

She shook her head.

"Do me a favor and call him. Ask if he would mind if I had a crime lab technician come in and dust the desk for prints."

"Do you need his permission?"

"It's just easier this way."

"Okay."

She went to one of the other desks and picked up a phone.

While she made the call, he looked the desk over without opening it, then stooped to look beneath the chair. No wads of gum stuck to the underside. He put on a pair of disposable gloves and carefully opened the top desk drawer without touching any of the surfaces a person would usually handle when opening it. He looked into it and smiled.

"He wants to talk to you," Nola said, holding the receiver toward him.

He took it from her, and she strolled closer to the open desk but didn't touch it.

"Detective Brandon?" Serault was saying. "I can't tell you how shocked I am."

"Who does the background checks on your employees?"

"My HR person calls the references."

"And all of Eric Grady's checked out fine. Except it wasn't Eric Grady who came to work for you."

"I can't believe this. I can't, really."

"I'll want to see any payroll checks this employee endorsed. We'll also want to talk to the people he worked with."

"Anything. Anything."

He paused, then said, "Mr. Serault, given the subject matter you cover on the program—"

"I know, I know, I should have been more alert than most. I can't tell you how embarrassing this is."

"I was about to say that you might want to increase security all the way around. If not for your own sake, for the sake of your employees."

"Yes. Yes. I see that now. Whatever you say. You let me know what I should do."

Alex nearly told him that at just this moment he was a little too busy to be doing private security analysis for free, but a thought struck him. "I know someone who'd probably enjoy coming out here and giving you advice. Retired sheriff's deputy. I'll ask him to give you a call. His name's O'Brien."

Serault readily agreed to this, and after offering more avowals of his chagrin, finally allowed Alex to get back to the task at hand.

He called for a crime scene technician, then moved back over to the desk.

As Nola watched, he opened other drawers, but he found little of interest.

"What made you smile when you looked in the first drawer?" she asked.

It was still open and he pointed to the pencils in the pencil tray.

"Mr. Phony is a pencil chewer."

"That's right!" she said. "He gnawed on the end of pencils all the time."

"With any luck, we'll get his fingerprints off the drawer pulls and his DNA off the pencils. By the way—can you warn the security guard that a crime scene technician is on his way over here?"

She made the call, then said, "Let's go into my office. I printed out some photos for you."

He followed her across the hall. His cell phone rang. It was Captain Nelson.

"I was just about to call you, sir."

"I should hope to God you were."

"Excuse me a moment, sir." He covered the phone and told Nola that he would join her in a moment.

"You need privacy?" she asked.

"I'll go in the other room. I should lock it up to make sure nothing's disturbed anyway. Could I get the key from you?"

She handed a key ring to him.

Once back there, he said, "I'm sorry to make you wait, sir. I was about to take a look at some photos of a man I believe to be connected with this set of cases." He told him about Eric Grady.

"Good work. Let's get rolling on this."

"If I may ask, sir, what prompted you to call me?"

"I'm over at the crime lab. They told me they were sending a tech out at your request. Keep me posted, Brandon."

"Yes, sir."

He locked the room. Nola's door was closed, and he knocked softly.

"Come in," she said.

She was standing near the desk, looking at a photo of the man she had known as Eric Grady.

"I can't believe I didn't notice the difference."

"Not your fault," he said, handing back the keys.

She didn't answer. She gave him the stack of photos. "The one on top is the most normal."

He thanked her, glanced through the others, then said, "It's much better than the others. You said this is a digital photo, right?"

"Yes."

"I'd like to fax this copy to my office, and get a copy of the file, too."

"No problem."

The tech arrived. He dusted for prints and gathered the pencils and a few other materials from the desk that he thought might be promising for identification evidence. Before he left, he told Alex that he thought he had picked up some good latent prints from areas of the desk that had probably been touched only by the suspect.

Alex began questioning Nola again. She had a good memory for details, but he doubted much of what the pretender had told her was true. Still, sometimes liars gave away more of the truth than they intended.

The story of the Eric she had known was surprisingly similar to the one Ciara had told him of the real Eric. He thought the pretender must have known Eric Grady, or at least talked to him at length. Alex would have to learn more about the crowd Grady had been in contact with in Topanga.

She said, "He dyed his hair."

"What?"

"It wasn't the same color all the time. But a lot of guys do that, you know."

"Always dark?"

"Yes. But sometimes too dark. And his roots were lighter than his hair. I think his natural color is lighter."

"Any sports, hobbies?"

"None that he ever talked about. I didn't like him much."

She burned a copy of the photo files onto a CD and handed it to him.

She stared for a long time at the photo they had faxed, her head bent over it. He saw a tear slide down her nose, saw her brush it away. She took off her glasses and covered her face with her hands.

"Nola—" He put an arm around her shoulders. She took a great hiccuping breath, turned her face into his shoulder, and wept in earnest.

"Harmless! I told you he was harmless. Jesus Christ, he probably killed the real Eric. A killer, and I worked with him on a show about killers. God, I saw him almost every day. A fucking murderer. And I told you I thought he was *harmless.*"

He waited until she had calmed down. She stepped away, pulled four tissues from a box on her desk, and blew her nose noisily. He almost smiled.

"I can't stay here," she said. "I'm going home."

"You okay to drive?"

She nodded and gave him a watery smile. "Thanks. I don't cry much, but when I do, I guess I really go for broke."

This time, he did smile.

In the parking lot, she suddenly turned and gave him a brief hug, then hurried to her car without looking back. She wouldn't touch him again, he knew. It was a liability of the job.

He had come to such moments many times, when he stopped being the person with the interesting job, the curious occupation. No one really wanted murder to come close to them. It had come close to Nola now. She would no sooner reach for him than she would reach to touch a corpse.

He told himself it was just as well.

1 5

In the memory-dream, the digging dream, he was a child again.

The boy Kit sat in a corner, reading A Tale of Two Cities, *turning the pages as quietly as possible. He was much quieter, much more studious than most eleven-year-old boys, a fact remarked upon by his teachers in every school in which he had ever been enrolled. He had long ago lost track of how many schools he had attended.*

He had also, long ago, learned the art of establishing his place at a new school. He could spot the reigning bully within minutes of entering a school-room. Rarely did he actually have to fight now. Kit was lean and strong, and tall for his age, but this was, he knew, not what kept challenges from being issued. He found that he could somehow communicate in one long stare that a fight would be a bad idea. If it came to that, he would win. He had tested himself against larger, adult opponents, and if he seldom won those encounters, he learned method from them. Usually, only another child who had faced the same at home had enough anger in him to try anyway.

The invariable pattern at any school would be that soon the bully would learn that Kit wanted nothing more than to be left alone, and would comply with this wish rather than face this strange, cold newcomer's fists. If any other student sought his protection, Kit would give it, but always with the warning that he would be gone from the school within weeks. Despite the hero-worship this earned him here and there, the protection was never given with any real offer of friendship. He had learned few lessons as thoroughly as how to make his in-evitable leaving-taking as painless as possible.

Like all of the homes Jerome chose, this one was isolated from its neighbors. There were no streetlights this far out of the city. Eventually, the room grew dark, but Kit didn't want to turn on a light. A light would attract attention. The last thing he wanted right now was to distract his mother and his stepfather.

Serenity and Jerome were excited about something. He wished they were both drunk or high or even having sex. Usually, at any of those times, they ignored him. When they shared this hard, mean-spirited laughter, any number of things might go wrong. They might fight. They might cause the sort of trouble that would then require another move. They might turn on him in one way or an-other.

His mother, in all his experience of her, was a weak woman, more inclined to aggravate any attack on him than to intercede on his behalf. He could hear the slurring of her words now, between the moments of laughter.

By the time he was eight, Kit had known that Serenity had chosen to give birth to him in order to ward off loneliness. He was certain that she wished she loved him but knew that his guaranteed attachment to her helped her to survive between relationships. She scorned the only other source of stability in her life — a family that would have welcomed her home at any time. But Serenity, most misnamed child, had been a runaway, a drug addict whose wealthy family had not been able to buy any cure that would bring her back to them.

Kit, throughout any part of his childhood he could remember, did whatever he could to take care of her. She would be most tender toward him when he was most needed. He liked being useful, looking out after her, protecting her to what-ever extent he could. He was not always successful.

That night, his mind strayed from the French Revolution as Dickens por-trayed it. The laughter pierced through his enjoyment of the book. He kept it open only to avoid eye contact with the two at the table.

Kit thought that Serenity already understood that as charming as Jerome could be when he felt it would do him some good, he did not marry her for love. He married her because he needed to master someone, and in her moments of so-briety — always filled with self-recrimination — she seemed to believe his mastery a penance. Kit sensed that somehow this time she had met a man who was worse than all the other men who had dated, slept, lived with her before now. Some had matched his heat. None had matched his ice. There was something in Jerome that enjoyed cruelty in the way her most hotheaded lovers had not.

A temper had its expression and its end. The building toward its release was nearly worse than the release itself. But with Jerome, there was seldom release in *a blow. The tension in the household built, and built, and built. Then this brittle laughter would start.*

When Jerome and Serenity were first married, Kit had not been living with his mother. Serenity had frequently left him in the care of his grandmother, usually because of an arrest, or a boyfriend who objected to feeding another man's son. In these months, he would be transported into a world so different from the one he usually lived in, the return was twice as cruel. Eventually, he began to shield himself from these disappointments in much the same way he shielded himself from the pain of parting with school friends—he resisted any deepening of the attachment. Elizabeth bore it patiently, making him both ashamed and unable to resist hoping he could live with her.

"Come here, Worm."

"Yes, sir." Kit quickly closed the book and hurried over to his stepfather.

Jerome had not only married Serenity, he had insisted that she collect her son from his despised mother-in-law. What Elizabeth Logan had ever done to him, Kit didn't know. But he constantly made remarks to Serenity about how much Elizabeth had spoiled his stepson. The nickname "Bookworm" had been shortened for several months now.

"Your mother and I are getting tired of putting up with your nonsense."

This was a favorite phrase of Jerome's. He seldom explained what he meant by "nonsense." It was not a question or a command, though, so Kit knew not to make an answer of any kind. This time, however, the cause of Jerome's displeasure was soon made clear.

He held up a phone bill.

Kit went pale.

"You know anyone in Malibu, Serenity?"

"No one I give a shit about," she said.

Jerome smiled. "Well, then. Since I don't know anyone in Malibu, and you don't know anyone in Malibu, I guess we know who called from this house."

After a particularly bad day at Jerome's hands last month, he had missed Grandmother Elizabeth so much, he had dialed her number. Her answering machine had answered, and he had hung up without leaving a message. At eleven, he was learning how little time is needed to incur a long-distance charge on a phone bill.

"Do you know what worms are good for, Worm?"

Trying not to let his uneasiness show, Kit answered, "No, sir."

Serenity laughed. He didn't know what she had taken. Some sort of downer. Jerome was stone cold sober, though.

"They eat dead things, for starters."

Jerome stood and walked to the back porch. Kit knew better than to move. When he returned, he held a shovel.

He thrust it toward Kit. "Take it, Worm."

"Yes, sir." Kit obeyed. The shovel suddenly seemed larger, heavier.

"Let's go. Serenity, you come along, too." Kit followed him into the dark back-yard, fear constricting his muscles, so that his movements were awkward. He could hear his mother laughing behind him.

Jerome didn't seem to notice his clumsiness or his mother's laughter. He came to a halt near the far fence, in the darkest part of the yard.

"Lie down."

Trembling, he obeyed.

Above his face, the shovel came down, its sharp edge veering away from him at the last second and piercing the earth so near to the top of his head, dirt sprayed over his face.

"I didn't hear you say, 'Yes, sir.' "

"I'm sorry, sir."

"Not as sorry as you're going to be, you little asshole."

He pulled the shovel free and moved so that he now straddled Kit's waist. He was smiling. He lifted the shovel, held it just over Kit's heart, letting it rest against his thin shirt, so that Kit could feel its cold blade against his chest. Jerome was staring down at him. Kit started to cry, and Jerome's smile widened. "You worm."

He lifted it high and brought it down—this time, just outside Kit's right shoulder.

"Damn me, I missed. I'll have to try a different target."

Serenity laughed.

Jerome settled the blade on Kit's throat. "That ought to do. Cut your fucking too-smart head off."

Again the shovel came up, again furiously down. Just to the left of him.

Jerome moved so that he was over Kit's knees, and the shovel touched down on the boy's crotch. He used a little pressure this time, and Kit cried out in pain.

"Shut up. No one's going to hear you out here, anyway."

Kit squeezed his eyes closed, but Jerome did not see this as he negotiated the move of bringing the shovel down and stepping back at the same moment. The shovel was left planted near Kit's feet.

"Stand up."

"Yes, sir," Kit said, tears still falling. He was shaking so violently now, it was almost too difficult to obey this simple order.

"Now, you damned baby, you can start digging."

"Yes, sir." He struggled to pull the shovel free.

"You dig in between those four marks."

"Yes, sir."

"You know how deep it has to be?"

"No, sir." Hardly able to breathe now, still he tried to make his muscles work.

"Six feet."

Kit looked up.

"You look around you, Worm. This is the end of the line. You're going to dig your own grave. I'm going to bury you right here. And the only choice you have right now depends on how well and how fast you dig, because that's going to be what decides whether you are buried dead or alive."

And so he had dug. He had dug and dug and dug, until his hands were as blistered and raw as any galley slave's, his shoulders and back sore, and his skin and clothing covered with dirt. He dug because he wanted to be dead.

The ground became harder, but he worked and worked at it. He was only a boy, though, and the rim of the hole was barely above the level of his head when the sun began to rise.

Jerome walked up to the edge and said, "Stop."

He leaned on the shovel, muscles shuddering in fear or exhaustion, he wasn't sure which.

"Give me the shovel."

He handed it up.

"Lie down."

He stood swaying. Jerome kicked his shoulder, easily knocking him over.

A shovelful of dirt landed on him. He found he could not move, could not even bring himself to brush it away.

Go ahead, he thought. Bury me. I don't care. I don't care.

Jerome laughed. "Maybe I'll let you live another day, Worm."

Kit, too exhausted to crawl out, lay in the bottom of the grave and slept.

As almost always happened when he dreamed the digging dream, at the moment when he fell asleep in the dream, he awakened from it. He did so now in Denver, miles and years away from the events of the dream, but feeling the power of the memories press in on him all the same. He quickly reached for the light, then held on to a small Chinese soapstone carving of a tortoise. A lucky tortoise, he had been told. Before long, he was breathing more steadily.

Sometimes, the dream would last a little longer, and he buried Jerome. In reality, this had not happened. In reality, when the hot sun had awakened him early that afternoon, he was roughly pulled from the grave by Jerome, who told him to wash up, because they were moving that day, and he didn't want worm dirt all over the car.

There would be more digging in days to come.

He told himself now that he could not rely on omens, on dreams to tell the future. He just barely resisted the impulse to call Meghan. Then he showered, awakened Spooky, and after promising fast food for breakfast and lunch, started for Albuquerque far earlier than he had planned.

16

"Place it on the counter, please."

Spooky turned a wide-eyed look of innocence on him. When she saw that her acting skills were unappreciated, she sullenly reached into the pocket of her windbreaker and placed the object she had pilfered on the crowded sales counter.

Spooky calmly met the sales clerk's startled look of dismay, returning a look that said, Doesn't everyone shop by placing unpurchased items in their pockets before bringing them to the counter?

It was an unusual shop, but Kit doubted it was quite that unique. Primarily, it sold colorful tiles. But a great many objects of Mexican art were available, too, and it was these that had drawn Kit's attention to the store. Today it was doing a great business in *milagros*.

The woman behind the counter had explained that the small, brass, gold, tin, and silver-plated charms were primarily used to petition for miracles. They might be worn as jewelry, or more traditionally, pinned to the robe of a statue of a saint—a Spanish tradition, one that continued in various forms in Central and South America.

Some *milagros* were body parts—a leg for the healing of one's leg, for example. But the *milagros* were of many other shapes, too—for anything for which one prayed for help—houses, animals, fruits, vegetables. There were also saints and praying figures. "And for help with love," the clerk had said, and handed him a small, silver-plated heart.

Kit, ever aware of the power of charms of any kind, and a strong believer in divine intervention, bought the *milagros* by handfuls.

While the clerk had been counting up his purchases, Kit kept an eye on Spooky. She was getting rusty, he thought, because he had clearly seen her hand dive into her pocket.

He saw now that the object she had taken was a Day of the Dead figurine, a skeleton dog wearing a saucy, colorful, wide-brimmed hat and a carefully decorated leather shoulder bag. A female dog, then.

"Add that to my purchases, please," he said to the clerk.

Outside, they walked in silence for a time. She asked for the dog and he gently removed it from the sack and handed it to her.

"Is it Molly?" he asked.

She nodded, not looking at him, studying the figurine. A few minutes later, she tucked it into her jacket. "Thanks for buying it for me," she said.

"You're welcome."

"I'm sorry about the stealing."

"I know."

"If we just go to California—just go by ourselves, you and me, I promise I won't steal anything more. Ever."

He paused and turned toward her. He decided to face this head-on. "You know me pretty well. Do you think I'm going to abandon you?"

For several moments, she didn't reply, and he didn't like the wait much. But he was also glad she didn't return a flip answer. She gave him a long, searching look, then said, "No."

"Good. Because I won't. Not ever. That was why I became your guardian and we spent all that time in court."

"They let you because you have so much money."

"You're changing the subject. And besides, I don't care why they 'let me.' I'm talking about why we went to court. Why did we go to court?"

"Because," she said, "you're crazy."

He said nothing.

She relented. "Because you wanted to be my big brother."

"Right. So don't be afraid of my friends. My friends can never be my sister."

They walked a little farther. She said, "It's not like you're really my brother, though."

"Yes, it is. That's exactly what it's like. Genetics aren't everything—right?"

Despite the warmth of the afternoon, she gave a little shudder. "Right."

They were almost back to the Suburban now. "By the way, you might want to give up on the stealing anyway," he said. "I think you're losing your touch."

She dropped her head, so that he couldn't see her face. After a moment, she said, "Maybe you're right."

"Good."

He reached into his jacket pocket and couldn't find his keys. He patted down his pants pockets, the other pockets of the jacket, then happened to look up to see her clasping both hands over her mouth, stifling laughter.

"Very funny. I suppose you have my wallet, too?"

She fell asleep in the Suburban not long after he started to drive toward the mountains. He called Meghan's cell phone. They had checked in with each other several times since last night, much to Spooky's annoyance.

"You okay?" he asked.

"Fine. The view from my new room is gorgeous, and I want to be outside. Feeling restless, in fact."

"Just a little while longer. The taxi will pick you up at the service entrance. You've cleared that with the hotel?"

"Yes."

"Good." He gave her the name of the man from the security company who would be meeting her. "He will already be in the cab, and he'll make sure you get safely to the tram."

She thanked him and started to summarize a soap opera she had just watched. He wasn't familiar with the show and could make little sense of the story line as she presented it, but he knew she was nervous and going stir-crazy, so he let her talk. Before long, though, he started losing the signal, and they were forced to end the call.

Frederick Whitfield IV was in a foul mood. Grimly, he thought he could wait it out. Since leaving the little victory party in the bar yesterday evening, he had been subject to one mood swing after another.

Stealing the old man's Thunderbird had not worked out as planned. Frederick suspected the man had figured out he was being followed. Well, perhaps not that, but the damned old geezer had taken so long getting out of his car, he had seen Frederick's lame-ass rental car drive by, and stared at it in a hard way. "Quit mad-doggin' me, you old butthole," Frederick had muttered to himself.

Not an hour later, these words would seem prophetic. Sure that he had given the old man enough time to stop worrying about his T-bird, Frederick moved nearer to the car, ready to pop the lock and hotwire that baby, simple tools at hand. He hadn't stolen a vehicle in a few years, and as he pulled his gloves on, he found himself joyfully anticipating this test of his old skills. In the next instant, he heard a screen door open, and turned to see a ferocious, noisy mutt bearing down on him, barking loudly. The dog had been allowed to chase Frederick back to the rental car. To be forced to haul ass out of perfect setups twice in one day was nearly more than Frederick could stand.

So, using the handheld GPS device he had with him, he drove to the closest shopping mall that had a big theater complex in it. He watched a middle-aged couple leave their pickup truck and walk to the theater box office. It took less than ten minutes to transfer his belongings from the rental car into the truck and be on his way.

The cab of the truck, though, was redolent with an odor he could hardly withstand, an aroma emanating, he was sure, from the half-empty bags of corn chips, wadded-up Kleenexes, and other souvenirs that awaited him courtesy of the previous occupants. He felt some punishment was due, and, reaching into the glove compartment, learned the owners' address for the car registration. He used the GPS again, drove to the address, and spent a therapeutic forty-five minutes tossing the place completely. He made the happy discovery of a Ford Bronco in the garage. Not only did he now have keys for it, it was cleaner than the pickup truck. He switched vehicles and gleefully drove off.

He found a room for the night in a small but clean hotel. He had no intention of sleeping there. He merely shampooed in the hair color he had brought with him, coming closer to his natural blond. He wasn't especially pleased with the result. He considered another set of tinted contact lenses, but he was uneasy about these props after the mishap at the Sandia Towers. He yawned at the face in the mirror, a wide, uninhibited donkey yawn. Everett would have hated to see him show such a lack of refinement.

"Tough," he said aloud.

He lay on the lumpy mattress to watch the latest update on CNN, thinking he would see happier news of himself, but he fell asleep during a stock market report.

At four in the morning, angry at himself for having dozed off, he peered cautiously outside, saw no one else stirring, and quickly changed into jeans, a white T-shirt, worn leather aviator jacket, and black boots. The pair of Ray-Bans that went with this outfit were already in the jacket's right pocket. He didn't put them on now, but knew that when he did, he'd looked an awful lot like James Dean. A really buff James Dean. He left the room.

He realized that if he showed up in the parking lot at the Sandia Towers at this time of day, he would attract undue attention. He drove to the highway, eventually found a truck stop, and ate a hearty and—he could not help but believe—manly breakfast. He mistook the other patrons' quick dismissal of him as a sign that his aura of dangerousness had been perceived. After all, he hadn't shaved that morning, so he was probably looking pretty much like a bad-ass kind of guy.

Don't even think about messing with me, he thought, as a beefy-armed trucker went by. *I have killed, and I will not hesitate to kill again.*

He wished he could say that aloud, stand up on the table and shout it.

Much better, though, to know something others didn't know. Frederick had always loved secrets, both keeping and finding them. Everett called Frederick his spy. He always said it with respect, with gratitude. Frederick had never met anyone who appreciated his talents as much as Ev did.

He wondered briefly what Ev would make of his disobedience. The thought made him uneasy, and he paid his bill in cash and went back out to the Bronco.

He stopped at a twenty-four-hour supermarket to buy a few supplies to help him survive the hours of surveillance ahead of him. He bought a cheap foam cooler, some ice, and a lot of bottled water. He bought some bread, a small jar of mayo, cheese, some lettuce, some sandwich meat, and a knife.

He felt pride in his purchases. He hadn't learned to make a sandwich until he met Everett. Everett had no more need to prepare his own food than Frederick did, but he had forced the members of Project Nine to learn, as he put it, to "stop acting rich," for those times when they would need to blend in with less important people. Thinking of Ev as he entered the checkout lane, he placed two packs of nearly every brand of chewing gum into his basket. This was another act of defiance—Ev hated gum chewing.

He prepared his new cooler and then drove over to the Sandia Towers Hotel. He had managed to kill about four hours. Eight in the morning was not such an odd time, though, so he approached the parking lot attendant's booth. He was a little disappointed to see that a different attendant was on duty, because he had looked forward to testing his change of appearance. He found a space from which he could watch Meghan's car. He rustled through the plastic shopping bag with the gum in it and began a taste test.

At noon, he called his parents, who were staying in their Italian villa through the end of the summer, when they planned to return to France, where they lived most of the time. Since he had rarely contacted them after the day he turned twenty-one—and received the bulk of his grandmother's estate—he surprised them. They had not forgiven him for suddenly becoming wealthier than they were. He understood that completely. He hoped his mother would mention the big news about the FBI's Most Wanted list, but when he asked if they had watched any news of the U.S., she told him that they had decided that the only way they would ever really relax and enjoy life was to go on what she called "a media fast." When he (quoting Everett) told her that intentional ignorance was the opium of the coward, she hung up on him. This was not a first.

At one o'clock, hotel checkout time, he stretched. Seeing that Meghan hadn't brought her luggage down to her car, and concluding that this meant she was staying another night, he devised a ruse that he thought might work well. He would disguise his voice, ask for her room, and when connected, ask her if she wanted extra towels. In his experience, women always did want them, if you suggested it. "That's room seven-eighteen, right?" he would say, and she would correct him and tell him her new room number. He would grab a stack of towels from a housekeeping cart and hold them in front of his face so that she couldn't see him. She would answer the door. Then he would make her tell him where Gabe was hiding these days.

But when he called and asked for her room, the operator said that he would have to leave a message with her, as Ms. Taggert was not accepting calls.

He was angry, so he said, "Ask her if she wants more towels," and hung up.

At about three o'clock, a disturbing thought occurred to him. What if Meghan planned to meet Gabe without ever driving anywhere? What if they were up in her hotel room right now?

But then he thought back to the previous evening's first fiasco. The reactions of the people at the front desk, the guard who chased him — Meghan had obviously been in touch with hotel security, and now they were keeping an eye on her. Somehow, he doubted she would bring her fugitive brother here under those circumstances.

His uneasiness grew, however, when he considered other possibilities. He decided to drive around the hotel perimeter to better assess the situation. When he used the ticket to exit, he remembered his impatience with the gate the day before and saw that parking in the garage itself might be a bad idea. If Meghan got into her Beemer, he would see her, but if he followed her out, she would very likely see him, and even if she didn't recognize him, she would notice that a guy who looked a lot like James Dean was following her in a Bronco. And if he waited to follow, by the time he got past the parking gate, he'd lose track of her.

So he put on his shades and looked for a good surveillance spot.

Shortly after he left the garage, he found a wide alley that ran along the back of the hotel. Several dozen floral centerpieces were being delivered at a receiving area. Frederick considered for a time all the ways he could gain entry through the back of the hotel, disguise himself in an employee's uniform, and work at learning Meghan's room number. None of these seemed like pleasant undertakings, or even likely to pay off, but he didn't mind having backup plans.

Driving along the front of the hotel, he saw two taxicabs parked in the shade of the area near the lobby entrance. This made him consider another complication: Taxicabs were another means by which Meghan could evade his watchful eye.

He eventually found a place along the street that would allow him to watch both the front entrance of the hotel and the exit for the parking garage.

About twenty minutes later, just as he had decided he was tired of the confines of the Bronco, that he'd just go home and forget all about Meghan, his attention was caught. A taxicab with a male passenger started to pull into the front drive, then suddenly veered away from the entrance, the passenger gesturing as he spoke to the driver. Frederick tried to get a better look at the passenger but failed. The driver then drove to the alley behind the hotel. Curious, Frederick started the Bronco and then moved it so that he could watch the cab without going down the alley itself or being too easily observed by its occupants.

The passenger did not get out. Frederick began to be sure this was Gabe, waiting for Meghan. He considered going down the alley right now and kidnapping him, or even killing him outright. But he'd have to kill the cabdriver and anyone else who might be around the area, and he had no gun with him. He hadn't tried to obtain one here, either, an oversight he was regretting. But why should he have to skulk around a strange town arranging in low-life bars to buy untried weapons, when he had perfectly good guns at home? If he'd been able to bring his personal arsenal along with him, he would have had plenty of firepower to accomplish the task. For at least two full minutes, his thoughts were taken up with the injustice of the various measures that impinged upon rights guaranteed to him and every other American by the Second Amendment.

Just then he saw Meghan Taggert, escorted by a hotel security guard, leave the hotel through a service entrance door and walk toward the cab. The guard was carrying a small overnight bag. The cabdriver got out, put the bag in the trunk, and—after she shook hands with the guard—Meghan got into the cab.

Frederick noted the cab number, then moved a little farther down the street.

His heart was beating faster now, the thrill of taking up the hunt in earnest singing through every nerve. The cab came out of the alley and moved down the street, nothing indicating a fear of pursuit.

"That's where you're wrong, you fucking idiots. I'm after you now!"

He pulled smoothly and slowly away from the curb, following at a discreet distance. He nearly lost them once, then saw that they were getting on to Interstate 40. It was easier for Frederick to hide the Bronco in the freeway traffic, and there were few taxis on it. He smiled and hummed the *William Tell* Overture.

The cab exited on Tramway Boulevard. Frederick stayed farther back now but had no difficulty keeping the cab in sight. When it pulled into the Sandia Peak Tramway parking lot, he kept driving. He waited, found a place to park along the road, and pulled out a set of high-powered binoculars.

The cab pulled into a passenger unloading area. As the driver got out to retrieve the bag, both Meghan and the male passenger exited. A burly man with graying sideburns—not Gabe.

The truth was instantly clear to Frederick. Meghan was going up to the mountains to this big dude's cabin, where he was going to fuck her brains out. Obviously the guy was married and cheating on his wife with Meghan, or they wouldn't have met behind the hotel. It was really sordid. Frederick had a hard-on thinking about it.

He decided that he'd let the man take her up there, let them start to drink a little, let them get naked, and then he'd give the big old dude the last surprise of his life. For Meghan, he had many other surprises in store.

1 7

The heavyset and graying man who called himself Gerald Majors studied the two new arrivals. He watched from the balcony of his room, where their voices had come to him as he lay thumbing through a magazine full of photos of naked young boys.

The men by the pool were German tourists, evidently. He had heard one of them call to the other in that language and receive a quick answer in the same. The young men were having drinks now, carrying on a low-voiced conversation. He thought they were probably in their early twenties. Not young enough to suit his fancy.

Majors would tell anyone who asked that he felt no desire whatsoever for sexual relations with adult males. The occasional fantasies about men were never as frequent or exciting as the ones he had about boys. His adult sexual partners had always been women, and he was, in fact, still legally married, although Regina had filed for divorce.

The problem, if you believed it was a problem—and he no longer did—was that every so often he felt an irresistible hunger come upon him, an appetite that had to be satisfied, he believed, or the appetite itself would eat away at him, would demand his attention until he could think of nothing else, do nothing else.

At first, it was a desire for sexual encounters with male children of a certain age, boys of not more than nine or less than six. As risky as that was, he had managed it. He was self-employed, and in a not-so-exciting line of work—an installer and repairer of commercial heating and air-conditioning systems who offered his services especially cheaply to low-income school districts, orphanages, and the like. He traveled for business purposes and was careful to ensure he never did anything that would make those closer to home suspect his proclivities.

The use of roofies—Rohypnol illegally obtained on occasional trips to Mexico—was a little dangerous with boys of this age, but the drug made them unsure of what had occurred and definitely prevented Majors from being identified. The actual encounter with the boys took place away from the schools. For a time he even made up employees for himself. "We'll send Mr. Brown there on Tuesday." If there were any questions, he would say Mr. Brown had quit without notice. But there were never any questions, so he had stopped bothering. Now the false IDs came in handy, though.

Before the trouble started, when he was experimenting in new and different ways, he realized true fulfillment was not going to come from a young zombie who had little idea what was happening to him. Acts of violence became a necessary component. The pleasure evolved and demanded greater sacrifices—first, he needed only to consider the idea. Then, he had to plan it, and the planning and anticipation were enough. Later, he needed to see their fear. Eventually, it was just better all the way around when they made the ultimate sacrifice—he found nothing could make him feel as complete as the moment of their death. It cleansed them, really, and it cleansed him, too. It allowed him to function—for a time.

Thanks to the Internet, he discovered that all along the spectrum of what he considered to be his own evolution, there were others, most of whom lacked his determination and courage. He made videotapes, and later DVDs, and sold them to carefully vetted customers. He thought of himself as a priest who performed the ritual for his special congregation—those who lacked his courage would pay to see the recordings he made of his activities, and feel pleasure. Some might find the courage to try to seek their own fulfillment because of him. This added a whole new dimension to his own pleasure.

He was a star. And he was rich. Richer than he'd ever been making rooms turn cool in summer and warm in winter. The market for his video recordings was small, but the suppliers were fewer.

For his victims, he felt not the slightest concern. Most were impoverished children, whose single parents could not afford help to find them, living in places where police were unlikely to have the means to chase him as far as he would go to commit his crimes. He was only sparing these children a future of poverty and abuse. He thought of all the children he had seen living in poverty in Mexico. He could stay in Oaxaca for a long time.

He continued to watch the German men below. If they had been wiser, the young men would have sought the shade, as he did, or taken a siesta, which would have been wiser still—if one could afford to sleep.

Majors wore only a pair of swimming trunks, but he was feeling the warmth of the day. He ran a thick, damp palm from his nipples to his navel, drying his hand on the mat of hairs that covered his chest and slightly rounded belly.

The temperature must have been nearly ninety, he thought. Warm for this mountainous part of Oaxaca. Oddly, these Germans didn't seem to mind the heat. Their tanned and muscular bodies were nearly perfect. One of them, though, the dark-haired one, bore scars on his wrists and ankles—thin, white lines that encircled each in crisscrossed bands. Majors wondered who had re-strained the boy. And with what had it been done—handcuffs? Rope? No—wire, he thought. Too thin for anything else.

Being in his line of business—his new business—one had to be wary. Every encounter with others raised questions in his mind, and he especially questioned the purposes of those who came into his orbit at this particular time in his life.

Even with his vigilance, he had been betrayed. While on a trip for his furnace company, which more and more served merely as a cover, his wife, Regina, had become convinced that he was cheating on her with another woman. She broke into his office, managed to guess the password on his computer—his reward for being a good provider and loving husband for twenty years was a wife who could do such a thing—and saw photographs that (she later told him) made her physically ill. She was too stupid to ask him about all the other things she saw, of course.

The bitch went straight to the police with the hard drive. He had missed being arrested by mere minutes. Fortunately, he had planned for making a quick escape if need be. His soon-to-be-ex wife wouldn't get her hands on much of his money, which was hidden away in offshore accounts. Slick and P.T. were among those whose help had been invaluable. Both had too much to lose to betray him.

He wished Slick were here, to help him find out all he could about the newcomers. But Slick would not return from his journey to Puerto Escondido until late this evening.

Castillo del Chapulínes—castle of the grasshoppers—was a small luxurious hideaway for the well-to-do. There were never many guests, he was told when he was met at the Oaxaca Airport by Alberto, a helicopter pilot who spoke just enough English to communicate a few basics about the resort. The helicopter provided the only easy route into the resort's location, in the mountains of the state of Oaxaca. This was an area of Mexico where many native tribal groups lived—few of the inhabitants spoke Spanish or any other European language. A beautiful part of the country, Majors thought, when he viewed it from the air. There were still unspoiled beaches along Oaxaca's coast—Slick had chosen to visit one today.

Majors did not want to be in places like Puerto Escondido and the city of Oaxaca, though, where too many Americans could be encountered. He was glad to be out here in a more remote area.

The golden-haired man by the pool laughed. The other was solemn, only smiling softly now and then. They were handsome, he thought, wondering what they had looked like when they were six. At six, they would have been irresistible. They were angelic even now. Perhaps not so irresistible even now.

The thought disturbed him. He tried to be critical of them. Was the scarred, dark angel a child abuse victim out for revenge on all other abusers? Or a child abuse victim who was now himself an abuser, looking for victims? It could go either way. One had to develop a certain ability to perceive the signs that differentiated them.

And so he studied them.

The men must be filthy rich—even beyond the usual for this resort. Majors had already noticed the deference being paid to them by the staff.

The resort was all Slick had said it would be. A place where he could feel safe and yet be pampered. There were no women guests here, at the moment, although one could send for one for a reasonable fee. The two other guests ignored him, but from Alberto he had learned that they were a Brazilian and a Canadian, apparently here to hold private business discussions. They had arranged the trip to Puerto Escondido and had politely—if somewhat coldly—agreed to allow Slick to take the fourth seat in the helicopter.

"Sorry to leave you," Slick had said to Majors, "but I could use a change of scenery."

He didn't mind. Slick was tiresome, really. One couldn't expect anything but nervous tension when dealing with a person you were blackmailing. He had several holds over Slick—ones that would have made him a three-strikes lifer in California. Slick knew that if Majors was arrested or harmed, his own freedom and well-being were in peril. It did not make him good company.

• • •

The Germans were going swimming now, in nothing more than those skimpy European swimming suits. He couldn't take his eyes off them. The dark one was in the water already. The blond stood, then turned toward Majors, his gorgeous green eyes looking at him with amusement. He smiled and said, in the mildly German, strongly British, accented English of the private language school, "You're American, aren't you? Come, swim with us—you don't seem terribly comfortable up there on your—oh, *scheisse*, what's the word?"

"Balcony," Majors said, hearing the carefully pronounced *th*'s and *w*'s. Definitely not Americans.

"Of course. Balcony."

"Perhaps later."

"Suit yourself," he said with a shrug and joined his companion.

Majors watched them move through the water, then heard the blond call to someone else in Spanish, another invitation to swim. The man's Spanish was excellent, although with the soft lisps of Spain rather than the harder sounds of Mexico, and yet again the faint German accent came through. European Spanish. Majors relaxed a little.

He heard an answer from inside the building, a deep male voice. Majors couldn't catch all of it, something about trusting Señor Emillio to take care. A moment later, Majors tensed in surprise.

A young Mexican boy, giggling, dressed in only swimming trunks, came running toward the pool. The dark one smiled and opened his arms. The boy jumped into the pool. Majors watched, and for the first time since he had been observing him, the dark one's face lit with pleasure, transforming him. Majors realized that he was more excited by the young man than the boy.

This was a first for him, slightly upsetting, and yet he found himself unable to stop watching the boy and man together.

The man said something in a low voice, and the boy replied, laughing. Majors caught enough of this to understand that the boy was amused by his Spanish. "No, no, señor, no burro—caballo." To a soft-spoken question came the answer, "Sí, el poney." As he moved to shallower water and set the boy gently on his feet, the boy spoke rapidly and enthusiastically to him, telling him of some adventure he had on his new pony, a gift it seemed, from the señor.

The blond watched, smiling, and came closer to them. He glanced up at the balcony and beckoned again to Majors. "Come and meet our friend Justino. He is telling us what a fine horseman he is."

Majors smiled back, made a decision, and hurried into his room.

After brushing his teeth and quickly washing his armpits, he sped down-stairs—but by then, the blond was taking the boy, wrapped in a towel, inside. "Sorry," he called from the doorway, "he's scraped his toe and no one but his papa will do for him now. But I forget my manners—I'm Emil." He nodded toward the pool. "There is my friend, Conrad."

"Gerald Majors," he said.

"I'll take Justino to his father. May I bring you something to drink?"

"Sure—Scotch on the rocks."

"Conrad, *bitte*," he said, "be entertaining, won't you?"

Conrad smiled at Majors, and in much more awkward English, said, "How do you do? You would like to swim with me, please?"

Majors smiled back and got into the water. He swam toward Conrad, but Conrad, smiling coyly now, evaded him, and for a time they played a little game of chase. The young man easily swam past him again and again, but oc-casionally brushed against him.

Emil returned with the drink, and refills for Conrad and himself. Majors was quite out of breath by then, and nervous as well—a little afraid of what he was feeling. He drank deeply, felt better, and then belatedly toasted the young men.

"Your first time to the Castillo?" Emil asked politely.

"Yes. Yours?"

"Oh no, we are friends of the family who own it. We adore it. We come here from Frankfurt every chance we get."

"Frankfurt? I was just there."

"No! You do business in Germany?"

"All over the world."

"But how wonderful! Do you speak German?"

"No, I'm afraid not. But so many Europeans speak English so well these days—you and Conrad, for example."

Conrad smiled and shyly said, "Emil, yes. Mine is . . . not so good."

Majors moved a little closer to him, patted him on the shoulder. "Your En-glish is fine."

Conrad smiled and stepped a little away, but Majors read invitation in his dark eyes.

Majors made short work of the Scotch. It was excellent, smoother than most. He began to feel a slight buzz—he hadn't eaten much at midday, the heat having taken the edge off his appetite. The young men kept smiling at him, and he found Emil's conversation more and more charming. Perhaps both of them, together? Why not?

He turned to set his glass on the pool deck and found that he couldn't quite coordinate the action. Suddenly light-headed, he wondered who it was who said, in perfect English as the sky began to spin, "Oh, at last. I'll up the next dose. Now, catch him, Cameron—drowning is really too quick and painless."

The grip on his hair, just before he passed out, was definitely not painless.

18

"Decision time," Frederick Whitfield IV muttered to himself, as he stared as if fascinated by a souvenir spoon rest that said "Sandia Peak Tramway" on it.

He had climbed the stairs from the parking lot to the tramway entrance, making sure he stayed out of sight of Meghan. He saw her the moment he came into the building. She had been standing with her lover at the ticket counter, their backs to him. They had just missed a tram, the woman at the counter said, and would have about a twenty-minute wait. Meghan, pointing out a sign that said diners with reservations at the Peak Experience Restaurant received discounted round-trip fares, asked about the one-way fare for a person with dinner. Frederick wanted to shout that the rich slut shouldn't quibble over a lousy four bucks. But the old dude with her had heard him walking by and started to turn around, so Frederick quickly ducked into the gift shop.

Eventually the lovebirds had walked outside. Frederick used the opportunity to pay fourteen dollars for a round-trip ticket—full fare, without a murmur of protest. He stayed inside, keeping a wary eye on them until they began to come back inside. Once again he ducked into the gift shop. The tram would be here before much longer, and he would be forced to decide whether to give them as much as a thirty-minute lead or get on a nearly empty tram and risk Meghan recognizing him. Hence his dilemma near the spoon rests.

As if in answer, though, a group of hikers came into the building, about twenty or so people who had made plans to take a moonlight hike along one of the trails at the top. A woman with the group wandered into the gift shop and began flirting mildly with him. She wasn't bad-looking—and he definitely liked her bod. She was in good shape, one of those healthy, outdoorsy types, but with delicate facial features. She had thick, wavy hair of a color that was a mixture of peaches and honey, large green eyes, and long fingers. She wore silver earrings shaped with the zodiac symbol for Gemini. Seeing an opportunity that might pay off in several ways, he gave her a dazzling smile and asked why her group was going hiking on a weeknight.

"Blame it on the moon," she said. "We have to choose the night when it will be at its best for the hike, and when we can get the permit for it." She then went on and on, telling him much more about it than he wanted to know, including that the full moon was not best for night hiking, and what animals might be seen, and blah, blah, blah.

Christ, he thought, *no wonder she has to go man hunting outside the group.*

But he kept smiling and took off his sunglasses, to give her the full effect of his baby blues, which obviously dazzled her. Even though he was now noticing that her outdoor wear was not made by the best companies, he pretended that he had never met a more fascinating individual in all his days. He managed to actually laugh a little at the moments when he was fairly sure she thought she had been funny.

"Do you cook or is it for your girlfriend?" she asked now. At his look of incomprehension, she said, "The spoon rest?"

"Oh—for my grandmother," he said. "She collects them. I bring her one from everywhere I go. In Russia, they have really adorable ones that rest one within the other. They call them *boyakinas.*" He smiled, seeing that his bogus (as far as he knew, anyway) Russian word was not detected as such. And then, remembering his conversation with his mother, he suddenly let his face fall and added, "I don't like to think much about Russia, though. My parents were killed there—shot as spies—when I was just a baby. No hard feelings, an honest mistake on the part of the Russian government, really. And maybe it all worked out for the best, because I was raised by my grandmother."

He went on to weave a tale about a grandmother who lived in a little cottage in New Mexico, surrounded by spoon rests, a kindly old woman whom he had just been visiting, to tell her that her grandson, whom she had raised in near poverty, had struck it rich through wise and honest investing, and was now going to see that she could command all the comforts of life. "Beginning," he ended, "with this spoon rest."

The woman, for once speechless, hugged him. He heard a familiar voice and looked over the woman's shoulder as he hugged back. Meghan stood not far away, talking to her lover. He was a little afraid that she had heard his tall tale, recognized him, and was about to expose him as a fake, but apparently she had not seen him. She was too engrossed in a disagreement with her lover.

To his puzzlement, he heard her say, "You don't need to wait, really. I don't think anyone will bother me."

The old dude, his back to Frederick, said something Frederick didn't hear.

Meghan said, "If you insist. Let's go out to the platform. The tram should be here any minute. Do you need cab fare back to your office?"

His answer was apparently a negative, because she didn't give him any money.

Frederick then had to turn his attention back to the woman in his arms, who was suddenly self-conscious. He behaved as if he were, too.

"I'm—" she began, but he placed his fingers gently over her lips.

"No, don't tell me. Not yet. And I won't tell you my name, either. That would spoil everything special about this, don't you think?"

And she nodded, although he could see she was a little unsure of exactly why it would.

"A complete stranger," he sighed. "I promise you, I have never told a living soul what I've told you today, and why a complete stranger should free me of these painful memories, I can't say, but—but thank you."

For a brief moment, he thought he might have overplayed his hand, but she merely hugged him once more.

He freed himself by paying for the spoon rest, but took her hand as they walked to the platform. He saw that a few of her fellow hikers were watching them, but she fended off their stares with a look of triumph. Who could blame her?

The man with Meghan was looking the crowd over but didn't seem to take more than casual notice of Frederick and the woman. Frederick waited until there were a number of people between him and Meghan before getting on. The man stayed on the platform as the doors closed, and the aerial tram began its ascent, a trip of more than two miles.

So, he thought, I have Meghan to myself after all. He smiled, watching the other men in the tram looking at her. Poor bastards. None of them stood a chance.

Following her now was going to be a damn piece of cake. Morgan would have fucked it up from start to finish, of course. Good thing he arranged to be the one who was here instead. All he had to do was send the hiker on her way with the other moonstruck idiots and Meghan—who was staring up at the top of the peak, as if she, too, couldn't wait to get off this thing—was going to see what Agent Frederick Whitfield IV was willing to do to get a stuck-up bitch to answer some questions.

She turned then, and her eyes rested briefly on him and then on the view beyond before she again turned away.

"Do you know that woman?" the hiker asked.

He squeezed her hand. "What woman?"

"The one you were just staring at."

He pulled the hand up, kissed it lightly on the knuckles. "Was I? I didn't even see her." He turned her then, away from the eyes of the other passengers, and stood behind her, so that the two of them were looking out the tram window—and away from any study Meghan might have decided to make of him. He bent his lips close to the hiker's ear and said quietly, "I'll tell you what was on my mind, since I don't seem to be able to keep any secrets from you. I was just wondering if—well, if maybe you'd give me your phone number. I have some business with the owners of the ski resort up here, but maybe when you get back from the hike, and I get back from my meeting? I'd like for you to meet my grandmother."

The woman turned her face up to him and smiled, his previous lapse of attention forgotten. "Sure," she said, sounding a little out of breath.

"She's able to tell fortunes, you know," he said.

She wasn't as impressed by this as he had hoped. "I'll try not to offend her," she said. "But I don't believe in fate and fortune and all of that."

"No? I thought maybe . . ."

She saw the direction of his glance. "The earrings? I just liked them. I'm not even a Gemini." She began searching her daypack and pulled out a pen and a small journal. She tore a piece of paper from it before tucking the journal away.

He took a moment to admire the stunning view beyond the tram as it climbed over the Cibola National Forest. Maybe a night hike wouldn't be so bad. Someday he'd have to try one.

She handed him her number. He smiled to see she hadn't written her name down. He asked her to hold onto the bag with the spoon rest in it while he put the number away in his wallet.

When he took the bag back, she turned and tucked her hands beneath his jacket, resting her head on his shoulder and pressing her lips closer to his own.

His arms around her, he peered inside the bag, wondering how quickly he could ditch the spoon rest into a trash can.

"Grandmother is going to love this," he said, and reading the look in the upturned face, bent to kiss her.

1 9

The old man liked clocks.

A few moments ago, on the half hour, a chorus of competing chimes sounded throughout the house. Over the last two hours, hearing them perform their various renditions every fifteen minutes, Alex had come to think of them as a genteel version of the horn that sounds for a rodeo bull rider—a signal that Shay Wilder had managed to hang on to life for another little patch of time. That Shay Wilder was dying, there could be no mistake.

Ciara Morton and Alex's uncle, John O'Brien, sat outside, talking quietly on the back porch after strolling through the small orchard outside Wilder's home. Early on, they had managed to get away from the bells and ticking and the thick haze of cigarette smoke.

Ciara had been hesitant to bring John along, until it became clear that Wilder wouldn't bother opening his door to them if his old friend didn't accompany them. She had tried to beg Wilder's help after he had refused requests from both their lieutenant and Captain Nelson. Alex figured she was hoping to show them both up. She prepared to approach Wilder by doing some homework—learned all she could about him by asking around.

But Wilder still demurred. "I'm retired," he told her. "I really have no desire to see what the latest sadistic son of a bitch has been up to, thanks all the same."

She had persisted.

"Detective Morton, within days—if not hours—you'll have the country's top profilers working on these cases. Perhaps Sheriff Dwyer will make life difficult for the FBI for a brief period of time, but we both know that they'll be involved soon."

"Some think you're better than anyone who's working out of Quantico right now."

He laughed, then broke into a fit of coughing. "There are even other retirees who are more talented."

So she had played what she thought was her ace—she had told Wilder that she was partnered with his old friend's nephew. Wilder laughed again and said he would do this as a favor to John O'Brien's nephew only if Alex would bring his uncle along.

"Can you believe it?" Ciara had complained to Alex.

"You should have anticipated that when you mentioned John."

"Shit. I give up. You're the one with all the connections around here. Without nepotism, the old boy network, or a penis, I guess I'm out of the running—I sure as hell won't get anywhere in this damned department."

Alex ignored almost all of this, a variation on an old theme, and later decided only a lack of sleep had made him say, "You think I'm here because John had some influence on my being hired or promoted?"

He saw the flash of anger, her impulse to make the accusation openly. But she regained control of herself and said, "Don't you think you had certain advantages, growing up with a deputy in the house?"

He thought for a moment and said quietly, "I suppose so. But not in the way you seem to be suggesting."

She backpedaled. "Look, I don't think you got any promotion you didn't earn. If I implied that—I'm sorry, I guess I did imply that, didn't I? I did. And that was wrong. You work hard, you solve cases—way above the bureau average. All I meant was, you know how to play the game, because you grew up with John."

"He has helped me to be realistic about department politics," Alex said. "Which is what I think you mean by 'the game.' And, Ciara, for that reason alone, you don't know how many times I've wished to God your uncle, aunt, mother, sister, granddaddy—you name it—had been with the Sheriff's. As it is, you never seem clear about who your enemies are."

He had seen her flinch somewhere in that recital and figured she was given this same sort of speech by the guys who called her B.B. Queen. *Let it go*, he said to himself, and tried to go back to concentrating on a list he had made of climbing gear suppliers. *Just let it go.*

Typically, she wouldn't. "It's my greatest weakness, isn't it? 'Does not play well with others.'"

He didn't answer.

"I know you aren't the enemy, Alex."

He looked up at her. "No one else in the department, either, Ciara."

"Okay, okay. I let one old man get the better of me. I'm sorry."

"He's not just one old man. If Shay Wilder told me he wanted to meet the Queen for tea before he'd look at the autopsy reports, I'd put him on a flight to London. As it is, he just wants us to bring an old friend of his along for the ride. It's easy. John will love the chance to get out of the house."

He was right—no persuasion was needed to get John to come along.

John knew the way to Wilder's home, in the hills just inland from Ocean-side, near one of the biggest of the old Spanish missions. He greeted his old friend by saying, "Damn, Shay. Guess you didn't get the comb I sent you last Christmas."

Wilder, whose dull gray hair rose from his head in disordered tufts, wheezed and coughed a laugh. "Buy me a mirror next time," he said, then curtly ordered them to come inside. Alex managed to hide his shock at the change in the old man's appearance. He had not see Wilder in about five years, although he knew John visited him often.

The once bright blue eyes were now watery and surrounded by reddened lids. His prominent brow ridge seemed to have sharpened, or perhaps the too thin face made it seem so. Only the dark, untamed hedges of the brows themselves seemed the same.

Wilder wanted to deal with business before pleasure, so he brought them all to his study, a dark room lined with books and file cabinets—all of it, like the rest of the house, reeking of cigarette smoke.

He was gaunt, his skin wrinkled and yellowish gray, stained between the two fingers of his right hand which were seldom without a cigarette between them. He used the hand in the way a chain-smoker will, moving it palm down over papers, the thumb and last two fingers working together as an especially adroit claw.

Alex felt a sudden and unaccountably painful flare of anger, then knew it for what it was—the banked fire of his grief for J.D., stirred to life by a smoker's gesture. Alex's old partner had moved his hand in just the same way. Useless to berate the dead for not having lived the way you wanted them to, or as long as you wanted them to, he thought, and rolled his shoulders, trying to relax.

Wilder looked up sharply at him, reading his thoughts—or so it seemed to Alex. But the old man said nothing. He went back to studying the files.

"What we're hoping you'll tell us . . ." Ciara began.

"If I'm going to tell you anything," Wilder said, "I need quiet. As for your hopes, they are no concern of mine."

"Polite as always," John said.

Shay Wilder grunted a response that sounded far from polite and went on reading.

After a few minutes, Ciara stood up and began pacing, arms crossed over her chest. Wilder looked over at John.

"I need to stretch a little," John said. "And besides, I don't think there's room enough in here for all of us and Shay's ego, too."

Alex looked at Wilder to see if he was offended. He was smiling.

"If I make Shay promise not to yap any conclusions to Alex while we're gone," John said to Ciara, "would you mind leaving this stink hole to sit outside with me for a little while?"

She hesitated, then agreed. Alex wondered if she was trying to play well with others.

Wilder said nothing to him, asked no questions during those two hours, except once, when, not feeling he was being of much use, Alex stood to go outside. Wilder, without looking up from the papers, said, "Don't disappoint me. Sit down."

So Alex sat silently, listening to the ticking at each swing of the pendulum of the mantel clock, the dry-leaf rustle of a page being turned by the old man's fingers, the snap of the wheel on the flint of his silver cigarette lighter, the clink of the lighter's lid as he closed it. The wheezing breath, the hacking cough that sounded as if Wilder's lungs were being turned inside out and shaken.

"Less than six months, they tell me," he said once, as if Alex had asked aloud the question that came to mind each time he heard the cough. "Unless I let them start carving. I told them they could test the sharpness of their knives on someone else."

"I'm sorry."

"Don't be. What in the course of nature could frighten me, after years of looking at this sort of thing?"

They were the only comments he made for a long time. At one point, he sat back and closed his eyes. Alex waited, wondering if he had fallen asleep.

Without opening his eyes, Shay asked, "Tell me—who called in about the first body?"

"At first, we were told it was a neighbor, but later we learned it was a call from a pay phone, so we're not sure now."

"Near the location?"

"Yes. The caller said he was reporting a neighbor but didn't want to be identified as the complainer—excuse me, sir, but I have an obligation to bring Ciara back in if we're going to start discussing the cases."

He opened his eyes. "Interesting that you put it that way. You may see to your obligation in a moment. And you may certainly tell her anything I say now, if you choose to."

Alex didn't reply.

Wilder smiled. "I appreciate your patience. Now, tell me about rock climbing."

Alex hesitated. "Some people would say that it's just you and the rock, and you find out what you've got. But that's not all there is to it. As much as I love rock climbing, I'm not sure I can give you an easy answer."

"Because you love it, you mean. Let me be more specific, then. How did you feel when you realized that a climbing rope had been used to string up Adrianos?"

"The way the Pope might feel if he saw someone spit on a crucifix."

"Yes, I think the killers knew that you would feel that way."

"No, that can't be right. They had no idea I'd be given the case. In fact, I wasn't the first detective there."

"But you were called to the scene as soon as the identity of the victim was known. And there was certainly a great deal of publicity about the fact that you and your partner were after Adrianos when your witness and his family were killed, correct?"

"We weren't the only ones after him."

"Rock climbing FBI agents showed up, too?"

"What are you saying?"

"You already know what I'm saying. Now, call your partner in, and your uncle. I'm tired."

Alex stood, but before he reached the door, Wilder said, "What's your partner's problem, do you think?"

"Old men," Alex said, and walked out, hearing Wilder laugh and cough behind him.

When they came back in, Wilder began by saying, "I want more time," then seemed to find this a good joke, so that they had to wait for him to stop coughing. When he was able to speak again, he said, "I suppose, Detective Morton, you will want my rough guesses now, because you lack your partner's patience. All right, I'll give them to you. You must let me know if the gentlemen with the FBI agree.

"These killers are probably highly intelligent males—plural, because I agree there is probably more than one, but I'm not sure there are only two—you could easily be looking at a close-knit group. Ages—I'll need more time. Some factors say older, some younger."

"Twenties? Thirties?" Ciara asked.

He ignored her. "They are intelligent, but they probably didn't do well in school. They would have exhibited behavior problems. They have difficulty with authority.

"They feel superior to law enforcement and are proving it. 'Above the law' is more than a phrase—they are not only not subject to it, they can do better without it. They have had problems in the past with the Los Angeles Sheriff's Department—they may have been rejected from the academy, or something of that nature. A little more difficult to know about the FBI, but the same thing may hold true there. Or, it may simply be that they consider the Most Wanted list to be the ultimate way to prove their point—these are the criminals most wanted by all the law enforcement agencies in the U.S., and they are smarter and better at catching them than the FBI is."

"So far, Shay," John said, "they seem to be making a good case for that."

"Yes," Wilder said slowly. "Curious, isn't it? It argues tremendous long-range planning—such as putting someone into the staff of that television program as a mole of sorts, finding a victim for the theft of the license, and so on. And I would guess that to drug and transport two individuals to Catalina, to buy pharmaceutical blood-thinning agents—if that's indeed what they used—to get someone inside Adrianos's organization to betray him—all of that took some money, don't you think?"

"The kind of money Christopher Logan has now?" Ciara asked.

Wilder's brows pulled together as he frowned at her. "Have you located him?"

"Not yet. His lawyers say he's not currently available to talk to us."

Wilder was silent for a moment, then said, "I interviewed him, you know. Years ago. After he killed Naughton."

"And?"

"He was remarkable. Extraordinarily intelligent. IQ off the charts."

"And used it to kill someone."

Wilder shrugged. "I think he found a way out of a horribly abusive situation, and it's just a damned shame he didn't get a chance to do so earlier than he did."

"Agreed," Ciara said, "but he has the capacity for violence—he went way overboard when it came to killing Naughton. I read the reports on that. He went berserk, bashed the hell out of his stepfather's skull with that shovel."

"Overkill is not at all unusual in that type of situation," Wilder said. "Teenagers or children who kill an adult abuser will often not believe their abuser can be killed. Think how much power the abuser has had over them— and yes, pent-up rage is part of it, too. But that doesn't necessarily argue continued violence."

"How could a kid like that not end up twisted?"

Wilder gave her a look of impatience. "You don't believe that Naughton had a contagious disease, do you?"

"No, but—"

"And since Kit Logan was Naughton's stepchild, you obviously aren't arguing that he inherited some physical impairment from his stepfather—some brain dysfunction that would predispose him to violence."

"No—I meant—"

"You meant that during his tender adolescent years, Kit Logan was both physically abused by Naughton and continually exposed to his stepfather's obsessions, and that he can't now be a normal man."

"Something like that," she said flatly.

"You may be right—it would be remarkable indeed if he survived that childhood without being damaged to some degree. But I don't think that's what's going on here—too much in these crime scenes doesn't fit."

Ciara frowned. "What do you mean?"

"One always has to ask—why this victim?"

"If the killers are trying to look like heroes," Alex said slowly, "the mimicking of Naughton doesn't fit."

"Exactly. There is a desire to be seen as heroes, or they wouldn't be killing those on the FBI's list—the victims would be different if you were truly trying to emulate Naughton. And Naughton was no hero to Kit Logan. I spoke to him often enough to feel confident that there was nothing about Naughton he wanted to emulate."

"But isn't it true that his history of abuse could have led to a sense of rage?" Ciara said.

"If he felt some sort of displaced rage, I would think Kit Logan would have chosen a target who reminded him of Naughton—a way of killing Naughton again and again. Or worst case, his mother, who failed to protect him. That would be more typical."

"But didn't he get to be a hero when he killed Naughton?" John asked.

"His grandmother made sure he stayed out of the spotlight," Wilder said. "But I have to say, John, you make a good point. Maybe he felt as if he was a hero, even if he didn't get attention for it."

"And law enforcement failed to protect him, too," Alex said.

"Yes. In fact, Kit did say to me that for a time, he hoped the police would catch Naughton and that he would be rescued. By the time he killed Naughton, he had stopped believing it was going to happen." Wilder began coughing again. "As I said, I need more time. But frankly, I still think it would be foolish to focus on Kit Logan. Look for this other young man, the one who posed as Eric Grady."

As they were going toward the front door, Alex felt Wilder take hold of his arm. "Let me lean on you a little," Wilder said. Alex slowed his pace.

"You miss J.D.," Wilder said.

"Yes."

"So do I. It will get easier, Alex."

"I know."

When Ciara and John were some distance ahead of them, he said, "Do you climb these cliff faces alone or with a climbing partner?"

"I have a partner—a teacher, really. He introduced me to climbing. He's a much better climber than I am."

"You aren't bothered by the difference in your skill level?"

"No, we're friends, and it's more a matter of attitude, I guess. It's cooperative, not competitive, between us. Besides, even if I learned everything I could, because of my work schedule, I couldn't get in as much time with him as his other partner can."

Wilder held up one of Alex's bruised hands. "You've climbed recently?"

"Last weekend."

"Good, so you got a climb in before all of this happened. I have a feeling it may be a while before you get time to do so again."

"You're probably right."

"You should ask among your other friends who climb—try to discover if anyone has been asking about you lately."

"I appreciate the concern," Alex said.

"But you don't believe me. Do you think that a killer careful enough to take three FBI fugitives in hand—careful enough to vacuum an attic—left pieces of a rappelling rope at each scene by chance? Or that it's a fluke that he is bringing his trophies to the sheriff's department?"

"I wondered about that. Not in Lakewood, of course. But Catalina Island . . ."

"Yes. Too much trouble to leave a body there unless one has a message to deliver with it. When are you going to get the message, Alex?"

"Are you so certain it's addressed to me and not the sheriff?"

Wilder sighed and shook his head. "Where's your climbing partner now?"

"Majorca. He and his wife left on Sunday night."

"I'm glad to hear it," Wilder said.

"Why?"

"Perhaps he will be safer there."

"Safer?"

But Wilder only said, "Your uncle is already at the car. Ask him to come back to say good-bye. I find I'm quite worn out."

On the way back to the homicide bureau, Ciara wrinkled her nose and said, "You'll have to take that suit to the dry cleaner, Smoky."

"And take a long shower, too. But I'm glad you talked him into meeting with us."

"Thank John for that," she said.

But John, uncharacteristically, was sitting quietly in the backseat, staring out the window, not involving himself in their conversation.

"Knee bothering you?" Alex asked him.

"What?"

Alex repeated the question.

"Oh, no. Not the knee."

Alex's cell phone rang. He answered and heard Lieutenant Hogan say, "I've got some interesting news for you. We just got a call from the FBI."

"They're claiming jurisdiction?"

"No, although they keep threatening it," Hogan said. "But they were admitting something that I'm sure they hated to tell us."

"What?"

"The press conference got national coverage, right?"

"That's what I've heard. They tell me our phones have been ringing off the hooks."

"They have been," Hogan said sourly. "Mostly people telling us we should be hiring these killers to work for the department. And the FBI has been getting those, too. But they've also heard from a few people who saw our Catalina duo. Not together, but in the places where they lived—when they were still alive."

"People who knew Valerie Perry and Harold Denihan?"

"Not both. But who knew one or the other. It seems Perry has been in California for the last month or so. Up north, in Placer County. Denihan has been in El Monte. So guess what that means?"

"No easy way to claim federal jurisdiction."

"Right," Hogan said. "To the best of our knowledge, the people who are killing these criminals haven't broken any federal laws so far. These are L.A. County homicides and only L.A. County homicides, as far as we're concerned. The FBI might have pending investigations involving the victims, but these homicide cases are ours. Apparently the director of the FBI has been calling Sheriff Dwyer all afternoon. The Feds hate how this looks for them."

"I'm sure they do. But I'm not so sure it looks all that great for us."

"That depends on you and your team, doesn't it? Any luck with Wilder?"

"He needs some time. We're on the way back now. He didn't have much to tell us yet. I can fill you in tomorrow morning."

"Okay. See you then."

"One other thing, Lieutenant. The *Los Angeles Times* knows more than it should—one of their reporters has been leaving messages for me asking me to verify that anticoagulants were used on the victims."

"A leak? Already?"

"The *Times* will have worked harder to have sources in the department than most, but I'd hate to start seeing every detail of the investigation in the morning paper."

Hogan wholeheartedly agreed and promised to look into the matter.

Alex no sooner disconnected than the phone rang again.

"Brandon," he answered, fully expecting it to be Hogan again.

"Uncle Alex?"

He still wasn't used to being called "uncle," but oddly, he found himself pleased that the boy was making an effort to stay in touch. "Hello, Chase. What's up?"

"Where are you?"

"Driving back from northern San Diego County. Where are you?"

"At your house."

"My house?"

"Is he okay?" John asked from the backseat, suddenly sitting forward. Alex realized he hadn't been paying attention to anything he said until he heard Chase's name.

"Yeah," Chase said, "I got worried, because Uncle John wasn't answering, and, you know—I thought maybe something had happened to him."

"He's right here. You want to talk to him?"

"Sure—but, I wanted to ask, do you think I could stay here tonight?" He added quickly, "I could sleep on the couch, or the floor—whatever."

"I don't think your parents would like that much."

"They're out of town. My mom flew to New York. That's where my dad is now."

"They still probably wouldn't like it."

"Okay. I understand."

Plain and simple. No anger, no whipped pup, no guilt trip. Any of those, Alex later told himself, he could have resisted. "Listen, Chase—what if they call home, and you aren't there?"

"I never answer their phone. But if they call my phone, to check up on me, you mean? Call forwarding. I'll get the call on my cell phone."

"You have a separate line—never mind, I should have guessed."

"So that wouldn't be a problem," Chase said.

He could hear the hope. "I'll tell you what. Talk to your uncle John and ask him what he thinks. Up to him."

He handed the phone back.

"Chase?" John said. "We'd love to have you stay over. . . . Sure, I'm sure. He's just like that sometimes. You'll get used to him. . . . You warm enough?"

Ciara said, "I didn't know you have a nephew, Alex."

"My brother's son."

"Well, that would fit, since he's your only sibling."

He glanced at her and saw her blush, and knew she was belatedly remembering department gossip. "What about you? I know one of your sisters lives with you. Any nieces or nephews by other members of the family?"

"Yes," she said. "Two nephews—my brother's children. But I don't see them very often. They live in Texas." After a moment, she added, "My sister Laney can't have children, and I'm past trying to hit the snooze alarm on my biological clock."

"Ever thought of adopting?"

"Sure. But this job is a little tough on family life. Maybe if I screw this up and get busted back to uniform, I'll find some big old deputy, marry him, and start taking in strays."

"Hell, go back to uniform now," John said, having ended his call in time to shamelessly eavesdrop. "Being in Detectives can't be worth all that. It's not making you happy."

"John, we've talked all afternoon, so I'll assume you aren't saying that because I'm a woman, or because you think I can't find true happiness without doing housework or finding a man."

"No, nothing to do with that. And from all Alex tells me, you're a fine detective, better than most. And he tells me you worked your ass off and put up with all kinds of attitude to get to where you are."

She smiled. "Alex said all that?"

"John, damn it—" Alex said.

Ciara laughed. "Don't get mad at him. As for the job, I don't think I could leave it in the middle of all of this excitement—could you, John?"

"No," he admitted. "But it will be the FBI's inside a week, mark my words."

"You think so?"

"Right now Sheriff Dwyer is trying to claim that there's no proof that the victims were brought to his jurisdiction under duress. All the FBI has to do is figure out where they were before they came to L.A. County, show that there was a struggle, and the sheriff will have to cooperate."

"Don't get your hopes up on that count," Alex said. He told them about his conversation with Hogan.

"Okay," John said, "but that just delays the inevitable. The public won't understand the lack of cooperation. They'll think the FBI ought to look into murders of people on the FBI list, period. One opinion poll ought to do it. I hear the *Times* is conducting one, so you may be working with federal agents soon."

"An opinion poll, huh? That or another body, I suppose," Alex said.

"That seems more likely," Ciara said. "After all, there are ten possible victims, and we've only found three—and unless the FBI stops adding people to its fugitives list, our vigilantes will have three new targets to go after as soon as replacements are named to those three spots on the list."

Their pagers went off simultaneously.

"Sorry," she said to Alex. "I jinxed us, didn't I?"

2 0

Castillo del Chapulínes Resort
Near Oaxaca, Mexico
Tuesday, May 20, 4:32 P.M.

The man who called himself Majors jerked awake when the cold water came rushing down on the back of his head. This sudden movement produced sharp pain in his wrists and ankles. He could see only water and bright whiteness. He was dazed, but the pain brought the beginnings of a rough focus with it. His scalp hurt, too—he was being pulled up by the hair. As his face was brought up into the gurgling flow of water, he panicked, thinking he would drown, but the pulling continued, so that he was bent like a bow, back from the stream of water still rushing from the bathtub spout.

He could not open his mouth to let out the scream that was caught in it—a wide band of duct tape had been wound over it, wrapped around his head. He could hardly breathe. Then the water was turned off and the grip on his hair released. He fell forward, twisting his face just in time to avoid smashing his nose on the porcelain bathtub. He took a nasty crack on the chin, though. He wondered, vaguely, if it broke his jaw.

Disoriented, he lay unmoving for some minutes before he realized that he was hog-tied, naked, facedown in a bathtub. A glaringly bright light shone on him, making him squint. His shoulders, thighs, and back ached with the strain placed on them, and it seemed impossible to relieve the pressure on the points where the wire bit into his flesh. He was bound as the young man with the scars must have been at one time, with strong wire around the wrists and ankles.

As these things became clearer to him, his nostrils flared with his labored breaths.

"Don't hyperventilate," he heard a mocking voice say. There wasn't a trace of the German accent now.

He struggled, felt the renewed bite of the wire, then held himself as still as he could.

One of them was laughing.

He tried to move his head, to see their faces, although he knew who they were. Or who they had said they were. He had just managed to angle his neck so that he could peer over the edge of the tub when he saw it.

A video camera. The red light that indicated it was recording was on.

He began to tremble.

"Oh, yes. We know who you are," said the one who had called himself Emil. The golden angel. How stupid he had been to lower his guard around them.

No use thinking like that now. He had to get himself out of here.

For a moment, despair nearly overwhelmed him. Then he thought of Slick. Sooner or later, Slick would be back. And so would the others. Or a maid or someone would come in.

As if reading his thoughts, Emil said, "We won't be disturbed. I'm quite sure of that."

They walked away.

He started to weep and managed to stop himself only when he realized he would not be able to breathe if his nose became congested from the tears.

He wasn't sure how much time passed before they came back, or even how long they had been in the room before he became aware of them. By then, the pain was so intense, his mind wholly belonged to it.

They were doing something with the camera. The bright lights went out.

Majors felt gloved hands taking hold of him, grasping hard and lifting him. The pull on his wrists and ankles was excruciating. The young men were strong, much stronger than he had believed them to be. He was not light, but they easily lifted him out of the tub. They carried him to a four-poster bed that had nothing on it but a fitted sheet. There was a plastic drop cloth beneath it. Seeing that, he felt bile rise in his throat and for some seconds was afraid that he might choke on his own vomit.

They made a change in the way he was bound. Weakened by the time spent pulled like a bow, he could not struggle against them as they released his arms and legs. The relief of the strain on his muscles nearly made him start crying again. He was moved to the bed and laid on his back, then tied spread-eagle—the wire, again, only this time each band was attached to hooks that were already in place at each bed corner. He glanced down at his naked torso and saw that his body had been shaved—there was no hair between his neck and his genitals.

He heard a knock on the door. He waited until he saw Emil open it, then screamed as loud as he could. Gagged as he was, it was a sound much softer than he wanted it to be, but loud enough to be heard by anyone at the door. Of that much, he was sure.

To his relief, it seemed he was heard, for who should come in but the helicopter pilot, Alberto.

Alberto's brows drew together.

Emil said, "Justino saw nothing of it. He helped us without knowing what happened next. Your brother made sure he was well away before we began."

"Thank you," said Alberto. He moved closer, staring down at Majors with utter contempt. "And I see you have exercised great self-control. I tell you, it has been difficult for me."

Majors felt all hope slipping from him. Fear made his mouth dry.

"I understand, Alberto," Emil said sympathetically. "As does Conrad." He turned to his partner, the dark-haired one. "Don't you, my friend?"

"Yes. But we won't have to delay much longer."

Again, a knock at the door. The Brazilian and the Canadian entered. If they were, Majors thought bitterly, really from those places. The Brazilian was carrying a black case.

"Ah, Paulo, you're here!" said Emil, and asked him something in Portuguese. He received an answer, and then said to the others, "Paulo tells me he would prefer to do his work now, to give Mr. Knox—or, as he calls himself now, Mr. Majors—time to think about what is to come. Do any of you object?"

There were no objections.

Emil turned back to look at him. "I think I'll keep calling you Majors, if you don't mind. I think I like the name better than your real one. And after all, you aren't going to hear our own real names, so it's only fair."

Conrad moved closer to Majors's head, then looked back at Emil.

"Yes, you're right," Emil said, as if he had heard a question asked.

Conrad reached down and grabbed an edge of the duct tape. In a swift move, he ripped a piece of it away. He did this again and again, mercilessly pulling hair and skin with the tape as he unwound it. When he finished, he stepped away.

Majors's cries of pain eventually faded to whimpers.

"That's better," Emil said. He turned to the others. "We will be happy to gag him again if he says anything to offend you, or if his screams bother you."

"I'll pay you!" Majors said. "Get me away from here alive, and I'll pay you. I'm a rich man."

"Oh dear," the Canadian said. "I think he already offends me."

Emil sighed. "Mr. Majors, you are not a rich man. Paulo is rich, Alberto is rich, and Pierre—this gentleman you think of as a Canadian—is rich. They have the money that used to belong to you. This surprises you, I can see. I can also see that you believe the funds in your Swiss and Cayman Island and other accounts couldn't be in their hands. But that's exactly the case."

Majors's eyes widened in disbelief.

"You may be hoping someone nearby will hear you. They won't. You may be expecting rescue from your friend Slick. Alberto?"

"I'm happy to report that his friend was careless in the helicopter. He has had a very long fall from a very high place."

Majors swallowed hard, then said, "He's not the only one who knows I came here."

"He's not," Conrad said, "the only one who is dead."

The coldness of that voice left Majors without his own.

He heard noises and turned his head to see that Paulo was removing an instrument of some sort from his case.

"A tattoo needle," Emil said. "Paulo is a tattoo artist. Do you remember the last time you were near a tattoo parlor?"

What little color was left in Majors's face drained away.

"Yes, the young boy in Rio." He spoke for a few moments to Paulo in Portuguese, then said, "Paulo says that if he had been given every dime you had earned, it would not repay him for the loss of his son. And it would not buy one second of the pain you inflicted on his boy."

"It's true," said Pierre. "But I appreciate the chance to have a revenge denied to me for the loss of my nephew. He will not remember the young boy from Minnesota, will he? My sister couldn't live with what happened to him. She felt responsible for not guarding him closer, for letting him fall into this one's filthy hands. She killed herself. So I owe him for two lives, you see."

"You asked me the name of the resort," Alberto said. "I told you *chapulín* means grasshopper, but the word has another meaning—trickster. Last year, in late August, a sweet and innocent boy—Justino's cousin, my only child— went to the city of Oaxaca. He went with his older cousins to sell *chapulínes*— chili grasshoppers—a local delicacy. They had caught the grasshoppers the night before and prepared them to sell on the streets that morning."

"He did not return," Emil said, "which is not exactly the same as saying he was not seen again." He paused. "We cannot, of course, do anything to a grown man that would equal your cruelty to those children."

"But we'll try," Conrad said, smiling.

They held him down while the one called Paulo began his elaborate design. He began on the tender nipples of Majors's chest. A five, Majors saw, in one of the moments of rest. They paused every now and then so that he didn't become too accustomed to the pain, so that the anticipation of it would stay fresh. He tried to think of why it was a five. Did they believe he had killed only five boys? He asked—politely, really—but they would not reply to anything he said.

Except once.

He found a little bravado at one point and said, "I'm surprised you didn't put the tattoo on my balls. The chest isn't such a painful place to get one."

Emil looked at him and said coolly, "But you will keep your chest."

It was the last time anyone spoke directly to him. When the tattooing was finished, Alberto, Paulo, and Pierre left. He began to hope it was over.

Emil and Conrad waited—for what period of time, he couldn't judge.

The lights came on again. A stand of camera lights, he saw now. Emil and Conrad donned hoods and turned the camera on.

They said the names of his victims as they did their work.

They knew there were more than five.

2 1

Frederick nearly lost sight of Meghan while trying to ditch the woman he had been kissing.

"We won't be leaving for another hour," the woman said to him, gazing up at him, her lips swollen.

A good kisser, he thought, with a little regret. If he weren't on a mission, he was sure he could have taken her somewhere semi-secluded and given her the best sex she'd ever had in her life. God knew she was hot for it. He admitted to himself that he was hot for her, too. Well, at least he had her number—he'd see if he had any juice left when he was done boning Meghan. He glanced up to see Meghan walking into the Peak Experience Restaurant, then smiled down at the woman who clung to him.

"Sorry, *boyakina*, business before pleasure."

She laughed. "Did you just call me your 'spoon rest'?"

He turned her around and pressed his crotch against her backside. He wrapped his arms across her chest, moving his hands inside her jacket, brushing his thumbs over her nipples with practiced care, then pulling at them a little as they responded. Breathing gently into her ear, he whispered, "*Boyakina*, because I like spooning with you. Do you mind if I call you that?"

"No," she said breathlessly.

He laughed softly and released her, setting her a little apart from him. "Now go on, join the others. What time do you think you'll be back home and ready for company after the hike?"

She was dazed, but answered, "Midnight, maybe a little earlier."

He smiled and said, "Then, we'll end our masquerade at midnight, all right?"

"I don't want to leave you," she said.

He checked his temper and transformed his expression into one of deep disappointment. "You don't trust me, do you? Of course not. I can't blame you, really. It's just that I had hoped you were feeling—"

"Oh! Of course I do! I'm sorry! Please—I won't say another word. I'm going. I'm going right now."

She smiled—bravely, he thought—and turned to walk off to join the others. While her back was turned, he hurriedly moved out of sight. He was afraid she might try to enact a prolonged scene, and he wondered how much Meghan might be able to see from the windows of the restaurant. He remembered that Meghan had dinner reservations at the restaurant, so he knew where she'd be for at least another forty-five minutes or more. It would be worth hiding near the tram platform for a few of those minutes, just to make sure he wouldn't be followed by his latest conquest. He spent most of this time fantasizing about what Meghan would look like naked and completely under his control.

"Why do we have to wait in here for her?" Spooky asked. The words were a little distorted. She had polished off her third Shirley Temple and was, for the third time, trying to tie a knot in a maraschino cherry stem using only her tongue.

Thirteen, Kit thought to himself. "Because this is where she's expecting to meet us."

He kept his eyes moving, staying aware of the other patrons in the restaurant, watching those who seemed to be watching the door. He was out of cell phone range, so he couldn't check to see if she had made it safely to the tram. He considered using a pay phone to call the man who had been sent to guard Meghan, but he decided to wait a few more minutes.

Spooky took a loosely knotted stem from her mouth in triumph, then complained that he wasn't paying attention. When that didn't prove effective, she said, "I have to go to the bathroom."

He glanced at the restaurant doors and then at his watch. Meghan was running a little late. Should he go out to the platform? Try calling her cell phone? Maybe he'd call her while Spooky was in the bathroom. "Okay. But promise me two things—"

"Let me guess. I won't rob anyone in the restroom," she said impatiently. "And I won't start any fires."

"Thanks. Hurry, all right?"

She frowned, said, "Why should I? Your girlfriend's not in any hurry."

She then strolled off at a leisurely pace. He knew he had doomed himself— she'd take as long as possible now.

In the next moment, his thoughts were completely distracted from Spooky. Meghan Taggert walked into the restaurant.

He had wondered if she would look different. She did. She wasn't the teenaged Meghan whose image he held in his mind, or the girl in half a dozen cherished photos taken during visits to her family's home when he was in high school with her brother. She had matured from the pretty girl every boy in Malibu had wanted to date to a woman who, dressed in blue jeans, a loose sweater, and hiking boots, radiated elegance and an indefinable something, a quality of which Kit could already see the usual effects: women studying her with slight frowns on their faces, men with drinks half-lifted to their mouths— halted mid-action as they stared.

If she was aware of these effects, she didn't reveal it in any way. She scanned the room as if its population didn't exist, then saw him and smiled.

He was glad he didn't have a drink in his hand.

He stood and began walking toward her, and her smile widened, and he found himself smiling back. As he came nearer, he saw that she was opening her arms, and he realized she was going to hug him, so he quickly forced his mind to put up one of the mental partitions that he built whenever he needed to cope with what at times seemed to him an embrace-crazed society. But although no one else ever had noticed this slight withdrawal, she seemed to sense it immediately and changed the motion a little, so that she merely lightly touched his shoulders before dropping her arms. Her smile seemed to waver, and he felt something in the region of his chest waver with it. Then she said in her husky voice, "Kit Logan, it's been far too long since I've seen you."

He felt a sudden urge to do something that—from the age of ten—he had never done of his own volition with an adult woman. He wanted to open his arms to her.

But then the memories came pushing and shoving their way into his awareness, and the desire passed.

"Yes," he said, "I've missed you."

She smiled up at him, and he let out a breath he had not realized he was holding.

"This must be Malibu week in Albuquerque," she said. "You'll never guess who I saw making out with his girlfriend in the tram."

"Who?" he asked sharply.

"What's wrong?"

He tried to keep his voice calm. He was thinking of the ones who killed Molly, though, and the incident at the hotel, and wondered if the FBI had ever been watching Meghan, or if his suspicions were right. "If you saw someone from Malibu, I don't think it was a coincidence."

"It was just Freddy," she said. "You know, Freddy the Fourth." She said it lightly, but he could tell that she had started to worry, too.

"Where is he now?"

She looked around. "I don't see him. Probably with the group of hikers he was with. By the way, where's Spooky?"

"In the women's room. Listen, I'm going to take a look around, to see if I can find him, just to make sure he's actually going on the hike. Would you mind going into the women's room and waiting there with Spooky until I figure out where he is?"

She was studying him in the way she used to study him when he was a teenager. Assessing something he had told her, sorting out for herself whether or not it was part of his craziness. "Okay," she said. "But what if—what if something happens to you?"

"Nothing will happen to me," he said. "I'm not going to confront him unless he tries to hurt you or Spooky. In fact, I don't want him to know I'm here, if I can help it. I just want to try to figure out what he's up to." He described Spooky and what she was wearing. He then asked Meghan to describe what Freddy was wearing.

"And the girlfriend? What did she look like?"

She told him, then said, "Now that I think about it, she was dressed for hiking. He wasn't really, was he?"

"I'll find out."

She came with him as he hurried to the table and collected his jacket and Spooky's, and paid for the drinks. He gave Spooky's jacket to Meghan.

He also wrote a quick note to Spooky on a cocktail napkin and gave it to Meghan.

"Don't let her intimidate you," he warned.

She laughed. "I won't."

"Thanks," he said. "I'll be back as soon as I can."

"Be careful," she said, and walked off. He watched until he was sure she had safely entered the women's room. He waited another minute, just in case Spooky came bounding out in rebellion. He didn't even hear raised voices, though, so he made his way to the restaurant entrance.

There, he approached the woman who was seating newly arrived customers. "Mr. Logan," she said, smiling at him. "I saw your friend arrive. So did all the men in the place. Is your party ready to be seated now?"

"I'm so sorry," he said. "But I'm afraid we're going to have to leave without dining." He took two one-hundred-dollar bills from his wallet and gave one to her. "Someone may come in and ask for Ms. Taggert—his name is Fred. He's an old boyfriend who has followed her up here. Rather than make a scene in the restaurant, I'd like to treat him to dinner. That's what the hundred's for."

"Generous of you," she said. "I don't get it, though."

"He might try to tell you that he's her brother. He may even claim that he's with the FBI."

"The FBI!"

"Ridiculous, isn't it? He may even have some realistic-looking ID. If he says that he's with the FBI, offer to verify that with the local FBI field office, and I think he'll take the next tram downhill. But if he says he's her brother or gives his own name, please seat him at my table—without letting him know I'm here, please. Perhaps you could pretend she's been waiting for a gentleman to join her, and tell him the table's hers and that she'll be right back?"

The hostess laughed and erased "Logan—3" in her reservations book, then replaced it with "Taggert—2."

He smiled and gave her the other hundred. "That one is for your trouble."

"Mr. Logan—that's not necessary."

"No, I know it's not. So you don't need to feel bad about taking it. One other thing—could I use the service road?"

"No problem."

He told her to watch for a young man with light, short hair, blue eyes, and wearing an aviator jacket. "He might be wearing sunglasses," he added.

"Indoors?"

"Oh yes."

He hurried outside.

Kit stood still and listened. Meghan said Freddy was with a group of hikers, and now he heard the voices of a group of people gathering to the left of where he stood. He walked around the building until he saw them. He casually approached one of the men who seemed to be a group leader and began asking questions.

A moonlight hike. Yes, it was a big group, but they had another fifteen who had started a little later and would probably be coming up on the next tram.

Yes, a hiking club based in Albuquerque. Freddy? No, he didn't think there was a Freddy in the group.

After waiting to make sure his little *boyakina* wasn't going to come back toward the tram platform, Frederick entered the restaurant, looking self-assured. He achieved this by asking himself, "What would James Dean do in this situation?"

The answer came to him immediately. James Dean would be cool. You would look at James Dean and say, "That guy is so cool, I will give him whatever he wants."

He walked up to the hostess, who was smiling delightedly at him, and said, "Ms. Taggert is waiting for me—I'm her brother."

"Of course," she said, her eyes twinkling. He wondered if he should have used the FBI routine instead, but then the hostess said, "She's been waiting for you. Let me take you to her table."

He couldn't believe how easy this was. But as they neared the table, he didn't see Meghan.

"She just went to use the ladies' room," the hostess said. "She said to tell you that she went ahead and ordered, and that you should do the same while you wait for her. Shall I send a server over?"

He ordered a beer and said he'd wait until he saw Meghan before he ordered anything more.

"Coming right up," the hostess said.

He could make women happy, he decided, just by smiling at them.

Spooky was making faces at herself in the mirror when Meghan came into the restroom. She quickly stopped and turned to frown at Meghan.

Meghan could see how it was that Kit had mistaken Spooky for a boy. Three years after he had found her in a men's room, she still looked as if she could have walked into one without causing anyone to doubt that she belonged there.

"You're Meghan," Spooky said, and went back to making faces.

"Yes. I have your jacket."

Her face squished between her hands, she looked at Meghan and said, "Tell me something I don't know."

"I have a note for you from Kit."

Spooky raised a brow, then crossed her arms. "Let me guess. 'Dear Spooky, Get your ass out of the bathroom. Now that *Meghan* is here, we can finally get on with life.' "

"No, but— I'm sorry, am I making you late for something?"

Spooky said, "To take a dump. Excuse me, I have to use the can." She closed herself into a stall.

Meghan didn't think it likely that Spooky had delayed bodily functions on her account, but since Kit wanted them to wait in here anyway, she didn't object to this part of the drama. In fact, she was glad they'd get the business of meeting each other over with, without Kit hovering protectively in their midst as some sort of referee.

"How did you recognize me?" she asked.

"Wouldn't your big ego like to know?"

"I recognized you because Kit has told me about you," Meghan said. "I don't think there's anyone else he cares more about than you."

"He cares more about his dead dog."

Meghan didn't say anything for a moment. "I was sorry to hear about Molly. She had been with Kit for a long time."

"She was old. Older than me."

"When she died, it must have been hard on you, too."

"You know what I'm *not* going to do? I'm not going to sit on this crapper talking to you about my dog, okay?"

"Okay."

Spooky faked farting sounds.

"Charming."

"Isn't it, though? I fart all the time. Maybe you should find somebody else to take you to California, because I'm probably going to fart all the way there. You're probably too prissy to fart."

"Most of the time, good manners do keep me from doing that when I'm around other people, but I can see that manners don't matter to you at all—so get ready, because if we're all going to be so free about it, that car's going to smell like the bean factory's company picnic."

She heard a little snort of laughter from behind the stall. It was quickly suppressed, but Meghan figured she had made some progress.

She waited in silence, then heard Spooky say angrily, "You can't fix him, you know."

"Kit? I don't think he's broken."

"He's crazy."

"No, he's not."

"Shows what you know."

"He makes mistakes, that's all. He told me you were thirteen."

"I am."

"Could have fooled me. Aren't you a little old for potty humor?"

"You tell me, bean eater. And he *is* crazy."

"Why do you live with him, then?"

"Craziness runs in our family."

"Well, I don't know about you, but Kit isn't crazy. He has problems, but who doesn't? He's not like everyone else, but I think that's why I like him."

"Do you love him?"

"You won't talk about Molly in here, I won't talk about what I feel for Kit. Maybe another time."

"Shit. You do love him."

Meghan didn't answer.

After several minutes, Spooky said, "I knew you were Meghan, because he has pictures of you."

Meghan was surprised by this and was glad Spooky couldn't see her face.

"You're prettier now," Spooky said, then added quickly, "but don't let it go to your head. It probably makes other women hate you."

"A few I don't worry about. Maybe I should meet everyone in bathrooms. They could get to know me without seeing my face."

"You should work at a place for the blind."

"I have."

"You're kidding."

"No, I'm not."

"Cool. What was it like?"

"I enjoyed it."

"So if you don't want to be judged by your looks, maybe you should go back to work there and leave those of us in bathrooms alone."

"I meet more people this way. Not everyone is blind—at least, not literally. But sooner or later, everyone has to—"

Spooky laughed. "Hand me Kit's note. There's no TP in here."

"Come out and get it."

Another woman entered the bathroom then, and Spooky came out of the stall. She washed her hands, then took her jacket from Meghan. "This doesn't mean I like you."

"I wouldn't want it to be that easy."

"Let me see the note—please."

Meghan handed it to her. Spooky's eyes widened as she read it. She shot a look of pure rage at Meghan. "You didn't tell me! He could be in trouble! You stupid bitch—"

"Spooky—"

But she evaded Meghan's grasp and ran out of the room.

Meghan hurried after her but hadn't taken more than two steps from the bathroom when Frederick Whitfield IV grabbed her by the arm.

"Sex with young boys in bathrooms, Meghan? Even I wouldn't have guessed it."

Spooky heard him and turned just in time to see Meghan move back, bend, and then twist, throwing Frederick off balance. With another quick motion, she sent him head over heels, so that he landed with a loud whump on his back. He rolled to his stomach, winded, and tried to get to his feet, but Spooky ran forward, asked, "Are you all right, sir?" and landed both knees in his back.

"Go!" Meghan shouted, and they both ran out of the restaurant.

Some restaurant patrons saw a woman and a boy run out of the Peak Experience. A few more saw the man who followed them, sometime later. The hostess, seating a couple who had just arrived, heard about it when she came back to her station and wondered if she should call the sheriff. She decided to give Mr. Logan a few more minutes to settle his problems privately.

Kit was driving up the service road to the restaurant when Meghan and Spooky came charging toward him. He braked hard, and Spooky yelled to Meghan, "Get in the front seat!

"Turn around!" Spooky shouted as she got in back, but Kit was already turning the wheel as they slammed and locked their doors. He stepped on the accelerator, leaving Frederick Whitfield IV in a cloud of dust.

The women cheered.

He slowed a little, then eased onto the main road. "What exactly did you two do back there?" Kit asked.

"Oh man!" Spooky said, laughing. "Meghan kicks ass!"

He smiled, then said, "Okay, but do I need to send a check to the Peak Experience to pay for the damage?"

"Let Freddy pay for it," Meghan said, catching her breath.

"He'll have a hard time doing that," Spooky said, holding up Frederick Whitfield IV's wallet and a set of keys to a Bronco.

"Spooky . . ."

"I said I wouldn't rob anyone *in the women's room.*"

"Spooky," Meghan said, "kicks ass."

Spooky frowned, then said, "Just because you can fight—"

"—doesn't mean you like me. I know. Likewise, I'm sure."

Kit sighed, then drove a little faster.

2 2

Alex Brandon stood a few feet from the edge of a sheer drop to the Pacific Ocean, one member of a tight circle of coroner's assistant, deputies, and crime lab workers who surrounded an aluminum-framed litter—and the tarp-wrapped corpse within it. After some struggle, and a climb that Alex would have envied them otherwise, the technical rescue crew had brought the body up from the cliff. They had wisely refused the earliest suggestion made to them, that they just haul it up on the rope left by the killers. It had taken a little time to rig a separate set of ropes and the litter.

Some distance away, the press and a few rubbernecking members of the public were standing at barriers closely guarded by sheriff's department deputies. They'd get a better view of the proceedings at home—a television news crew in a helicopter had already taken footage of the litter being pulled up to its present location.

"Detective Brandon?" Alex turned to see one of the uniformed deputies approaching them. "The FBI agent is here."

"Bring him on over," Alex said. He turned back to the coroner's assistant. "Can you wait for a moment, until he joins us?"

"Sure."

The sheriff, Alex had learned, had made certain concessions to the FBI in an effort to counter some of the criticism he had received from the local press. Lieutenant Hogan believed that their fearless leader had apparently outnegotiated the director of the FBI in superb style by agreeing that until any federal jurisdiction over the cases seemed warranted, he would generously give copies of all earlier reports to the FBI and would allow an FBI liaison to work with Alex and Ciara on any new cases.

Ciara's own take on this was that the FBI was providing the sheriff all the rope he'd need to hang himself. Alex wasn't so sure she was wrong.

As they watched, a young man of medium height came stepping gingerly over the damp, uneven ground along the cliffs. Alex, recognizing an Armani suit and Cole Haan shoes when he saw them, wondered if every nickel the FBI paid the guy was on his back and feet. The agent had sun-bleached golden hair and a light tan. If he was over thirty, Alex thought, it wasn't by much.

Ciara said, "What did I tell you? If that's not a third-stringer, you can have my badge. Christ, he isn't even shaving yet."

Alex saw the agent blush, and turned to Ciara.

"Save the reprimand," she said. "I'll shut the hell up."

"For novelty's sake," Alex said quietly, "give politeness a try."

"Hi!" she said a little too brightly to the agent as he reached them. "I'm Detective Ciara Morton, Los Angeles Sheriff's Department. This is my partner, Alexander Brandon, who's in charge of the task force."

His brows rose higher above his dark brown eyes, then he warmly shook their extended hands, returned their smiles, and said, "Special Agent David Hamilton, FBI. I know some of you say that stands for Fan Belt Inspectors, but really, only the guys in the vehicle lab back in Virginia have earned that rank. Would you like to see my badge or my razor?"

There was an uneasy silence, then Ciara said, "Your razor, to slit my wrists."

"Oh no," he said. "Besides, I haven't heard a thing. Have any of you heard anything?"

Alex glanced behind him and saw that everyone else shook their heads.

"I understand we have a true cliff-hanger," Hamilton said.

"Yes," Alex said. "Some boaters noticed a long, tarp-wrapped bundle hanging over the side of the cliff here. Took a look through binoculars and saw that it had feet. When our department sent a team to take a look, they saw a six painted on the canvas in blood."

"They were kind enough to draw a little line under the six," Ciara said, "just so we wouldn't get confused and think it was another nine."

Hamilton grinned at her.

Alex said, "Our officers realized there were some other similarities to the previous cases, so they called us in." He paused, then added, "We've made a preliminary identification."

Hamilton moved closer to the litter. "Another longtime resident of California?"

"Couldn't say. But he's been on your list for a long time." Alex used a gloved hand to pull the canvas back from the corpse's face.

"Victor Elliot," Hamilton said. "You're right. On the list for about three years."

Alex, seeing him pat down his pockets, handed him a pair of latex gloves. "Thanks," he said.

Alex watched him carefully remove a large gold and ruby school ring before putting them on. Hamilton bent nearer to the body. "Featured on *Crimesolvers USA* in February of last year." He looked up at Alex. "I hear you're the one who figured out that connection. The photos and description you sent out of this 'Eric Grady' are in all our field offices now."

"Maybe we should try to get him featured on *Crimesolvers*," Ciara said.

Hamilton laughed. "Maybe so. God knows Victor Elliot slipped past us for over a year."

"Armored car robberies, right?" Alex said.

"Yes—six of them, and only three out of eighteen guards lived to talk about what happened. Victor Elliot masterminded the robberies. We captured everyone who worked for him, but we could never lay hands on Elliot himself."

"Lay hands on him now," Ciara invited.

Hamilton touched the canvas near Elliot's arm and said, "My God, rigor hasn't passed off yet?"

"He's frozen," Alex said.

"Defrosting," Ciara corrected.

"Despite the heat of the day," Alex said, "he's far from thawed. We want to get him to the coroner's office as soon as possible, so that he doesn't end up smelling like the last three."

Hamilton stood. "I heard they were fairly ripe. I'll admit I wasn't looking forward to getting a snout full of that when they called me to come out here."

As the coroner's assistant and the others moved the litter away, Alex showed Hamilton what he could of the scene. He pointed out the place where the rope had been anchored.

"There are a number of obvious differences this time," Alex said. "Frozen body, openly displayed outdoors in a visible location. But while the others were hanging nude, this one was wrapped in a tarp—as you saw. The other bodies were also left hanging over bathtubs, but this setup is not as elaborate as those were. The person or persons who left this body here simply set up a rock climber's anchor at the edge of the cliff and lowered the body over."

"Person?" Hamilton said. "I thought you figured this was a duo at least."

"Still do, but Victor Elliot was a small, thin man, so the body could have been placed here by someone acting alone. This time, the victim didn't seem to have been subjected to torture—the autopsy will tell us more, but we didn't see knife wounds, and the body was not exsanguinated. There does not seem to have been any use of blood-thinning agents, either. There was one wound to the back of the skull, probably a blunt instrument applied with some force."

"That's the presumed cause of death?"

"Too early to say."

"Extreme cold seems more likely," Ciara said.

"They froze him to death?"

"Too early to say," Alex repeated, with emphasis, as he looked at Ciara.

"And the similarities to the other cases?" Hamilton asked.

"Left in an area known to be in the sheriff's jurisdiction. Hanging upside down, tied around the feet and hands. A rappelling rope was used again— probably another length of the same one—the lab will be able to tell us if the ends match. There's another difference, by the way—while the knots around the hands and the feet are similar to the previous three cases, the ones that actually held him over the edge of the cliff are tied differently. My guess is, someone else tied them this time."

"I wonder how long it takes to freeze a human body?"

"Depends on weight, I suppose," Ciara said. "Like a side of beef. For a skinny little guy like Elliot, maybe not too long at all. Just put him in the old home freezer overnight."

"I guess so."

"I don't know that it would have been so easy, Ciara," Alex said. "His arms and legs were extended when he was frozen—so he was frozen without his knees or elbows being bent. Elliot was thin, but he was about five seven— even if a home freezer was empty, it's not likely he'd fit inside in that position."

"So, you think he has been in a commercial freezer?" Hamilton asked.

"Maybe. Or, if he's been in the freezer of a private home, it's a big house."

"A mansion," Hamilton said, looking back at the lights along the peninsula.

"Yes, there's a lot of wealth in this area," Alex said. "It's not the only wealthy area in Los Angeles County. But you know that, right?"

Hamilton blushed again. "The tan or the accent?"

"To my ear, the lack of accent. And the USC college ring."

Hamilton laughed. "Yes, I went to SC. And I grew up in L.A. It's one of the reasons why I was given the assignment, I'm told. I know the LASD and my agency aren't on great terms right now . . . but I'm hoping we can improve the situation."

"We're on the same side," Alex said.

"Thanks. Anything I can do to help out?"

"Do you know the last date anyone in your agency received a report on Elliot? Last time he was seen alive?"

Hamilton pulled out a Palm PDA and turned it on. He tapped the stylus on the screen a few times, then said, "We received reports in February, after the show aired." He read for a few minutes, then said, "Looks as if we had a reliable report on February twenty-seventh, in Lafayette, Louisiana. A bank teller called to say someone who looked like Elliot had been in just before Christmas and set up a safe-deposit box. We took a look at the security camera tapes and agreed. We got a warrant and got his prints off the box, but something or someone must have tipped him off, because we watched the address he gave to the bank and he never showed up. We checked it out later, and he had definitely been there. Nothing after that."

"So they've probably been working on your top ten list at least since February," Alex said grimly. "They've got a big head start."

"Anything in the safe-deposit box?" Ciara asked.

"About a hundred thousand from one of the robberies."

"Seems likely he saw his story being featured on TV, don't you think?" she said.

"The show aired February twentieth," Hamilton said, "so I don't know—if that was going to make him nervous, wouldn't he have left on the twenty-first?"

"If the box had been empty, I would have said the show spooked him," Alex said. "But you say he left a hundred grand, right? So he must have planned to return. How long between the teller's call to the FBI and the Bureau's response?"

Hamilton looked uneasy. "About ten days—we received a lot of calls after the show aired, so it took some time to check them all out."

"Not all that many commercial flights in and out of Lafayette, are there? I mean, nothing like JFK or DFW, right? So let's look at passenger lists from February twenty-seventh to March—whatever day it was the agents arrived—and pay special attention to anyone ticketed through to LAX, Burbank, Long Beach, Ontario, or other nearby California airports during that time."

"Okay. And when we have this list?"

"Find out who paid for the tickets, for starters. Did he have a phone at this house you watched?"

"No phone."

"How did they contact him?" Alex said, rubbing his forehead. "And out of all the places he might have been, how did they choose Lafayette?"

Hamilton shrugged. "We'll have to look at all the calls that came into the show, try to learn how they thought it out. Maybe we can look at the calls logged for some of the other shows and get ahead of them."

"I'll try to go back there tomorrow, see what I can get from them." Alex stood looking out at the moonlight on the water for long moments.

Behind him, he heard Ciara say, "Four down, six to go. Unless all ten are already dead."

Alex considered asking Hamilton to give Ciara a lift back to the office. He had reached his limit for the day, and if he hadn't been so sure that she would repay the insult by making tomorrow worse for him, he would have foisted her off on the agent.

But as he turned to face them, he heard Ciara say, "Agent Hamilton, could I trouble you for a ride to my car? Alex has had a long day, and his house isn't far from here. Besides, his nephew is waiting for him."

"I'd be glad to be of help."

Alex almost protested out of guilt, but instead said, "Thanks, I appreciate it."

"Come on," Ciara said to Hamilton. "I'll buy you dinner. Have you ever eaten at Café Misto? I think we can make it before they close."

Before they left, he exchanged cards with Hamilton. He watched them walk away, past the deputies who were still keeping the scene secure.

Alex went over the same things he had gone over earlier, only this time, in relative solitude. He tried to picture the killer coming out here with his burden—or a pair of killers doing the same. The crevice in the cliffs would have been chosen beforehand—perhaps from offshore? They probably would have parked as close as possible to the place where they dropped the body. They set the anchoring system first. Then the rope and body were set at the edge, the rope tied, and the body lowered. At some point, the person who tied the knots this time had cut the excess rope, and had probably done so pulling the rope taut with one hand and pressing the rope with the thumb of the other hand, the hand that also held his knife.

And made a small mistake that had given investigators a piece of luck this time, one they hadn't had before. The knife had been sharper than expected or he had been a little clumsy—he had cut himself and bled on and near the

rope. He had tried to wipe it off, but enough had remained on the rope's surface and on the rocky ground nearby to catch the attention of a crime lab technician.

DNA.

Someone had suggested that it might be the victim's blood, leaking out.
But a frozen body would not drip blood.

Alex wanted to make sure their own lab had what it wanted for processing
before mentioning the blood to the FBI. If there was enough for the FBI to
run its own tests, fine, but if not, he wouldn't be placing the sheriff's department in the position it was in a few months ago.

He began walking back to his car, ignoring the shouts of the press.

He wondered if Ciara was talking to David Hamilton about bloodstains
over dinner.

Albuquerque, New Mexico
Tuesday, May 20, 9:36 P.M.

As he sat on the steps leading down to the Sandia Tramway parking lot, Frederick Whitfield IV heard his cell phone ring.

"Am I glad I still have my cell phone, or not?" he asked aloud.

He looked at the caller ID display and felt a chill that had nothing to do with the evening's dropping temperatures. "Not," he whispered. He didn't answer the call.

Hands shaking, he put the phone back in his jacket.

Unlike the hive of activity it had been a little earlier, the parking lot was quiet now. The last tram had come down from the mountain, and only the cars of the moonlight hikers remained.

The Bronco he had stolen was gone.

This was not a surprise to him—not now, anyway. He had been more than surprised a few hours earlier, when he had helplessly watched from the descending tram as a police tow truck took the Bronco away.

He had been totally humiliated when Meghan used karate or jujitsu or whatever the fuck it was on him. Where the hell did that bitch learn how to do that? Belatedly, he remembered that in high school, Gabe had talked about the two of them taking lessons of some sort—she had hurt her brother during practice or something.

Big deal. Frederick also knew all kinds of martial arts moves, but it really wasn't fair if you weren't expecting someone to pull that kind of shit without warning. So in front of all those people, she thinks it's funny to try this fancy crap, and she gets lucky.

Then that little freak who was in the bathroom with her—what was *that* all about?—nailed him in the kidneys. Kid comes at him from behind, when he's already down. Really unfair. Totally, totally unfair. They didn't teach that in any dojo—that much he knew. Leave it to a woman to not understand that this is not the way to fight.

He hadn't been able to get a good look at the driver of the Suburban, and he wondered for a minute if it had been Gabe Taggert. But he had read the dossier that Everett had prepared on Taggert, and he knew that if Taggert had a kid, Everett would have found him by now, and used him to get Taggert to come back to California.

The reservation book—which he had looked at when he came back into the restaurant, intending to complain that he hadn't thought this was the kind of place where you'd get attacked on your way to use the restroom—said "Taggert—2," though, so he was confused. He decided that Meghan was maybe meeting the boy for dinner, as a favor to the kid's father. Kind of like a baby-sitter or something. Maybe the kid was retarded, and she had to help him use the bathroom. He still couldn't figure out the bathroom part.

But he was just about positive that the kid's old man was the one driving the Suburban. Another asshole. Frederick didn't get a chance to catch more than a glimpse of the guy, just enough to know it was a man doing the driving, a white guy. Maybe Meghan was more like her brother than anyone suspected, and they were a gang, preying on rich people who came to ski resorts. As a rich person, Frederick really resented that kind of thing. There should be better laws—after all, wasn't it a violation of your civil rights if someone robbed you just because you were rich?

He didn't think it was an accident that the license plate on the Suburban was too muddy to read. He hoped a cop stopped them for it. Then they'd have to explain why they had his wallet and keys and about why there were all these different people's driver's licenses in the wallet, and shit like that. He really, really hoped it happened. He might even call in an anonymous tip. That would teach that little butthole to steal wallets.

He hadn't known his wallet was missing at first, of course. When he had walked up to the hostess's stand, he thought he was just going to be complaining about the physical abuse he had suffered, maybe get a free beer out of it. But then the hostess had said, "Oh, Mr. Taggert! I'm so glad you came back. I have your change."

He had almost forgotten that he had told this woman that he was Meghan's brother. He smiled a little feebly at her, because he was sore from the pummeling he had been given. Then, to his amazement, she extended a little tray to him, on which he counted a sum of ninety-five bucks.

"Is everything all right, Mr. Taggert?" she asked.

The first and most important intelligence he received from this question was that she didn't know what had happened to him—maybe not so many people had seen him face planted into the floorboards after all.

The second was that he was, for whatever reason, about to receive a windfall. Ninety-five dollars wasn't even pocket change to someone with his resources, but it was money, and he never held his nose up at money. He was not unaware of the predicament in which the rest of the world found itself, and he knew that in a place like the Peak Experience, this was a lot of change for a guy who had only ordered a beer.

So he said that everything was fine, and took the cash, and reached for his wallet to put it away.

No wallet. A quick check of all of his pockets revealed that his keys were also missing.

The hostess was watching him closely.

For a moment, in his fury, he considered pitching a fit that would allow him to do a healthy amount of venting. He'd say he had been mugged and robbed by professional thieves. Meghan and her gang would be captured and humiliated, as he had been humiliated.

But then he realized that if the thieves were caught, he'd have to explain why he was using a dead man's driver's license, had a collection of credit cards in names other than his own, had the keys to a stolen vehicle, and answer any number of other awkward questions that were sure to arise.

So he put the loose bills in his jeans pocket and walked out with what dignity he could muster. He thought he heard some sniggering from the area of the hostess's stand but didn't bother looking back. No use being paranoid.

He was feeling fairly stiff and sore by the time he went up the stairs to the tram. He had just reached the entrance when he realized his return tram ticket had been in his wallet. But he lucked out, because the skinny old long-haired dude who was taking tickets said, "Don't worry about it—I remember you from the trip up. Where's your girlfriend?"

"She's hiking down," he said. "I'm going to wait for her below."

"You don't want to take that moonlight hike?"

"I'd love to, but . . . well, I don't tell many people this, but I have a rare heart condition. I've had to give up hiking."

"Man, that sucks," he said, and Frederick felt moved by this show of sympathy—something he found he needed, even under false pretenses.

Seeing his face, the other man added, "I hope she appreciates how danger-ous it is for you to be up at this altitude, even to see her off."

"I don't want her to know how much danger I've been in up here," he said in all truthfulness.

"That's beautiful, man. I think I'll ride down with you, just to make sure you're okay."

This was carrying the sympathy a little further than he would have pre-ferred, but he graciously accepted the offer.

It was on the tram that Freddy saw something that nearly did stop his heart—the Bronco being towed. There was a police car following it.

"Hey, hey . . . sit down there, fella. You really shouldn't have come up here."

"You're so right," Frederick said with feeling.

Would someone be watching to see who came off the tram and didn't have a vehicle? Of course. A trap must be in place. He was starting to wonder what Everett would say if he learned that one of his men had been arrested in Albu-querque. It didn't bear thinking about.

His anxiety over the number of crimes he might be charged with had taken up so much of his mind that he had forgotten the story he told the hippie. So he looked a little confused when the man said, "You can wait inside until about nine, okay? That's when the last tram comes down. Just take it easy until then, man."

"Thanks, you've been so kind," Frederick said.

The man smiled and said, "Think nothing of it. You're an inspiration. I mean it."

After the tram office closed and the workers had left, he considered stealing one of the other cars in the lot, but he still had some fears that the lot was being watched. After all, as far as the police knew, the Bronco might belong to one of the hikers. He knew that car theft wouldn't usually warrant so much attention, but the theft of the Bronco would lead to the house he had tossed, the pickup he had stolen, and possibly the hotel. Not good.

The cell phone rang again. Again he ignored it. It started beeping. He looked at the display and saw a text message:

ARRIVING LGB TOMORROW 10 AM. BRING THE VAN. DO NOT DISAPPOINT ME.

He stared at the message for a moment, but no matter how many times he read it, it said the same thing—Everett and Cameron would be at the Long Beach Airport at ten in the morning. He called the company he used when he needed a private jet and arranged to have a plane ready to take him home at six tomorrow morning. He told them his wallet had been stolen, so he would not have his ID. They assured him that the pilot and crew they were sending were his favorites and knew him personally, so there would be no problem. Was there anything else they could do for him?

People were really wonderful, he thought. Then he saw the text message again, and thought of Everett, and how he would react when he learned what had happened here, and that he had lost track of Meghan.

He turned the phone off. He began to weep.

The first group of hikers arrived about then, so he wiped his face with the soft handkerchief he had brought with him. He had made sure not to bring one of the monogrammed ones. He looked up to see his little *boyakina* hurrying toward him. She looked angry. A pissed-off woman, he decided, was all he needed to make this a one-hundred-percent-fucked-up, completely whack day.

But she slowed when she saw his tears, her look changing to one of genuine concern. For some reason, that made him start crying again. He was glad Everett wasn't here to see what a total pussy he was turning into.

She sat down next to him and put an arm around his shoulders. "What's wrong?"

Where to begin? he thought. He briefly considered telling her that his grandmother had died in a fire, some accident that occurred while she had been reading the Tarot cards by candlelight, but then he remembered that she didn't like the fortune-telling thing. He found he liked the feel of that comforting arm and suddenly no longer had the energy for lies. He leaned against her and said nothing.

She used her free hand to stroke his hair. "I think the hike helped me to start thinking a little more clearly. Your parents weren't Russian spies, were they?"

He shook his head. "They're alive."

"And that was also bullshit about your grandmother, right?"

He nodded. "She's dead."

She sighed. "If my usual ability to pick men is at work here, you're also out of a job and completely broke."

"I have ninety-five dollars."

She laughed, and he found himself laughing, too. He dried his face again.

He came to a quick decision. "I'm—" He started to give her the full title, but then said, "I'm Frederick Whitfield. What's your name?"

"Vanessa. Vanessa Przbyslaw."

For a moment he was distracted. "How do you spell that?"

She told him.

"Okay, Vanessa, here are three things that are true. One—I have no wheels at the moment, and I don't want to tell you why not. Two—my plane leaves at six tomorrow morning, and I have got to be on it. Three—I'd like to spend the hours I have left here in New Mexico with you. Can I go home with you?"

She studied him for a moment, then said, "Why am I going to say yes?"

"Because I remind you of James Dean?"

She laughed again and said, "Okay, that's as good a reason as any. Come home with me, James Dean, and I'll cook you a late dinner."

He kissed her long and hard. As he did, a practical consideration occurred to him. All his condoms were in his wallet and luggage—and these were in the possession of Meghan and the Albuquerque police, respectively. "Know of an all-night drugstore we could stop at on the way home?" he asked.

He decided she really was pretty when she blushed.

He stood on the threshold of her apartment, holding the paper sack from the grocery store, staring in amazement. It was a small place, nothing special in its layout or location. But the décor was completely unexpected.

She watched his face and said, "If you wanted turquoise and beige and howling coyotes and cacti and all that goddamned Southwestern shit, you went home with the wrong woman."

The apartment, in the middle of Albuquerque, probably eight or nine hundred miles away from the nearest ocean, was covered with nautical paraphernalia. A fishing net covered one wall, and attached to it were a life buoy, driftwood, shells, starfish, an oar, and other objects of the sea. At one end of the living room, there was a large aquarium.

"I like it," he said. "But . . ."

"But why is it here in New Mexico? Because I've promised myself I'll live near the water again someday, and this reminds me of that promise. I grew up near the ocean, not far from Portland, Maine. I've sailed since I was seven. I'm not saying there isn't great stuff here, but I miss the water."

"Okay, then why live in Albuquerque?"

"I came here with my mom four years ago. Her doctors told her she needed to live in a dry climate. I moved with her to help her out, and got a job here."

"She lives with you?" he asked uneasily.

"Not now. She's in a hospice."

"I'm sorry," he said. He moved nearer to the aquarium.

"Freshwater," she said. "Can't afford a saltwater aquarium at the moment."

"I live near the Pacific," he said. "Have you ever seen it?"

"Not yet. I will someday, though."

"You really know how to sail?"

"Yes." She grinned as she walked into the kitchen. "Later on, I'll show you some knots."

They ate dinner on placemats made from nautical charts. Spaghetti sauce from a jar. To his own amazement, he liked it.

"Thanks," he said. "I'll repay you for all this trouble, you know."

"Don't worry about it."

"I'm serious. I might surprise you, you know. Maybe I'll come back and take you away from New Mexico. You know, take you sailing in the Pacific — Hawaii, Tahiti, Bora Bora — something like that. I've got some business to finish up, so it might take a while, but — oh, that reminds me — could I get your number again?"

"Lost it already, huh?" But she wrote it down again. "Here's to the Pacific," she said as she handed it to him. "I put my e-mail address on there, too. Get in touch with me if you need help, but no obligation otherwise."

After sex, he usually wanted nothing more than to leave a woman's bed as soon as possible, so perhaps out of habit, he got out of Vanessa's bed and walked over to watch the fish for a while. He thought she would probably complain or ask him to hold her — women always whined to him about the "just hold me" thing. But she didn't, and after a few minutes he found he wanted to go back to the bed and hold her anyway. She felt good alongside him.

He kept waiting for her to make some demand, but she didn't. And she didn't like him because of his money, or because he drove a sweet ride, or because of some expensive place he had taken her. He hadn't done any favors for her. He had lied to her and kept secrets from her, and she knew it. But instead of slapping him or screaming at him, she had fed him, provided him a place to stay for the night, and given him what he had to admit was the most incredible sex he'd ever had. She talked a lot, and she was a little weird, but he decided he was kind of attracted to her because of it.

At first, he figured it might have been that she was just so hard up and horny that she would have gone home with anyone. But he had changed his mind about that.

Over the last couple of hours, he had escaped his own troubles by listening to her, and he had come to the conclusion that she had no social life. Even so, she wasn't looking for a relationship, because she wasn't going to stay here, and she didn't want more complications in an already complicated life, or to bring a lover into the picture while her mother was dying.

She had told him that her dad had dumped her mom and married some young bimbo when Vanessa was in high school, and had basically forgotten that he had a daughter. Frederick considered looking him up and beating the shit out of him for doing that. If her father had stuck around, maybe he would have protected his daughter from guys like Frederick.

He traced his fingers along her spine. "You should be more careful, Vanessa. Don't go taking any more strangers home, okay? For all you know, I could be dangerous."

"Of course you are," she said drowsily. "Nothing's more dangerous than a lonely man. They cause most of the trouble in the world."

She fell asleep, but he lay awake for a while, thinking about that. He was dangerous, but he wasn't lonely, he told himself. Women liked him, and he knew how to play them. She ought to understand that—like her—he just didn't really want to get involved with anybody right now.

That's the way it had to be. If a man was involved in something really important and secret, he had to be free. Frederick knew he had done things that Vanessa couldn't even imagine, and he wasn't about to tell her about them. Because of Project Nine, he was going to keep having adventures and living on this incredible edge, feeling that adrenaline.

Everett understood his need to make his mark on the world. Everett had never failed to understand him completely. Without Everett, he would have been just another useless rich kid. Another Sedgewick loser.

No, he wasn't lonely, he told himself. She was wrong about that.

He sighed. Women really didn't know anything about men, but they were always full of so-called insights about them. He pulled her closer and fell asleep.

2 4

Spooky was engrossed in examining the contents of Frederick's wallet, a pastime she had engaged in several times over the last few hours.

Some people play license plate bingo, Kit thought, *and we play with twice-stolen identification cards.*

Meghan, who had slept for the last few hours, stirred awake and smiled at him. She stretched and sat up. "Do you want me to drive?"

He was feeling tired, and was almost certain that no one was following them now. If they were going to make it to Malibu without staying overnight somewhere between here and there, he needed to let her take the wheel for a while.

"Okay, thanks."

"No fair!" Spooky called out from the backseat. "You let *her* drive, and you won't let me?"

"Are you a licensed driver?" he asked Meghan.

She managed to keep a straight face. "Yes."

He looked in the rearview mirror at Spooky. "Are you a licensed driver?"

"Sure. I've got at least five licenses here in Eric Grady's wallet."

"I told you, his name is Frederick."

"So why was he after Meghan?"

"What do you think might have changed since the last time you asked that?"

"You said he was looking for her brother, but that's really dumb, unless her brother has tits as big as hers."

He didn't reply but knew she caught his look of disapproval in the mirror.

She sulked. "Okay, so nothing has changed, but you aren't telling me everything, either."

"I don't know everything yet. When I know more, I'll tell you. Apologize to Meghan."

She crossed her arms and glared at him, then said to Meghan, "I'm sorry for referring to your—"

He cleared his throat.

"—*body* in that way."

"Apology accepted," Meghan said.

He pulled over at a service station, filled the Suburban's big gas tank, and paid cash. They all took a bathroom break, and he noticed that Spooky used the restroom in record time. He knew that this was due to her fear of being left behind. He thought of saying something to reassure her but knew she would be mortified if he said anything like that in front of Meghan. He reached into his bag of *milagros* and found a tin dog. He slipped it to her as they were getting back into the Suburban. For a moment, she looked as if she might throw it away, but then he saw her tuck it into her jeans pocket.

Meghan took a moment to readjust the seat and mirrors, then they were off.

He moved his own seat into a more comfortable position. He verified in the side mirrors that there were no cars or trucks behind them, then relaxed back into his seat. He needed sleep. Everything would be fine.

He had just closed his eyes when there was a loud popping sound, and the SUV swerved as Meghan jumped.

Kit's heart raced, but there were no other cars nearby. No indication that they had blown a tire. He looked toward the backseat.

"Spooky . . ."

"What?"

"Exactly. What was it?"

She started laughing. He looked at the seat and saw a foil wrapper next to her.

"Did you just blow up a condom like a balloon and pop it?"

"Yes," she said, still laughing.

He waited until she stopped, then said, "Don't do it again."

"Aw, Kit. There are a bunch more of them."

"It wasn't funny. Not at all."

He heard a small snort and watched as Meghan struggled not to give in.

"Then why is Meghan laughing?" Spooky asked.

That proved to be Meghan's undoing.

"Great," he said. "Hand me a pillow, would you, Spooky?"

She did and said in a low voice, "Don't be mad."

"Are you done pulling stunts that could get us killed?"

She glanced at Meghan, who was faking deafness. "Yes," she said. "I promise I won't do anything like that again. Here. You can have all the rubbers, too." She handed over two strips of them. She frowned. "You aren't going to use them, are you?"

"No. Try to get some sleep."

"I slept too much today."

This was probably true, he decided, but was too tired to argue with her. Within minutes, he had dozed off.

Meghan glanced at him and kept that image of his face—seldom seen so free of care—in mind as she returned her attention to the road.

She told herself that there was absolutely no reason to feel depressed at his ready assurance that he wasn't going to use the condoms.

2 5

Manhattan Beach, California
Tuesday, May 20, 11:25 P.M.

Alex had nearly reached home when his pager went off again. He called in and was patched through to a detective with the Albuquerque police, whose department had made some promising discoveries. "Eric Grady" had been there. They were dusting for prints in a Bronco, a pickup truck, and an abandoned rental car, and already had some from a home that had been ransacked before the Bronco was stolen. They didn't have a matching record of an Eric Grady as a passenger arriving on a flight for the day the car was first rented, and assumed another identity had been used for purchasing the airline ticket.

As for the prints, they hadn't found a match in New Mexico's Automated Fingerprint Identification System—AFIS—files, but were sending copies of the prints on to the LASD. There was a computer compatibility issue. One of the frustrations Alex and everyone else in law enforcement faced was that AFIS and other computer technologies varied from state to state, and the systems were often incompatible.

The better news was that the man posing as Grady had left opened water bottles, half-eaten sandwiches, and—strangely—wads of several varieties of chewing gum. "We'll have lots of DNA samples, and dental impressions, too," the detective said. "We'll send most of them to you, but the FBI has asked for some, too."

Alex thanked him and called Hamilton.

"Great, isn't it?" the FBI agent said. "I just got word from our field office there. I'm going to ask our guys to rush the DNA work and to run it through CODIS."

"Sure, why not?" Alex said. If the gum chewer in New Mexico had ever been convicted of rape, assault, homicide, or certain other felonies, his DNA might be in the FBI's CODIS—Combined DNA Index System—database.

"You don't sound enthusiastic. Do you have a problem with using CODIS?"

"Not at all—I hope we get a hit. But I suspect this guy has managed to stay below the radar, that's all."

"Committing crimes of this nature without ever having any prior trouble with law enforcement?" Hamilton asked skeptically.

"Trouble, maybe—but caught for violent crimes? I don't know. You have profilers working on these cases?"

"They're just getting started."

"Like I say, I hope I'm wrong. If these cases are starting to go better than they have been, there won't be any complaint from me."

Hamilton laughed. "No kidding. See you tomorrow."

"One other thing," he said. "We may have some DNA from the scene at the cliff this evening."

After what seemed like a long silence, Hamilton said, "Oh? I don't remember hearing that mentioned."

"That was my call. Things are touchy right now. Especially where lab work is involved."

There was another long pause, then the agent said, "Sure, I understand. Thanks for letting me know now."

Alex hung up, feeling dissatisfied. He had probably managed to piss off both the FBI and his own department. But if there was DNA in New Mexico that might compare with what was found on the rope, he wasn't going to be the one who stood in the way of making the comparison, even if the FBI claimed these as federal cases because of it.

The flickering blue-gray light beyond the blinds told him that John was probably still awake and watching television. Maybe Chase would be, too. He hadn't meant to keep the kid waiting this long.

He walked into the house and saw that John was talking on a cell phone. Chase stood next to him, looking anxious. The television set was muted. Alex clicked it off.

"That's not true," John said to the caller, seeming exasperated. He saw Alex, rolled his eyes, and said again into the phone, "That's not true."

Alex said quietly to Chase, "Who is it?"

But before Chase could answer, John said, "I'll tell you what, Miles. You want to start insisting on setting down conditions for Chase to visit me, then let me give you a few about leaving a minor . . . What? Yes, he just walked in, but this is between you and me, boy."

Alex saw John's face turn red. Alex was surprised—John wasn't a man who angered easily. In the next moment, he thrust the phone toward Alex.

Alex smiled, took it, and said, "Miles?"

"Alex? I don't know what you're up to, but—"

"Miles? Miles? Hello?"

"Hello, Alex?"

"Must have hung up," he said to Chase and John, who could hear Miles shouting even as Alex pushed the disconnect button.

John started laughing. "Why didn't I think of that?"

Alex closed the phone and took the battery off. He handed the two pieces to Chase, who was staring at him in amazement.

"Chase, think you'll be able to get that phone to work again before tomorrow?"

"No, sir," Chase said, smiling.

"Good. What did you two have for dinner?"

"Uncle John made steaks. He's got one marinating for you, too."

Alex turned to John. "Thoughtful of you. This day may turn out all right after all."

"Take a load off," John said. "I'll get dinner together for you. And don't fret—I've been staying off my feet."

"He has," Chase said. "Besides, I'll help him."

"Okay," Alex said. "I'll be back in a minute."

He changed into jeans and a T-shirt and joined them in the kitchen. As he sat at the table, Chase brought him a beer.

"Thanks. You aren't drinking these, are you?"

"No—Uncle John would never let me drink your beer."

"Diplomatically answered," John said with a grin.

Chase laughed. "Hey—we saw you on TV!"

"Out on the Peninsula?" Alex said. "Yes, that's why I'm so late."

"You have another morning meeting with the sheriff?" John asked.

Alex nodded. "Probably will have every couple of days, until this is settled."

"That figures. Unlike what you usually investigate, these aren't run-of-the-mill population adjustments."

Alex smiled. "True." But not wanting to talk shop, he turned to Chase. "So fill me in on your news. What's the problem with your dad?"

He shrugged.

Alex took a few sips of beer, watching him.

"He's mad because I came down here."

"To my house."

"I guess so. It's so dumb."

John opened the broiler and turned the steak over. "You need to talk to your dad about it, Chase. Alex has had a long day, and he doesn't need to be hassled about family matters."

"He's not hassling me," Alex said.

John shot him a look.

"I know what he means," Chase said. "Uncle John wants to talk about it when I'm not listening in. It's okay."

"Oh for pity's sake," John said.

Chase went to the freezer and took out a package of mixed frozen vegetables. As he opened it, he said, "I just want you to know—well, I know. I didn't know last time, but now I know."

Alex paused in the act of lifting the beer to his mouth. "You know what?" he asked warily.

Chase put some of the vegetables in a bowl, added a small amount of water, covered the bowl with plastic wrap, and set it in the microwave. He started the oven and, without looking at Alex, said, "That you and my mom used to be married."

Alex put the beer down. His appetite left him.

John frowned. "Where'd you come by that little piece of news?"

"My mom told me—the night Uncle Alex took me home." He was still staring at the microwave.

"That bother you?" Alex asked.

He shook his head.

"Funny, it looks as if it does."

Chase looked at him. "It doesn't bother me about *you*."

"But?"

"It does about her." He caught a glimpse of John's face and said defensively, "I haven't said anything disrespectful."

"No," John said. "But you seem to forget that I can read your mind."

"One of his most annoying habits," Alex said.

Chase shrugged. "I just wanted you to know that I understand now."

"Understand what?"

"Why you didn't come over. Why I never met you. Before—I thought maybe you didn't like kids or something. My mom said—she said that you and my dad weren't so comfortable around each other, because a few months after she divorced you, she started dating my dad."

Alex took a drink of beer. He could feel John's eyes on him, but he avoided looking at him. He said, "Your mom was right about the awkwardness, but as your uncle John will be pleased to tell you, I was a damned fool to let that keep me from meeting you."

He heard Chase let out a sigh of relief. The microwave beeped.

John took the steak from the broiler, then Chase loaded the vegetables on the plate and carried it to Alex. They sat down on either side of him.

"Thanks," Alex said, realizing that his appetite had returned in full force.

Chase and John made small talk to allow Alex time to eat. Most of this consisted of Chase asking John about his time training with Special Forces. Alex noticed that John was much more open with Chase about his experiences than he had been with Alex and Miles—perhaps because John had been in the role of a parent to them, or perhaps because it was then too close to the experience.

When Alex was nearly finished eating, Chase asked, "You want to come out to the range with us this weekend?"

"Do some shooting? Sure, if I can get time off. But that's not looking likely at the moment."

He saw the flash of disappointment, but Chase said, "Sure. No pressure. It would just be fun if you could."

"Your dad teach you to shoot?"

"No, Uncle John. My dad doesn't practice anymore. Uncle John said he used to be good at it."

"Better than me."

"Not these days," John said. "Chase is quite a marksman himself."

Alex watched the boy blush but could see that he was also pleased.

"At first," Chase said, "I was scared of guns."

"Never hurts to maintain a healthy respect for them," said John.

"I shook so bad the first time I held one in my hand," Alex said, "John almost gave up on me."

"Now, that is untrue," John said. "I had remarkable patience."

Alex smiled. "I closed my eyes every time I pulled the trigger. Makes it tough to aim."

Chase laughed. "How old were you?"

"About your age."

"My age? But . . ." He frowned at John. "Wasn't that kind of mean?"

Alex found himself oddly touched by Chase's concern. "Because of the way your grandfather died? At the time, I thought your uncle John was being terribly mean."

"You two always thought I was being mean to you," John said.

"We'd whine that he was meaner than any of our friends' parents," Alex confided to Chase, "and he'd tell us that he sure as hell hoped so, because he'd met our friends."

John and Alex laughed, as Chase looked between them.

"Years after he took me out to the range," Alex said, "I realized that he had helped me to get over a fear that I might have carried with me all my life. He didn't teach me because he thought that I'd need to be able to shoot a gun—he taught me because I needed to get over that fear, or it would have been something that stood in my way forever."

They stayed up talking about those years Alex had lived with John. Not so many years, Alex realized now, but John had been a greater influence—more of a father to him—in those few years than his dad had been in fourteen as an absentee parent.

Alex gave Chase his bed to sleep in, over the boy's protests. Alex took his alarm clock and a pillow, then grabbed a spare blanket. He settled in on the big leather couch but lay awake, his thoughts moving between the cases and Chase, and in the moments when he failed to turn them to other subjects, to Clarissa and Miles.

He heard John move into the room.

"Trouble sleeping?" Alex asked.

"No, not really." He sat down in a nearby chair. After a moment, he said, "That first time I took you shooting, I was damned proud of you."

Alex grinned. "Oh, I'm sure that was one of your more memorable days on the range. I remember the range master asking if you wanted your virgin paper targets back."

John smiled. "He was an old friend, just giving me some shit."

"Miles approve of you teaching Chase?"

John frowned. "Miles had weapons in the house and hadn't taken the boy to any gun safety courses. I gave him so much hell over that, he didn't dare try to prevent me from taking Chase out to the range."

"Miles doesn't secure his guns?"

"Oh yes. Fancy-pants gun safe. You aren't going to sit here and tell me you think that's enough?"

"No. Especially not with a bright teenager who's in the house alone a lot."

"Good. Because even with all that security up there, guess what happened about three months ago?"

"Someone cleaned out that safe."

"Exactly right. Only thing they took from him, and they knew right where to go—trouble with a guy like Miles is, if he has a fancy safe, sooner or later he was bound to show the damned thing to his friends."

"Miles report the theft after all that bragging?"

"Sure. Wanted the insurance money. Blamed Chase for supposedly not setting the house alarm, but guess what the combination to the gun safe was?"

"Miles's birthday."

They tried to keep themselves from laughing too loud, not wanting to wake Chase.

"Chase tell you Miles's plan about the next school term?" Alex asked.

John shook his head.

"Chase didn't want to tell you—he's afraid you'll be ashamed of him."

"What? As if I could."

"That's what I figured. Anyway, Miles wants to send him to Sedgewick."

"Sedgewick!"

"John, you've got to talk him out of it. Unless a lot has changed in the last few years, I can't picture Chase surviving there. I can't tell you how many times I've gone to juvenile court to testify in an assault case or one involving some other violent offense, and watched a judge allow some vicious little jerk to be sent to Sedgewick instead of somewhere that might have done him some good—or at least protected the neighborhood from him."

"I've heard stories. But I also heard they straightened some kids out."

"Some kids did all right there," Alex admitted. "Supposedly, the school rides herd on them. But unless you haven't been telling me the truth about him all these years, Chase isn't in the same league as these kids. Even the best of them is likely to have some kind of violence in his background."

"Amazing what you can do with money, isn't it? It's off in one of the canyons, right?"

"Isolated as hell. Christ, John, why doesn't Miles just tell the kid he's sending him to Alcatraz? I don't think he'd be half as scared."

"Chase isn't going there, not if I have anything to say about it. I'll talk to Miles."

"Might as well talk to Clarissa, too. Chase seems to think it's her idea."

"Clarissa? What mother would want that for her own son?"

"I never imagined Clarissa could be all that motherly. Am I wrong?"

"Clarissa's not easy to understand."

Alex laughed.

"Glad you're amused. But I'm worried about the boy."

"Me, too."

"Are you?" he asked, brightening. "Well, then I feel better. Maybe I'll be able to get to sleep. Good night."

He went off to his room, and Alex turned out the lights. He lay in the darkness and thought of how neatly his uncle had managed to thoroughly involve him in his worries about Chase.

"You damned old fox," he murmured.

2 6

Kit slept in the passenger seat for about three hours, awakening just before they reached the California border. He had dreamed another of the old dreams and worried for a few moments that he might have talked in his sleep. But if he had, neither Meghan nor Spooky gave any sign of it. He woke to the sound of Spooky's raised voice telling Meghan that she was on the wrong road and was going to cause them all to die in the desert. Meghan calmly denied that this was the case. Kit sat up.

"Now look what you've done!" Spooky said.

"Sorry," Meghan said.

"She's on the right road, and you're the one who woke me up," Kit said.

"I did not!"

He perfectly mimicked her dire predictions of death in the desert.

She folded her arms over her chest and kicked the back of his seat.

He stayed awake, answering Meghan's questions about the cabin in Colorado. He tried to draw Spooky into the conversation by deliberately misstating how many rooms it had and how it was furnished, but she didn't give in to whatever temptation she might have felt to correct him, so he gave a little shrug and told Meghan the truth.

Near Barstow, they stopped to stretch and get some coffee at an all-night diner. He took over driving again. Although Spooky had ordered a Coke and some fries—not eating many of the fries but apparently enjoying swirling them in a mound of catsup until they broke, one after the other—she stead-fastly refused to enter into conversation. She put on headphones and started listening to her MP3 player.

She broke her silence somewhere between Pomona and Riverside to ex-press her dislike of all she had thus far seen of California. She had never been to any city larger than Denver and was overwhelmed by Los Angeles and the heavily populated area that seemed to stretch endlessly around it. There was too much traffic, too many shopping malls, you couldn't see stars in the sky. Kit knew he shouldn't have let her have anything with caffeine in it when they stopped in Barstow—now she was overtired and cranky. Worse, for as long as they were in the car, Meghan would pay the price for that with him.

But when they reached the Pacific Coast Highway from Interstate 10, and she saw her first glimpse of the ocean just as the day was dawning, her criticism suddenly ceased with an abrupt "Wow." She had remained fascinated all the way to Malibu.

"Is your house on the beach?" she asked, taking off the headset.

"One of them is, yes," he said. "We're going to be staying at the house in the hills most of the time, but don't worry—we'll go down to the one at the beach, too."

"Will you teach me to swim in the waves?"

"Sure. You're a strong swimmer, so it shouldn't be hard for you to learn."

"It looks kind of scary."

"It can be," Meghan said. "If you have a healthy respect for it, though, you'll have a lot of fun."

"What would you know about it?" Spooky snapped.

"I grew up here, near Kit's house."

"Are you going to stay at your own house, then?" Spooky asked, brighten-ing.

Meghan laughed. "No, you're not going to be rid of me after all."

"Spooky . . ." Kit said, embarrassed.

"She made it sound like she lived here," Spooky said defensively.

"I used to. After my mother died, we sold the house. I still live near the water, but north of here, near Carmel."

Now he turned up the road leading to his home. "I should warn you," he said, "that I've hired a security team. It might take a little getting used to . . ."

Meghan frowned. "I hope you haven't gone to a lot of expense because of me."

"No, they're here most of the time."

"You trust them with the house while you're gone?"

"I'd trust Moriarty with my life," he said.

"Moriarty!" Spooky shrieked in delight.

"Moriarty?" Meghan said, and gave an exaggerated shiver. "Didn't you ever read *The Adventures of Sherlock Holmes?*"

He smiled. "This one is no villain."

"He's the best!" Spooky said.

They approached a flat, concrete pad that extended several yards on either side of the car. A black wrought-iron gate and concrete-and-steel posts formed one set of barriers. Just beyond them, tall trees formed another. Meghan noticed that no branches were allowed to overhang the brick and wrought-iron fence that ran the length of the property. The thick fence appeared to be about twelve feet high. The gate was flanked by two pillars — cameras were perched on top of each.

A set of bright lights came on, illuminating the SUV and the flat concrete area around it, then the gate rolled open. A second, equally sturdy gate stood not far ahead. As Kit drove forward, the first gate closed behind them, penning the vehicle in a brick and iron box. A guard dressed in a dark green uniform and combat boots, wearing a sidearm, knife, and baton came forward.

"Good evening, Mr. Logan."

"Good evening, Joe. 'Long time the manxome foe he sought.' "

"Thank you, sir. Good to see you again."

The guard spoke into a radio attached to the shoulder of his uniform, and the second gate opened.

"What did you say to him?" Spooky asked.

"It's from *Jabberwocky*. A password of sorts. If I hadn't said it, he would have known I was in some sort of trouble, perhaps being forced to drive in."

"Teach it to me!"

"I'll teach you *Jabberwocky*, if you'd like, but the password will change now."

They came up a long, steep drive bordered by trees that kept the house hidden from the road. At the crest of it was a house that had been built in the 1950s along modern lines — a two-story structure that curved with the hilltop, with wide decks and tall windows of dark glass overlooking canyons and cliffs, and beyond them, the Pacific.

Kit caught Meghan looking at it with a wistful expression. "What are you thinking?"

"I'm remembering your grandmother. She always made Gabe and me feel so welcomed here. Do you miss her when you visit this house?"

He nodded, not trusting his voice. How had she known?

He stopped the car near the front steps. "We're home," he said, then wondered immediately what had led him to use the phrase.

Meghan smiled to hear Kit call this home. Elizabeth Logan would have liked that, she thought. Memories of visiting her while Kit and Gabe were in school came back to her. Despite the difference in their ages, Meghan had always enjoyed talking to Elizabeth and found it easier to confide in her than in her own mother. Meghan's mother had always been a beautiful butterfly, fragile and delightful in her way, but unable to stay still or concentrate. "Be thankful you got her looks and my brains," her father used to say. "If the dice had rolled the other way, you would have crapped out in both departments."

Elizabeth encouraged Meghan to come by anytime, and in her, Meghan found the listener she so needed then. Most often, Elizabeth could be found standing near the deck of the pool, wearing a wide-brimmed sun hat. The pool was built at the top of the cliff that ran along that side of the property. Although Elizabeth seldom swam, this was where she spent a great deal of time in the afternoon, peering over the railing at the canyon below. Meghan had wondered why she didn't choose one of the other decks, which had more striking views of ocean and hills. Then one day Meghan realized that Sedgewick was just below that cliff, hidden beneath trees. She somehow knew that Elizabeth would not want Kit to know of those afternoon vigils, but as she thought of them now, she felt Elizabeth watching over them as surely as she had then.

Spooky was already out of the car, not bothering to close her door. "Moriarty!" she called, running toward a tall man with short silver hair who was coming down the front steps. He had an athlete's build and grace.

"Hey, you scamp!" he said, smiling at Spooky as she gave him a quick embrace. "What? You aren't going to try for my wallet?"

"You always catch me," she said.

"Hello, Moriarty," Kit said, coming up to them, wondering how it was that being around Moriarty always made him feel a weight lift from his shoulders, to feel as if everything would be all right.

"Good to see you made it safely," Moriarty said, shaking his hand.

"Moriarty, this is Meghan Taggert. She's the friend I called you about yesterday."

Meghan's brows rose in surprise.

"I hope the man we sent to meet you at the hotel worked out all right?" Moriarty said.

"Oh—yes. He saw me safely to the tram. Thank you."

"Why don't you get the ladies settled in, Kit? I'll start unloading some of the luggage."

"I'll get it later. You aren't hired to be a bellman," Kit said. Moriarty was his last real link to Elizabeth Logan. He had never asked the nature of their relationship, but he knew it had not been merely employer-employee, whatever they might have said to the nosy.

"I'm not here because I'm hired, either," Moriarty said, as if reading his thoughts. "Go on, you all look as if you walked from Colorado. We can talk later."

As they drew nearer the front door, Meghan saw Kit holding a rabbit's foot and stepping carefully on the large marble tiles of the entry, avoiding cracks. At the door—over which, she noticed, he had at some point added a horseshoe—he slipped the rabbit's foot back in his pocket.

Spooky hurried past him, but Meghan moved more slowly—she took care as well not to step on cracks as she approached. She paused when she reached him, and heard him draw in a breath. She looked into his eyes, only inches away from hers now, and said, "I'm lucky to know you, Kit Logan."

She kept moving, and when she was sure he could not see her face, allowed herself a small smile.

Later, Kit was in his study, while Spooky and Meghan were fast asleep in their bedrooms at the opposite end of the house. He looked out at the ocean, which could be seen from most rooms of the house, but didn't really see it. He was still thinking of that moment on the threshold. He loved her scent. Maybe it was something she used on her hair or the soap she used, but he thought it might be more than that, something that was essentially Meghan.

As he shifted in his chair, his foot struck a soft object. He looked down and saw one of Molly's toys. He felt his chest tighten.

Was it wrong, he wondered, to feel so much grief for a dog?

When Kit had called to say he was coming here, Moriarty had offered to gather the dog's bedding and toys and clear them out of sight for him. Kit had declined. Perhaps, he thought now, that had been a mistake.

He saw that it was seven o'clock and turned on the small television set in the room to watch a local newscast on Channel Three.

"Our top story this morning—the FBI and the L.A. County Sheriff's Department have released the identity of the fourth fugitive from the FBI's Ten Most Wanted list to be found here in Los Angeles County. We'll have that and more when we return."

He held fast to the rabbit's foot throughout the commercial. "Not Gabe, not Gabe, not Gabe," he whispered over and over.

He waited impatiently while the newscaster basically repeated himself, then breathed a sigh of relief as the photo of an older man appeared on the screen. Kit had memorized the Ten Most Wanted list by now. He knew the man in the photo was Victor Elliot even before the newscaster said so. A man who had masterminded armored car robberies.

"There have been other developments overnight," the anchorman said, "and the FBI and sheriff's department will hold a joint press conference at three this afternoon. We are expecting more details on Elliot's death at that time."

Some footage of police cars outside a home were shown. "This bizarre string of murders began with the discovery on Sunday of . . ." They recounted the previous cases, showing pictures of the victims. They cut away from these to a reporter named Diana Ontora. She was asking people on the street what they thought of the "Top Ten Exterminators," as she called them.

"They're great. They're doing what the cops can't do," a man in a shopping mall said.

Diana Ontora came back on. "While most of the people we talked to said they think of the Exterminators as good citizens who had simply had all they could take of crime, Alex Brandon, the lead detective on these cases, doesn't agree."

Hearing Brandon's name, Kit moved closer to the screen. The newscast cut to a clip of Detective Brandon saying, "They're not heroes."

Apparently taken from the press conference Meghan had seen yesterday, the clip showed Ontora badgering the detective at a press conference. Kit concentrated on Brandon himself. He remembered him—the youngest of the detectives to talk to him after he killed Jerome Naughton.

The newscast cut back to a live broadcast of Ontora, who was standing on a city street. Some kids were making faces behind her and mouthing "Hi Mom." Ontora appeared irritated as she said, "This set of cases has thoroughly frustrated the sheriff's department, which has finally called the FBI in to help investigate. Diana Ontora, Channel Three News."

The anchorman thanked her. Another photo appeared, this one of a young man. Kit was about to turn off the television when he realized this was a related story.

"Sources close to the investigation tell Channel Three that law enforcement officials believe one of the suspects may be using the identification of Eric Grady, a young man who died under mysterious circumstances in Malibu last year . . ."

Eric Grady. Spooky had said that name yesterday—that was the name on one of the licenses in the wallet she had stolen from Freddy. Kit waited, but the newscaster didn't give much more information.

He thought about Freddy pursuing Meghan at the hotel and on Sandia Peak. And the wallet. The way the bodies of the fugitives were left, hanging upside down.

If he had any remaining doubts, they were gone now. Everett and his friends were involved in hunting down the fugitives, and they had plans for Kit, Gabe, and Meghan.

Simply calling the FBI or the sheriff's department was not an option—not only was Gabe's life at risk, someone with his own background would be a suspect. If Kit came forward, connections would be made. Everett had taken steps to remind the investigators of the crimes committed by Kit's stepfather, Jerome Naughton. Kit knew there were those who believed he had participated in those crimes.

He believed it himself. Was he any less guilty of murder than Gabe?

The memories, always ready to torment him, came back to him in sickening, stark, snapshot images.

Think of lucky things, he told himself. *Think of numbers*. He clutched the rabbit's foot and began to recite the multiples of seven. He reached one hundred eighty-two before he felt his heart rate slow. *No time for this. You have to keep Spooky and Meghan and Gabe safe*. Avoiding thoughts of those he failed to protect from his stepfather, he focused on the problem of Eric Grady's license.

Spooky had lost interest in the wallet and left it in the car. Kit put on a pair of gloves and retrieved the wallet from the backseat. Moriarty, watching him bring it into the house, said, "Spooky told me about the guy at the restaurant. Sounds as if Ms. Taggert knows some self-defense."

"I talked her and her brother into taking lessons in high school," Kit said absently. He spread the contents of the wallet on the kitchen table. There was a driver's license and three credit cards for Eric Grady, among other identification for other names—including the true one for Frederick Whitfield IV.

"I assume this isn't the wallet of a guy with a multiple personality disorder," Moriarty said.

"No. Moriarty, I need your help. Can you find out where the sheriff's department and FBI are going to hold their joint press conference today?"

"Piece of cake. I'll just pretend to be a member of the media when I call."

"Thanks. Can you get rid of Spooky's fingerprints on these?"

"With the processes they have now, maybe not. I can wipe off most of them, anyway. But you know it will take the other guy's fingerprints off, too?"

"Yes. That's not important." He pointed to the real license. "His DMV thumbprint won't come off."

Moriarty smiled. "That's true."

"I'll be in the study."

"Okay, I'll call about the press conference. Then maybe you can get some sleep?"

"Maybe."

In the study, he glanced at a copy of the *Los Angeles Times*. A reporter had written a story claiming that experts were speculating that the Exterminators were a national network of rogue law enforcement agents based in Los Angeles. No law enforcement agency would be able to stop them, because none really wanted to. Kit knew better but wondered how much inside help Everett was getting.

He set the paper aside and opened a packet that had been forwarded to him overnight. It was a short stack of mail. Unopened bills. While many of his bills were paid by his accountant, these were forwarded to him by a private mailbox company without the knowledge of any of the team of financial experts who worked for him, and paid for out of an account that would have been extremely difficult to trace back to him. They were small bills—one for water, one for a telephone, one for gas, another for electricity. As he opened them, he smiled in relief. There had been low usage of all of these services, except for the phone. No calls, just the basic service fee. The accounts had all been at the same level until January—when the electricity, water, and gas had increased.

Anyone could be living in the cabin near Arrowhead.

He knew, somehow, that it was Gabe.

He put the bills in his desk drawer and locked it.

Moriarty came upstairs, told Kit that the press conference would be held at the sheriff's department headquarters, and gave Kit directions. Kit asked for a small number of items, including some electronic equipment, and told him which ones he needed most immediately. Moriarty assured Kit that he could provide them, and that he would keep Spooky and Meghan safe while he was gone. The calm exchange of information was typical of countless conversations held over the ten years they had known each other. When they finished, Moriarty stood and went to the door, then turned back to him. "Kit . . . I'd rather go with you, if you want to know the truth, especially if you're going to do what I think you want to do. Someone should be watching your back."

Kit hesitated. It was the first time in memory that Moriarty expressed worry. "Keeping Spooky and Meghan safe is the most important thing you can do for me." When Moriarty didn't argue, Kit said, "Thanks—besides, it's better if you're here to bail me out if I do get in trouble."

"Let's hope that it's no more than a matter of finding you a lawyer."

"I'll need to leave here at about noon," Kit said. "I'm going to try to catch some sleep until then."

"Well, at least you're doing one sensible thing."

Kit looked in on Spooky, resisted the temptation to do the same with Meghan, and in his own bed, fell quickly into a blessedly dreamless sleep.

27

Frederick worried that he might do something embarrassing—might cry, or something worse. And there was really no reason to, he told himself. Not yet, anyway.

Everett sat at the head of a long mahogany table in a room he set aside for meetings of their group. The four core members of Project Nine were present now, all back from their journeys. Frederick hadn't managed to get much sleep last night, but he had been on time with the van at the Long Beach Airport.

As far as anyone at the airport knew, the small plane had arrived from a trip to Sacramento. The corporate jet would arrive later. This plane, which had been able to skirt radar, was still big enough to carry the cargo they had in it. It hadn't been anywhere near Sacramento, of course.

Morgan had already told Everett that Frederick had been to New Mexico. He figured that out the moment he picked them up, from the way Cameron smiled at him. But Everett hadn't said anything to him about it yet. The only comment he had made was "What have you done to your hair?"

"Now, let me understand," Everett said, calmly surveying the others seated around the table. His hands were clasped before him. Nothing in his posture, his face, or his voice gave any hint of his feelings. "The sheriff's department has found four bodies, correct?"

"Yes," Morgan said.

"Nine, eight, seven, and six," Frederick added. No use sitting there cringing, he told himself.

Cameron smiled again.

"Five and four are ready to go," Everett said. "Three?"

"Three is at his safe house," Morgan said. "He's been loaded up with morphine for the last two days. His guard said he's been completely out of it."

"Excellent. And the others?"

"No problems."

"You understand my concerns?" Everett asked.

"Yes," Morgan said, hesitating only slightly, but Frederick wondered at it. He suddenly began to study Morgan, suspecting he was hiding something.

"Well?" Everett said to Morgan. "What are they?"

"You're, like, worried because the guards might catch the news and start freaking out. But you know what I think?"

Everett gave him a hard look. "Enlighten me."

Morgan swallowed hard. "Just that—you're giving them a ton of money, so they have to know something big is going down."

"Exactly," Everett said.

Frederick watched as Morgan turned as pink as a little schoolgirl, a little teacher's pet who had just given the right answer. Frederick thought of making a kissy sound but was afraid Everett might not like it.

"Besides," Morgan added, encouraged now, "it's only a matter of time before the FBI or sheriff's department starts offering money, too."

"I'm not worried that they'll outmatch my counteroffers," Everett said. "Still, one of the guards might decide to try to milk a little more out of both sides." His eyes narrowed. "I could replace them with members of this team, but I'm afraid the two of you have lost interest. You're taking on projects of your own."

Frederick felt himself break out in a sweat. "We just switched places."

"Frederick," Everett said. "Please. I know you, don't I?"

Frederick nodded.

"How long have I known you?"

"Since . . . since we were at school. At Sedgewick."

"Does anyone understand you better?"

Frederick shook his head.

"No, no one does. I even understand your need to rebel from time to time. As I do yours, Morgan."

Morgan opened his mouth—probably, Frederick thought, to tell some big fucking lie. But apparently he thought better of it, because he snapped his mouth closed again.

Everett smiled at him, then turned to Frederick. "I think the biggest problem is that I haven't given you enough to do lately. You've grown bored while Cameron and I pursued number five. Perhaps you believe that I don't appreciate your skills?"

This was exactly what Frederick felt to be the problem, but he said, "You know best, Everett. I know that, but when you're gone—"

"You grow restless."

"Yes. I'm sorry about losing track of Meghan."

"Cameron," Everett said, without taking his eyes off Frederick, "what make and color is Kit Logan's vehicle?"

"A dark green Suburban."

Frederick looked anxiously between them.

"Yes, Frederick. And he has a young boy living with him."

"But he's in Colorado!"

"Obviously not anymore."

"How did he get in touch with Meghan?"

"I suspect they've never been out of touch since high school."

"He's boffing Meghan?" Morgan asked.

Everett's hands curled into fists as he turned to Morgan. Frederick thought Everett might have been angry before, but there was no doubt about it now. He was definitely giving Morgan the stink eye. Everett had major attitude when it came to Meghan.

"That—that *eunuch* hasn't got the nerve to have sex with anyone!"

Everett drew a deep breath and exhaled slowly. He looked down at his hands and opened them. He seemed to regain control of his temper. He turned to Cameron and smiled. "Not anyone living, anyway."

Cameron smiled, too. Frederick felt uneasy, seeing that smile. You never knew what might amuse Cameron.

"One of the two of them knows where Gabe is," Everett said. "If they are together, I'm even more convinced that Kit and Meghan know where he is hidden."

"You think Gabe is still in California?" Frederick asked.

"We lost track of him here. But even if he is elsewhere by now, we'll have the bait that will lure him out of his hiding place."

"Kit's the bait?"

"Yes. Half of it, anyway. That's why Cameron made sure he'd come here."

"The dog," Frederick said, understanding dawning. "He killed his stepfather because the old man kicked that dog, right?"

"Stepfather?" Everett chided. "Rumor has it that Naughton was actually his father all along."

Frederick almost snorted. He knew exactly who had started that rumor. Who was Everett trying to kid?

"What if he's like his old man, then?" Morgan asked. "Maybe he'll hang Meghan upside down over a tub."

Again Frederick saw the flash of temper cross Everett's face. Again, Everett brought it under control. "Maybe that's exactly what she deserves, then, for listening to him."

Frederick knew that Everett blamed Kit Logan for Meghan's refusal to go out with him. Frederick had all sorts of wonderful sexual fantasies about Meghan himself, most of which involved her begging for more after submitting to him, but he couldn't bring himself to wish her hanging upside down over a bathtub with all her blood spraying out. He didn't think Everett really meant it, either. Everett hated her, but that was because she had dissed him. Everett never gave up easily on anything. Still . . .

"None of that need concern us at the moment," Everett said. "It will all play out as it should. We have a great deal to do in the meantime." He smiled. "I have special assignments for both of you. Cameron, would you please brief Frederick while I work with Morgan?"

When he left the house an hour later, Frederick felt that same mixture of fear and excitement that came to him whenever Everett entrusted him with this sort of work. He climbed into the empty van—whose cargo from the airport now joined another former fugitive in Everett's walk-in freezer—and looked into the rearview mirror.

"I have killed, and I will kill again," he said to the assassin who looked back. Then he sighed. The assassin's hair really was fucked up. He'd have to change that before he did anything else.

Cameron hung up the phone and turned back to Everett.

Everett raised a brow.

"The guard will stop the morphine immediately. By the time he gets there, most of its effects will have worn off."

"Thank you." He watched Cameron for a time, then said, "Are you tired?"

Cameron shook his head.

"I was thinking of inviting the twins to come over."

Cameron smiled. "Are you sharing?"

"Of course. But do you prefer before or after?"

Cameron considered this. Everett thought that one of Cameron's best traits was that he seldom blurted out an answer to a question.

"Before, I think," he said at last. "It will be a long day, and I'd hate to make you wait."

"You," Everett said, standing up and stretching, "are always so thoughtful. Yes, before is better. We can enjoy a little sport before we load the van."

He walked to the phone but paused before lifting the receiver. He turned back to Cameron and asked, "Did Morgan tell you how he cut his thumb?"

"Said he was slicing a loaf of that hard bread he buys at the organic food store."

"Do you believe that?"

"No."

"Funny, neither do I."

2 8

"Yes, Mr. Whitfield," the lawyer said. Mr. Blaine—at fifty-eight, the younger Mr. Blaine—tried hard for patience. "I have long thought you should have a will. I've been urging that from the day we settled your grandmother's estate. But to act so hastily—"

"Look, I've got like a really busy day ahead of me, okay? You are making me really late. Can you write this fucking will now, or not? If not—"

"I can, of course," Blaine said, thinking of the surcharge he was going to add to this young fool's invoice. He had already rescheduled two other clients to see his wealthiest and most impulsive one.

"Okay, so here's the thing," Frederick said. "My grandmother hated my dad, right?"

"I don't know if I would say—"

"Well, she did. And that just shows that my grandmother was one fucking smart old lady, because my dad is a turd."

Mr. Blaine pursed his lips. He recalled the outrageous behavior Frederick Whitfield III had exhibited when he learned that his mother had not left him a penny, the things he had said to Mr. Blaine, the attempts he had made to overset the will Mr. Blaine had drawn up in favor of old lady Whitfield's grandson. "I agree," he said at last.

Mr. Blaine thought Frederick had seemed a little nervous, but at that, his client smiled charmingly.

"Great—because, like, I've been thinking—I could get killed."

"What?"

"I mean," he said quickly, "in a car accident, or like, on an African safari, or something—you never know, right? And I don't want my dad to get my grandmother's money after you and Grandmother worked so hard to keep it from him. So I'm making a will. But I've got to get this done today. Right now."

"Why?"

"Dude! I just told you!"

"No, I mean, why today?"

There was the slightest hesitation before he said, "Because I'm going to travel to the South Pacific and go sailing with someone, and we leave this afternoon."

Mr. Blaine thought this was not the whole truth, or perhaps even part of it. But he knew Frederick Whitfield IV well enough to realize that his best course of action at this point was to call in his secretary—who was also his second wife—to hear Mr. Whitfield dictate his will.

When she arrived, Mr. Blaine said, "Now, Mr. Whitfield, let's carefully consider how you want to leave your estate."

"Fuck all of that," he said. "I'm leaving it all to my *boyakina*."

"Your what?"

"*Boyakina*. You're too old to understand that, my man, so don't even bother. But I've thought about this—a whole lot. Like, all the way down here from Malibu. Everett and my other friends, they're already so fucking rich, they wouldn't even notice the difference, right?"

Mr. Blaine had once met Mr. Corey and thought him a bigger—to use his client's expression—turd even than Frederick Whitfield III. He therefore didn't bother to remark that only an institutionalized catatonic wouldn't notice being made richer by the size of Mr. Whitfield's fortune.

His secretary cleared her throat and said, "Pardon me, Mr. Whitfield, could you spell the name *boyakina* for me?"

Frederick grinned. He spelled it, then said, "But that's not her name. Her name is Vanessa. Vanessa Przbyslaw. P-r-z-b-y-s-l-a-w." He gave them the address he had noted when he left for the airport that morning. "I don't have the zip code, but here's her phone number."

"And is she some relation of yours?" Blaine asked.

"No—man, don't you get it?"

"I understand that you don't want your parents—"

"Or any of the others. Grandmother would have loved Vanessa."

Mr. Whitfield seemed to believe this quite strongly. Although Mr. Blaine doubted much of what Mr. Whitfield said to him on any given occasion, he began to believe that his regard for Ms. Przbyslaw was genuine. Mr. Blaine glanced at his wife, who nodded encouragement.

And so they made out the will, which was simple enough. Mr. Whitfield wrote a personal note to include with it.

"When you return from the South Pacific," Mr. Blaine said, once the document was signed and witnessed, "please come to see me again. Although I'm pleased you have a will, I don't think such an important matter should be handled in quite this way, sir."

"Will my parents be able to fight this one?"

Blaine stood a little straighter. "Not successfully."

"That's why I came here. Look, I gotta get out of here, but thanks. Just mail my copies to me, okay? I don't want to lose them on the boat. And if everything works out okay, maybe I'll come back and you can bore the shit out of me with all your lawyer talk. But if I don't, you be good to Vanessa and look out for her, because her old man is a turd, too."

When he left, Mr. Blaine put the will in his safe. He heard the click of the lock on his office door and turned to see his wife smiling at him.

"When he came in, I canceled your other appointments for this afternoon. Come here, my *boyakina*."

29

The sensation that he was being watched had stayed with Kit. Again and again, he checked his rearview mirror on the drive to the press conference but never saw any car that stayed behind him for long. He pulled over once and looked up into the sky, to see if a plane or helicopter had been following him from above. Twice, he suddenly took an exit from the freeway without signaling and watched for another car to do the same. Despite all this maneuvering, he still managed to reach the sheriff's department parking lot in time to find a space close to the front door, although not as near as some television trucks and vans. By then, he was convinced that his fear of pursuit was unfounded.

He felt embarrassed and wondered what Meghan would say if she knew how unstable he really was.

He came to a security checkpoint as he entered the building. A rectangular shoulder bag—Moriarty had assured him it was similar to ones used by some reporters—had an extra lining in it, which would show a wallet and perhaps a few other small objects when X-rayed, but not the envelope they were in. The digital camera, pens, notebook, keys, and other items would not be questioned.

He had wanted to use his own name, afraid he would be taken into custody trying to present a phony driver's license to a sheriff's deputy. But Moriarty had been adamant that he use a fake ID. He had to admit that he would not have been able to tell the difference between his own license and the one for "Ed Thomas," whom he was pretending to be. Next he worried that the press credentials Moriarty had created for him might be rejected. He did, however, own a percentage of the small paper he supposedly represented. He knew the publisher would back him up, but he hoped it wouldn't come to that.

To his relief, both the license and the credentials were accepted without more than a glance. He decided the sheer number of people who needed to be admitted was of help. The story was being covered nationally now—and to some extent, internationally as well—and reporters from newspapers, magazines, radio, television, and Internet news services were on hand. All the same, he flipped the laminated press pass around. He'd just as soon not have too many people remember his presence here.

Once in, he became calm. He had so often been the new kid at school, he had developed skills that helped him in new and possibly hostile environments. There was something about this throng of reporters that reminded him of the school yard, and his old ability to keep bullies at a distance seemed to work here as well as it had there, perhaps even better than when he was younger.

The room was crowded and excessively hot, no doubt because of the television camera lights. He pulled out his reporter's notebook and flipped through it. There were notes here, about Alex Brandon. For two days now, Moriarty had tried to learn all he could about the man. Moriarty had resources within the LASD. A former Green Beret, Moriarty never ceased to amaze Kit with his ability to find someone who would give him information.

So Kit now knew about Brandon's father's suicide, the breakup of his marriage, and most of his career. He had been sorry to read that Brandon's old partner, whom Kit remembered vividly, had died about a year ago. Kit learned that in the time since he had first met him, Brandon had taken up rock climbing. Brandon lived alone, but at the moment, his uncle was staying with him. For the first time in any report Kit had received from him, Moriarty had added a personal note. "Thanks for this assignment—it has helped me discover what became of an old friend. Before he left the army, Brandon's uncle, John O'Brien, made my life miserable when I was training for Special Forces. I won't contact O'Brien until this is all over, but I can tell you that if Brandon is anything like his uncle, you can trust him completely."

Kit wondered if he should try approaching Alex Brandon through his uncle. Or whether that would destroy any possibility of keeping Gabriel Taggert safe until he decided to turn himself in.

A public information officer stepped up to the microphone and asked everyone to take their seats. Soon, a group was approaching the platform at the front of the room. Because of the cameras and other equipment near the front of the room, he could not see all of them, but he easily picked out Alex Brandon. Sheriff James Dwyer came to the podium, but Kit continued to watch Brandon.

He remembered him, of course. He could not clearly recall most of what happened in the days after he killed Jerome Naughton, but he remembered Brandon. Brandon was younger than anyone else who talked to him, had remarkable blue eyes, and was perhaps a little less hardened than he seemed now. He had brought with him two old men, his late partner and Shay Wilder, both of whom smoked constantly but were kinder to Kit than any of the others. Thinking of Shay Wilder, he decided he would ask Moriarty to try to locate him.

As for Brandon, Kit wondered if—should they meet—Brandon would recognize him in return.

He had seen pictures of himself, taken when Moriarty had first found him. Moriarty had been sent to help bring him back to his grandmother. Kit had been bruised, as usual, and wearing filthy, blood-spattered clothing. Holding tight to a mongrel he had named Molly. Fourteen, he had been tall for his age and muscular . . .

The room and the voice of the person at the podium dropped away from him as image after image from the years of building that muscle by doing as Naughton commanded flashed through his mind. And of the other photographs, the hated ones, the ones Naughton had taken.

"That's right, put your arm around him. You see? All I want to do is take a picture of you with the boy. He's not a bad-looking kid, now, is he? You pose with the boy a few times, and I'll let you go free. I promise. That's good . . . right. Now kiss him. Christopher, damn it, hold still . . ."

He closed his eyes and felt himself sway a little in his seat, as if he were falling asleep in his chair. He jerked himself upright and reached blindly into his pocket and found the rabbit's foot. He took a deep breath.

"Hey, buddy—are you okay?" a low voice asked.

He turned and looked into the face of the man sitting next to him, a slender man with a beard. He glanced at the laminated tag around his neck. *Los Angeles Times*. Author of the article he had read this morning.

"Fine, thanks," Kit said. "Just a little warm in here."

"TV assholes always make it unbearable for the rest of us. In more ways than one."

Kit smiled, then focused his attention back on the conference. Something in the reporter's manner made him even more unsure of him, and he decided it would be best to avoid further conversation.

Alex Brandon was talking now, telling them about the man who posed as "Eric Grady" at the *Crimesolvers USA* studios. Kit didn't pay as much attention to what he was saying as to his body posture and his eyes, the tone of his voice. Cues that would tell him more than words, whether Brandon was indeed as trustworthy as Moriarty thought he might be. Kit could not learn this from watching Brandon on television newscasts—the camera would not always be on him or pick up subtleties of behavior and expression.

Brandon wasn't telling all he knew, but that was understandable. What interested Kit was how calm he was in the face of all the pressure. It wasn't the disinterested calm of the cynical or the bored. Kit wondered at it, then remembered the rock climbing. He supposed that if you could withstand falling from cliffs, or put up with the pressure of literally hanging on by the tips of your fingers, a roomful of reporters wasn't likely to faze you.

Brandon stepped back, and his partner, Ciara Morton, came up to the microphone. The two partners didn't make eye contact during this change of places. They didn't seem close, but it was hard to tell much about that in this setting. Detective Morton began speaking about the real Eric Grady. She seemed unhappy, Kit thought. Her face was tense. He became so caught up in her story of finding the bones of the real Eric Grady, though, he didn't study her in the same way he had Brandon. She addressed her audience in an intense, direct way, demanding their unwavering attention. She was being truthful, he thought, but like Brandon, wasn't telling all she knew.

"Hey, Thomas," a voice said next to him, "you just here as a sight-seer?"

Startled, it took Kit a moment to remember that he was supposed to be Ed Thomas. He glanced down and saw, with a dread he quickly masked, that his name tag had flipped around.

"I've never heard of the *Mountain Chronicle*," the reporter from the *Times* said.

"Small Colorado paper," Kit said, with an assurance he was far from feeling. "Not in your league."

"They have the bread to send you all the way out here for a story they can get off the wires?"

"There's a local angle," Kit said.

"Oh? Like what?"

Kit smiled. "Come sight-seeing in Colorado sometime, and maybe you'll find out."

They were shushed by someone behind them. Kit stood up and made his way out of the auditorium. For one awful moment, he had been certain that the guy from the *Times* was going to follow him.

He walked unhurriedly to a restroom, splashed cold water on his face, and went into a stall. He put on latex gloves and carefully removed the padded envelope addressed to Detective Alex Brandon from the inner lining of the bag, but left it within the bag itself. He pulled out the reporter's notebook, the pens, the camera, and took off his press credentials. He took off the gloves and stuffed them into his pocket.

He stepped out and moved toward a bank of pay phones. He stood at one for a moment, pretending to make a call, hunching forward as if taking notes while talking, but not actually handling the receiver. He left the shoulder bag there and began to walk out.

"Leaving before the show's over?" a deputy called to him.

"On a deadline," he said and shrugged. "My editor's pissed off at me for taking this long." He glanced toward the pay phones.

The deputy followed his glance, then said, "Hey—you left your bag."

Kit looked slightly puzzled. "Not mine." He started to walk toward it.

"Never mind," the deputy said quickly, stepping in between him and the pay phones. "I'll take care of it. Good luck with your deadline."

"Thanks."

He walked out, the deputy watching him before he turned toward the phones again. Kit hurriedly crossed to the parking lot, ducking out of sight when he reached the television vans. He got into the Suburban with relief and felt even more relief when he reached Interstate 10 without being pulled over by the sheriff's department.

He had not gone far, though, before the sensation of being followed came to him again.

30

Sheriff's Department Headquarters
Monterey Park, California
Wednesday, May 21, 4:05 P.M.

"Describe him again," Alex said.

The deputy shifted his weight. He thought it was awfully crowded in this lit-tle office, with Brandon, Morton, that guy from the FBI, and even Captain Nelson, for God's sake. He wondered if he was about to lose his job for trying to be helpful. It wasn't as if he had accused Brandon of carrying one of those damned reporter's purses. Maybe he ought to make that clear. "I didn't think you'd carry a bag like that . . ." he began.

"Describe him again, please," Alex said, with no apparent loss of patience.

The deputy sighed. "White male, about six three, mid-twenties, dark hair, gray eyes. Built about like you. Maybe a little bigger in the shoulders."

"Thanks."

"Anything else?"

"You didn't actually see him touch the phone?"

"No, sir, I didn't."

"Thanks, that's all."

Alex waited until he had left, and started to put on a pair of latex gloves.

"Brandon," the captain said, "maybe we ought to have the lab take a look at it."

"Or the bomb squad," Hamilton said.

Alex paused and looked over at him. "It went through security, right?"

"To end up on that side of the checkpoint, it must have," Ciara said. She had been in a good mood all day, Alex thought, and immediately looked at Hamilton. They were getting along, which, for Ciara, might as well have been the sign of a mad crush on the guy. If there was some budding relationship in progress, though, they were hiding it—or at least weren't putting on a soap opera episode in front of the captain. He wondered if Hamilton was playing her to get information from the department.

"The new lab's not that far away," Nelson said with some emphasis.

"Think it's a love letter from an admirer?" Hamilton asked.

That struck a little too close to his thoughts, so Alex set aside an almost unbearable amount of curiosity and agreed they should take it over to Scientific Services.

Alex filled out evidence forms, wishing it was the captain's task, a punishment for suggesting the safer course of action. He halted, pen over paper, and wondered what was making him so irritable. He had managed to get more sleep last night on the couch than he had on any other night since they found Adrianos.

He looked over at Ciara, tête-à-tête with Hamilton.

As the envelope was being irradiated to destroy any biotoxins, Alex grew nostalgic for a time when a man could simply open his mail.

The lab ran a quick check for latent prints on the exterior of the package. There was one set—which they assumed to be the deputy's—that would be checked. No others were revealed. The lab tech cut open the bottom end of the envelope, preserving the sealed end so that it too could be checked later for fingerprints. He tilted the envelope over a large sheet of paper that would catch any fibers or other trace evidence.

The first thing that fell out was an eye. Next came a leg, an arm, a horse, and a sheep. All were tiny, made of brass on silver.

"What the hell?" Hamilton said.

"*Milagros,*" Alex said, and wondered what message they were meant to convey. Working in an area with a large Hispanic population, he had seen them many times but was puzzled by this particular combination of them.

"Okay. What are *milagros?*" Hamilton asked.

He explained what they were while, wearing gloves, he began to look through the wallet that had tumbled out after them.

"My God," Captain Nelson said as Alex carefully removed a license. "Eric Grady."

There were four other licenses as well, and credit cards to match. Alex studied them for a moment, then said, "This one, I think. He looks the most like the employee photo from *Crimesolvers USA*."

" 'Frederick Whitfield IV,' " Ciara said. "Well, la-dee-da."

"Let's run checks on all of them," the captain said.

"Yes, sir," she said. "But look at the address for the Fourth, here. He comes from Malibu. Where Eric Grady's remains were found."

Alex continued to look through the wallet and found a slip of paper with a phone number written on it. "What do you know—an Albuquerque phone number. Maybe your office could follow up on this one, Hamilton."

When there was no response, Alex looked up at the FBI agent, who seemed lost in thought.

Ciara noticed it, too. "David?"

So it was *David* now. Well, Alex thought, so what? They had gone out to dinner together. She could call him David.

Hamilton blushed.

Well, God damn, Alex thought, suddenly feeling protective of his partner. If this guy had anything less than the best intentions . . . and a guy with the best intentions would wait until these cases were solved.

"Sorry," Hamilton said. "I was kind of distracted by these little charms. *Milagros*, right? Do you think the person who sent the wallet is Hispanic?"

"I don't know," Alex said. "But if Frederick Whitfield IV turns out to be our man, then our tipster definitely brought me luck."

He called the phone number and got a woman's answering machine. The outgoing message didn't mention a name, just repeated the number. Not wanting to tip off any member of this group of killers, Alex didn't leave a message. Hamilton was going to follow through with the FBI office in Albuquerque to learn the woman's identity.

The Malibu Station tried the residence listed on Whitfield's license, but a caretaker said that Mr. Whitfield had been living in France for more than two years.

Hamilton got in touch with his office, to see what could be done to contact Whitfield in France. Ciara checked Whitfield's vehicle registrations and learned that Mr. Whitfield IV had unpaid parking tickets dated as recently as three weeks ago. Alex looked at the driver's licenses again but still felt sure that Whitfield was the one.

The sheriff's department put out a bulletin saying Whitfield was wanted for questioning and sent information about him to the Albuquerque police and all FBI field offices. He had no adult arrest record, though, and the captain had started to question the possibility of crimes of this nature being committed by someone who didn't have anything worse than a parking ticket on his record.

"We've got a lot to learn about him yet," Alex said.

Alex drove Ciara and Hamilton back to the homicide bureau—they had carpooled together to the press conference. The rush hour traffic was bumper to bumper, but for once Ciara was not providing running commentary on all the other drivers' lack of intelligence. Instead, she talked excitedly about the recent breaks in the case and the prospect of using DNA from the New Mexico samples and the blood from the rope to prove that Whitfield was involved.

Alex stayed quiet, observing that her conversation and questions were directed entirely at Hamilton, and that apparently she hadn't noticed that Hamilton was mostly returning noncommittal answers and seemed subdued.

"And so what about France?" she said. "A guy that wealthy probably takes the Concorde all the time."

"That doesn't seem likely," Hamilton replied.

"Okay, so he has his own jet. I'm just saying that travel between here and France would not be a problem for this guy."

When they reached the homicide bureau parking lot, Hamilton pointed out his car—a black Jaguar XJ8.

"Nice ride," Alex said as he pulled up next to it. "That's a rental?"

"Yes, Hertz at LAX," Hamilton said and held up a key with a rental tag on it.

"My tax dollars at work, or did you trade in frequent flyer miles for the upgrade?" Alex asked, but Hamilton got out of the car without replying.

Alex glanced around to see where Ciara had parked. He had just realized that he didn't see Ciara's car, when Hamilton opened Ciara's door. She started to get out, too.

"Ciara, wait," Alex said, "I need to talk to you for a few minutes—if you don't mind?"

Hamilton stood there, eyes narrowed.

"Sorry, Hamilton," Alex said. "It's about an earlier case. I promise it doesn't have anything to do with this one."

"Sure," Hamilton said.

"I might take a trip up to Malibu later on," Alex said. "Want to come along?"

Hamilton shook his head. "I think jet lag has finally hit me. I'm going to turn in early and try to make a more clearheaded start tomorrow."

"Sure."

"Ciara," Hamilton said, "you need a ride home?"

"I'll give her a lift," Alex said. "You get some sleep and we'll see you in the morning."

He hesitated.

Ciara glanced at Alex, then said, "Alex is right. See you tomorrow."

As Hamilton drove off, Alex realized that he had never been to Ciara's house. Over the last year, within a week or two of being partnered with anyone else, he had known exactly where his partner lived, and usually they had gone out for a beer together, or had spent some other time together after work. That hadn't happened with Ciara.

"Long Beach, right?" he asked.

She smiled. "Right city. Are you going to take a wild stab at one of the dozen or so exits?"

He felt his face redden.

"Atlantic Avenue," she said.

They hadn't gone far before she said, "It's none of your business."

"Hamilton?"

"Right."

"If you're thinking of having a relationship with him—"

"I'm not," she said quickly. "I enjoy talking to him, that's all."

Alex was silent. He found himself comparing Hamilton's age to hers. Not fair of him, he knew, but couldn't help wondering what all Ciara and Hamilton had in common. And why, apparently, she felt more relaxed around an FBI agent than him.

"Alex—really. Don't do this."

"What?"

"Go all protective on me."

"Can't help it. Is that so bad?"

She didn't answer.

"Maybe I'm jealous," he said.

"Jealous!"

"Sure, why not? I don't mean—not in that way. Just makes me realize that a guy who blew into town yesterday has better rapport with my partner than I do."

She bit her lower lip. "That's my fault."

"No. John made me realize the same thing when we were down at Shay Wilder's place. My uncle probably knows more about you than I do."

"We haven't been working together all that long."

"More than a damned day. That's all it took either one of *them* to get you to come out from behind the barricades."

"The barricades . . . that bad?"

He shrugged.

"Look, it was easier to let my guard down with them. They're not really in-house. They didn't meet me knowing that everyone else in the bureau hated my guts."

"That's not true."

"I came to you as a problem child. No use denying it."

"Maybe you weren't the problem. Hey, listen—let's not talk shop. That's what always happens."

She smiled. "Oh, so you were bullshitting poor Agent Hamilton?"

"You know I was. He does, too. Cut it out. Tell me—I don't know—tell me about your sister."

She was quiet for so long, he almost wondered if he had accidentally stumbled on to some taboo subject.

"Laney's the reason I'm a cop."

He waited.

"Her attackers were never brought to justice, so I figured the only way I could deal with my anger over that was to catch people like them. Who knows? Maybe I'll get lucky one day and just happen to round them up, too."

"You have a description of them?"

He saw her struggle for a moment before saying, "My sister is one of those victims who was never able to describe her assailants. You know how much patience some cops have with victims like that."

He did know. It wasn't hard to get so caught up in trying to catch the bad guys that you focused only on what could help you do the job, even if it meant turning away from the victim's misery if it wasn't going to provide a lead. Especially when you'd had a steady diet of misery for a few years. John had talked to him about it, warned him. "Some days you are going to be tired and frustrated and fresh out of sympathy," he had said. "If you ever want to make a cop hater out of somebody, go ahead and show it."

"So," Alex said now, "does your sister approve of your career?"

"Maybe you should meet her," she said.

"Sure, I'd like that."

"We'll see if you do. We'll pick her up on the way to my place, if you don't mind."

"Not at all."

"You have much in the trunk?"

Surprised, he said, "No."

"Good. We'll need the room for her wheelchair."

"Okay," he said mildly.

She smiled. "Alex Brandon will present a lecture this evening on how to re-main calm while your hair is on fire . . ."

"Ciara—"

". . . and you are simultaneously being pursued by a swarm of bees. Killer bees."

He smiled. "Well, what good would it do you to panic in that situation?"

That made her laugh.

They pulled up in front of a small house with a wheelchair ramp built over its front porch steps. "She's sometimes afraid of men she doesn't know," Ciara warned.

The woman Ciara paid to care for Laney when Ciara had to work late—which was often, Alex figured—opened the door to their knock and protested that she had just picked Laney up from the Clooney Center. The nearby Betty Clooney Center, Alex knew, specialized in helping those with head injuries and their families.

It prepared him, a little, for meeting Laney. She was watching television, or was facing it, anyway. Unlike her sister, she was a redhead. Alex thought that if she could have stood, they would have been about the same height. But Laney was thin to the point of gauntness. Like Ciara, she had big brown eyes.

At the sound of Ciara's voice, she turned her head and gave a lopsided smile. She made a sound that was something between a shout and a squeal.

"Hello, Sis," Ciara said. "Ready to go home?"

This was met by a low sound. She was staring at Alex now.

"Hello, Laney," Alex said. "I'm Alex. I work with Ciara."

Her brows drew together, and her face twisted, then relaxed. The squealing sound again, if a little less enthusiastic.

"Well," Ciara said, "so you won't mind if he drives us home?"

Another lopsided smile.

Ciara thanked the caregiver and managed all the effort of getting Laney into the car, while Alex stowed the wheelchair. Ciara had seen him con-sider helping to lift Laney into the backseat and said, "Let's not press our luck."

Throughout the short drive to Ciara's home, Alex held a conversation of sorts with Laney, an exchange of signals of interest in each other, if not something comprehended on both sides. He spoke to her as if she could understand every word he said. She apparently did the same.

Between directions to her house and managing the trip inside, Ciara explained that Laney had some motor skills left—she could grasp objects, for example. She could also chew and swallow, which made life for the two of them easier than it was for some of the other head injury patients and their families. But Laney's speech, ability to walk, and anything involving fine-motor skills were lost. Ciara did not exclude Laney from the conversation while explaining all of this. "Laney, you obviously catch a word or two now and then, or read people's voices and body language, right?"

Laney made a soft sound they took for agreement.

The house was a small single-story Craftsman, probably built in the 1930s. There was a white picket fence around what had been a front lawn, but was now completely covered in concrete. A long, gently sloping ramp led up to the deep front porch.

The interior of the house was neat and clean, with what little furniture there was moved to the walls, where it would not block the way of the wheelchair.

Ciara took a framed photograph from a shelf—a picture, she said, of Laney with their mother—taken when Laney was about twelve. The young girl in the photo was at a stage of life when her prettiness was already maturing into beauty, and he supposed that the changes her injuries brought to her appearance must have been all the more difficult for her family to bear because of that beauty. But having met Laney now, becoming acquainted with her now, he found himself unable to think of the image in the photo as the same person. Ciara might as well have shown him a picture of one of Laney's ancestors.

"Around the time Laney was able to leave the hospital," Ciara was saying, "my mom was already widowed and living with me, so Laney moved back in with us—right, Laney? Then my mom died about two years ago, just about the time I started working in Homicide. That was a rough time for both of us, but we had our routines set by then, so it wasn't as hard as it might have been."

Laney reached for the photo, and Ciara gave it to her. She held on to it without really looking at it. After a moment, she seemed to lose interest in it, and Ciara gently took it back and returned it to the shelf. "My brother and I look more like my dad," Ciara said, "except I've got Mom's hair and eyes, too."

They ordered pizza—an apparent favorite of Laney's.

"I'd better hit the road if I'm going to get up to Malibu this evening," Alex said quietly, when he noticed that Laney was nodding off. "And I have that lecture to give about fire and bees."

Ciara smiled. "Thanks for the ride. I know it was out of your way."

"That stuff about the shortest distance between two points being a straight line? Really overrated." Tired as he was, he meant it.

He decided to stop at home before heading up to Malibu. As he drove, he thought about Ciara and wondered how she managed to cope with all the pressures of the job and the pressures of being the primary caregiver for her sister. And still managed to be a damned good detective into the bargain.

Had any of her previous partners known about Laney? He doubted it. Word would have spread, most likely. The first time someone had called her B.B. Queen, someone else would have said to cut her some slack, and mentioned that she cared for a sister with severe disabilities.

And God, how she would have hated that.

"You can slit your throat with your tongue," John had once told him. Hell if he'd be the one to talk about Ciara's home life to anyone in the homicide bureau.

3 1

Julio Santos was bored. He was used to seeing a lot of action when he was working as a bodyguard for Bernardo Adrianos, because somebody was always trying to kill that bastard. At first, he had enjoyed the high-intensity life, but nobody likes to live like that for long. Or gets to. That much was clear to him, and to his partner Ricky Calaban, even before they were contacted by their new employers.

The basics of the original deal had been appealing. Adrianos dead, Julio and Ricky alive and wealthy. None of Adrianos's friends or associates knew where Julio and Ricky were. Most people figured the bodyguards had died trying to defend him. This is exactly what the strangers had told him would happen.

Then the strangers offered more—if Julio and Ricky agreed to come to work for the strangers' private company for one year, they would earn five million each, and Ricky's brother and Julio's mother would each receive another million. If they wanted their family members relocated to a safer place, this would be arranged.

Julio asked what they would be required to do during that year.

It would be a dangerous job, the leader said, but not as dangerous as continuing to guard Bernardo Adrianos. They would each guard one man, and that man would be drugged most of the time. They would learn to do certain simple medical procedures involving narcotics and intravenous feedings.

They did not need to learn how to do these gently, just effectively. In addition to the leader, three men would be allowed to visit the prisoner from time to time, but otherwise, they would be somewhat isolated.

Ricky, he learned later, had jumped at the offer. Julio had been more cautious but had ultimately accepted it. He didn't have a lot of options.

At first, he thought it might all be some FBI setup, but so far, all the strangers had told him had been true. Julio's mother now lived like a queen back in Mexico, and he had a bank account that was going to be much bigger in a few months. The man he was guarding here in this abandoned small factory in Palmdale was too heavily sedated to be a threat. He looked like a mean motherfucker, all right, but most of the time, he was completely out of it.

To the outside world, Julio appeared to be a watchman who was paid to keep an eye on a property that might be sold. The room Julio guarded and his own living quarters were concealed within the building. His quarters were extremely comfortable. He had music and magazines, electronic games, a satellite dish, and a phone—although they warned him that the phone was tapped and that the entire place was, in fact, full of listening devices. If he wanted to call his mother, they would pay for the call. Anywhere in the world. But they would be listening. They were sure, the leader said, that he could understand their desire to protect their investment.

They would send a whore to him whenever he wanted one, provided he never let her see the prisoner or even hinted that there was a prisoner being held there. And the whores were much classier hookers than the ones he had enjoyed while working with Adrianos. At first he had taken a lot of advantage of that perk, but even his appetite for whores seemed to be waning these days.

As happened on visiting days—when one of the four strangers would stop by—the prisoner's morphine had been cut back. Sometimes, if he wasn't waking up fast enough, Julio gave the prisoner a low-dosage injection of an amphetamine. That would counteract the morphine's effects for a while. Julio was so tired of this routine, he was tempted to go in there and kill the prisoner himself, and tell whichever of his bosses who showed up today that the man had tried to escape. But he wasn't going to blow five million—six, if you counted his mother's share—by being impatient.

He heard the prisoner pacing. He watched him on a security camera. It had bothered him a little at first that he was going to spend time watching a naked guy night and day, but by now it hardly registered with him.

He understood the man's restlessness. At first, whenever he was awake, the prisoner had ranted about wanting his lawyer. Julio wondered if the guy had finally figured out that it wasn't the good old cops who had him now. Then again, where he came from, maybe this was the way the cops treated all their prisoners.

Watching the news, Julio figured he had a good idea what was going on. Adrianos had been on the FBI's Most Wanted list. The prisoner was on it, too. His name was Farid Atvar, and he was one of those fucking terrorist assholes, one of the few who were on both the top ten and the special list for terrorists.

The day he had learned that, Julio, who was not unpatriotic, had been ready to go in there and fucking put Farid's lights out permanently, and to hell with the money. He had no patience for these head cases, these so-called religious men who blew up buildings and shit like that in the name of God.

That was bullshit, anyway, Julio thought. Who the hell would be dumb enough to worship a god that wanted you to do senseless crap like that? You didn't do shit like that because of God. Julio figured this kind of guy must embarrass the hell out Arabs who really did believe in Allah, the way some of those preachers on television embarrassed Christians.

Julio never would believe anybody bombed anything on account of God. No. You blew things up because you were a powerless little fuck who found another bunch of dickless wonders and let lunatics who hid themselves half a world away talk the group of you into being suicide attackers. You let them do it because they were good at mind games, and they knew exactly what you thought of yourself—that you and your useless life weren't worth the paper you used to wipe your ass. Well, they got that part right, at least.

Julio had no respect for them at all. He had done his share of killing, but he had killed to live, because his life was worth something. Somebody came toward the man he was protecting, he knew it, he was there. He was ready for you—bring it on.

At least, that's the way it was before. Now, who knew what he'd do when he was done with this job?

Well, he'd deal with that when the time came. But no matter what happened to him, he'd never blame God. The way Julio figured it, God was this guy at the show, and when it was your time to leave the stage, *adiós*. While you were on the stage, go for it, but just keep in mind you weren't writing the play—He was. And He loved a good laugh. As for encores, well, Julio would wait and see.

He'd had a lot of time to think about these things lately, whenever he wasn't playing video games or watching porn.

He watched the news, too, which was usually just about as repetitive as the porn. When he kept hearing about the dead guys from the Most Wanted list, he figured he was fly to the time of day. His new bosses were sick of the cops being so lame. They were rich boys trying to prove they had balls. He wasn't sure they were all that different from the prisoner. Really, didn't they get that there were just going to be ten more brand-spanking-new assholes on the Most Wanted list? There were already new ones taking the places of Adrianos and the others. What did they think was going to happen—the country would run out of criminals?

Crazy.

But he didn't mind taking their money to help them do their bit while they were front and center stage. No one was going to connect him with it, or by the time they did, he'd be long gone. Even if he was caught, what could they accuse him of—holding this guy hostage? A guy who planted a bomb on an Oceanside bus—a bus that he knew young marines often took to get back to Camp Pendleton at the end of leave? Who killed three kids and half a dozen retirees at the same time? *Shit*, Julio thought. More likely he'd get a medal for keeping the bastard from planning some other fucking bombing.

He was pretty sure his bosses would get away with it somehow, too—they had money. He hadn't seen a hell of a lot of wealthy people punished in his day, unless they fucked with other wealthy people. These guys were killing people everybody hated.

To keep himself from going in and killing Farid just to make God laugh His ass off, Julio always tried to call Farid "the prisoner" in his mind. He figured he earned his five mil by self-restraint.

He stood up and stretched, and got ready for a visit from one of the four. Chill—his name for the boss of them all, as cold a bastard as he had ever met—had called but hadn't said who would be coming by. He never did.

Julio went up to the roof. The prisoner didn't have a prayer—no matter who he prayed it to—of getting out of his cell, and there wasn't a thing in there that could be used for a suicide attempt. But Julio took a little portable monitor with him anyway.

He watched until he saw a van approaching. It wasn't the usual one, but he caught a glimpse of the driver and recognized him. So, it was the Surfer this time. Julio went downstairs.

The Surfer was wearing a suit, looking exactly like a guy who puts on suits only for funerals and weddings. But Julio didn't think that was what was bothering him as he watched the prisoner on the monitor.

His voice was kind of high-pitched when he said, "I thought he was supposed to be drugged."

"My instructions were to sober him up," Julio said.

The kid—really, he was no more than a kid—looked at him, and Julio saw that he was scared shitless.

"What's supposed to happen here?" Julio asked, his tone inviting confidences.

"I'm supposed to kill him."

God, the kid looked like he was gonna barf just saying it.

"You ever done anything like that before?"

He thought he knew the answer, but the kid surprised him. "Yes."

"Really?"

"Yeah, but—I just helped."

Julio found himself suppressing an urge to laugh. "You want me to help you? It would be my pleasure."

For a moment, he thought the kid was going to say yes, but in the end he shook his head.

"What would you like me to do?" Julio asked.

"Just let me in there, and—and watch. If there's any trouble . . ."

"Help you out."

"Yes."

The entrance to the prisoner's cell was through a triple set of doors, each with a short hall between them. The doors were heavily reinforced. Julio let the Surfer into the first door. The Surfer waited in the hallway while Julio closed and locked the first door.

Julio went over to the monitor closest to the door and watched.

The Surfer entered a code that released the electronic lock on the second door. He closed it behind him, and entered the code again, locking it. He stepped up to the third door.

On the days when he was not fed intravenously, the prisoner received his meager rations through a slot in this door. The Surfer leaned over and called through it, "Mr. Atvar? I'm an attorney with the ACLU."

Julio wondered if it was the drugs that made the prisoner start crying. He was shouting some stuff that Julio thought might be prayers, and saying, "Help me, help me, please."

"Maybe some of those people on that bus wished someone would help them," Julio said.

But when the Surfer stepped into the room, the prisoner said, "You? You are no lawyer. You are too young."

"Mr. Atvar, settle down, or I'm walking right back out of here."

That put an end to Atvar's rebellion. He began scratching himself. Over the ten weeks he'd been here, Julio had followed a program that had turned his prisoner into a morphine addict. Julio had no regrets about that.

The Surfer started pacing. *Get on with it,* Julio silently urged. At the same moment, his attention was drawn away by the sound of a motor. He checked the monitor that gave him a view of the parking lot entrance. Someone else was approaching. He was driving a Maserati Bora.

No one comes around for a week, and now the whole world shows up. Damn it, he wondered, now what should he do?

He made certain that he had easy access to his weapon, but he was fairly sure that anyone approaching in a Maserati was one of the rich kids.

Julio turned back to the screen just in time to see the kid make his move—an awkward attempt to garrote the prisoner.

It wasn't pretty, but he did get it around the prisoner's neck, probably because the prisoner was in a weakened state. Still, Julio had to admit, the prisoner was fighting like hell. He bashed his head back into the Surfer's, making his nose bleed. Julio almost went in at that, but the Surfer was holding on, even though the prisoner kicked and twisted.

Tighten it, kid. Pull on it!

The buzzer for the door rang, and Julio looked at one of the other screens and saw, to his relief, that it was one of his bosses. The dark-haired one. He was dressed in dark leather and was wearing driving gloves. Julio had mentally dubbed him the Mechanic, because he had seen his kind many times before. He figured this one had a love of his work that even Chill was missing.

He hurriedly let him in, then said, "I think your friend needs some help. Want me to go in?"

"No," this one said. "That's why I'm here."

Julio opened the door for him, then locked it. On the monitor, he watched as the prisoner pissed himself. It got all over the Surfer's suit. The Surfer swore and loosened his grip, and the prisoner took advantage of this to free himself. He had just thrown himself on the thin mattress on the floor when the door opened.

"Cameron?" the Surfer said. "What are you doing here?"

The prisoner began to stand up. Cameron—the Mechanic—pulled out a .38 and shot the prisoner in the kneecap.

Farid Atvar screamed.

Julio heard all of this over the monitor only. Even the shot had been nothing more than a slight popping sound. The cell was virtually soundproof.

Cameron walked calmly over to the Surfer and handed him the gun. "Finish your job."

The Surfer said, "I thought I couldn't use a gun." Julio could barely hear him over the prisoner's screams.

Cameron looked at him in exasperation. "Finish it, Morgan."

Morgan—the Surfer—aimed the gun and fired. He hit the prisoner's shoulder. More screams.

Cameron took the pistol from him, aimed, and fired a shot through Farid's left eye.

The screaming stopped.

He watched as the one called Cameron holstered the weapon and then pulled out a big black marking pen. He bent over Farid's skinny, bloody chest.

"Are we going to do all the rest of it?" Morgan asked.

"No time. If Freddy makes as big a mess of his assignment as you did of yours, he'll be needing my help soon."

Julio let them out again. He tried not to look at Morgan's suit pants, which reeked of piss. The smell of gunpowder never bothered Julio, but he couldn't stand the piss smell.

The Surfer was looking green again and wringing his hands like an old woman.

"Mr. Santos," Cameron said, "I know he's shorter than you are, but would you have a pair of sweatpants and a T-shirt my associate could change into? I don't think he'll want to sit in these clothes in his Maserati."

"You drove my Bora?" Morgan said in outrage.

"Shut up. Mr. Santos, we need to leave as soon as possible. The body can stay here. I'll need you to drive the van to Malibu. We'll pay you there and you can be on your way."

"Sure," Santos said, smiling and thinking that it really hadn't been bad work for five million bucks. He had just started up the stairs toward his apartment when the old instincts kicked in—a moment too late.

He could swear he felt the bullet sting his back, then tear through the front of his chest even before he heard it, but maybe that was his own gun, going off too late. He was losing consciousness, his knees buckling, and he was suddenly struck by the thought that he must look ludicrous. He drew a painful last breath and called out to his laughing God, although he knew it came from his lips as little more than a whisper.

Cameron walked forward and felt for a pulse. There was none.

He turned and tossed the keys to the Bora to Morgan. "You drive the Maserati, I'll drive the van. Follow me. We're going to take Mulholland Highway."

"Mulholland? Why?" He was shaking.

Cameron was distracted for a moment, unlocking a cabinet and removing tapes from the security cameras' tape decks. But he answered, "We've got to meet Freddy there."

"Don't tell him about the piss, okay?"

"I won't."

"Or—or that I couldn't do it."

"You just need practice, that's all."

Morgan looked at Santos's body and said, "Why did you kill him?"

Cameron hesitated, then said, "You said my name when I walked into the room."

"You said mine."

"After you spoke mine, it didn't matter."

"Oh."

They began to walk out. Morgan took one last look at Santos. "What was it—at the end—what did he say?"

Cameron smiled. Morgan started shaking again.

But Cameron simply walked past him, saying, "Encore."

3 2

Meghan heard someone step out onto the deck behind her and quickly closed the cover of the photo album. She turned to see Kit.

She saw his gaze go to the album. He flinched and looked at her uncertainly. She felt her face turn warm with embarrassment, but smiled and said, "You're back safely. I'm so glad. Spooky has been worried about you—we all have been. Moriarty said you were doing something foolhardy, but wouldn't tell us more."

"Everything went fine," he said. He seemed distracted. He walked to the edge of the deck and leaned his forearms on its railing. He stood looking out over the canyon, toward the ocean.

"Spooky will be relieved."

"I've seen her," he said, still not turning around. "She's swimming with Moriarty. A way of putting off working on her summer reading assignments, I suppose."

She set the album aside, stood, and walked over to him, but she kept a distance of a few feet between them. "I apologize," she said.

"For what?"

"Looking in the album. I—I wasn't trying to pry."

She saw him reach into one of his pockets. He pulled out a little soapstone tortoise. He began to turn it over and over in his hand. "You didn't do anything wrong."

He looked at her then, studying her face in a way that would have embarrassed her and made her step away had anyone else stared at her in the same way. But Kit was unlike anyone she knew, and something in his own face told her that any lack of patience on her part at this moment would cause her to lose a chance—a chance at what, she wasn't entirely sure, but she didn't move.

"Did Moriarty give you the album?"

She shook her head. "I found it in the library. I thought I might find pictures of you when you were little."

That brought a quick, mirthless smile. "Did you?"

"A few. I hadn't gotten far." She hesitated. "Your mother was beautiful."

"Well, then. You really didn't get far, did you?"

She was taken aback—she had never heard him speak in this bitter, sarcastic tone.

He saw her dismay and instantly said, "I'm sorry . . . I'm sorry." He looked out at the sea again and drew a deep, steadying breath.

After a moment he asked, "Do you know why Freddy Whitfield was in Albuquerque?"

"No. I guess I've stopped believing it was coincidence. I wanted to ask you about it, but I figured you didn't want to talk about it in front of Spooky."

"Thanks for understanding—you're right, I'd rather she didn't worry." He smiled ruefully. "For one thing, she tends to relieve her stress by starting fires."

"So, was Freddy there because of me?"

"I think so. Indirectly, anyway. I think he was probably looking for Gabe and hoped you'd lead him to your brother."

She frowned. "Why would Freddy want to find Gabe? Do you think he's trying to collect the reward on him?"

"That reward would be pocket change to someone like him. Knowing Freddy, he spent more getting to and from New Mexico than the amount of the reward."

"So why?"

He hesitated, then said, "He's involved in the killing of the people on the FBI's Most Wanted list."

"Freddy?" She started laughing. "Oh, Kit—I'm sorry, but—Freddy?"

He waited.

"But he's such an idiot!"

"He isn't as stupid as you'd think. Besides, I didn't say he was masterminding it. But he's involved. This morning, on the television news, I saw that the police were looking for someone who had stolen the ID of Eric Grady."

She looked puzzled for a moment, then said, "One of the driver's licenses in the wallet."

"Yes. And for all he might seem to be an idiot, he's always been sneaky. He loves to spy on people, to try to learn their secrets."

She studied him for a moment and said, "He learned some of yours?"

He looked out at the sea again. "A few. Not many."

She saw him rolling the stone tortoise between his thumb and fingers. She set aside her curiosity about him and asked, "Why would Freddy — or whoever it is he's working with — go after criminals on the FBI's Most Wanted list?"

"I think he's working with Everett Corey and Cameron Burgess. Maybe others — I don't know. Morgan, I suppose. I'm certain of one thing: Everett's in charge. As for why . . . If you build a machine, maybe sooner or later you want to see what it can do." He saw she was puzzled, and added, "Everett feels superior to just about everyone else alive. He enjoys making his closest friends do as he asks — they're totally under his control. His own secret society." He frowned. "No, more like a band of mercenaries. He used to do all this drilling and playing at soldiers at Sedgewick — kid's stuff, I thought. I knew Moriarty, who had been a real soldier, so I thought what Everett was doing was laughable and figured the only good part of it was that it took up a lot of energy and time that he would have been using to push other people around. Now — well, it's not funny at all."

"But why the Most Wanted list?" she asked again.

"I don't know, exactly, but I think it has something to do with old grudges against Gabe and me."

"I know why Everett didn't like Gabe in high school —"

"Do you?"

"Yes. Gabe stole a lid of marijuana from him."

Kit shook his head. "Gabe paid him back for that."

"Because you insisted on it. I know the story. I know that's how you met Gabe — you kept Everett from beating the hell out of my brother on your first day of school."

"That was part of it. But Gabe's biggest offense, as far as Everett is concerned, is that your brother talked you out of dating him."

She was silent for a time. When he looked over at her, she said, "That's not true. Among other reasons, I didn't go out with Everett because I didn't want to go out with him. I never liked him."

"I don't think his incredible ego can accept that explanation."

"Is that why he bears a grudge against you?"

"Me? Because of you?"

He looked surprised, and she found herself irritated that he did. "Yes, you."

"No. He hates me because, as you've said, from my first day at Sedgewick, I started breaking his stranglehold on the school. Gabe was my biggest ally. Before that, Everett's word was law."

"But you wouldn't accept that."

"No. Everett didn't present much of a challenge to me—I thought I'd seen his type before, and I—I had been in worse situations." He gripped the little tortoise for a moment, then went on. "When I came to Sedgewick, it was at a time in my life when I was unable to tolerate bullies. I thought that was all he was."

"Well," she said, "I thought he was a bully, too."

"He is one, but that's not all there is to it. He's . . . he's missing something—whatever it is that makes a person think about anything or anyone but himself. He only studies other people so that he can manipulate them."

"To be honest, Cameron always scared me more."

"Maybe he should have. He's disturbed in an entirely different way. But for a long time now, he's been under Everett's control. They're both ruthless."

"You're twenty-six, right?"

"Yes. You're thinking that it's a long time for someone to bear a grudge, that it was just high school."

"Well, yes—"

"But you went to Malibu High." She saw him look toward the cliff that dropped down into the canyon to the east of the house. "At Sedgewick . . . at Sedgewick, it was different. The students were all male, and almost all of them were kids who couldn't fit in anywhere else, usually because they couldn't control their tempers." He paused. "How can I explain it? If you're disappointed about something, you feel bad, but ultimately, you accept it. At Sedgewick, most kids didn't react to setbacks that way. Something upset them, they couldn't let it go."

"Are you bearing any grudges from high school?"

"No, I have my own kind of problems. I'm not better off—I just don't think in the way Everett does." He turned back to her. "Has he been in touch with you lately?"

She blushed. "Not all that recently."

"He's called you, or come by?"

"He called not long after my parents died. I don't know how he got my number."

"He has more than enough money to buy what he wants to know. What was the excuse for calling?"

"Condolences. Started to say something about small planes, thought better of it, said my dad was a great pilot. Wanted to know how to reach Gabe."

"You're still blushing, so I assume he also said that he always thought the two of you should get together, or something like that."

"Something like that." *"Meghan," Everett had coaxed. "Think of it. Our children would have beauty, brains, and wealth. What more could you want for them?"*

Kit was watching her closely again. "Did he insult you?"

"No. Listen, Kit, I can understand—barely—that he might have some ridiculous notion in his head that I should have gone out with him in high school. But after all these years? I can't believe he's been carrying a torch for me—"

"It's not impossible," he said quietly, staring out at the water. "Not by any means."

"Kit . . ." she said, but he wouldn't meet her eyes.

"It's not impossible," he said again, a little more firmly, "but in his case, I think it has more to do with anger over a rebuff than a broken heart."

"Let's say you're right. Is he still angry that you wouldn't kiss his ass in high school?"

"I guess so. He sent Cameron to Colorado to kill my dog."

"What? Cameron killed Molly?"

"I saw him get in his car and drive away from my place in the mountains. I almost think he waited for me to notice him."

"My God," she said, shaken.

"There are other ways they've issued challenges to me. The way the victims of their crimes have been found."

"What do you mean?"

He glanced back at the photo album, then looked at her. "Meghan," he said, and swallowed hard. "Meghan, from the day I first met you, I've hoped . . . and hoped . . . and prayed to God that I'd never have to tell you . . ."

He stared out toward the sea again, clenching his fist around the stone tortoise.

"And all that same while," she said, "I've waited for you to trust me, even a little."

He turned to her in surprise.

"And if," she said, "it's still too soon, then take the photo album. I can keep waiting."

He pushed away from the rail and shoved his hands into his pockets. "No—no, go ahead. Look at it." He started to pace.

Seven steps in each direction. She noticed this, and despite the tension between them, she had to hide a smile.

"It isn't a matter of not trusting you," he said. "I do trust you."

"To care about you no matter what?"

He stopped. "I know you would want to. You would try. But it would change everything."

"Everything changes anyway, Kit."

He sat down, holding his head in his hands. She took the seat next to him.

After what seemed to her a long while, he picked up the album and turned to a page near the end. He handed the album to her.

33

The page had two photos on it. Meghan's eyes were drawn first to the one of Kit, smiling softly, looking up from a book. Meghan thought he must have been about ten. He was seated in front of a fireplace—the one in this house.

"My grandmother took that one. I had been living with her for a little while. She gave these photos to Moriarty when she hired him to search for us. The woman in the other photo is my mother."

Meghan was speechless. It did not seem possible that Serenity Logan, the beautiful girl in the photos at the front of the book, the lively teenager with a spark of mischief in her eye, could have become the dissipated, rail-thin hag in this one. Her dark hair was uncombed and unwashed. Her formerly creamy complexion was mottled, her perfect nose appeared to have been broken and healed crooked. The once alluring eyes had a bloodshot, glassy look. The skin beneath them was darkly shadowed. One side of her mouth was puffy, as if she had been given a fat lip. She didn't look as if she had smiled much for a long time. She was flipping the photographer the bird.

"That's the last photo I have of her," he said dispassionately. "She would sometimes clean up for a month or two, and she'd look better than that. She looked worse before she died."

"How old is she here?"

"About twenty-nine, I think."

"Twenty-nine!"

He shrugged. "My grandmother told me she took that picture when my mother came to take me to live with her and Jerome."

"Jerome?"

"The man she married." He hurried on. "She had just turned eighteen when she got pregnant with me. I was her second pregnancy, as far as I know. She got rid of the first one. She was sixteen that time. She thought about getting rid of me, but she decided it might be nice to have a kid to keep her company." He paused. "That's what she told me, anyway."

Meghan turned the page, unable to look another moment at Serenity.

The photograph on this page was larger. "Moriarty took that one when he found me. I was fourteen."

She stared at the boy in the picture, so much more like the Kit she had first met, and yet so utterly unlike him. This boy was bruised, and both his skin and ragged clothing were covered with dirt and what looked like bloodstains. His large gray eyes were lifeless, the eyes of a person in shock. He was holding fast to a skinny mongrel that was mostly yellow Lab.

"It was taken just a few hours after I had killed Jerome. I'm not sure how much time had passed—some of that part of my life is still hazy in my mind."

She looked across at him. He looked away.

"I guess everyone who went to Sedgewick heard that I was a murderer. Part of what Freddy the snoop uncovered. Gabe probably told you that much, although you never asked me about it."

"Gabe also told me your stepfather had killed your mother."

"Yes. But that was about two years before the photo was taken."

Kit watched her closely, but she didn't say anything or give any sign of disapproval. He could tell it was news to her that there had been so much time between the two events. He felt an urge to try to shock her, to explain that he had struck Jerome Naughton again and again with a shovel, and continued to strike him long after he was dead. But he thought it would be cruel to give her those images to carry around in her head, and there was so much more to give her a disgust of him that he would not need to make any real effort to alienate her. It would happen anyway.

"This is Molly, isn't it?" she said.

He nodded. It wasn't the question he had been expecting. "Jerome tried to hit me, and she bit him. So he kicked her. I don't know why, exactly, but I snapped. I killed him."

She held her head to one side, considering him. "How did Moriarty find you?"

"Like I said, he had already been looking for me. My grandmother was frustrated with the police, so she hired him. He's one of the best at what he does, I think. That night—he wasn't all that far away from me, as it turned out."

He paused, then said, "My stepfather had . . . he had done things and said things that made me terrified of trying to contact my grandmother before that night. I thought of Jerome as someone who was all-powerful, and he had made it seem possible that he would kill her if I called her. I believed that—I had absolutely no doubt that it was true. So, that night, after he was dead and I . . . I don't know how to describe this, exactly, except to say that somehow, as I stumbled around in a daze, I realized that I could finally call my grandmother. So I called collect, and she told me she would send someone to help me, and she stayed on the line with me until Moriarty reached me. Then I remembered to tell them about the woman."

"The woman?"

This would be it. Their last conversation would be about this. "The woman Jerome had been torturing. He left her hanging upside down over a bathtub to come after me."

She went pale. "He tortured a woman in front of you?"

Keep it straightforward, he told himself. Still, his voice wasn't quite steady when he said, "He tortured and killed eight women in front of me. One of them was my mother."

"Oh, Kit . . ."

"Don't pity me," he said angrily. "I helped him."

"Helped him?" She searched his face, looking, he knew, for some sign that he'd lied to her.

He fell silent.

"I don't believe it." She was angry, too. Of course she was.

"Believe it," he said in a tone that would allow no argument.

She frowned. "How?"

"What?"

"How did you help him?"

He reached for the tortoise, gripped it. "In a thousand ways."

"Name one."

His mind filled with images. He closed his eyes tightly.

She waited. Why didn't she just give up? he wondered.

"Just believe me," he said. It was a plea this time.

"This once, I don't."

He came to his feet. "You want to know, Meghan? You want to know? All right. I did whatever the hell he asked me to do. Anything. 'Tie her up, Worm.' 'Take a picture of me with her, Worm.' 'You stay in that chair and watch, Worm.' And I'd do it."

"You were a child."

"I didn't act like one. Would you like to see the photographs of them being forced to kiss me? To hold me? I'd strip naked and sit on their laps. And he'd tell them where to put their hands. What to do to me. They hated it. They hated me. Even the one who understood—but he killed her just the same. All the others, all so scared of him, they couldn't talk or cry or anything else. He'd take pictures of them and everything he made them do with me."

"Kit—"

"And after they were dead, I helped him then, too. I buried them. I'd be shoveling dirt into a grave, and he'd be in his room, beating off while he was looking at those photos. Why didn't I run away while he was in there with his pants around his ankles? A thousand times I could have escaped from him. Ten thousand."

"You were a child."

"I was old enough . . ." He sat down again, buried his face in his hands. He was surprised to feel the dampness on his face. When had he started crying?

"He beat you, didn't he? The bruises in this photo—"

"So fucking what? I had been beaten before, and by bigger men than Jerome Naughton."

"But he did more than use his fists, didn't he? He terrorized you, day after day. He made you afraid to disobey him."

He didn't answer.

"Just tell me that when you were asked to do those things, you weren't feeling afraid of him, that you would have done them if he wasn't there—say that's true, and I'll blame you for your part in it."

He opened his mouth to say it, just to get her to see how bad it was, how unclean he was. But he couldn't.

He stood up, and she came to her feet as well. "I have to go," he said.

"Wait—" she said, and blocked his way.

She was inches away from him. "Please let me leave," he said. Physically, she was no match for him. He could have tossed her aside, martial arts training or no. He waited.

"I'll let you leave. But first, promise me that you won't start avoiding me now that you've told me this."

"Meghan—"

"Promise."

He looked up at the sky. *God,* he pleaded silently. *God, help me.*

"I promise," he said, and moved past her into the house.

3 4

Frederick Whitfield IV wondered when he had ever felt better. True, he had been barfing his guts out a few minutes ago, but now he was fine. Now he was great. That barfing business, well, nothing to be ashamed of there. A lot of people might not know it, but great actors tended to puke after giving their best performances. Athletes barfed a lot, too. He had a friend who ran marathons, and he said a lot of those runners would cross the finish line and two seconds later, they'd be delivering street pizza. Just a fact. Bodybuilders, too. Famous for upchucking after a tough workout.

And what a workout he had just had. Two of them, both of them pros!

Granted, the one had been in restraints inside a locked cell, a little dull-witted from drugs—but so what? He knew a lot of people who would have been afraid to go in there with a guy who had been a sniper.

Thanks to Frederick Whitfield IV, Mr. Sniper wasn't going to have another chance to hide in bushes and kill people.

Cameron had told Frederick exactly how to do it. He had given him a gun and everything. Cameron was the best shot of any of them. So Frederick had been pleased when Cameron told him that he knew that there was only one other marksman in the whole group who could handle this. Since Cameron was going to be busy taking care of business in Palmdale, he said, he was depending on Frederick. Cameron usually made Frederick uncomfortable, but now Frederick was beginning to think they were going to get along better.

Cameron was going to see that Frederick was no poseur—which is how he had made him feel in the past.

Everett had been talking to Morgan, but after Morgan left, he had taken Frederick aside and stressed that they were all depending on him. Project Nine failed or succeeded because of him. He was their assassin.

Well, he was going to join them at the rendezvous on Mulholland, where they'd get rid of the weapons and report a big green light for Project Nine. Thanks to Frederick Whitfield IV, all systems were go. He spent a few minutes while inching along the 405 freeway not noticing rush hour traffic, but in a beautiful dream, a dream in which Everett said, "Frederick, I just wanted to ask your opinion about something . . ."

He recalled with a little embarrassment his meeting with his lawyer this afternoon. But hell, he had to change his will anyway. Fuck if he was going to let his parents get a dime of his grandmother's money. If she had wanted them to have it, she would have left it to them. Now that he had survived, he realized that he probably didn't need to be so insistent about the appointment. One good thing about being stinking rich was, everyone made time for you. And a man facing death had to have his affairs in order. That was just the responsible thing to do.

He had been a little afraid this afternoon. He could admit that now. But he had shot that sniper just like Cameron told him to, in the left eye. And the guy had died, just like Cameron said he would.

Then Frederick had barfed, and that was probably a good thing, because when Ricky let him out, and he asked for a glass of water, it was a perfectly reasonable thing to do. And so while Ricky was handing him the water, he shot Ricky in the left eye, too, and it worked just as well that time. He could see that he had totally surprised Ricky. Some bodyguard he must have been.

Frederick barfed again after that, and then got the tapes and drove off. He had to go back, because he had forgotten to put a number on the sniper, and damned if that didn't make him sick again, because he had to get the key off Ricky's body, and then go in there with the mess the sniper had made, and smell his own puke in there with him, and let's face it, he thought now, what kind of asshole wouldn't get sick after something like that?

He took off his gloves as he drove, and stuffed them in his pocket. He was glad he hadn't worn his complete assassin's outfit. He had an all-leather black outfit, and he had put it on, but he was really too damned hot in it. Except for the gloves, he had gone back to the James Dean look. You just couldn't go wrong with James Dean, he decided.

He thought about listening to the news on the way to the rendezvous, because they might have something on it about a double homicide in Del Aire. But then again, it was probably too early. He wondered if Everett was already at the rendezvous. He doubted Cameron and Morgan would have made it yet, because they were coming all the way from Palmdale, which was about sixty miles from where they were going to meet.

They were meeting at a little house Cameron owned. Frederick was right—Everett was already there. Frederick brought the tapes in, and they watched them together. They both laughed when Frederick got sick. Really, it was funny on the tape.

By the time Cameron and Morgan got there, it was getting dark. Frederick thought maybe the Bora had broken down, but Morgan got huffy about that and said that he had just gotten it back from the shop and it was running perfectly. They had hit a lot of traffic on the way in, Cameron explained, then said that the Bora was indeed running great. Morgan gave Cameron a dirty look, and that's when Cameron told everyone that he had broken into Morgan's place and ripped off the car. They had a good laugh over that.

Frederick and Everett got another laugh at Morgan's expense, because he smelled like pee, and he kept trying to blame it on the prisoner. Frederick felt so sorry for him that after a while, he played the tape for him. Everybody got a kick out of that, too. It was just as funny the second time.

Cameron congratulated Frederick on doing the job just right and asked for his gun back. Frederick noticed that Morgan was looking unhappy again. He wondered what was eating him.

They sat around drinking toasts from a bottle of Dom Pérignon Everett had opened, eating caviar, and hearing about how things had gone in Mexico. Morgan didn't take more than a few sips of champagne. He said he needed to be sober to drive on Mulholland.

Finally, Everett said, "We'll leave one of the vans here. I'll ride in the other van with Cameron. Morgan, you take Frederick and follow us, all right?"

Morgan rarely let anyone other than Everett ride in the Bora, and Frederick could see it chapped him a little that Everett was going to ride in a van instead of with him, but he didn't complain. He really was in a weird mood, Frederick thought.

He didn't talk in the car. Frederick asked if they could roll the windows down, because, after all, there was this pee smell. Morgan wouldn't even crack his open, but Frederick rolled his all the way down. It was noisy but worth it because it was a warm night, and the fresh air felt good. They were way up in the Santa Monica Mountains, past Seminole Hot Springs and still going. Frederick thought he knew the plan—they'd drive on Mulholland all the way back to Pacific Coast Highway, nearly to the Ventura County line, and then go back down the coast to Malibu. The air smelled great, and you could really see the stars. He was leaning his head out a little so that he could see them better, when Everett signaled them to pull into a turnout. Cameron and Everett got out of the van and walked back toward them.

Everett asked Frederick if he'd change places with him. Frederick had liked riding in the Bora, even with the smell, but he graciously got out of the car. Morgan was smiling as Everett got into the passenger seat.

Frederick wasn't all the way to the van when he heard the shot. Cameron turned back toward the car, and Frederick followed him, although he had this sick feeling again. Everett stepped out of the Maserati, and Frederick moved faster. Cameron let him run past him.

"What happened?"

"Get in the car," Everett said.

"What happened?" he asked again.

" 'What happened?' " Cameron mocked from behind him. "What happened is that this dumb ass left his DNA on the rope at the peninsula."

Frederick felt all the blood drain from his face. He turned to Everett. "You shot him because of that? You've known him since high school! He's on our team!"

"He lied to me, Frederick."

"I don't like this, Everett. I don't like it. I'm not playing anymore."

He suddenly felt the gun at his back. "It's almost nine o'clock," Cameron said. "Get in the car and turn on the news."

He started crying, but of course they didn't care. He tried not to look at Morgan as he got in the car. Cameron held the gun to his temple and made him turn the radio on. Frederick kept looking in the rearview mirror, hoping someone would drive by, would see them.

"Our top story this hour . . . Sources close to law enforcement say that a Malibu man, Frederick Whitfield IV, is being sought for questioning in the deaths of four criminals on the FBI's Most Wanted list . . ."

He said, "I'm famous!"

Cameron pulled the trigger.

3 5

"You've got everything?" John asked Chase, for at least the third time.

"Yes, sir," Chase said.

"You could stay here tonight, if you'd rather. Alex won't mind taking you back tomorrow. He's going to have to be up there a lot this week, I imagine."

"He's right," Alex said. "Want to stay?"

Chase hesitated, then shook his head. "They're coming back early tomorrow. If I'm not home, my dad will be mad, and he'll put me on restriction or tell me I can't come here anymore."

John sighed. "Probably right. But if you need us, you give a call, okay? I'll come up there and talk to your dad about all of this as soon as I can drive again. Couple of weeks at most. Will you be able to hang tight until then?"

"I'll be fine," Chase said, and smiled, but Alex didn't think it was a particularly convincing smile.

As he drove toward Sepulveda, he answered Chase's questions about his day. He told him about the task force meeting—discussing the cases with the other investigators, assigning people to take on new areas of investigation, preparing for the press conference. He told him about the wallet and the *milagros*.

"Wow. So that was just like a gift from someone?"

"Sort of. In an investigation like this, you are always a little suspicious of gifts."

His cell phone rang. "Brandon," he answered.

"Alex? Dan Hogan."

"What can I do for you, Lieutenant?"

"We've got another one. Another two, actually, but only one of them has a number on him. How far are you from Del Aire?"

"You said Del Aire, not Bel Air, right?"

"Right. Near LAX."

"Just a few minutes away, but I've got my nephew with me. I'm taking him home to Malibu. Then I was going to try to follow up on Whitfield."

"I need you to stop by the scene as soon as you can. It's indoors this time. Is the nephew old enough to wait in the car for a little while?"

"He's fifteen." He glanced over and saw Chase's look of intent interest. "Yes, I suppose he could wait, but this doesn't sound like a 'little while' kind of scene."

"Maybe you can work something out with Ciara—"

"You've called her already?"

"No, is there a problem?"

He realized how close he had just come to causing her trouble. He said, "No, I just got back from giving her a lift to Long Beach, that's all. Too bad we didn't get the call half an hour ago."

He wondered how difficult it would be for her to make arrangements for Laney's care. She must have had to do this a thousand times already, of course, but still—

"Alex, you there?"

"Yes, Dan. Sorry—tell me where I'm headed."

He wrote down the address on a pad on the dashboard.

"The place belonged to an air freight company that went out of business," Hogan said, "so everyone thought it was an empty warehouse. You shouldn't have any trouble finding it. The damned press got wind of it through a radio call—we've already reprimanded the deputy—so we've had to set up a bigger than usual perimeter to keep the media the hell away. Once we knew that it was one of the ten, we cordoned off the area. But be prepared."

"Any idea who the victims are?"

"The one with the number on him is Seymour Merton—the sniper who's been killing doctors."

"The anti-abortion fanatic?"

"Right. No idea about the other one. There are things worth noting about the scene, but I'm not going to discuss them with you over the phone. I'll be down there myself soon."

"You've contacted Hamilton from the FBI?"

"He's my next call after Ciara," Hogan assured him.

"Okay. See you in a few."

He hung up. He calculated the distances. He needed to get to the scene in Del Aire as soon as possible, to see it before all the world had tramped through the place. He definitely had to get there before the FBI showed up, or they might use it as an excuse to take control of the scene—Captain Nelson would never forgive him. If the press was already there, Hamilton could have already learned of it, too. No time to go back home. "Chase, I'm sorry—I've got to stop by a crime scene. I can't take you in with me. Do you mind waiting in the car?"

"Oh man! No, I don't mind."

Alex laughed. "Trust me, Chase, this will not be exciting for you."

"I promise I won't cause any trouble."

Alex saw one of John's old friends among the deputies who were keeping the press and onlookers from getting too close. Alex parked the Taurus near where he was standing guard. He brought Chase over to introduce them to each other. "Chase is going to wait in the car for me, but if he should need me for any reason, can I ask you to make sure the message gets relayed to me?"

"No," the deputy growled. "I'll personally go in there and I'll personally drag you out." He turned to the boy and smiled. "Your uncle John never shuts up about you—but probably only because we told him he'd have to stop bragging about Alex here."

Chase grinned and dutifully returned to the car.

Inside the building, Alex wondered if they were about to see a change in approach from the killers. One of the members of the Most Wanted list, all right, and with a number three written on his chest—but tied up in a specially constructed cell, shot to death, and not left hanging upside down. He almost questioned whether it was the same group, until he saw the other victim.

"Ricky Calaban," he said. "One of Adrianos's bodyguards."

Kit sat in the rented Jeep Cherokee, waiting until he saw the signs of boredom on the faces of the sheriff's deputies who were keeping watch on the perimeter of the crime scene. That might not be for a while yet. He watched members of the press attempt to get more information out of the lieutenant who had made a brief statement some minutes ago, but none succeeded.

Kit had been here almost before any of them. He heard the call go out on a scanner—supplied to him by Moriarty. He had been listening nonstop, hoping for a little piece of luck, and he got it.

Getting out of the house hadn't gone as smoothly. Spooky caught up with him just after he had talked to Meghan. Meghan had been a few steps behind him, and only Moriarty's quick intervention had prevented Spooky from launching herself at Meghan.

"What did you do to make Kit cry?" she had shouted. Kit couldn't convince her that Meghan was not to blame, but at least she hadn't been violent. He made her promise not to start any fires, or hurt Meghan (she nearly wouldn't give him that one), or rob anyone who was in the house. He remembered to add, "Or on the grounds."

Meghan had long since retreated to her room. He stood outside her door, not knowing if he should talk to her again or just leave. He had eventually gone into the study and used the phone there to call her on the intercom line—almost every room in the house had a speakerphone that was also part of the intercom system.

Apparently, he startled her, but she said, "Kit? Where are you?"

"I'm down the hall, in the study," he answered. "I just want to make sure you're okay."

"And this is how you do that?"

He didn't answer.

She opened her door, came down to the study, said, "I'm fine, Kit," turned around, walked back down the hallway, and closed her door again.

Moriarty, damn him, not only had watched but found amusement in all of this.

By the time Kit left, much later than he had wanted to, it was nearly dark. His plan was to observe Alex Brandon, maybe follow him to the next crime scene. Kit was still unconvinced that Brandon was trustworthy. He had to see that for himself. Too much was at stake. Gabe's life, for starters.

As he drove down Pacific Coast Highway toward Manhattan Beach, he again felt that sensation of being followed. It was strong enough to make him hesitate to go near Brandon's house. Moriarty had stressed how important it was not to let anyone else learn Brandon's address—an unnecessary warning to give Kit, who was fully aware of the perils of drawing anyone else into the net Everett was casting. Kit believed that Everett could get Brandon's address if he wanted it badly enough, but Kit wasn't going to be the one to lead him to the detective's home if he could help it.

Kit would do all he could to keep Brandon safe, even if the detective chose not to be of help. He had even given Brandon some *milagros* to help ward off danger. A man could never do too much to improve his luck.

So even though he had yet to see whomever it was that shadowed him, even though he was not entirely free of the suspicion that his imagination was getting the best of him, he made a decision when he reached LAX. He parked the Suburban near Terminal Four. He called Moriarty on his cell phone, so that by the time he took a van to the Hertz rental center, EL Enterprises had made arrangements for its representative, Mr. Ed Thomas, to pick up a Jeep there. He showed them his Ed Thomas driver's license, and was on his way back to where the Suburban was parked. He loaded his equipment into the Jeep and drove away from the airport.

He turned on the scanner and heard a deputy call in a report of a 187 — a homicide. Two victims. The deputy was shaken and asked the dispatcher to contact the task force. Within minutes, Kit found his way to the crime scene, but the Lennox Sheriff's Station had already gone into action to close off the area.

He was already at its edges, though, and watching with binoculars when Alex Brandon arrived with a teenaged boy. That puzzled Kit. The boy's eyes were the same bright blue as Brandon's, and there was a resemblance, but he knew that Brandon had no children. He watched as the boy went back to the Taurus and stayed there — occasionally leaning out of the open car window to watch what was going on. The deputy they had spoken to when they first arrived took time to stroll over and talk to him whenever things slowed down a little.

Kit flipped through Moriarty's notes and saw a reference to a nephew — one that Alex Brandon had supposedly never met, since he had nothing to do with his brother and ex-wife.

He looked up to see Diana Ontora, the reporter from Channel Three, hurrying alongside a young man in an Armani suit. The man in the suit was trying to make his way to the deputy checking the credentials of detectives, evidence technicians, coroner's office personnel, and all the other people who had a legitimate reason to be on the other side of the yellow tape. He ignored the reporter and left her shouting questions while he signed in. The man seemed familiar to Kit, but he couldn't recall where he had seen him. The questions indicated the man was an FBI agent.

The agent didn't enter the building immediately, because Alex Brandon and Ciara Morton walked out, and he met them and spoke with them for a few minutes before going inside. As Kit watched through the binoculars, Detectives Morton and Brandon walked toward Brandon's car. It seemed to Kit that the two detectives were on better terms now than they had been earlier in the day, at the press conference.

The teenager stepped out of the car again. Watching them together, Kit felt sure that this must be Brandon's nephew. Chase Brandon.

Ontora was next warned away from Brandon's Taurus by the deputy. Kit had to admire her tenacity.

All attention suddenly focused on some activity near the door of the building, and the television camera lights glared bright. Flashes strobed. The coroner's assistants were bringing out the bodies. Both bodies were encased in dark bags. They were placed in the coroner's van, which drove away within minutes after its doors were closed.

The television crews began leaving. The lieutenant made a final statement, and most of the reporters left, too. Close to the building, crime scene tape and wooden barriers were still in place, but beyond them, there was not the same number of patrol cars or officers on foot—most of the deputies were being released to other duties. Even the FBI man left. Ontora made another try, but again came up with nothing. Ciara Morton left next—he noticed Ontora didn't even bother approaching her.

Kit got out of the Jeep and stretched his legs. The long hours of driving over the past few days had left his muscles stiff, and he decided to walk a little. He drank from a bottle of water and opened a package of beef jerky. He stayed in the shadows. If anyone else asked, he had credentials to show he was Ed Thomas, reporter for the *Mountain Chronicle*.

He found a short, darkened alley and stepped just inside its entrance. Its shadows hid him as he leaned against one of its walls. Perhaps some new story was breaking, because Ontora quickly ordered her crew back to the news van and drove off.

Something scraped against the pavement of the alley, and Kit flattened himself against the wall. It occurred to him that he might be invading some homeless person's territory—or the territory of someone violent. He didn't feel fear so much as annoyance. He had skills now that he had not had at fourteen and felt capable of defending himself. Besides, he wasn't far from a dozen or more members of the sheriff's department. But he'd prefer to avoid making any kind of scene.

His clothing was dark, so he might not be noticed. He listened carefully, and now he recognized the sound. He stared into the darkness, and gradually he made out the form of a large dog creeping slowly toward him.

As it moved into the light, he felt his heart stop.

A skinny yellow Labrador retriever.

Not Molly, he told himself, but he already knew that. The dog had a different face, was closer in looks to a true Lab than his beloved mutt, was younger,
not much more than a pup. Again he felt the unyielding grip of grief, felt it
take hold of him as it did with any thought of her, and for a moment he could
not breathe or think or move.

Was this some omen? he wondered. Labradors were one of the most popular breeds in the country, but why, out of a thousand breeds of dogs, was this
dog so similar to the one he had buried only a few days ago?

He stepped forward, and the dog flattened itself against the ground. Kit
slowly lowered himself so that he was squatting over his heels. The dog crept
closer, looking up at him uncertainly. Its tail was tucked between its legs. He
saw it look nervously toward the street, and was surprised to see Chase Brandon standing nearby.

"Is that your dog?" Chase asked in a soft voice.

"No," Kit said.

Chase moved a little closer, slowly approaching until he was only a few feet
away from Kit. He kneeled down and sat back on his heels. "It's okay, fella," he
said to the dog, half singing to it. "We won't hurt you."

The dog's tail uncurled and gave a small wag.

To Kit, Chase said, "I think he wants your beef jerky. Or maybe your
water."

Kit saw his earnest look of concern for the dog and smiled. He extended
both the water and the opened package of jerky to him. "Here, you try. I think
he already trusts you more than he does me."

"Really?"

"Yes."

Kit saw the dog's eyes follow the package with longing. Chase held out a
stick of jerky, and the dog took it quickly but gently. A few moments later, the
dog was eagerly lapping water from Chase's hand.

All the while, Chase spoke to it, told him he was a good dog, asked
him where he had been and why no one was feeding such a handsome
fellow.

Kit looked at the dog's dirty coat, the scrape on his hindquarters, the tendency of one ear not to lie quite as flat as it should, behaving more like a wing
than an ear. The alley itself smelled better. "He is handsome, isn't he?"

"He needs more to eat," Chase said, and looked up at Kit.

"Sorry, I'm out of beef jerky."

Chase went back to talking to the dog. "You've got rust on you," he said,
stroking the coat gently. "Is that who you are—Rusty?"

The dog, it seemed, had fallen in love as well. Revived by what Kit guessed to be the best meal it had enjoyed in days, undoubtedly hoping for more, it was showering kisses on its benefactor.

"He doesn't have a collar or a tag," Chase said.

"No," Kit said. "I don't think anyone has cared much about him for some time."

"I know how you feel," Chase said in a low voice to the dog.

"Chase!" a man's voice called frantically. They looked up to see Alex Brandon standing near his car, obviously searching for his nephew.

"Sounds to me as if someone cares after all," Kit said. "You'd better let him know where you are. See you around."

"Wait! What about Rusty?"

"Fight for him," Kit recommended, "or forget you met him."

He hurried away from Chase and the dog, back to the Jeep. If the boy left the dog here, he would do what he could for it.

"I'm here, Uncle Alex!" Chase called.

Alex all but ran to where he was. "Jesus Christ, you scared the hell out of me!"

"I needed to take a leak. I told the . . ."

"Whose dog is that?"

There was an uneasy silence, then Chase said, "His name is Rusty. He likes me."

Alex was just ready to leave the scene, when Lieutenant Hogan came in to tell him that Frederick Whitfield IV had been found dead in a Maserati off Mulholland Highway—Whitfield and another young male, Morgan Addison, apparently had a suicide pact. "You realize what this means?" Hogan had said. "If we can tie these two to the crime scenes, we've seen the end of this business. And not a moment too soon, if you ask me. I know it's late, but you'd better head out there."

Unlike Hogan, Alex hadn't felt excited. If Frederick Whitfield IV had committed suicide, all the answers died with him.

What brought you to this? Why would you—a rich, good-looking young man with the resources to do almost anything—turn into a killer, and then kill yourself? How is it that your family never noticed what you were up to?

The answers to a hundred questions would be nothing but guesswork from now on. It was a damned waste all the way around.

So he had gone outside in a foul mood, not—as Hogan suspected—because he now had to drive another forty or fifty miles to a new crime scene, but because this was not the way he wanted this one to end. And he wondered if Frederick Whitfield III would give a damn, over in France or wherever the hell he was, when he learned that his son had shot himself.

He talked Hogan out of calling Ciara back, saying that he'd call her himself if needed, but this way one of them would get some sleep. He agreed that Hamilton should be notified as soon as possible. He was debating whether to take Chase home to Malibu or back to his own house, when he saw that Chase was no longer in the car.

He felt panic, anger, and guilt for leaving Chase alone so long. And let his temper get the best of him. Chase was looking up at him now with a mixture of defiance and uncertainty. He was petting one of the most pathetic examples of a Labrador Alex had ever seen. The dog's fur reeked of smells Alex didn't really want to identify. Chase had to be starved for company if he'd befriended this thing.

The thought suddenly reminded Alex of another rich kid whose parents had left him behind. "I can see that he likes you," Alex said. "And I'm sorry— I didn't mean to snap at you. I've just had a rough night, that's all. And it's not over, so we need to get going."

"We're going to another case?"

"Let me restate that. I need to go to another crime scene. You need to decide if you'd rather go back to my house or Malibu tonight."

"What about Rusty?"

Alex opened his mouth to say, "Leave him," but shut it without uttering a word. The dog was watching him, too, now. He'd have to be diplomatic if he was going to talk Chase out of this. He'd start with the blame going elsewhere. "Will your folks let you keep a dog?"

Chase shook his head. Still, Alex noted, there was hope in his eyes. He couldn't bring himself to crush it. "You want me to keep your dog at my house, is that it?"

Chase looked down at the dog, who briefly wagged his tail, then seemed to pick up on his new friend's mood. In a voice Alex could barely hear, Chase said, "It doesn't sound fair to you after all, I guess."

I've lost my mind, Alex thought, but said, "Just promise me that the minute we get home, you'll bathe the dog. Then you'll bathe yourself and put your clothes in the wash . . ."

How much of this Chase heard, he wasn't sure, because he was shouting with glee and the dog was barking. Chase jumped up and hugged Alex before Alex guessed what he was going to do. "You're welcome, but now you're going to pay my dry cleaning bill, too. And probably for a car wash. God almighty, that dog stinks. You sure that damn thing is alive? Jesus, he must have rolled in garbage . . ."

But Chase was hugging the dog now and waving to someone. Alex turned to see a man driving off in a Jeep.

"Who was that?" he asked.

"Some reporter. Rusty liked him." He paused, then added, "He gave me his water and beef jerky, so that I could give them to Rusty."

"I'll have to thank him someday," Alex said under his breath.

3 6

The Bora was bright red beneath the lights the crime lab had set up, a low, sleek streak of color in dark surroundings. If you ignored the two dead men, Alex thought, and the dark brown stains on the inside of the driver's side window and elsewhere in the interior, you couldn't help but appreciate it as a thing of beauty.

"Less than six hundred of them ever made," Enrique Marquez said. "I couldn't let them just haul it off on a standard tow truck. The flatbed should be here before too long."

Alex had been in touch with Marquez through the task force, but this was the first scene they had worked together since Adrianos's body was found. Recalling Ciara's insults to the man, Alex was relieved she wasn't here. He wouldn't break any confidences about her sister, but he could still mend some fences.

"I'm with you," he said. "Besides, we'll want to go over every inch of it anyway."

"You aren't thinking of dismantling it?" Marquez asked in horror.

Alex smiled. "I doubt that will be necessary."

"I hope not."

"Any idea how long they've been up here?"

"The Malibu Station says they patrolled past here at about six o'clock and would have noticed it then—I've got to believe that's true, because at six it wasn't dark yet, I'm damned if I believe one of our guys could go past a red Bora in broad daylight without seeing it."

"So who did see it first?"

"Malibu Station deputy taking that same routine ride between here and Kanan-Dume. He found them at about ten-forty-five. So we're looking at sometime between six and ten-forty-five. Coroner thinks—unofficially—they've only been up here two to three hours. When you're done looking them over, he'll take them out of the car and be able to tell you more. It's a little cramped trying to work in there now. But we've had a chance to take some photos, do a little fingerprint work, make some calls. My partner has been running his ass off down in Malibu and the Palisades, and I learned a few things from a deputy who has worked here for a while."

"I'm glad you caught this case, Enrique. Anyone else might not have made the connection to Whitfield so quickly."

"Your buddy from Channel Three beat you up here," Marquez said. "I wish I knew who was tipping her off to everything."

"You and me both. You've held her at bay?"

"You know I did." He grinned. "Ontora and I have had a few run-ins. I think she was disappointed that I was here. Wouldn't let them close enough for a shot, and at this turnout there are too many trees to let them get anything by helicopter. I loved it."

"The deputy radioed it in and waited here, right? Maybe Ontora heard it on a scanner. Same thing just happened to us in Del Aire."

"That's possible, I suppose. Thank God the deputy stayed here, though, because between the money these two had on them and the car, these guys were like a hundred-thousand-dollar prize waiting to be claimed."

"Not an easy car to unload, though," Alex said, and frowned. He walked nearer to the Bora. "A little conspicuous for arranging murder, too, don't you think? If they had pulled up in this thing in the Lakewood neighborhood where we found Adrianos, I think someone would have noticed it."

"Sure, but you know these guys have more than one car. In fact, this one was in the shop until today."

Alex stopped walking. "What?"

"No, wait, it's after midnight isn't it? Until yesterday morning—Wednesday."

Alex frowned—something wasn't right. "You're sure he just got it back?"

"Yes—hang on a minute." Marquez opened the file folder he had in his hand. "The driver is the registered owner of the vehicle. Morgan Addison." He flipped through some department forms and came to a flat evidence envelope. He pulled out a yellow carbonless form and handed it to Alex.

The form was a receipt made out to Morgan Addison from Blackstone European Auto Repair and Restoration in Santa Monica, time-stamped at nine-fifteen on May 21. It appeared to be a routine maintenance check, but combined with the bill for washing and detailing the car, the total cost was more than Alex paid for a year of visits to a mechanic. "How many miles driven since it was in the shop?"

Marquez consulted his notes. "One hundred forty-six."

"Then we'll want to see what's within that range and try to find out if anyone in those areas remembers seeing a red Bora. Maybe we'll be able to fill in the gap between their victims—we've skipped from number six to number three."

Enrique put a hand on his shoulder. "I feel for you, man. I'm glad they didn't decide to go out in a hail of bullets or holding hostages, but this is lousy."

"Yes."

"And nothing but shitwork from now on, tying up all the loose ends. Just isn't as rewarding as catching somebody."

"I'm not so sure there's no one left to catch."

Marquez raised his brows.

"Why does someone who's planning to kill himself take his car into the shop?" Alex asked, handing the receipt back to him.

"Wants to make sure he can get to the scenic location in style. You know how suicides are about staging things. Probably why he got it washed."

"Yes, but that receipt isn't for washing and repairs. He paid for oil and fluids, wiper blades, things like that."

Marquez studied it again and said, "Okay, so on Tuesday, he didn't know he was going to kill himself. On Tuesday, the brilliant Detective Brandon had not yet been visited by the tooth fairy at a press conference, and so he wasn't naming Mr. Frederick Whitfield IV as one of the murderers yet."

"Tooth fairy, huh? Well, maybe you're right about the change in outlook. But it bothers me. He spent his last day or so driving the Bora over a hundred miles, only to take it up to a spot on the road this close to Malibu?"

"Like you said, maybe he had to leave a body somewhere."

"And hauled it in this sports car?" Alex asked.

"So he used another vehicle for that, but this was going to be the one they made the exit in."

"Maybe—but why this spot?"

"It's pretty up here."

"You've driven Mulholland. Is this the most scenic spot? Even at night, there are places with amazing views of city lights. This is a shallow turnout with no real view, even in daylight."

Marquez gave him a scathing look of disbelief. "You think someone else is involved because these guys picked a lousy view?"

"No, it's just—I don't know, it feels wrong. If they're from Malibu, why come here the long way?"

"What do you mean, the long way?"

"Look at the side of the road they're on. They're heading toward the ocean—toward Malibu. So where did they come from?"

"Maybe they headed up here, saw this turnout, and did a U-turn," Marquez said.

Alex conceded that this might be true. "Any other tire prints?"

"Dozens of them. Nothing we can use."

Alex couldn't shake the feeling that something about this scene was wrong, though. "So talk to me about what else you've discovered."

"Looks like they had a suicide pact. They're apparently old friends—lived in Malibu, went to the same private school. We found them so late this evening, we weren't able to learn a lot, but we got that much from a couple of people who knew them—one neighbor and a deputy that had dealings with them when they were juvenile delinquents."

"So they have juvenile records?"

"Rumor has it they do. We'll see what the courts will let us learn. Not in trouble much as adults. We're just getting started on all of that."

"Not complaining. You've already covered a lot of ground."

"Morgan Addison was twenty-four years old last February. He owns a house on the beach in Malibu. Lives alone. Neighbor told us that Mr. Addison came into a trust fund when he turned twenty-one and spent most of his time surfing and polishing the Maserati, hanging out with friends, and so on. No employment ever. Parents live in the Palisades, but apparently they're estranged from their son—that's another story. Anyway, one of their neighbors said they're on a cruise. Couldn't remember where. We're trying to get in touch with them, but that's as far as we've gotten. The other one—"

"Wait, before we talk about the passenger, tell me a couple of other things about Morgan Addison. You said a deputy told you there had been trouble before now?"

"Speeding tickets in the Maserati, that's all. But the guy from the Malibu Station who rode up here with me has worked there about twelve years, and he says the kid was a lifetime asshole and good riddance. Said that he was dumped in that private reform school up here—what's it called?"

Alex suddenly felt a cold knot form in his stomach. "Sedgewick."

"Yes, that's the one. Guess Addison used to deal dope at the local high school before he was old enough to be in high school himself. Got caught at it twice, but they could never make the charges stick—parents bailed him out of every jam he ever got himself into. Then one day, he beat the crap out of his sister—broke her arm, knocked out a couple of teeth—'cause she borrowed his bike without asking. Mumsy and Daddy had apparently had enough at that point and sent him to Sedgewick. He boarded there and never went back home after that."

Alex realized that Enrique and his partner must have been really pushing to learn this much so quickly. "Thanks, Enrique. Like I said, I'm glad you're the one who caught this one."

"Yeah, well, between you and me, I'm glad your partner isn't here with you."

Alex caught his look but decided to avoid the topic of Ciara. "Sorry I kept you waiting," he said. "Guess I'd better not hold up everyone else any longer."

He walked around to the passenger side of the car, bracing himself, as he found he must always do in suicide by gunshot cases. There had been enough of these over his years in homicide investigation to no longer make it as difficult as it had once been, and now only a case involving a man of about his father's age would disturb him to any great degree.

He knew that he would always think of his father in these cases, would always recall finding him. But he had learned to concentrate on the cases of new victims by telling himself that their families deserved to have him do his job—without allowing his personal emotional reactions to interfere with it.

"A shame, with all they had going for them," he heard Marquez say.

"A damned shame," he agreed.

He sat on his haunches to lower himself to eye level with the occupants of the car. This was the less messy side—entrance wound side. Frederick Whitfield IV's lifeless hand lay in his lap, his pale manicured fingers holding a gun.

"Both right-handed?" Alex asked.

"Apparently."

Addison was slumped over the steering wheel. Alex noticed something odd. He moved around to the driver's side and carefully opened the door. He studied Morgan Addison's face and clothing. "Strange that they're dressed so differently, isn't it?"

"So one wants to look corporate, and the other like he's too cool for words, that's all."

"You think they fought beforehand?" Alex asked.

"Why?"

"Addison's nose is swollen—looks as if he was punched in the face. He's got blood on the front of his shirt, too."

"Sure it isn't from—well, there's a lot of blood in there."

"Exit wound spatter, yes, but that's not from his bullet wound. And not from Whitfield. Look at the driver's side window and then at the windshield. The blood and tissue on the driver's side window is more concentrated—I think Addison was looking straight ahead. The blood and tissue on the windshield couldn't have come from his wound, especially not in the pattern they make. That must be Whitfield's. Whitfield must not have been facing forward—maybe he was sitting at a slightly different angle. He must have turned away a little bit—maybe trying not to look at his friend's body."

"How do you know the driver was first?"

"I don't know for sure, and won't until the lab checks the inside of the car and tells us exactly whose blood is where. But there's a misting of blood on this side and on the back of Addison's suit, which is probably Whitfield's blood—spraying out over the car's interior after Addison was already slumped forward."

"I'm going to make sure the techs got photos of all of that," Marquez said.

Alex wrinkled his nose. For a moment, he thought the dog's smell was embedded in his suit. But this was not quite the same.

Marquez saw the look and said, "The urine is on Addison's suit."

Alex looked over at him. "What do you mean, 'on' it?"

"Look at the stain. You think a guy can piss himself and miss his own crotch?"

"No."

"I wonder if these two were lovers. You know, and old Frederick Whitfield IV here gave his beloved Addison a little golden shower as a going-away present."

"On his clothes?"

"Stranger things have happened."

"My uncle once told me this saying—'If you hear hoofbeats, don't first look for a zebra.' "

Marquez laughed. "I get your point. We've already got a promise from the lab to try to figure out who peed on whom."

Alex looked at the positions of the bodies and how their hands held the guns. Something about Whitfield's arm position didn't seem quite right, but he couldn't say why. "Has Whitfield been moved at all?"

"Not that I know of. Crime lab took photos, though, so you can double check that. Something bothering you?"

"I don't know." He tried for a few minutes more to figure out what didn't seem to fit. He couldn't shake the feeling that the Bora was just an expensive dustbin, into which someone had swept two people who were proving to be problems. But if this was murder and not suicide, was it because the media had learned that they were seeking Whitfield? Had Whitfield been killed because the LASD knew his name? But then why kill Addison, too? And who could get close enough to these two to kill them in the car like this?

Sedgewick. Another school chum?

He shivered. The night air was cold, but he knew the chill he felt had nothing to do with the weather. *Admit that these might be suicides and nothing more,* he told himself. *Maybe you can't be objective after all.*

He stood up and stretched. He looked back through the bloodstained windshield, unable to prevent the memory of his father's death from intruding on his thoughts. But his father had been wracked by guilt—deeply depressed, penniless, and ashamed. What would have made these young men feel so hopeless?

"Damn, I'm tired," he said, then saw that Enrique was watching him closely. They had known each other for a long time, and he wondered how much the other man was guessing about his mood.

"You just need some sleep, Alex, that's all."

"Yeah. Listen—thanks again for holding things up for me, Enrique. We'll call a meeting of the task force for late tomorrow morning and see what we have then, all right?"

"Okay. I'm with you. No use trying to think things through on three hours of sleep. These guys aren't going anywhere."

Alex got back in his car and rolled down the windows, but the stench of Chase's new friend was pervasive. He wondered what the hell had possessed him to tell that kid to go ahead and bring that stinking mutt home with him. A drive of ten minutes had been enough to make his car reek like the bottom of a Dumpster. Maybe Chase had a problem with his sense of smell.

Then he thought of Chase borrowing crime scene tape to make a leash and his excitement as they rode back to the house. Kid could have just about any material thing he desired, and he was crazy over a skinny stray.

He laughed out loud when he recalled the look on John's face.

A little later, two questions began to nag at him.

Why had the guy in the Jeep, the reporter that Chase had waved to, been hanging around in an alley near the crime scene?

And why hadn't Hamilton shown up on Mulholland?

3 7

Gabriel Taggert stood looking out at the trees beyond the deck outside his bedroom. The moon was in its last quarter. Tonight it brought a translucent silver coating to the dark green of the pines, changing the sloping, shadowy landscape before him, making it the sort of forest that inspired stories of enchantments and haunted places.

He had found a beginner's astronomy book in Kit's library and had learned the names of the phases of the moon, and how to tell if it was waxing or waning, and when it was that the sun and moon were closest in the sky, and when farthest apart. He had grown fond of studying the sky, in part because he realized how little attention he had paid to it before he took refuge here. That was, he thought now, an indicator of just how narrow the focus of his life had been.

He had not spent much time outdoors since hearing of the first three murders of the FBI fugitives. The more he had heard about the cases, the more afraid he had become. Thinking about a long prison sentence was one thing. Thinking about being tortured while hanging naked upside down was another.

The names and faces of those on the FBI's fugitives list had been shown on television again and again. He feared recognition—even with his change in appearance, this much exposure would inevitably lead to someone identifying him as one of the ten. The newscasters repeatedly mentioned that new names were added whenever someone was caught or killed, but the "replacements" were hardly ever mentioned. Gabe couldn't help but think there was a kind of countdown going on, and a rapid one at that. When he had gone to bed on Tuesday, there had been three names crossed off the list. Now, two more. Half the list in half a week. And one of the bodies had been frozen, they said, so who knew how many more were already dead and just waiting to be displayed?

But that wasn't all that was making him fearful. He was beginning to believe that he was more than just a number on the list.

Yesterday afternoon, he had watched a live broadcast of the Los Angeles County Sheriff's Department press conference. He was shocked when they showed a photograph of Eric Grady. Gabe had met Eric Grady, had partied with him. Gabe had even convinced him to hang out in Topanga Canyon one summer. Must have been a year or two ago. Now someone was using Grady's identification—someone involved in these cases.

He began to feel a little queasy. Bad enough to think that he might have introduced Eric Grady to someone who had killed him. That was just the first of the implications, though. Gabe was on the Ten Most Wanted list, and whoever was doing the killings was using the identification of a man Gabe had met. He didn't believe that strongly in coincidence.

And sure enough, within hours, the newscasters were announcing that police were seeking Frederick Whitfield IV for questioning in connection with the killing of four members on the fugitives list.

Freddy? There had to be a mistake. Impossible to believe that he was masterminding something like this. Freddy had always been completely under the control of Everett Corey.

That idea no sooner occurred to him than he became certain of it. Everett, and probably Cameron, too. The two of them were almost inseparable, and he knew they must be behind this somehow. Maybe Morgan was in on it, too. But why?

Then came the special report on the news radio station, the story of an apparent suicide pact between two wealthy young men. Freddy was one of them, and although the reporter said the other man's name was being withheld pending notification of his next of kin, when the car was described as a red Maserati Bora, Gabe was sure it was Morgan. There was some speculation, the reporter said, that these two were the so-called Exterminators who had been killing members on the FBI's Most Wanted list.

He had never liked either of them much, and yet hearing of their suicides was as unsettling as it was unexpected. You didn't want to think of anyone you knew committing suicide, he supposed, let alone someone you grew up with, went to school with.

He couldn't understand it. Freddy just didn't seem the type to do something like this. Freddy made excuses for anything that went wrong, blamed other people. Even with the law after him, he could have found a way out of the country—he was probably wealthier than any of the people Gabe had gone to school with, with the possible exception of Kit. Hard to tell about Kit, but Gabe remembered his dad saying that Sedgewick would have kicked every other student out to have a chance to have old Elizabeth Logan as one of its patrons.

The more he thought over the events of the last few days, the more desperate his situation seemed to be. He wasn't convinced that Freddy and Morgan were the only ones involved. He was sure that Everett and Cameron were behind what was happening, and he didn't want to think about what they had planned for him.

He suddenly felt unbearably lonely. He turned away from the view of the trees and went into the living room. It was chilly there, so he built a fire and paced for a while to keep himself warm—and to try to work off the tension he felt. He went to the phone. He had lifted its receiver dozens of times over the last few months but had fought off the urge to call Meghan. This time, he lost the fight.

It rang four times, then went to voice mail. He could tell from the outgoing message that he had reached her cell phone—she must be forwarding messages to it from her home phone. He hung up without leaving a message.

He sat staring into the fire for a moment, then called again—the cell phone directly this time. He'd leave a message for her this time—

"Hello?" she said drowsily.

"Sis? I woke you up—I'm sorry."

"Gabe! Oh, thank God—Gabe!"

He could hear her crying.

"Meggie . . . don't cry," he said, but he was crying, too.

"Don't mind me. I've done more weeping in the last few days than I have since Mom and Dad died. Gabe, I've been so afraid for you! I'm so glad you've called."

"I'm okay, Sis," he said. "I'm fine. Especially now that I'm talking to you."

"Where are you?"

He hesitated, then said, "I can't tell you, Meggie. I'd like to, but I promised the person who let me stay here that I wouldn't talk about it. I'm safe, though. I just wanted to let you know that. And that I miss you. I've missed you for a long time."

"Gabe, if you're in the States—anywhere in the country—we've got to get you out. Do you know—"

"About the Exterminators? Yes. Look, I probably shouldn't talk to you too long—I don't know what can be traced from a cell phone, but—"

"Don't hang up! Listen, I'm staying with Kit, and he—"

"Staying with Kit? In Colorado?"

"No, in Malibu—the house that used to be his grandmother's. Gabe, you should talk to him—"

"Maybe. Tell him I said hello, okay?"

"I will, but Gabe—"

"And tell him to keep my little sister safe, okay?"

"I'm your big sister. Listen—"

"Gotta go. I'll call again."

"When?"

"Whatever you hear— No, wait, that's not important. Forget that."

"Gabe, I don't care what you've done, I don't. But—"

"You're the best, Meggie. I just called to let you know that—well, that I love you, that's all. I never say that to you anymore, I know, but please don't ever doubt that I do."

He heard her calling his name as he hung up. He kept his hand on the receiver for a long time before letting it go.

So Meghan was with Kit.

But none, I think, do there embrace.

Too bad, he thought, staring into the fire. Too bad.

3 8

Kit wondered what had delayed Moriarty. He had left three hours ago with one of his men to pick up the Suburban from LAX. It would have taken him about an hour to get to the airport from the house. He had called once to tell Kit to listen to a radio news station—to hear the reports of the suicides—but Kit hadn't heard from him since.

Kit had spent the time waiting for him to return by gathering Molly's things and placing them in a large cardboard box. He moved the leather couch in the study to reveal a treasure trove of flip chips and the knotted ends of rawhide bones. Under tables and chairs, beneath beds, and in the corners of closets, he found tennis balls, squeaky toys, and the lamb's wool exteriors of formerly plush toys—he pictured her ridding them of their stuffing, shaking her head vigorously as she pranced in victory over her "kill."

Many of these prized possessions of Molly's would have to be thrown away, but he wasn't sure he could be the one to march them out to the trash bin. To distract himself from his grief, he thought of Chase Brandon's excitement over Rusty. He thought the two of them would be good for each other. And he had learned a great deal about Alex Brandon in those few minutes. Brandon hadn't wanted a dog. That much was plain. He hardly knew his nephew, unless reports were mistaken. But he had agreed to take Rusty home all the same.

Kit checked on Spooky, who was sound asleep. She was unhappy with him, he knew, but he wasn't sure how best to smooth things out between them.

Over the last few years, he'd worked hard to help her feel more secure, to be trusting of him. He felt almost as if they were back to square one today. He found the reversal unsettling and wondered how an experienced foster parent or guardian would have handled this problem.

He heard the muted ringing of a cell phone and rushed down the hallway, toward the study. As he passed Meghan's room, he realized that the ringing was coming from behind her door. He stopped, puzzled, and wondered how his phone had come to be in her room.

Then he heard her shout Gabe's name.

Her phone ringing, then.

Gabe was alive. For a few minutes, that was all that mattered.

He moved away from the door, not wanting to eavesdrop. Or, he admitted to himself, wanting to eavesdrop but overcoming the temptation. He called Moriarty from the study.

"Just getting ready to call you," Moriarty said. "There's a reason you were feeling like you were being followed."

"You saw someone?"

"No, we waited around for a little while, just watching, and then we decided to look the car over—I've got a suspicious nature, you see."

"That's why you're good at what you do," Kit said. "What did you find?"

"A transmitter. Secured near the back bumper."

"Any idea how long it's been there?"

"Judging by the amount of undisturbed mud near it, maybe before you left Colorado."

"Someone followed me from there?"

"I doubt it. This type of device has a range of about thirty miles, forty if you're tracking it from the air. If they had attached a little larger model GPS system, they could have found you just about anywhere. From that and everything else we know, I think they were waiting for you to come back here."

"How hard would it be for them to get this type of equipment?"

"You can order it off the Internet. Companies get these devices for their company cars and delivery vans, to make sure the drivers are going where they say they're going. Shippers use them to make sure their cargo doesn't get lost. This is a fairly sophisticated one—it will pulse at about forty beats a minute when the vehicle is still for fifteen seconds or more, but if the vehicle moves, it pulses at more than ninety beats per minute."

"So it alerted them every time I moved."

"Whenever they were close enough to pick up the signal, yes."

Kit was silent for a moment. Moriarty waited patiently.

"Did you take it off?"

"No. I didn't think that would be smart. For one thing, this type of transmitter has a tilt sensor that would tell them if it was pried off the car. So we couldn't just take it off and stick it on a mail truck or something."

"Better to leave it on anyway," Kit said. "If they've tracked it to the airport, they may think I've taken a plane somewhere."

"That's my boy," Moriarty said with pride.

"Any listening devices?"

"No, we swept for those. And the house is clear, so I'm not worried about that. Can you live without the Suburban for a while?"

"Yes, I'll be fine. Sorry to send you all the way out there . . ."

"No, it's a good thing I went. If you and Meghan had picked it up, you would have brought them right back onto your trail. See you in a few — and try to get some sleep, kid."

Kit walked back down the hall. He stood outside Meghan's door, then summoned the courage to knock on it. "Meghan?"

"Kit?"

"Are you all right?" He added, "I'm asking in person."

He heard her give a small laugh. "Come in, Kit." Her voice sounded odd to him.

Her light was on, and she was sitting on the edge of the bed. Her hair was tousled, and she was wearing an old flannel robe. She was holding her cell phone. She looked up at him, and he saw that she was crying, but she smiled. "Gabe just called. He's all right . . ." She started crying harder. She set the phone down and, propping her elbows on her knees, covered her eyes with her hands.

He found that he couldn't just watch her cry. He sat next to her and tentatively placed an arm around her shoulders. He felt her surprise, but only for the briefest moment, then she leaned against him. She was warm, especially where her head rested on his shoulder and chest, and he wondered if there was the slightest chance that she didn't hear his heart hammering in a rhythm that echoed both his pleasure and his panic.

"You'll be okay," he said, as much to himself as to her.

"Until just now, I didn't realize how scared I've been that Gabe was tortured or dead," she said.

He reached into his pocket and produced a clean handkerchief.

She took it gratefully, then said in a wistful tone, "Cloth handkerchiefs. I'd forgotten. Elizabeth hated tissues, didn't she?"

"Yes. Environmentally wasteful, she said, but I think she was just old-fashioned."

He wished he could relax. She must feel, he thought, as if she's being hugged by a mannequin. He was aware of every centimeter of contact between them.

She blew her nose.

It was such a robust, undignified, unexpected sound that he started laughing.

"What?" she said, but she was laughing, too. "I promise I'll wash it before I give it back."

"Sorry, I shouldn't have laughed."

She looked up at him. "I like your laugh."

He moved his hand away but stayed sitting next to her. "So tell me what Gabe had to say."

"He sounded good, in spite of everything—he sounded sober and didn't seem to be on anything. Usually, if he calls me this late—I guess I don't need to tell you what state he's usually in at this hour."

"I don't think I get as many of those calls as you do. And none lately. Does he know . . . ?"

"Yes. He's heard the news. He says he's safe, but he won't tell me where he is. He said he's promised the person who's hiding him not to reveal his location, but I have to tell you, that makes me so nervous! What if it's someone who wants to turn him in for reward money, or sell him to Everett, or—I don't know!" She glanced at him and said, "What is it? Why are you smiling?"

"If he's where I think he is, he's safe, at least for now."

"How could you possibly know where he is?"

He picked up the bedroom phone and called the number for the house in Blue Jay.

It rang several times, and when it was picked up, no one said anything.

"Gabe, it's Kit."

He heard Gabe exhale in relief. Meghan's eyes widened.

"God damn, you scared me," he said. "But I also hoped it might be you."

"Are you all right?"

There was a little hesitation before he said, " 'It was the best of times, it was the worst of times.' I'm grateful to you for giving me the key to this place, Kit. I think you saved my life. I think you saved it even before all this bullshit started happening." He paused, then added, "I don't know if you're happy about that, though."

"Of course I am. Talk to your sister again before she punches me, okay?"

"Sure."

"You two . . ." she sputtered angrily. "I've worried myself sick, and Kit has known all along where you were?"

"No, no. He gave me the key to this place five years ago. I never told him I was coming up here. Don't be mad at him, Meggie. Think of where I'd be if he hadn't given me that key."

She looked at Kit, nervously watching her. "You're right. Gabe, I was trying to tell you before—Kit has some theories about all of this. I think you should listen to him."

She gave the phone back to Kit.

Gabe said, "Before we talk about anything else, I want you to know—"

"That you didn't shoot anyone. I know."

There was a silence, and Kit saw Meghan watching him intently.

"Thanks, Kit," Gabe said in a choked voice.

"Meghan never thought so, either."

"But I was there. I was part of it."

"You'll have to decide the best way to make up for that, then. In the meantime, let me tell you my ideas about Everett."

Meghan listened as he talked to Gabe, then said, "Tell him about Freddy," and Kit realized that she didn't know that he was dead.

"There's a lot more to this, but I don't want to talk about it on the phone," Kit said. "I don't think you'll be safe there forever."

"I've been thinking the same thing myself," Gabe said.

"I want to come by and pick you up, if you're willing to come with me. I'll bring you here, where we can do more to keep you safe."

"You want me to turn myself in?"

"I'll leave that up to you," he said, reaching for his rabbit's foot. "I've been working on trying to find a trustworthy person in the sheriff's department—"

"Are there so few?" Gabe asked.

"That's not what I meant. I think someone in the FBI or the L.A. County Sheriff's Department may be working with Everett. One or two people at most. But I want to make sure I don't approach the wrong one. If you agree to turn yourself in, I'll pay for your attorneys. If you don't want to, I'll help you get out of the country."

"You'd be guilty of a felony."

"It won't be the first time."

After a long silence, Gabe said, "Come up, Kit. Bring Meggie, too, if you don't mind letting her see the place."

"Thank you, Gabe."

Gabe laughed. "I think I'm the one who's supposed to say that. Hey—I just remembered something. You're a stepdad or a big brother or—"

"Guardian. I've got someone here who'll keep an eye on her. I'd bring her, but you and Meghan should have some privacy. And a little peace. I'll have to wait an hour or so for my friend to get back here before I leave, though."

"I'm not going anywhere. See you when you get here."

He handed the phone to Meghan, who listened for a while, then frowned. "No, I was asleep. I hadn't heard about that . . ."

While she talked to her brother about Freddy and Morgan, he reached into his jacket pocket and found a few *milagros* he'd grabbed at random to have on hand, in case he had a chance to give any more of them to Alex Brandon. He looked through them, quickly putting them away when he heard Meghan saying good-bye to Gabe.

She looked at Kit, and he wondered if she had seen him—he knew she didn't have his faith in charms, though she never belittled him for his. But she only smiled and said, "I'm going to thank you all the way up to Lake Arrowhead, but for now, why don't you get a little sleep? I'll watch for Moriarty and wake you when he gets here."

He agreed to this plan and started to leave for his bedroom, but paused in the doorway. Over his shoulder, he said, "Number six on the intercom. I won't mind."

She laughed.

She waited until he had left, and changed quickly into jeans and a T-shirt, and put on a pair of boots. She looked over her meager supply of clothing and decided she'd have to shop or do laundry. She smiled and wondered if Spooky would like to go shopping.

She pulled out a sweatshirt with a hood and pockets, and hoped it would be warm enough for the mountains. She transferred Kit's handkerchief from the pocket of her robe to the pocket of her sweatshirt. He could keep his rabbit's foot—she'd keep this token of luck.

Something shiny on her pillow caught her eye.

A *milagro*. A little silver heart. She held it for a moment, then tucked it into the small pocket of her jeans.

A little miracle indeed.

39

Something cold was pressed to his temple, and Alex Brandon sat straight up on the couch where he had been—until that moment—sleeping.

Rusty, seeing this hoped-for result, began wagging his tail furiously—and knocked a wineglass, a paperback, and half a dozen papers to the floor. The papers scattered and Alex's place in the book was lost, but it was the breaking of the wineglass that scared the dog—or perhaps, Alex thought later, it was his shout of dismay that made Rusty cower and pee on the carpet.

Chase, awakened by the commotion, came in looking scared enough to pee on the carpet, too, Alex thought.

"Rusty and I just startled each other," Alex said. "Careful where you step in here, there's broken glass."

"I'll clean it up—the carpet, too. I'm sorry, I just thought he wanted out of my—I mean, *your*—bedroom. I should have taken him outside. I'm sorry!"

"It's okay," Alex said. "Nothing to get upset over. I'll take care of the glass. You get the paper towels, all right? And let Rusty out in case there's more where that came from."

He picked up the biggest pieces of glass and then set a Dustbuster to work on the rest. John came in, looked as if he had a comment to make, and wisely kept it to himself. As Chase scrubbed at the carpet, he said, "Don't you need to get a big vacuum cleaner to do that?"

"Naw," John answered. "This is bachelor living, son. You can do just about anything you need to do with paper towels and a Dustbuster."

"Only because the wineglass was empty. Chase, let's try a little baking soda on your part of the carpet, though. It will keep it from smelling bad."

"Did you smell Rusty?"

"I'm trying not to."

"I mean, his coat."

"No—which is good. I noticed that improvement when he greeted me last night."

"He wants back in," Chase said, and hurried toward the back door.

"You're out of shampoo, by the way," John said, and laughed.

Rusty came back into the living room and greeted each of them with the enthusiasm of one who might have just returned from a long sea voyage—especially letting Alex know that he was ready and willing to let bygones be bygones. Alex noticed that the dog's coat was soft and smelled just like the shampoo he was now out of.

"I'm surprised you were able to get him this clean with one bottle of the stuff," Alex said, and gave John a quelling look when he started to laugh again.

"It wasn't easy," Chase confided. "Uncle John helped me clean out the tub afterward. He washed the towels, too. Twice."

Alex smiled and scratched Rusty between the ears.

"I'll make breakfast," John said. As he made his way past Alex, he murmured, "You tell anyone I did dog laundry and I'll see that you are on disability longer than I am."

Dressing after a shower, Alex saw that Rusty had relieved his boredom during the evening by gnawing on one of his dress shoes. His only pair of dress shoes. He swore under his breath and decided that as soon as he was dressed he would make sure none of his climbing equipment was in range of quadrupeds.

He wouldn't mention it to Chase, he decided. He was puzzled by the boy's reaction when he first walked into the living room this morning. He hadn't done anything to give Chase a fear of him, so what was going on?

He looked at the shoe and sighed. A dog was no minor responsibility, and this one was going to end up being his. Chase would go back to live with Miles and Clarissa, and probably forget all about the dog. John would move back to his own house, and Alex would return home to find fleas in his bed.

Rusty came in then and sat handsomely at his feet.

"You must have been warned out of the kitchen by John."

The dog wagged his tail.

"Are you going to be a pain in my ass?"

Rusty, he would swear, was grinning at him.

He reached down and petted him. At least he was a nice height. He didn't know what he would have done if Chase had wanted to bring home a Chihuahua.

Rusty rubbed against his dark pants, coating the front of them in fur.

"Criminy, yes you are going to be a pain."

But Rusty was cocking his head and then scrambling toward the front of the house. He began barking.

Alex looked at the clock on his dresser. A little early for a barking dog. He hoped his neighbors would bear with him.

Then he heard a knock on the front door—no, more like pounding. The intensity of the dog's bark increased, even as Chase called to it.

Alex came down the hallway. John was frowning, looking from the kitchen. Chase had hold of the dog by now, but over the sound of someone leaning on the doorbell, Rusty was still voicing disapproval. Alex was inclined to agree with him.

He looked out through the view port in the door. The man on the front porch had put on weight and lost some hair since Alex had last seen him, but he would have known him anywhere.

"Shithouse mouse. It's Miles."

He opened the door but did not step aside to let his brother enter, a fact that stymied Miles for a moment.

But only a moment. "Where the fuck is my son?"

Alex heard limping footsteps behind him and glanced to see John coming into the entryway.

"That will be enough of that, Miles," John said in a tone of voice that worked as well now as it had when they were twenty years younger.

Miles ran his hand through his hair. "I'm sorry, John, I didn't realize you were here."

"You knew damned well I was here. You just thought I might not have been close enough to the door to hear you talk like that to your brother."

"Forgive me if I've forgotten the connection," Miles snapped.

"Let's say he's a stranger, then."

"John—" Alex said.

"Let's say he's a stranger," John repeated. "You come to the house of a stranger who has been looking after your boy while you went gallivanting all over the country, and you greet him like that? Who taught you to act like that?"

Miles turned red and muttered, "Sorry," without looking at Alex. Then he fired up again. "But Chase is my son, and I won't have either of you encouraging him to run away from home!"

From behind them, Chase said, "I didn't run away!"

"You stay out of this, you little dumb ass! You've caused me more trouble than you're worth."

"Don't talk to him that way," Alex said.

"You don't get to tell me how to talk to my son." Miles tried to peer over Alex's and John's shoulders, but they were both taller than him. Miles, always competitive, had been unable to triumph in this one area, Alex thought wryly—remembering a period in high school when Miles had tried wearing lifts in his shoes in a hopeless effort to remain taller than his younger brother.

"What are you smiling at?" Miles asked suspiciously.

Alex turned to Chase and said quietly, "Are you all packed up and ready to go home?"

Chase looked miserable, but he answered, "Yes, sir."

"Jesus—'Yes, sir,' " Miles mimicked. "He doesn't talk that way to me!"

"I wonder why?" John asked.

"Go and get your things, then," Alex said to Chase. "I'll keep an eye on Rusty."

Chase hugged the dog, then brought him over to Alex before hurrying back to the bedroom. Alex was just noticing that the dog had a collar that looked a lot like one of his leather belts when Miles said, "Damned if that is not the jankiest-looking dog I have ever seen in my life."

Rusty growled at him.

"Look at it! Skinny and ugly to boot."

Rusty barked—Miles stepped back nervously.

"Dog's a good judge of character," John said.

"You keep giving me grief, John. But is there some reason why Alex has not been able to address a single remark to me?"

Chase came out then and said, "Thank you, Uncle Alex and Uncle John. Good-bye, Rusty."

The boy looked pale, Alex thought. "Come back anytime," he said. "Rusty and I will both be happy to see you."

"Thanks."

He stepped past Miles, who cuffed him on the back of the head as he passed him. Chase cried out in pain, and in the next instant Alex pulled hard at the back of Miles's collar.

"Hold the dog, John," Alex said. By then he had also grabbed Miles's wrist and pulled his arm up hard behind him.

Miles tried to speak but couldn't. Chase turned around.

"Chase, go on to the car," Alex said. "Everything will be fine. Your dad will be there in just a minute."

Alex waited until the limousine driver, who was trying hard to hide his curiosity, let the boy into the backseat.

He then yanked back harder on the collar, so that Miles fought to keep his balance as he was pulled backward into the house. Alex shut the door, then shoved his brother face first hard into it. He pinned him there, and said into his ear, "I am addressing a remark to you now, Miles. You touch that boy in anger just once again—just once—and you'll have to learn sign language, because I will personally kick your nuts in so hard they'll lodge in your ears. You got that?"

"Let go of me!"

"Did you say to let go of Rusty?" John asked innocently.

"No!—No! I didn't even hurt him, for Christ's sake."

"Did that sound like a promise to you, John?"

"Nope. A promise would go something like this: 'You lay a hand on Chase, and I'll beat your ass so hard, it will look like a new moon.'"

Alex laughed. "Oh, damn. I wish I thought you'd need my help to do it."

"All right, all right!" Miles said. "I promise I won't touch him. Let me go!"

Alex released him. Miles straightened his shoulders, then turned back to Alex and smiled coldly. "I'll give your love to Clarissa, Alex."

Alex smiled back. "You mean I get cuts in line?"

He easily blocked Miles's punch, caught him off balance, and landed a blow that doubled Miles over. Alex used the opportunity to open the door and shove him outside.

"You want to get back at me for that," he said, "be a man and come after me, not your kid. I'm holding you to your promise."

He closed and locked the door behind him.

John let the dog go then and said, "I guess you've waited a long time for that one, but I'm sorry it came to this with you two."

"Don't deny me my pleasures. It's been a lousy morning until now. And give Rusty whatever is left of that steak."

"He had that last night."

Alex shook his head. "I'll bet you made his collar, too."

"That belt never looked good on you."

"Now you're the fashion police. Okay, let's go into the kitchen and see what else we can spoil him with."

"All right."

But neither of them moved.

"It's mostly that he belittles him," John said. "I don't think Miles makes a habit of hitting him. Chase would tell me."

"It doesn't need to be a habit. I don't care if I just saw the only time it ever happened."

"I'm with you," John said. "Even if he were only using words—Chase is having a hard time with it. It's just since he's been a teenager. Anybody gets the least little bit angry around him . . . Well, sorry you got dragged into this, and I know I'm the one who dragged you."

"I can get into a fight without any help from you, old fart."

"Yes, well, I never felt so much like an old fart in my life. When I saw him hit that boy, I wanted to grab on to him, too. Between this damned knee and you handing the dog off, I couldn't get to him quick enough."

"You made me laugh at him, and that bothered him a lot more than anything I did with my fists."

John shrugged. They started to walk into the kitchen.

"New moon?" Alex said, and they both started laughing.

4 0

Spooky had looked all through the house. She couldn't find Kit. Finally, in the kitchen, she noticed an envelope addressed to her, tucked under a clean cereal bowl set out on the table. There was also a spoon and a box of disgustingly healthy-looking cereal. Kit should know better than to try to get her to eat that stuff. The last time he had tried to sell her on the benefits of high fiber, she told him to use a plumber's snake if his drain was plugged up, because hers wasn't.

She opened the envelope and frowned as she read the note:

Good morning, Spooky—
Meghan and I have gone to visit an old friend of mine. I'm hoping to talk him into staying with us for a little while. I know you'll like him . . .

"Don't be too sure." She read on.

We should be back by early this afternoon. Meghan wants to know if you'd like to go shopping with her.

"I would rather poke myself in the eye with a sharp stick."

I'm sorry that I haven't seen much of you since we arrived in California. I know you are unhappy with me. I wish you weren't, but I understand. I hope you will try to be patient for just a little while longer. I do miss you. Kit

That part made her throat feel tight and funny. She took the note over to the kitchen sink and set it on fire. It had just burst into flames when Moriarty came running in and turned the water on it.

He was giving her the evil eye. He was good at it. He didn't look as if he had had much sleep.

"When," he asked, "are you going to grow up?"

"When people stop treating me like a kid!"

"It works the other way around, Spooky."

"You and Kit are keeping secrets from me!"

"This, from someone who won't tell Kit her name?"

"He knows it!"

"Not because you've said it to him. What makes you think you get to have all the secrets?"

She sat down hard in a chair and crossed her arms. She swung one leg back and forth.

"When have you ever seen a grown-up sit down like that?" Moriarty asked.

"Fuck you!"

"Oh, you're gonna make me cry if you're not careful."

She was silent. She stopped kicking, though.

He sat down next to her. "What's the trouble, brat?"

She thought it would serve him right if she didn't answer, then wondered if only kids said "serve him right." She eyed him for a minute more before staring at the end of her bare foot. To her big toe, she said, "He doesn't care about me anymore. He leaves me alone all day in this stupid house while he goes out with *Meghan*." She looked up at Moriarty and said, "That's the trouble."

"How much of his lifetime do you suppose he ought to spend thinking only about you?"

"He doesn't think about me at all."

He waited.

"Not since Meghan."

"Meghan was before you, kiddo."

"What do you mean?" she asked, frowning.

He hesitated, then said, "Do you think Kit is lonely?"

"No. He's got me. We're a family."

"He needs you, there's no doubt about that."

"That's what you think."

"Yes, it is what I think. I also believe that he might need other people to be part of his life, in some other way."

"What other way?"

"Well, you keep thinking about that. And think about Kit, and not just about what Spooky likes and Spooky wants. Except for this—want me to take you out for an evil breakfast?"

She brightened for a moment, then said, "You're tired."

He raised his brows. "I'll be damned, you sounded like a grown-up just then."

She smiled at him.

"I'll take you out to breakfast, and then I'll come home and sleep—but only if you keep your promise to Kit about the fires."

"That was yesterday."

"Was there an expiration date on it?"

"No," she sighed. "Okay. I'll put some shoes on."

He drove her to a little place near Decker Road that he was fond of, and they had a leisurely breakfast that seemed to revive her spirits. He was paying the bill when she told him she needed to use the restroom. He asked her to wait a minute, but she said she couldn't, so he watched her walk back to the door leading to it. He went back to their table to leave a tip, then gave in to a chill along the nape of his neck that he trusted as completely as he hated it, and ran toward the door that led to the hallway. He shoved it open, then called through the one to the women's room.

"Spooky?"

"In use!" came a woman's voice.

He threw his shoulder against the door, and it easily gave way. An indignant woman sat on the single toilet seat with her pantyhose down. She shouted, "What on earth! A little privacy, if you don't mind!"

"You see a girl—or a boy in here?"

"Which?" she asked, then quickly said, "Neither! Now for God's sake—"

But he had turned to the other side of the hallway, and was shoving the men's room door open. No one.

He ran out the back door and into the alley behind the restaurant. He saw a white van turning on to the small street that led to Pacific Coast Highway.

He was in the pickup truck and out of the parking lot in less than thirty seconds. He could see the van ahead weaving in and out of traffic. Keeping his eyes on it, he used his hands-free cell phone to call the house as he closed the distance.

He ordered his security team to send two men for backup. Years of training and experience didn't fail him—his voice was calm as he said, "White van. License plate—hang on—4GHR302. Wait—just went up some little dirt road. Yes, I'm following. Call Kit. Tell him—no, just call him right now. Yes . . . I'm staying on . . ." But as he turned up the road, the cell phone signal was lost. "Damn!"

He heard the sound of a motorcycle pulling out of a dirt driveway and saw the weapon raised. He turned the wheel just in time to keep the bullet from finding its intended mark. It only grazed his forehead, which still hurt like hell's own fire. His forehead began to bleed. The maneuver had nearly managed to knock the cyclist over, but the biker regained his balance. Moriarty's truck fishtailed, but he recovered control. They twisted and turned higher into the canyon, the dust cloud from the van obscuring the winding road. He glanced in the side-view mirror and saw the biker raising the weapon again, just as the van went around a sharp bend ahead of him. His stomach dropped—he didn't think the van would hold the road. He slowed for the turn, but was still going so fast he wasn't sure he'd make it himself. He did, only to discover the van had come to a sudden stop.

If he hit it going this fast with a truck this big, he might knock the van down the embankment and kill Spooky. So he swerved, just as another shot blew a hole in the rear window. As the truck went through a guardrail, the airbag deployed, briefly blocking all sight and nearly making him scream as it hit his raw forehead. He held on to consciousness as long as he could before one of thousands of bone-jarring jolts took it from him, a few long seconds before the truck finally came to a halt at the bottom of a deep ravine.

41

"Alex!" Hogan called to him as soon as he came through the front door. "Just getting ready to page you. Captain wants to meet with us—now."

Alex had just spent more than a hundred dollars on Chase's free dog and dropped off a dog bed, leash, collar, food, dishes, brush, biscuits, and more at home before heading out for work. He had taken his climbing equipment and put it in the trunk of the car—out of canine reach. Although no one would have expected him in too early after his long night, he still hoped Hogan didn't want to know what he had been doing this morning. "What's up?" he asked.

"All kinds of craziness. You know where Ciara is?"

"Home, I assume. Or on her way in. You call her?"

"I called her home, her cell, and her pager—didn't get an answer."

"I'll try her pager again," he said, and used his cell phone to dial it as he walked with Hogan toward Nelson's office.

"By the way," Hogan said, "we located the Whitfields. They're in Italy now, as it turns out. They didn't seem too broken up. Asked us to have their son's lawyer call them about his estate. Can you believe it?"

Just as they reached Captain Nelson's door, Alex's phone rang and he saw Ciara's name on the caller ID display. "Meet you inside," he said to Hogan, who didn't seem pleased but moved on.

"Alex? God . . . a morning . . . having." There was a static hum between words. He could hear traffic in the background.

"We've got a bad connection, Ciara."

"Sorry . . . know . . . Hogan wants?"

"A meeting with Nelson."

"Shit."

"Well, that came through nice and clear. Must have reached a new cell. What's going on?"

There was a long silence, and for a moment, he thought he might have lost the connection. But then, in a strained voice, she said, "Laney had some kind of seizure last night."

He thought she might be crying. Fearing the answer, he asked, "Is she okay?"

She seemed to regain her composure. "I think so, but I want to be sure. She hasn't had one in over two years, so I'm worried. I'm taking her to the doctor now—he promised to see her right away. Can you cover for me there?"

"I'll do what I can. Mind if I tell them you've had a family emergency?"

She hesitated, then said, "No, I guess not. I probably should have told them about my situation a long time ago, but . . ." Again, she seemed to struggle for control. After a moment, she said, "I just didn't want to seem like a whiner, you know what I mean?"

"They aren't as heartless a bunch of SOBs as they pretend to be around here, Ciara. Call me and let me know how she's doing, okay?"

"Thanks, Alex."

When he walked into Nelson's office, though, there was a pale, thin stranger seated in the chair next to Lieutenant Hogan. He was a man of medium height with sandy hair and a long head that made his face a nearly perfect oval. Within that oval his features were plain, with the exception of a pair of eyebrows that sat bristling and white above blue eyes. He was dressed in a cheap suit that didn't hang well on his bony shoulders. He was sitting with his arms folded over his chest, and his untamed brows were drawn together as he studied Alex with apparent disfavor.

"Alex," Captain Nelson said, "this is Agent Hayden Moore of the FBI. He's replacing David Hamilton on the task force." Listening to Nelson's tone, watching his expression, Alex heard the unspoken message: *Don't ask.*

Alex noticed that Moore kept his arms folded, so he didn't extend his own hand.

"I understand the suspects have taken themselves out of commission,"

Moore said. "And that this is all basically wrapped up. Until we were brought in and could provide you with that New Mexico connection, you seem to have always been more than a few steps behind them—so they've probably saved us all an inordinate amount of trouble and expense."

Alex said, "We're still not sure—"

"Good point, Alex," Nelson interrupted. "We're still not sure how much of your fugitives list is dead, but if they've left them in our jurisdiction, I guess that will be our work, not yours."

Moore's face settled back into a frown.

"So," Nelson said, standing and extending his hand in a clear signal that the meeting was over, "we want to thank the FBI for their cooperation and help, and we'll make sure any reports are sent to your attention. Please give our best regards to Agent Hamilton. We enjoyed working with him."

Moore turned a pink color. Whether it was due to the fact that he was getting the bum's rush or the captain's slight emphasis on the word *him*, Alex didn't know.

"Hold on!" he said. "If anyone else on that fugitives list shows up murdered—"

"Detective Brandon will notify you immediately. Stay a moment, please, Alex. Dan, on the way out, will you please make sure Agent Moore is given copies of the lab's reports from Catalina and Lakewood? I don't think we had enough time to get those to Agent Hamilton."

Moore gave in at that point and left with the lieutenant.

Nelson invited Alex to take a seat, then said, "We were informed this morning that Agent Hamilton has taken a leave of absence—for reasons unspecified. Back to our usual cordial relations with the FBI—they aren't telling us anything. But judging from the amount of bluster I got off of Moore this morning, something about Hamilton's leave obviously makes them extremely uncomfortable. How well did you get to know him?"

"Not all that well. He's from here originally, went to USC, and probably has money that isn't coming from his FBI paycheck."

"On the take?"

"I doubt it. He was too open about it—wore expensive clothing, drove a Jag." He paused, then added, "He spent more time with Ciara. They got along well. If he confided anything to anyone in the department, it was to her."

"Where is Ciara this morning?"

Alex hesitated. Even though Ciara had agreed that the captain should be told about Laney, he felt that it was her place, not his, to do so. Thinking of her fear of being pitied, though, he decided that perhaps it would be easier on both Ciara and the captain if he did the telling. And much better to face the awkwardness of talking about Ciara's difficulties, than to have Nelson think she was shirking her duties or having problems with Alex. So he told the captain about Ciara's sister and Ciara's dedication to her.

Nelson considered this in silence for a time, then said, "I wish I had known this a year or two ago. I should have suspected there was some stress on her from outside the job. But other than the problems she had in getting along with her partners, she's been one of the best we've had. Her clearance rate is above average. I had no idea that she was also coping with these personal pressures all this time."

"For the most part, I don't think she sees it as pressure. I think it demands a lot of her energy, but I don't think she sees her care of Laney as a burden. There are just going to be times, like this morning, when she might need the department to cut her a little slack. She was reluctant to have me mention it even then."

"I'll talk to her more about it when she comes in. Are you going to be able to handle winding this up if she ends up needing a few days off?"

"I'm not so sure it is winding up."

"What's that supposed to mean?"

"I'm not sure all the participants ended up dead on Mulholland Highway last night. I think we need to do a lot more work before we know with any certainty that those two were the only ones involved. And I hope the department will be careful not to book a band for the victory dance just yet."

"Temper our remarks to the public, you mean?" Nelson said. "Sheriff Dwyer is anxious to issue a statement, you know."

"What will it cost us to be cautious?"

"Public confidence."

"Think we'll recover that confidence if he announces this is all over and it's not?"

"True . . ."

"Think of it this way. If any of the remaining fugitives are still alive, they must feel they are in danger, and may surrender, believing themselves safer with us than in the hands of the so-called Exterminators."

"That reporter has a lot to answer for, doesn't she?"

Alex shrugged. "If Ontora hadn't made them out to be heroes, someone else would have."

"Hmm. I suppose so. I'll talk to the sheriff. What do you have in mind for the task force now?"

"We need to find out more about the two men in the Maserati—Whitfield and Addison. We need the lab to take a careful look at that suicide scene, because not everything adds up. I'm not ready to definitely say it was suicide. Even if it is what it appears to be, how are the two of them connected to each other? Where did they meet, how did they plan this? Can we link them to the crime scenes? Who paid to have that special cell built in Del Aire? What was Whitfield doing in New Mexico?"

"Okay—"

"That's not all. We need to know what made Hamilton stop having fun after we found Frederick Whitfield IV's wallet—"

"You're right," Nelson said. "He got kind of quiet after that, didn't he?"

"Yes. Never showed up at the suicide scene, either. I want to figure out who our benefactor is, too. If we hadn't received that wallet yesterday, in all likelihood, we wouldn't have connected Whitfield with these cases. So who helped us out, and why?"

"All right," Nelson said. "The full task force is still active, then—but keep me informed all along the way." He paused, then said, "I have a friend at USC. Maybe I'll give him a call, see if he can tell me anything about Hamilton."

"Thanks. Anything would be helpful, but especially anything that connects him to Whitfield. I've wondered all along how they learned certain things about investigations—just in terms of not leaving evidence, for starters. But also how they narrowed down the locations of the fugitives. They could have done some of that narrowing by working with what Whitfield learned from the *Crimesolvers* show, but shows like that get hundreds of tips, so I can't help thinking that someone with investigative experience looked at the possibilities and showed them which tips were most likely to pan out."

Hogan returned then, looking more excited than Alex thought he would after spending time with Moore. "Frederick Whitfield IV's attorney just called—a Mr. Blaine. Wanted to make sure the news reports were true, because Whitfield insisted on making out a new will yesterday."

Nelson looked at Alex. "A twenty-five-year-old thinking he might die? Sounds like he was planning to end his own life after all, Alex."

"Or knew that someone else might end it. Maybe he had a near-miss with one of the fugitives. Maybe he thought we might catch him. We've had information leaks on these cases—to the *Times* and others. If he learned that we were looking for someone using Eric Grady's ID, maybe he was worried that his days were numbered." He turned to Hogan. "Did this lawyer give you any other details?"

"Yes," Hogan said. "Whitfield was filthy rich—inherited a bundle from his grandmother. Remember the parents in Italy? Guess they are really steamed. The will leaves it all to a woman in Albuquerque, New Mexico." He looked at his notes. "Vanessa . . . P-r-z-b-y-s-l-a-w. No relation to Whitfield. He told the lawyer that she was his . . . I think the word the lawyer said was something like 'boyakina.' He said he didn't know what it meant, but he thought it might be some new slang term for 'girlfriend.' He contacted her early this morning, and said she was pretty upset. You want her number?"

"Yes, thanks. I'll try to get in touch with her," Alex said. He wrote the number, frowning as Hogan read it off. It seemed familiar—then he remembered why. "I think this is the one that we found in his wallet."

He was on his way back to his desk when a call came through saying that two bodies had been discovered in a warehouse in Palmdale—one of the victims appeared to be Farid Atvar, another name on the fugitives list. There were similarities to the scene in Del Aire.

"Check to see if the other victim matches a description for Julio Santos," Alex said. "He was another of Bernardo Adrianos's bodyguards—worked in a team with the man we found in Del Aire last night."

Alex was talking to Hogan about whether or not he should drive out there himself or send another team when another call came in—two more semi-frozen bodies had been found—not far from Seminole Hot Springs.

"I thought it was weird before," Enrique Marquez said. "This time, it's downright freaky. One body belongs to Todd Vicker."

"The arsonist. Killed seventy-three people when he set a nightclub on fire."

"Yes, because his girlfriend was in there dancing with another man. Apparently our Exterminators didn't think that was such a bad thing to do, because there's hardly a scratch on him, if you look below his neck. The neck isn't as pretty—he was garroted. The number two has been drawn on his chest—with a black felt-tip pen, from the looks of things. He's really frozen stiff, as if he's been in cold storage for a while."

"And the other one?"

"Just fucking bizarre, Alex. Wait until you hear the difference. I'll start with the easy part—not fully frozen. Mr. Defrost here is believed to be Jerry Knox, a.k.a. Gerald Majors and half a dozen other aliases."

"Producer of snuff films with young boys," Alex said.

"Yeah, well, first time I heard about this bastard I hoped his life was short, but it looks as if old Jerry here might have been wishing the same thing for himself at the end. He has a huge number five tattooed on his chest—tattooed, not just drawn on him. That had to take some time. They obviously tortured him—and it looks as if they took their time there, too."

"Beyond what we've seen so far?"

"Oh yes. But let me finish, because there's more. Or in his case, less. He's missing his tackle. Totally cut off, and not with the body. So even if he comes back as a zombie, he won't be raping any more little boys. And unless he was already dead when they shoved the critters up his nose and mouth, we may have L.A. County's first death by grasshopper asphyxiation."

"By what?"

"Grasshoppers. Little ones. I don't want to guess how many. Got the forensic entomologist on his way. Should make a nice change for him from studying maggots, but better him than me."

"Jesus. Make sure Shay Wilder sees the photos from this one," Alex said. "Get a messenger to take them down to him today."

"Wait—I'm not done. There's something for you here."

Alex felt the hair on his neck rise. "For me?"

"A videotape. Label on it says 'Deliver Immediately to Detective Alex Brandon, L.A. County Sheriff's Department Homicide Bureau.'"

Alex found himself unsettled by the news that the killers had singled him out as the one to receive the tape. He tried to force himself to consider everything he had learned this morning in a dispassionate, logical way, but his thoughts kept returning to Shay Wilder's warnings that the killers had a personal score to settle with him. After almost twenty years in law enforcement, he knew he had made some formidable enemies. But who would choose to come after him in this particular way?

Before he could leave for Seminole Hot Springs, he got a call from the firearms evidence lab, telling him that they had a match—the gun found in Frederick Whitfield IV's hand had fired the bullets that killed the two victims in Del Aire.

"You don't sound as happy about it as I thought you would," Alex said. "What's wrong?"

"Nothing is easy about these cases. The pathologist wants you to give her a call. I'll let her explain it."

He called the pathologist.

"Don't think we're looking at a suicide here," she said, "unless dead men can take their gloves off."

"What do you mean?"

"The victim had a pair of black leather gloves in his pocket. The lab found GSR—gunshot residue—on one of them, but we didn't find a thing on the hands. Since you say the firearms guys found a match with your Del Aire scene, I'd say Whitfield was the shooter there, then someone else used that same weapon to shoot him up on Mulholland. Sorry if I've ruined your day."

"No, I've had doubts about that scene, so you've just confirmed some suspicions. What about the other one—Morgan Addison?"

"Another problem with the suicide theory there," she said, "but not one that's impossible to explain away. He had minute traces of GSR on the surfaces of *both* hands. Looked to me as if he might have been wringing his hands after he fired a weapon. If he had been the only victim, you might have been able to say he shot someone, did the hand-wringing, and then shot himself. So, it's not as clear-cut there—except Addison wasn't the shooter in Del Aire, so we don't know if he was out at a shooting range doing target practice or involved in a crime."

"We've got two victims in Palmdale this morning," Alex said. "I have a feeling that when you examine them, some of these questions will be resolved."

"There's a real boom in corpses in this county lately."

"Wait until you hear about what's on its way from Seminole Hot Springs."

"I've heard. With any luck, they'll give me the Palmdale cases and let someone else work with the grasshopper man."

He set the phone at his desk to forward calls to his cell phone, then stopped by Nelson's office to give him an update. When he had finished, Nelson said, "My friend at USC tells me Hamilton grew up in Malibu. You did, too, right?"

"For the most part."

"Did you know his family?"

"No, I can't say that I remember anyone by that name, but he's younger than I am, so we wouldn't have been in school at the same time."

Nelson looked at his notes. "He went to Sedgewick."

42

Malibu, California
Thursday, May 22, 9:00 A.M.

After leaving his uncle Alex's house, Chase rode in the limo with his father to a house in Beverly Hills, to pick up his mom. She had chosen to have breakfast with the friends his parents had traveled with in New York, waiting with them while his dad came to get him.

Chase had expected to be berated during the ride from Manhattan Beach to Beverly Hills, but nothing happened. That had puzzled him, especially since his dad had made sure the window between their seats and the driver stayed up.

In Beverly Hills, Chase watched his dad grow angrier and angrier while his mom kept talking to her friends, taking her sweet time. Chase had seen her do this kind of thing before, and he was certain that she knew how mad his dad was, and that she was enjoying watch him get more and more pissed off. His dad would never take his anger out on her, Chase knew, so he really hated it when she played this game, because he would pay the price.

When they finally got back in the limo, his dad was in an awful mood. Chase knew it was unlikely that his dad would hit him in front of her—although she knew that had happened a couple of times before, she pretended it hadn't—so he waited for his dad to start yelling at him, something his dad felt free to do anytime, anywhere.

Somewhere along Sunset, his dad told him he was grounded for a month for running away. Chase didn't bother arguing with him. Then his dad told this totally bogus version of what had happened at Uncle Alex's house. He claimed that while Chase was getting in the limo, Uncle Alex had insulted her and then assaulted him. Chase watched his mom. She was smiling.

"You find it funny that my brother attacked me?" his dad asked.

"Of course not," she said, and looked out the window. She was still smiling.

Just then, Chase's cell phone rang. A friend called to ask if Chase wanted to go with a group of kids to the place up on Mulholland Highway where those two dudes had offed themselves—the Exterminators. Turns out a girl they went to school with, Sherry, had been dating Morgan Addison, and she also knew Freddy Whitfield. Wasn't that crazy? And a bunch of other people knew Freddy and Morgan. "We're going to go up there and start, like, you know—a little memorial."

"I'm grounded."

Chase was glad of the excuse for a couple of reasons. One was that he knew what Uncle John and Uncle Alex thought of these two dead guys—that they were really no better than any other killers, and maybe worse. He didn't want to be disloyal. The other was that although being grounded wasn't fun, telling a friend you were being punished in this way gave a guy a certain kind of status that Chase was not above enjoying.

"Oh, dude," his friend said, "that sucks. Is it because of stealing the car?"

"No, it's not that. I'm with my folks right now."

"Oh, I get it. I'll try to sneak over there later. Maybe we can talk."

"Thanks, man."

He hung up. He didn't even like that kid all that much, but he appreciated the moral support. Maybe he would even tell him about Rusty. He was thinking this as his father snatched the phone out of his hand.

"Why'd you do that?" Chase asked.

"I'm taking away your phone privileges, that's why."

"So you're making me use the phone at home?" Chase asked. "You get mad if I'm talking to my friends on it. You say I talk too long to them."

"No—you aren't using *any* phone. I think it would do you good to spend time away from some of your friends. No computer time online, in chat rooms, or anything like that. For that matter, I don't want you to sit around talking to your uncle John, either."

"But Dad! No, Dad, please! Uncle John—"

"You heard me."

"Miles . . ." his mother said.

"Don't contradict me, Clarissa! It's not natural for a boy his age to spend so much time with an old man. He needs to develop a better set of associates than the ones he has now."

Chase could see that he had made her really mad. When his mom got mad, she didn't yell or scream or throw a tantrum. She turned cold. It wasn't that she just ignored you. It was more like you weren't even there to be ignored.

By the time they were on Pacific Coast Highway, Chase was staring out the window just like his mom. There was more traffic than usual—a bunch of sheriff's cars and ambulances heading up toward Decker Canyon Road. He would have taken more interest in that, or in the slow speed at which they made their way up the road to the house—behind a van and a motorcycle—but he had started to think about not even being able to talk to anyone. It was one thing to not be able to go anywhere for a month—that was bad. But it was another to be completely isolated, cut off without communication during that time.

He might have waited to see if this would really happen, but as Chase climbed the stairs to his room, his father said, "I'm going to call John and tell him that if they're keeping that dog for you, to just take it to the pound now."

Chase had learned enough from watching his mother to withhold the sort of reaction his dad was looking for, but thoughts of Rusty being put to sleep in a pound horrified him. He knew that Uncle Alex had not really wanted the dog. He had to let them know that no matter what his dad said, he wanted Rusty. He'd take whatever punishment his dad wanted to give him after that.

If he ever came back to receive it.

In a way, by falsely accusing him of it, his dad had been the one to plant the idea in his head of running away. He had thought of it before, of course, but he knew Uncle John, the one person he would have run to, would have encouraged him to return home. He wasn't so sure Uncle Alex would make him go back. Uncle Alex seemed to understand how bad things were now. Maybe he had understood what Chase's dad was like a long time ago, and that's why he no longer had anything to do with his own brother.

His dad hadn't always been this way, Chase thought. It really hadn't started until this past year. When he had asked his mom what made his dad feel angry toward him all the time, her answer hadn't been serious. She had said, "Manhood."

He briefly considered leaving a note but decided against it. To leave a note for someone, you had to have something to say to them.

He took some cash and his ATM card, and left by a side door for the garage. He took out his bike and pushed the remote that opened the front gate. He quickly rode down the drive and out to the winding road that led to Pacific Coast Highway.

He had escaped the house many times before, but somehow this time felt different to him. Before, he had no doubt of coming back. This time, he thought of Sedgewick and of all the other depressing things that were in store for him if he returned.

Perhaps because his mind was on all these other things, he didn't see the van that was just behind him. One moment he was keeping the bike's speed just where it needed to be for the downhill ride, the next, it was wildly accelerating, careening as the van tapped the back tire and he fell hard and skidded against the pavement. He hit his head, not hard enough to pass out, just enough to daze him and make him think—in a spacey kind of way—that Uncle John would be pissed when he heard that he hadn't worn a helmet.

Someone was helping him up, a guy wearing a motorcycle helmet with the visor down. He stood, shaken, and the guy took him toward the van that had hit him. The world started spinning. "I'm going to be sick," he said, but he wasn't.

"We'll take care of you," the motorcycle guy said, and gave him a shot, which he thought was kind of strange, but now Chase could see that it wasn't a van but an ambulance, or something like that, because it already had another patient in it.

He was lying down on a mat, then, next to the other patient. A girl, he realized, but she was dressed like a boy. She lay without moving, except that her eyes briefly fluttered open. There was a bruise on her jaw, and her wrists and ankles were tied.

Why would you tie up a patient? He was feeling more and more drowsy. Nothing made sense.

The motorcycle guy shut the doors and it was dark and they were moving.

Just before he gave in to the unyielding tide that rushed him away from awareness, he wondered who would save Rusty now.

43

LASD Homicide Bureau
Commerce, California
Thursday, May 22, 11:25 A.M.

"I'm on my way out to Seminole Hot Springs," Alex said. "Tell whoever it is—"

"Her name is Vanessa Przbyslaw," the desk sergeant said. "She claims—"

"I'll be right there. Don't let her leave."

He watched her for a moment before approaching her. She was pacing. Her eyes were red and a little puffy, her face a little tear-swollen. But if she had cried earlier, she was past that for now—the look on her face was one of determination and anger. Her arms were folded in the manner of someone who is resisting an urge to strike out at anything that might come his or her way, and her stride was long and sure. Her features were delicate, but there was strength in her, and Alex wondered if Frederick Whitfield IV had been drawn to that quality, too.

He introduced himself and ushered her into an interview room. He gestured toward a seat on the other side of the scuffed wooden table. If he had more time, he would have left her sitting there alone for a while. Instead, using standard interrogation procedures, he sat between her and the door. The concealed camera was already running.

An hour later, he thought the videotape was unlikely to be of use. As strange as her tale was, he believed her. She could also easily account for her movements during the past forty-eight hours. He talked to her long enough to establish that Frederick Whitfield IV could not have been the person who hung the body over the cliffs on the Palos Verdes Peninsula, but learned little more.

"I know you're busy," she said. "That's why I came here before meeting with Mr. Blaine. It's why I came to Los Angeles in the first place. I just don't believe Frederick killed himself, and I want to make sure his murder is investigated. It might be easier for the sheriff's department to call it a suicide, but—"

"I don't believe it was suicide, either," he told her.

She looked bewildered. "But the news—"

"Isn't written by the sheriff's department. We've had doubts from the beginning. Sorry if that takes the wind out of your sails."

She frowned, and he wondered what he had said to upset her.

"Do you know who killed him?" she asked after a moment.

"Not yet. Who were his enemies?"

"I don't know," she said. "Like I said, I didn't even spend twenty-four hours with him."

He thought of how dangerous that one evening might have ended up being.

She seemed to read the look. "I won't say I knew him—I thought he was practically homeless until I got the call from Mr. Blaine. But the side of him I saw—or the side he chose to show me—wasn't cruel. He tried to be slick, tried to put on a Mr. Big Shot act, and it didn't work. By the end of the evening, he was just another lonely guy. I have a hard time believing that he had anything to do with anything as awful as murder, but . . ."

Her voice broke off, and he watched her struggle with her emotions, seeing anger and sadness and disappointment cross her face.

After a moment, she said, "You must see this often. I suppose most criminals have a mother or a sister or a girlfriend who can't believe the person they care about has done anything wrong. I'm sorry."

"I'm sorry he let you down."

She shook her head and said, "He didn't. Not really. Perhaps my story makes me sound cheap to you, but . . . we just took a little comfort in each other. It's not so easy to find, you know?"

"No," he said, "not easy at all."

She looked down at her hands folded on the table before her. When she looked up, it was with calm resolution. "What happened to him is wrong, Detective Brandon. Doesn't anyone care about that?"

"That's why I'm investigating it. I think it's wrong, too."

"But I mean—Mr. Blaine has told me something about his parents. But what about his friends?"

"His friends may be the ones who killed him, Ms. Przbyslaw."

She stared at him for a moment, then said, "If I'm the only one who feels sorry that he died, Detective Brandon, then I suppose it wouldn't matter if I had only known him for five minutes. It should make a difference to someone when a person dies, shouldn't it? What can I do to help you find his killers?"

At his request, she left information on how best to reach her while she was in Los Angeles. "I'll be going home tomorrow afternoon, though."

"With this new wealth," he asked, "are you planning to move?"

"I'm not so sure I'm going to be wealthy. But I'll still be in Albuquerque for a little while yet." She told him about her mother. "I'd never take her from that hospice—she's comfortable there and likes the staff. They tell me it's probably a matter of a few weeks now. It would be cruel to make a change at this stage."

He gave her his card, then said, "I don't think money was the motivation for murder in this case. But with this amount at stake, it would be unwise to ignore it as a possibility. That said, I hope you'll be cautious and report anything unusual both to us and the police in Albuquerque."

She thanked him. She began to leave, then paused in the doorway.

"Detective Brandon, do you know of a place where I can rent a sailboat for the afternoon?"

44

Kit was asleep when he got the call about Moriarty and Spooky. Meghan was driving—later, he was thankful for that—and Gabe was with them, hidden in the back of the Jeep. They were on the freeway, near Riverside, and he was in the passenger seat, dreaming of one of Jerome's victims, the one who had tried to comfort him. In his dream, she was escaping.

The cell phone rang and he came fully awake, immediately knowing something was wrong.

He was told that Moriarty's team was scrambling to learn what had happened, while still leaving some men to guard the house. They would do all they could to keep Kit's name out of this, but if at some point he wanted to bring law enforcement in to look for Spooky, that might not be possible.

Kit knew he need not worry about the security team's coverage, even if Moriarty was not there to lead them. Still, the fact that they had lost contact with Moriarty made Kit fear for both Spooky's and Moriarty's lives.

The rest of the drive was nearly unbearable.

Kit took out his rabbit's foot, stared at it for a moment, then put it away.

Gabe, who sat on the floor of the backseat of the Jeep, concealed from view beneath a blanket, tried to offer encouragement but grew quiet when Kit seemed not to respond.

Meghan turned on the radio to a news station.

". . . gruesome discovery in the Santa Monica Mountains brings the total count to eight. Sources close to the investigation speculate that the remaining two fugitives—Wesley Macon Sloan and Gabriel Cuthbert Taggert—are also dead."

"Death might be best," Gabe said, "now that everyone knows my horrible middle name."

"Gabe!" Meghan said in exasperation. "How can you joke at a time like this?"

"It's okay," Kit said. "Moriarty . . . Moriarty always makes jokes when he's in trouble, too. And he hates his first name so much, he won't let me use it."

"What is it?" Meghan asked.

"Percy," Kit said, and heard Gabe give a bark of laughter.

The news announcer went on to say that nearly one hundred people had gathered at the place on Mulholland Highway where Morgan Addison and Frederick Whitfield IV, the two young men believed to have been the so-called Exterminators, were found dead.

A young woman was asked why she was placing flowers there. "I didn't know them at all," she said. "But I admired them. In less than a week, they got rid of the worst criminals in our country. I think it's really sad that they ended their lives before we could show them our appreciation for all they did."

"Turn it off," Kit said.

But just then, Detective Alex Brandon—intercepted by a reporter as he was leaving the Sheriff's Homicide Bureau—was asked to comment on whether Morgan and Whitfield should be considered heroes.

"If it's proved that they committed these crimes," he said, "definitely not. People should remember that those on the fugitives list are suspects—not convicted criminals." He paused, then added, "Let me put it this way. If you were accused of committing a crime, would you want us to let your innocence be decided by a jury or by vigilantes who torture and maim their captives?"

Meghan lowered the volume of the radio. "He's the one you want Gabe to surrender to, right?"

"If we can make sure everyone will be safe, yes."

"Kit, turn me over to him now," Gabe said. "If Everett knows I'm not with you, he has no reason to keep Spooky and Moriarty."

"That's one of the things I'm afraid of," Kit said.

The phone rang again. The team had found Moriarty and the pickup truck. No sign of Spooky.

Moriarty was taken by helicopter to the UCLA Medical Center. Spooky had vanished. The license plate Moriarty had read to his team was found near the place where Moriarty's truck had gone off the road—it was a stolen plate.

Kit arrived at UCLA after dropping off Gabe and Meghan in Malibu. Meghan had wanted to come with him, but he had seen a glint in Gabe's eyes that made him fear his friend would do something foolish, so he asked her to stay with her brother. To Gabe, he said, "Please don't think you are Everett's sole target. He wants to get to me, too, and maybe Meghan most of all."

"Give me something to do, then," Gabe had pleaded.

Kit thought for a moment, then called one of Moriarty's team members into the room and asked him to show Gabe and Meghan all the information Moriarty and Kit had gathered on Everett and Cameron, and on the cases so far.

"Look it over, see if you can see anything I've missed," Kit said to Gabe.

"Meghan might be good at that kind of thing, but I'm not—"

"You're not giving yourself enough credit," Kit said. "I've never understood why you want people to think you're a brainless clown. You aren't."

"He's right, Gabe," Meghan said quietly.

Gabe turned red. "Might as well try this, then. Kit never laughs at my jokes anyway."

"Because I know why you tell them," Kit said, and left.

They finally let Kit into Moriarty's room. Kit told them he was Moriarty's son, so that he would be allowed to learn more about his condition, but as he sat waiting for him to come out of surgery, he realized that Moriarty had, more than anyone else, been the father Kit had longed for as a child. No one other than Elizabeth Logan had done more to gently guide him away from the disastrous paths his childhood might have set him upon; no one had protected him, in every sense, as well as Moriarty had. It was Moriarty, he knew, who had convinced Elizabeth that he should be allowed to keep his dog. For that alone, he would have remained devoted to Moriarty for life.

Knowing he could not do more than Moriarty's staff could to find Spooky, he had decided to wait at the hospital. Each minute of that waiting time was spent alternately between willing Moriarty to survive and thinking of what might be done to a thirteen-year-old girl by people like Cameron and Everett.

A doctor came out and spoke kindly to him, understanding that in his first rush of emotion after hearing the words "through the surgery fine" and "painful injuries, but unlikely to be life threatening," he could not really take in any other information.

Moriarty was not lost to him.

"He's incredibly lucky," the doctor said, which got Kit's attention.

"Lucky?"

"Yes. He's pretty banged up, but all things considered—"

"Banged up?"

"He's broken some ribs and his right wrist, and there are some fairly serious fractures of the right leg. That's what concerns me most. He's got a concussion, but we didn't see any skull fractures or more serious head injuries, although he's scraped and bruised. A few bad cuts. But to come through a ride down a ravine without worse injuries is pretty amazing. I think the seatbelt and airbag must have helped. And getting helped as quickly as he did probably saved his life—the bleeding might have caused problems—so he owes a lot to those people who found him. Best of all, they knew just what to do for him."

"That's what I was told by the nurse."

"I think one of them must have had some kind of medical training. And your dad appears to have been in excellent physical condition before the accident."

"Yes," Kit said, "Dad's something of an exercise nut." The word *dad* sounded strange to him, but the doctor didn't seem to suspect anything.

"Well, that will help with his recovery, if he doesn't get too impatient. He should be in his room in about another fifteen minutes. You can go up to the fourth floor and they'll let you know his room number at the nurses' station. He's had a head injury, and those often make people seem unlike themselves. He may be more emotional than usual. He's going to need rest, so—"

"I won't keep him awake," Kit said quickly. "I—I just need to see him."

He called the house to ask if someone could be spared to guard Moriarty and was told they already made arrangements—one of their men was on his way.

A nurse told him that Moriarty was in room 403.

He felt a little better. The numbers added up to seven.

He had tried to brace himself for Moriarty's appearance. It didn't help. Moriarty had always seemed invincible to him. Once in a while he might come back from an assignment with a bruise or stitches, but nothing more. Kit was not ready to see him this battered or still.

He sat down next to him. He took the little tortoise out, then remembered his *milagros*. He sorted through the ones he had with him and found a hand and a leg. He saw the stitches that closed a gash near Moriarty's left eye and chose an eye *milagro* as well. Three was a good number. A nurse gave him a piece of tape. He gently attached the *milagros* to the cast on Moriarty's leg. He had thought of pinning them to the hospital gown, but he was afraid they might be lost if the gown was changed.

Once this task was finished, he began to pace—anger and helplessness ruling in one direction, fear and restlessness in the other.

A man looked into the room and said, " 'And, as in uffish thought he stood . . .' "

Kit nodded.

The man looked at Moriarty with concern.

"He'll be okay," Kit said, trying to convince himself.

"Yes, sir, he will." He left to stand guard outside the door.

Kit turned back to see Moriarty's eyes open. "Kit?" he said through swollen lips. He looked confused.

Kit hurried over to him. "You're going to be okay," he said, with more conviction than he had felt when he had said the same thing to the bodyguard. "You're at UCLA Medical Center. You were in an accident. But things will be fine now. Don't worry about anything. Just sleep."

Moriarty seemed to consider this. Kit could swear he saw the moment when the memories—whatever ones he had of the accident—came back. "Brat?"

Kit had never wanted to be a good liar as much as he wanted to now, but he couldn't. "Everything will be all right," he said instead.

Moriarty's eyes closed, but his face twisted. "My fault."

"No. You know that isn't true. If she had been with me and this happened, what would you tell me?"

Moriarty didn't answer.

"Your team is looking for her. Do you remember anything about the ones you followed?"

He tried. His frustration was evident.

"Moriarty, please—they'll find her. You shouldn't get upset like this—it's not good for you."

Moriarty was silent for a long time, then he looked at Kit and murmured something.

Kit leaned closer. "I'm sorry—I didn't understand."

"John O'Brien."

Kit was puzzled.

"Brandon."

He remembered then. "Alex Brandon's uncle?"

"He'll help. Tell him I sent you."

His speech was slurred, but Kit understood it. Moriarty was wearing down now. Kit saw him struggle to keep his eyes open. "Okay, I'll go to him. Get some sleep now."

"Jabberwocky . . . tell O'Brien."

"He knows it?"

"Taught me."

"Okay, I'll recite it to him." He wondered if Moriarty was confused. If he approached John O'Brien and started reciting nonsensical poetry to him, he thought he might end up in a psych ward. Still, Moriarty had never given him bad advice, and Kit could certainly use help approaching Alex Brandon.

Kit promised to come back later, after Moriarty had been able to get some sleep. He started to go, then he came back to Moriarty's side. Moriarty's eyes opened again, but he seemed to have trouble focusing.

Holding on to the bed rail, Kit said, "I know you might have trouble re- membering this later, but I'd better warn you anyway—I told them you were my father. I hope that's not—you know—embarrassing to you."

Moriarty reached over with his left hand—the one that wasn't in a cast— and put it lightly on top of Kit's. "Won't ever forget. Always proud of you, Kit."

Forty-five minutes later, Kit was standing on Alex Brandon's doorstep.

He heard a dog barking and said, "Hello, Rusty."

The barks turned to whines. Kit heard a gruff voice say, "Some guard dog you are. Who is it?"

"Mr. O'Brien? I'm—I'm a friend of Moriarty's. He said I should come to you. I need your help."

John O'Brien opened the door. He watched as Rusty gave Kit an enthusias- tic greeting, then said, "I might know someone of that name. I might not. What's your name?"

"Kit Logan."

O'Brien's gaze narrowed.

Kit took a deep breath and said, " ' 'Twas brillig, and the slithy toves . . .' "

"Everyone knows that part," O'Brien interrupted, but Kit could see his in- terest was caught.

> " 'One two! One two! And through and through
> The vorpal blade went snicker-snack!
> He left it dead, and with its head
> He went galumphing back.' "

O'Brien looked at Kit, and at the dog, and back at Kit. "What's Moriarty's first name?"

"Percy. Short for Percival."

"Well, I'll be damned. Come in, boy. Come in."

45

Alex Brandon watched the viewers' faces. He had already seen the tape of Knox's torture and didn't want to watch it any more often than he would have to—that would be often enough.

The room was silent. He glanced at Ciara—she had walked in during one of the worst portions. He thought she looked a little pale.

Maybe that was from coping with Laney's troubles this morning, though. He had managed to get enough information out of Ciara to learn that Laney had indeed suffered another seizure and was now hospitalized. When Alex asked Ciara if she wanted to be with her sister instead of at work, she said, "I've done all I can for her. Now I'm desperate for distraction."

He was sure a tape of two men torturing a third was not what she had in mind.

"If any of you want to watch the rest of this," he said, pressing the stop button, "I'll make sure you can do so. We don't know who the torturers are, but neither are similar in stature to either Morgan Addison or Frederick Whitfield IV. So we've got two other individuals involved in these killings, and maybe more."

"That should work in our favor," Lieutenant Hogan said. "More people involved, more likely that one of them will talk to someone, or confess."

Silence. Alex, too, was unconvinced that any of the Exterminators would talk.

"We've got tattoo specialists who will be comparing the number five on Mr. Majors—or, I should say, Knox—to the work of local tattoo artists and others we have on file. I should mention that there is a possibility he was not killed here in the U.S., however."

FBI Agent Hayden Moore, who had watched the torture of Knox without so much as wincing, sat up at that. "What do you mean?"

"We've had a forensic entomologist look at the grasshoppers that were lodged in Mr. Knox's mouth and nose. He wants more time to study them, but he is almost positive that they are . . ." He looked helplessly at the crime lab's representative to the task force.

"*Melanoplus femurrubrum*," he supplied.

"Thanks. It's a small, red-legged grasshopper found in parts of the Midwest and in Mexico. The grasshoppers found on Knox were roasted and coated in what we are fairly sure is chili powder. That makes Mexico more likely. The entomologist said that in Oaxaca these are commonly caught in communal fields and prepared fresh to be sold in the city each day. A local delicacy called *chapulínes*. But these must have been caught last summer or fall and kept for some reason—perhaps for this."

"So someone in Oaxaca was saving grasshoppers, hoping for this creep to show up again?" Ciara asked.

"Maybe 'expecting' would be a better word," Agent Moore said. "We know from the snuff films that several of Knox's victims were Hispanic. His wife said he had traveled to Mexico, Peru, and Brazil."

"We're asking Mexican authorities to help us to discover if anyone matching Knox's description was in Oaxaca," Alex said. "Do you have identifications on any of the boys who were his victims?"

"A few," Moore said. "We're still working on most of them. I'll try to find out if any members of the known victims' families have traveled to Mexico lately. I'll also ask if the team that has been working on the snuff film cases has any more specific records of Knox's travel."

"Thanks," Alex said.

"When will we have the results of these DNA tests?" the captain asked.

"Our backlog is six months," the crime lab representative said, to a chorus of groans. "We've moved this work up to the front of the list, but it will probably be at least a week before we have anything for you."

Nelson hesitated only slightly before asking, "Could the FBI lab get them to us any faster?"

Agent Moore gave him a brittle smile. "No, the test itself takes a certain amount of time."

Nelson turned back to Alex. "What about the situation in Palmdale?"

"We've got preliminary identification on the two victims," Alex said. He gave them what little information the detectives had been able to gather at the scene. "I haven't been out there personally yet, but we've got a good team there. We've got a warrant on the phone records, just as we do from Del Aire. And we're hoping to discover whether or not the bullets match either of the guns from Mulholland."

"And we're almost sure we can rule out suicides on Mulholland?" Nelson asked.

"Yes, sir."

Agent Moore's cell phone went off. He answered it. "Just a minute," he said to the caller. "Let me get out of earshot." He walked out of the room.

"They want to know if you want them to overnight the FBI etiquette manual to you," Ciara said as the door shut behind him, causing the others to laugh. She got another laugh when she asked Alex in an overly polite manner if she might be excused.

"Alex, what's the plan now?" the captain asked when she had left.

"We need to look for connections—not just between Addison and Whitfield, but between them and any of the fugitives. So far, we're having some difficulties—many of the people who knew them are extremely wealthy, and there are a lot of layers of protection around them. Many are being advised by attorneys not to speak to us without an attorney present—"

Someone made a cash register sound.

Alex smiled. "Maybe. But even without their help, we've learned that Addison and Whitfield went to the same school. And one member of the fugitives list grew up in Malibu—Gabriel Taggert."

"That's the suspect in the killing of that film producer and his family?" Hogan asked.

"Right. I've tried contacting the school, but it's closed for the summer and none of the live-in students are present. Apparently, it's under new ownership and they're doing renovations—there are signs of construction work going on, although I didn't see any crew around when I drove up to the gates today. We're tracking down the owner of the company that bought it. Once we reach him, we'll try to talk to faculty and staff who might have known any of those three former students."

He was interrupted when a sergeant hurried into the room.

"We're getting reports of a surrender by one of the top ten fugitives. Not sure which one it is, but some lawyer has been calling the media to say he represents one of them and that his client will be giving himself up to the FBI in Long Beach."

Alex and the captain exchanged a glance.

"Any idea of the exact location?" Alex asked.

"Not yet."

Alex's cell phone rang and he answered it.

"Alex? It's John—"

"John, let me call you right back. All hell is breaking loose."

He had no sooner hung up, than it rang again.

"I'm following that snake from the FBI," Ciara said.

"Which one?"

"Moore, of course."

"Don't you think he'll spot you?"

"Doesn't matter if he does. When I stepped out into the hall, I heard him taking down directions. Something about one of the fugitives giving himself up."

"My God—" He motioned to Nelson and Hogan, who were about to leave the room. "Where is Agent Moore going?"

"Third and Pine Avenue in Long Beach. I might as well have stayed at home—it's just a few miles from where I live."

"So it is Long Beach. We won't have any jurisdiction there. Hell, I guess all we can do is sit back and watch. You have any idea which fugitive it is?"

"No, didn't catch any names. I'll keep you posted, though. I'm hanging up now—I want to make sure there aren't any last-minute changes in plans."

Alex told Hogan and Nelson about Ciara's pursuit of Moore.

"I'd better give the sheriff a call," Nelson said. "And although they probably heard about this before we did, let's make sure the Long Beach PD knows about this. Alex, maybe you should go down there, too. If the FBI will let us talk to him, at least we can find out what the lure has been for getting them to California."

"Both Taggert and Sloan are Californians, both from the L.A. area. May have been here already. In fact—I was going to pursue this earlier, but we've had so many scenes to process—let me get to my desk. I've got some files there on Taggert and Sloan."

They followed him out. Along the way, they were stopped by Nelson's assistant, who said Sheriff Dwyer was calling. The captain left them to take the call.

"So what is it you're after?" Hogan asked Alex.

"The lawyers. Both Sloan and Taggert have adult criminal records in California. Taggert had a couple of cocaine possession charges. Sloan had a murder conviction before he escaped from prison."

"He's the last of that gang that escaped from Lompoc?"

"Yes. There were four of them—Sloan was the leader. They became trusties, learned the routine for outside deliveries, murdered two guards and a truck driver, and escaped. Three were quickly recaptured, but Sloan managed to slip through the net."

"This is the one with the wife, right?"

"Right. The FBI thinks his wife helped him—she was one of those women who think of a murder trial as a singles bar—sigh over a defendant and start writing love letters to him. The Sloans were married in prison."

"Since she's no longer breathing, I guess they needed the old Graybar Hotel for their love nest. Why do these women do it?"

Alex smiled as he looked through the files on his desk. "Because nice guys are so boring." He found Sloan's and Taggert's files. He started with Taggert's. "Here—I knew I had this somewhere. Taggert used high-priced attorneys— his sister usually posted bail for him, and I imagine she paid the bill for these guys, too."

He then opened Sloan's file. "Sloan had a lawyer in Pasadena, but recently hired a new one to handle appeals work— Yes! He's in Long Beach."

He picked up the phone and called his partner. "Ciara—Sloan's lawyer is Desmond Wrait. He's got offices at One-thirty-three Pine Avenue in Long Beach. Suite six-fifty-six. That may be where Moore is headed."

"Are you sure about that address? It's not—"

"The one Moore gave. So watch for a sudden change of direction."

Everett Corey watched on television as the police in Long Beach did their best to cope with the sudden arrival of a convoy of television trucks and vans, as well as a rapidly increasing number of FBI agents.

He was a little sorry not to be there, but Cameron would handle this perfectly, he knew. He smiled. Cameron was such a funny one—so cold with adults, so protective of children. If it had been up to Everett, they would have stripped both of their prisoners after drugging them, to humiliate them and to make escape less likely—not that it was likely now. But Cameron would not allow it—this is exactly what Cameron's father used to do to him, so that Cameron would come awake bound with wire and naked before the other abuses began.

Cameron was unhappy about including children in their plans. It had taken a lot of convincing, all Everett's skills as a manipulator, to get Cameron to see that this was exactly the pressure they needed to bring to bear on Kit Logan and Alex Brandon.

Everett was pleased that they had managed to capture both hostages. They had been forced to bring their friend in on the action, something Cameron had also objected to, but Cameron was mistrustful by nature. Cameron could hardly object to the outcome—it had worked perfectly.

Everett had considered killing both prisoners while Cameron was gone. He recognized this impulse for what it was—at times, Everett felt a temptation to test Cameron, to see how attached Cameron truly was to him. If Everett did the worst thing imaginable, in Cameron's eyes, would Cameron break away from him? Cameron had a certain dependency on him, but he was something like a pet wolf. Everett would never deceive himself into believing that he had totally tamed Cameron.

Perhaps, he thought, that was why Cameron was alive, and Freddy and Morgan were dead. Neither could have ever presented the challenge Cameron would always be.

He was so absorbed in these thoughts, he nearly missed all the action on television. He knew in advance how most of it would play out, of course.

Of all the fugitives, only Wesley Macon Sloan had been harder to track down than Gabe Taggert. Not long after Sloan had made the FBI list, Everett had contacted Desmond Wrait. Law enforcement officials had already been in touch with him, of course, but although they knew that Wrait would be obliged to encourage his client to surrender, they really couldn't ask much more of Sloan's attorney.

Unlike Everett, they couldn't offer large sums of money, placed in an off-shore account, available to Wrait if he would do nothing more than follow a few simple instructions. Instructions that would not in any way leave Wrait vulnerable to charges of any kind—which would, in all probability, enhance his public image. All this, in addition to relieving him of a client who might not treat his lawyer any better than he had treated his wife.

Really, Everett thought, inflation might have upped the price from forty pieces of silver, but there was no shortage of Judases.

Everett was not a fan of the media, but he enjoyed watching the events unfolding now. Security was at its highest near Pine and Third in Long Beach, where the FBI and most of the media expected Wrait to appear. A few sharper reporters kept an eye on Wrait's offices. But only one television crew—for Channel Three, the station he was watching now—were nearer Long Beach Boulevard and Broadway. Diana Ontora had received a call from Wrait's secretary, tipping her off to the fact that the first glance anyone might get of the fugitive would be in an alley near that corner, where Sloan would be smuggled out of a nearby building and into a waiting car.

"This is Diana Ontora of Channel Three, bringing you exclusive coverage of Wesley Macon Sloan's surrender to federal agents . . ."

• • •

Above the alley, several windows were open on the higher floors of the building just opposite the one Desmond Wrait was leaving now. Wrait talked for a moment with Ontora, then motioned to his client to come out.

Sloan, the most ordinary-looking of men, glanced up nervously at those open windows.

Cameron sighted Wesley Macon Sloan's left eye through the rifle's scope and fired.

Now, he thought, *your appearance is remarkable.*

The Ontora woman was screaming. Cameron quickly fired a couple of shots over the heads of the lawyer and the reporter. That got them to stop looking up. He picked up the shell casings, concealed the weapon under the floorboards, and left. The purchase of the building had been well worth it, he thought. Perhaps someone might someday trace its ownership through several corporations to Everett and Cameron, but he doubted it would lead anyone to suspect him as the sniper.

By the time police and the FBI descended on the place, Cameron was calmly on his way back to Malibu.

If Everett had harmed those children, he thought, he just might give him a remarkable appearance, too.

46

Malibu, California
Thursday, May 22, 4:50 P.M.

Gabriel Taggert drank a cup of good, strong coffee while he watched the news at low volume. His sister slept in her room upstairs. Although the drive to Blue Jay and back had been tiring, she was exhausted, he thought, more by worry than anything. She worried about Spooky, this kid Kit was raising. She worried about Moriarty. She worried about Kit.

But Gabe also knew she worried most about her ne'er-do-well brother.

Guilt had come with his sobriety. He hated to think of all the concern he had caused her over the years. Being around her, seeing that concern on her face, had only heightened his shame.

He stood and walked over to a shelf that had a picture of Spooky on it. She was cute, Gabe thought, but he wondered why she dressed as a boy and cut her hair so short. And what was up with that name?

He was distracted from these thoughts when he realized that on the television, the newscasters were talking about the surrender of Wesley Macon Sloan.

Perhaps he should turn himself in, just as Kit had been urging him to do. If it could be managed, it would certainly defeat Everett.

Then he saw Sloan, standing one moment, looking up at the sky, the next minute collapsing as a series of shots rang out.

Over his own sickening fear came the sound of the reporter's screams. The camera moved unsteadily, capturing oddly angled images of brick walls and pavement for a few seconds as the camera operator tried to move to safety. The reporter was saying, "Oh my God! Oh my God!" over and over.

Gabriel heard a rattling sound and looked down at the cup and saucer in his hands. Trembling, he had sloshed coffee over the rim of the cup. He set the cup and saucer on a nearby table and pressed his palms to his eyes. He felt as though he could not get air into his lungs. He turned off the television and went outside, by the pool.

As he calmed a little, he began to wonder if he should leave the house and find a new hiding place.

But what was the use of hiding? Everett would be sure to come directly after Meghan then. And what would become of Kit and the kid?

He thought about the files Kit had left for him. Law enforcement couldn't help him, he decided. They were always one step behind Everett.

Someone in the FBI must have tipped off Everett about Sloan. The problem, he decided, was that Everett was forcing everyone to play his game, his way. He had been the same way in high school. Kit had been the one to change all that.

Gabe decided that if he surrendered, what happened to Sloan would undoubtedly happen to him. The detective Kit wanted to approach would have to let the FBI know Gabe was giving himself up, and Everett's buddy in the FBI would immediately be telling Cameron where to set up for a clear shot at Gabe's head.

He needed a way to draw Everett out into the open without endangering Meghan or Kit. He needed to be somewhere that would cause Everett to play the game Gabe's way. He needed surprise on his side.

He looked down into the canyon and glimpsed a tall gray structure.

The bell tower at Sedgewick.

He began to make a plan. Did he have the courage, he wondered, to carry it out?

He wrote a long note to Meghan, just in case things didn't work out as he hoped they would, and then crept into her room. He looked down at her as she slept and resisted a sudden, strong temptation to wake her and tell her how afraid he was.

He left the note propped up on the dresser and tiptoed out.

One of Moriarty's staff stopped him once. The guard politely apologized, and said that Mr. Logan had asked him to keep Gabe safe, and that meant keeping him here. Gabe said he understood perfectly and went back inside. After a few minutes, he went into the wing of the house occupied by the guards and borrowed some clothing. A little big, but the camouflage fabric would be helpful.

He was still afraid but found it felt surprisingly good to be doing something, to be acting on his own behalf.

If Moriarty had not been gone, if the guard had not been reduced by men looking for the child, he might not have made it outside the grounds. Even then, anyone else might have had difficulty slipping past the guard that remained. But as a teenager Gabe had spent more time here than he did at home.

Twenty minutes after taking the clothing, he was on his way down the winding canyon, wondering, as he recalled many a morning when he had overslept during high school, if he would still be able to find the shortcut into the grounds of Sedgewick.

4 7

"Don't move," a voice whispered.

Chase felt confused. Some moments passed before he realized he was lying on a bare wooden floor, his wrists and ankles bound. His muscles felt stiff, and he was scraped and bruised. Gradually, he remembered the accident on the road, although the details of that were unclear to him.

He tried to turn toward the voice, but again it said, not unkindly, "Don't move, it will only hurt." He heard the sound of someone scooting along the floor behind him, then a little whimper of pain, quickly suppressed.

"Are you okay?" he asked.

A low, short laugh—then, again in a whisper, "No. I'm as okay as you are. Hold still, and if you have to talk, keep your voice down. I'm going to try to get your hands free."

A girl, he decided.

He felt cool hands touch his own, moving near his wrists. After a moment, she said, "It's no use, my fingers are too numb. Wait a minute."

He heard her moving again. Some moments later, her face was near his hands.

There was the odd sensation of her lips against his wrists, her face and hair touching his lower arms, her breath against his hands, and, in a little while, moisture—her tears? She was using her teeth, he realized, to work at the bindings around his wrists.

It took a long time, but he felt them loosen, and then, seemingly all at once,

he was able to pull free. He heard her roll away. He moved his arms, feeling relief in his shoulders and back, and rolled toward her, his feet still bound. The
room swam for a moment, and he waited for his double vision to clear. As it
did, he got his first look at her.

She had really short hair, which suited her, he thought. He liked her eyes.
They were big and brown beneath dark brows, and there was nothing coy in
the way she studied him with them. She looked bold, as if she'd as soon hit
him as look at him, and somehow that made him feel less afraid. She hadn't
cried after all, he realized, and glancing at his own hands and then back at her
face, saw that the moisture he had felt was her blood—her lips were bleeding
where the wire that had been around his wrists had cut into them.

If a girl—a girl who looked younger than he was—could go through that
without shedding a tear, then he wasn't going to feel sorry for himself, either.

He hurriedly moved his hands—which felt numb, then quickly needle-
pricked by returning circulation—and began fumbling with her bonds. He
rubbed at her hands to help get the blood flowing to them again, then freed
her ankles before freeing his own.

"I'm Chase," he said. "What's your name?"

She hesitated, then said, "Emily. Some people call me Spooky."

He didn't get that weird nickname at all. "Thanks for freeing me, Emily."
He frowned as he looked for a clean corner of his ragged T-shirt, then tore off
a strip of it and offered it to her. "Your lips—I'm sorry—it looks as if that really
hurt."

She shrugged but accepted the cloth.

Every time he moved his head much, the narrow room dipped and swayed.
At one point, it was so severe, he thought he might get sick, but the notion of
doing that in front of this girl was too humiliating—he forced himself to wait
out the sensation. It seemed to subside, and he took that opportunity to try to
take stock of his surroundings. A storage room of some sort, he thought. The
only source of light was a long, narrow window. He stood up and moved toward it on unsteady legs. She followed, dabbing at her mouth with the cloth.
"It's a long way down," she said.

They were high in a tower, it seemed. He couldn't see much of what was
below—trees, mostly. A group of buildings. His vision doubled again, and he
felt another wave of nausea. Dizzily, he moved back from the window.

The place seemed familiar to him, but he wasn't quite sure why. His mind
wasn't working right.

He saw Emily move quietly to the door and try the handle. To his amazement, it was not locked. The door opened a crack. "Be careful!" he warned.

She eased the door farther open but hesitated on the threshold. Beyond was nearly complete darkness. He waited until he was a little steadier on his feet, then moved next to her. He allowed his eyes to adjust to the small amount of light coming from what appeared to be an opening in the ceiling above. He still could not see more than that opening's square edges. He heard pigeons somewhere above it.

He quietly moved out a step, and listened. Nothing.

He looked back at Emily, then stretched a hand along the wall outside the door. He took another step. Emily followed him. He reached back in the darkness and took her hand. He felt her jump a little, but then she held on tight. They edged along the wall.

Suddenly he found himself stepping out into space. Emily must have felt his loss of balance—she pulled back hard. That was all that saved him from falling some unknown distance into the darkness.

He tried to keep the panic out of his voice when he said, "Thanks. I guess we'd better go back."

"Wait here," she whispered, and lay down flat by his feet.

"What are you doing?"

"Getting a match."

"You have matches?"

"Always. I have them hidden in the hem of my jeans."

"Why didn't you light one earlier?"

"I only have three left."

"Wait—if you've only got three, maybe we shouldn't waste one now."

But she lit it anyway. For the brief time that it burned, they saw that they were at one edge of a platform that ran along the walls of a tower—a bell tower, Chase thought. There were rails everywhere but at the place he had nearly fallen from. Wooden stairs led up from the opposite wall, toward the top of the structure, but the stairs leading down and the platform that would have been just below them had been dismantled, leaving a long drop before they resumed again. For all he could tell, they were alone. A set of ropes hung through the center of the tower, out of reach.

The match died out just as his surroundings seemed to whirl before him.

Emily reached into a pocket, found a few coins, and pitched a quarter over the edge. It seemed an eternity before they heard the sound of it striking bottom.

He heard Emily get to her feet. "Are you dizzy?" she asked.

"A little."

She took hold of his hand again and carefully led him back to the storage room.

They sat next to each other. His headache hammered at his skull. He felt as if the pain was derailing his thoughts, keeping him from coming up with any sort of plan.

After a time, he said, "I guess we've been kidnapped."

She nodded. "They took me from a restaurant. Two of them. They gave me some kind of shot. You?"

"Ran me off the road while I was on my bike. I think—I kind of remember someone giving me a shot. I don't know. I hit my head." He rubbed a hand over his scalp and winced as he touched a good-sized knot.

"Why do you think they took us?" she asked.

He felt sleepy and lay back down on the floor. "I don't know."

"Are you going to sleep? How can you sleep at a time like this?"

"Sorry. I can't help it. Maybe I have a concussion." He yawned. "I don't know."

" 'I don't know, I don't know, I don't know . . .' Is that all you can say? Besides, if it's a concussion, you're supposed to stay awake, right?"

"I don't—"

"Know."

He smiled a little. "No. I don't."

"Think! Why did they do this?"

He frowned, trying to concentrate. "Maybe because—maybe because my parents have a lot of money. I don't think my dad will pay to get me back."

She thought this over. "Maybe they think Kit will pay them, too."

"Kit?" He struggled to keep his eyes open.

"My brother. He's my guardian. He's got a lot of money, too." She was silent for a long time. Then she said, "Kit would pay them. He would pay anything."

As he drifted off to sleep, Chase wondered why that made her look as if she might cry after all.

48

Manhattan Beach, California
Thursday, May 22, 6:21 P.M.

"I thought you said he was here."

John O'Brien didn't bother to hide his impatience. "I left that message over an hour ago, Alex. And thank you very much for taking your sweet damned time."

Alex saw Rusty try to hide himself under the coffee table. "You're scaring the dog." He sat on the couch and tried to coax the dog out. Failing that, he said, "Look, I don't know when I've had a more hellacious day. Sorry I didn't get back to you sooner. So tell me what happened. You say an old army buddy of yours vouches for Kit Logan?"

"Never mind all the details of why I trust this kid. You don't have time for that. Enough to say Kit Logan came here, and he's hoping he can trust you. I told him he could. He wants to talk to you about Gabe Taggert. And he thinks his ward has been kidnapped."

Alex sat up straight. "He knows where Taggert is?"

"Yes. He says Taggert's alive, and he wants to make sure he stays that way. Turns out he became good friends with Taggert when they were in school together at Sedgewick."

"Sedgewick . . ."

"But he thinks someone in the sheriff's department or the FBI is working with some old rivals of his. It's complicated, but mainly it boils down to a couple of guys who were good buddies of your supposed suicides up on Mulholland."

"Everett Corey and Cameron Burgess."

"You know their names?"

"While I was taking my 'sweet time'—as you call it—I was going over everything I could lay hands on about Whitfield and Addison. Anyone that knew the two of them very well mentioned that the four of them had been nearly inseparable since high school—at Sedgewick. In fact, even though neither set of parents seemed to pay much attention to their sons, they mentioned those two." He paused, then said, "I know Corey and Burgess."

"How? From living in Malibu?"

"No. When I was first in detectives, I busted Everett Corey on an assault case. He was only about fourteen, but he had nearly killed this other kid. His father tried everything he could to prevent the case from going forward—even a not-so-subtle attempt to bribe me. That nearly got his own ass thrown in jail."

"I remember this one now. Made you twice as determined to see the kid convicted."

"Money still talks, though. He had a good lawyer. That's how he ended up at Sedgewick instead of with the California Youth Authority. His father carried on as if I had ruined the kid's future. He's the one who ruined that kid. That wasn't our last run-in, either. He was a real asshole."

"Oh? You had other problems with him?"

"Later on, I caught another case up there—Everett's friend, Cameron Burgess? His father was found dead. He had been strangled, supposedly by an intruder. I thought both boys might have been involved, but I didn't have much more than a gut feeling to go on. Corey's old man—who never forgave me for arresting his pride and joy the first time—swore both boys had been at his place all night when Burgess died."

"Where's the father now?"

"Looked that up this evening. While I was taking my—"

"Okay, okay—I realize you've been busy."

"Thank you."

Rusty eased out from under the coffee table. Alex stroked his fur absently and said, "Corey Senior was bedridden when Cameron's father was killed, and it was clear that he didn't have much time left then. He died a few years ago—cancer, I guess. Everett Corey has all the money now."

John frowned. "Alex—when we spent that afternoon with Shay Wilder, and he asked me to talk to him for a minute—when you and Ciara were in the car?"

"Yes, I remember."

"He said he thought someone had targeted you personally. From everything Kit Logan told me today, Everett Corey is not exactly the forgiving kind.

Could bear a grudge for years. Used to walk around quoting the old saying about revenge—"

"That it's a dish best served cold?"

"Right."

"His father was like that, too." Alex thought for a moment. "John, you realize Logan went to the same school?"

"Yes." He shrugged.

Alex gave him a look of disbelief. "Don't you get it? There is absolutely no doubt that there is some connection between these killings and that school. Maybe not the school itself, but let me tell you—it has one hell of an alumni association. And this morning I learned that an FBI agent who hasn't been seen for a while is a graduate of the place. Now you tell me another Sedgewick grad has knocked on my front door and claims to be able to show me where the only living fugitive is hiding out—"

John interrupted. "You wonder why I trust him. It's not just that I trust Moriarty's judgment. Rusty likes him, too."

"Rusty? Oh, for Christ's sake—wait a minute. Describe Kit Logan."

"You've met him."

"Years ago. What's he look like now?"

"Good-looking kid. In his twenties, but I guess you know that. About six three, dark hair, light eyes."

"I think I saw him last night—I asked Chase about him. He talked to Chase in the alley, gave him food for Rusty. He was at the crime scene in Del Aire, John. How do you think he got word of that?"

"The scanner?" John said, but he looked uneasy.

"Maybe."

John's brow suddenly cleared. "Wait a minute. He told me he's been trying to find someone in the department he could trust. He said he watched you at a press conference and was the one who tipped you off about Whitfield. Said he left little good-luck pieces for you—or, not exactly that, but some kind of Mexican prayer objects. I forget what he called them."

"*Milagros?*"

"That's it!"

Alex stood and paced. Rusty tried to follow, then abandoned that effort to sit at John's side.

"You know that it's typical for killers to be among the onlookers at a crime scene."

"Yes. But I know Moriarty, Alex, and he would never—not in a million years—team up with someone like that. And no matter what you think about

Logan, you have to be worried about this kid—she's just thirteen, for God's sake."

"Are you sure there is a little girl?"

"What do you mean?"

"He suspects a kidnapping, but he hasn't called the sheriff's station in Malibu?"

"I told you! He's not only housing a fugitive, he thinks there may be someone in the department who's involved in this."

The phone rang.

"Brandon," Alex answered.

"Alex?"

It was a voice he hadn't heard in years. "Hello, Clarissa."

John, who had been petting Rusty, looked up at that.

"Alex," she said, "I'm sorry to disturb you, but I'd like to talk to Chase, if you don't mind."

"I don't mind at all, but he's not here."

"Not there!"

"No. Didn't your current husband tell you? He picked Chase up this morning."

If she heard the word *current*, she ignored it. "I know—I know—but listen, Alex. I'm worried. One of the staff tells me Chase left here hours ago on his bicycle—late this morning."

"Maybe his old man took another swipe at him, like the one he gave him this morning. Ask the staff."

There was a silence, then she said, "I was so sure he'd go to your place. If not to see you or John, at least to be with the dog."

"Hang on." He put a hand over the receiver and said to John, "You hear from Chase this afternoon?"

"No. What's going on?"

He told him what Clarissa had said.

John motioned for the phone. Alex wasn't sorry to hand it over.

"Clarissa?" John said. "Now, don't worry. He probably just got mad and went off to pout somewhere. You know how those Brandon men are. Did you try his cell phone?"

Alex watched John's eyes narrow. John covered the phone, swore fluently, then drew a deep breath. When he spoke again, his voice was remarkably calm. "Tell you what—get the cell phone from Miles and use the call-back feature to reach that kid who called Chase. Chase is probably just with his friends. Meanwhile, we'll keep an eye out for him. What kind of bike was he riding? . . . If he doesn't show up soon, we'll go looking for him, okay? Let me know what you find out."

He hung up.

"Chase decided to run away from home?"

"Hard to tell. Miles took his cell phone from him, but I don't think that's what made him take off. Miles gave him some bullshit about Rusty, saying he'd tell us to take the dog to the pound."

They both looked down at the dog, happily panting up at them.

"No way," Alex said. "And what the hell makes Miles think I'd let him tell me what to do with my—with Chase's dog?"

"Damn straight," John said, for a brief instant looking suspiciously as if he might be amused. "But Chase doesn't know that, does he?"

"I guess not." He shook his head. "You say Kit Logan went back home to Malibu?"

"He left the address for you. When you get to the gates, say 'the frumious Bandersnatch!' "

"What?"

"Don't tell me you've forgotten *Jabberwocky* . . ."

"You are a weird old son of a bitch, you know that? And I think this Logan kid is just about as weird as you are. Why couldn't he wait here for me?"

"When that ninth fugitive got shot right through the eye in front of God, the FBI, and the *L.A. Times*—the last two believing they are the same as the first—Mr. Logan wisely considered the possibility that number ten on that list might be a little freaked out by events and might even need convincing that he could be safely delivered to the L.A. Sheriff's Department. Alex Brandon or no Alex Brandon. Promise me you won't make a liar out of me—I told him he could trust you to hear him out. That's all he's asking."

"Fine, I promise to hear him out, but—"

The phone rang again. John answered this time. "Clarissa? Oh—sorry, Ciara. Yes, he's here."

Alex took the phone. "Hi, Ciara. I was just about to call you. Want to take a ride with me to Malibu?"

49

Malibu, California
Thursday, May 22, 7:20 P.M.

"I can't believe this," Ciara said.

"Sorry, miss," the guard at the gate said.

"Tell Mr. Logan he either lets us both in, or he'll have to meet me out here," Alex said.

The guard relayed the information. After a few moments, he said, "When I open the gate, just follow the drive up to the house."

As they entered the gates, Ciara said, "Was your family's place like this one?"

"No, this one is higher up and has more acreage."

"It's pretty up here."

He looked out. The sun was just above the horizon, about an hour away from setting. The view from the Logan property was spectacular.

"If you lived up here, would you run away from home?" Ciara asked.

He looked over at her. "Are you asking about Chase?"

"No—no, sorry. I meant Serenity Logan."

"When I had her case, I wondered the same thing. From all I could learn, though, it was a mixture of rebellion and addiction. Elizabeth Logan was more patient than most parents would have been—maybe too patient. She felt a lot of guilt about not taking her grandson away from her daughter earlier on."

"Guilt," Ciara said, "is just one more useless luxury."

He could see the tension on her face. "I had no business asking you to come with me," he said. "You've had a worse day than I've had."

"No—I'm glad you asked me. Especially after you told me Logan had been at the crime scene in Del Aire. And 'helping' with the investigation? This gives me the creeps."

They were met by another guard near the house. He guided them to a study. Alex didn't see Kit Logan right away—he wasn't in the room but was standing at the railing of a large deck. A woman was with him. Both wore dark clothing. In other circumstances, they might have been a young couple about to enjoy a sunset. But Alex saw that they were tense, standing close but not touching. The woman's voice was low, speaking in an anxious whisper.

As Alex and Ciara stepped onto the deck, Kit Logan turned toward them, and the woman's whisper stopped. Kit briefly studied Alex, transferred a rabbit's foot from his right hand to his left, then came forward and nervously shook Alex's hand.

"You met me a long time ago," he said.

"Yes, I remember that, Mr. Logan."

"Please—call me Kit."

"Not Christopher?"

Alex saw him flinch. "I prefer Kit," he said.

Alex watched with interest as Kit seemed to quickly assess Ciara—she had hardly moved to fold her arms when he withdrew what might have been an offer to shake her hand as well. Alex thought he looked as relieved as Ciara.

Alex then turned to the woman who had been standing next to Kit and found himself speechless. Kit's companion was gorgeous.

"Do you want me to get a bib for you," Ciara said in low voice, "or are you going to stop drooling on your own?"

She hadn't spoken quietly enough. Alex felt himself turn red with embarrassment and noticed that Kit and the woman seemed embarrassed, too.

"This is Gabe's sister, Meghan Taggert," Kit said, looking between Alex and the woman.

Meghan Taggert straightened her shoulders, then extended a hand to him. During the brief moment he had that hand in his own, Alex felt it tremble. Looking closer at her face, he thought she looked pale and as if she might have been crying earlier—her lips and eyelids were slightly swollen. She was upset now, he thought, but doing her best not to show it. She took a deep breath. "Thanks for meeting with us," she said to him, completely ignoring Ciara. "I'm afraid we have bad news, though."

"Oh?"

"Apparently Gabe saw the news and left here about two hours ago. I have no idea where he is now. We're so worried about—"

"So, you've wasted our time," Ciara interrupted.

Alex shot her a look, then said, "John told me that your ward is also missing, Mr. Logan. Do you have a photograph of her?"

"Yes," he said. "If you'll come with me into the study—"

"Alex," Ciara said, "I left something in the car. Mind if I borrow your keys for a second?"

He looked at her suspiciously but gave them to her.

She walked out. He noticed that a guard followed her, but at a distance.

Kit handed him a photo.

"John led me to believe your ward was a girl."

"She is. Spooky—that's her nickname—Spooky prefers to wear her hair very short."

"Is this recent?"

"Yes. That was taken about two months ago."

"And John said you thought Everett Corey or Cameron Burgess might have taken her?"

"Yes." Kit took the photo back. "I'm sorry to have wasted your time, Detective Brandon."

"Kit—" Meghan said.

"It's no use, Meghan. He doesn't believe us. We're wasting time we could be using to look for them."

"Mr. Logan, I'm sorry if I've given you the wrong impression," Alex said. "But you must realize why I'm feeling a little wary."

"Nine of the ten people on the FBI's Most Wanted list are dead," Kit said. "Perhaps you realize why we're feeling a little wary, too."

"Why trust me in the first place?"

"Your uncle. And the dog."

"The dog?"

"You let your nephew keep a smelly, underfed Labrador retriever that you obviously didn't want."

"So it was you. You were there."

"Yes. I heard the call on the scanner. I was just trying to watch people, to figure out who could be trusted. I was hoping you could be. I remembered you from—" He clutched the rabbit's foot harder. "I remembered you," he said softly.

Alex turned to Meghan. "You were willing to go along with this? Risk your brother's life because I let my nephew keep a dog?"

"I can understand why it seems like an omen to him. And yes, I think he could learn a lot about you just by watching you in that situation."

Alex looked between them.

"You think we're both crazy," Kit said.

"Detective Brandon," she said, "I was willing to give you a chance because I trust Kit's ability to read people. He's better at it than anyone I know. Is he wrong this time?"

"Let's just say I'm not as used to the idea of retrievers as omens as you are. Did your brother leave here on foot or in a car?"

"Don't answer, Meghan," Kit said. "I'm sorry, Detective Brandon, but—"

"I'm sorry, too," Ciara's voice said. They turned to see her standing in the doorway. "Mr. Logan, I'm afraid we'll have to ask you and Ms. Taggert to come in for questioning."

"I'm afraid we'll have to make it another time," Kit said.

"Ciara—"

"You've lost your objectivity, Alex. I know you felt sorry for Mr. Logan and his grandmother all those years ago, but the fact is, these two have knowingly harbored a fugitive wanted for murder. They themselves can be considered accessories to murder. If they aren't going to reveal information regarding Gabe Taggert's whereabouts, they should be placed under arrest."

"Damn it, Ciara—I gave John my word."

"You also took an oath when you were sworn in. You tell me, Alex—are you playing by the rules? Should we have come out here without backup, entered an armed camp—"

"You won't be harmed by my security staff," Kit said.

She ignored him. "Let's call the captain and see what he has to say about what we're doing here, Alex."

She was right, Alex knew. Only John's faith in an army buddy's loyalties and his own belief that someone in law enforcement was helping the killers had made him agree to this in the first place. But even if he had come out here with the whole department at his back, he wouldn't have handled it the way she was. Now, they'd probably never hear a word out of either of these two.

"Is this some kind of good cop, bad cop script?" Meghan asked.

"No," Kit answered, before Alex or Ciara could.

Kit Logan had been true to his word. The guards, though clearly unhappy with this turn of events, had allowed both Kit Logan and Meghan Taggert to be handcuffed and placed in the backseat of the car. "I'll call your lawyer," one of them had said to Kit. "And I'll call Moriarty to tell him what a great pal his friend turned out to be."

"Don't upset Moriarty," Kit had told him. "Spend your time trying to locate Everett Corey. He'll know where Spooky is."

Alex had managed to talk Ciara out of making the young man empty his pockets. Alex had patted him down and told her that if that wasn't good enough, she could drive off without either one of them. While Ciara was busy patting down Meghan Taggert, Alex slipped the rabbit's foot back into Kit Logan's hand. Logan shot him a quick look of gratitude and then withdrew into a world of his own. The childish token of luck, and all the other talismans Logan carried, obviously meant more to him than Alex had originally guessed. Alex told himself he allowed Kit to keep anything that was not a weapon because he was still hoping for cooperation.

Ciara repaid him for his resistance to her tactics by refusing to give him his keys back. "I'm driving. You can count yourself lucky if I make it sound as if arresting them was your idea."

"You can have all the credit," he said as he opened the passenger door. "In fact, I insist on it."

She seemed about to say something to this, but her cell phone rang, and he used the opportunity of her distraction to get into the car and talk to their detainees.

"Listen, I'm sure this can be straightened out quickly, but in the meantime, if there's anything you can tell me that will help me out here, let me know now."

Meghan Taggert said angrily, "If any harm comes to either Gabe or Spooky, it's because you came here with that bitch."

Logan was looking out the window but said, "No, Meghan. I'm sorry I didn't put a better watch on Gabe. I should have known . . ."

"Stop it!" she said. "Not everything bad that happens is your fault! Not now, and not when you were younger, either. Gabe does stupid things all the time. This is just one more. You think I don't know he's a loser?"

"That's not true."

"Look," Alex interrupted, "you two can fight all this out later. Kit, you told your guards to find Corey. Where do you think he might be?"

"He could be anywhere," Kit said. "He was in Germany on Monday. We've just received a report he was in Mexico on Tuesday."

"Mexico?" Alex thought of the grasshoppers. "Where in Mexico?"

"Oaxaca."

"Jesus Christ." Any small doubt he had of Everett Corey's involvement came to an end.

Kit was watching him closely now. "He's probably here—if not in L.A. or Malibu, then not far away. I know it was reported as suicide, but I think

Cameron or Everett killed Freddy and Morgan. I think they took Spooky and tried to kill Moriarty. Gabe is probably safe—he's good at hiding—he always has been."

"That's true," Meghan said, looking at Kit in a way that made Alex wonder if the guy was blind. "That's so true. You really think he's safe, Kit?"

"I hope he is. I think Everett wants to punish you and me more than Gabe or Spooky."

"Why?" Alex asked, but Ciara was getting into the car, and neither of them spoke.

Alex saw that Ciara was looking even more tense. "About your sister?" he asked.

He saw her struggle to keep her composure and felt alarm. He was sorry he had asked the question.

"Yes," she managed to say. "I'm supposed to call back when I get home." She glanced toward the backseat, then said, "I'll tell you more later."

They had reached the bottom of the road when his own cell phone rang. "Brandon."

"Alex?"

"Clarissa? Did you find Chase?"

"Alex . . ." She was crying. "You have to help him, Alex . . ."

"Clarissa, what's happened?"

"I . . . I've had a call from . . . from someone I was seeing. He has Chase, Alex."

He said sharply to Ciara, "Stop the car!"

She pulled over.

"Take a deep breath," he said into the phone. "I know it's hard under the circumstances, but you've got to tell me this as calmly as you can. Who has Chase? What's his name?"

"Everett Corey."

"Corey!"

"He says . . . he says no police . . . no one else. Just you. Not even Miles. I'm sorry, Alex! I'm so damned sorry. But please, Alex—Chase!" He heard her sobbing.

With great effort, he bit back every word of anger. He managed to say, "Where?"

"He owns a school . . ."

He knew the answer even before he asked, "What school?"

"He owns Sedgewick."

He swore. "Corey owns Sedgewick. And you wanted Chase to go there?"

"I didn't know! I didn't know he would do something crazy like this! I swear it. I never meant . . . oh God, I'm so sorry!"

He wanted to tell her that her sorrys weren't worth shit, that they never had been. That for a fling with a man more than ten years her junior, she had let her son fall prey to someone who tortured and killed his captives. Images from the videotape from Oaxaca ran through his mind, and he suddenly felt bile rise in his throat.

And then he remembered what Shay Wilder had said and wondered if maybe it wasn't Clarissa's fault after all. Had Everett Corey used her to try to get to him? Taken Chase for the same reason?

"Alex?"

"I'm here, Clarissa. I'll do what I can."

He hung up. He tried to put his thoughts in order, but for a brief moment, could not. The images of the past week were too fresh, his fears for Chase too well founded. Everett Corey would not be kind to his captives.

He heard from the backseat, "I know Sedgewick."

He turned to see Kit Logan studying him.

"I know Sedgewick," Logan said again. "If your nephew is being held there, then I think Spooky's probably there, too. I'll come with you. I'll help you find them. We'll have about an hour's head start on whatever they have planned for you—they don't know you're already in Malibu. They'll be counting on the fact that it should take you an hour or more to get here from your home in Manhattan Beach."

"Alex—" Ciara began to protest.

"What if it was your sister in there?" Alex asked.

She was silent.

"Drive us closer to the school," he said. "Take a right at the next corner."

As they made the turn, she said, "Do me a favor, hit redial on my phone. I need to tell them I'll be later than I thought."

He felt guilty for forcing her to come along, but Laney would be cared for by experts, while God knew what was happening to Chase and the girl, and maybe Gabe Taggert as well. He tried turning the phone on. It wouldn't work.

"Something's wrong with it," he told her. "I think your battery is dead."

She swore.

"You can borrow mine."

She didn't reply. She was concentrating on the shadowy, curving road, slowing as a set of gates came into view. "Is this it?" she asked.

"No," Kit answered. "Farther up the road. It's at the back of the canyon. Hurry."

She shot him a look of annoyance, but speeded up. Alex glanced at his watch. Only ten minutes had passed since Clarissa's call—it had seemed much longer.

At the last bend before they would be within sight of the school's gates, Alex said, "Stop here. Don't go any closer."

She pulled over. "Alex, think for a minute—you're making a mistake."

Alex didn't answer. He left his phone with her, then got out of the car, even as she continued to protest.

He went around to the door behind the driver and tried to open it. He pounded his fist on the roof of the car. "Unlock it, Ciara!"

He heard the locks go up. He opened the door and helped Kit out. He unhandcuffed him.

Ciara rolled down her window. "Alex, are you nuts?"

He didn't answer.

"I'm calling for backup," she said. "This should be handled by a crisis intervention team, and you know it. We need hostage negotiators—"

"Call them, then!" he snapped. "But I'm not waiting around for the cavalry."

"Do you have a Kevlar vest?" Kit asked. "Cameron is an excellent shot."

Alex swallowed hard, thinking of the shooting in Long Beach. "Open the trunk, Ciara."

She hit the release, and it popped open. He reached beneath the bag that held his climbing gear and found his vest. He held it out to Kit.

"No, you should wear it," Kit said. "He'll probably go for a head shot with me. Or he might try garroting—that's how he killed his father. And my dog."

Alex, hearing nothing but cool deliberation in Kit's voice, stared at him for a moment, wondering what kind of partner he was taking on now. He put the vest on.

"Bring a flashlight, too. And—do you have a first aid kit?"

Alex found each.

Kit looked down at Alex's shoes. Before he said anything, Alex said, "I'll change them. But I can't do anything about the suit."

"Keep the coat buttoned if you can—your white shirt will be easy enough to see as it is. Leave your pager here, please."

"Good point."

"I'm keeping his girlfriend hostage," Ciara called out. "You hear me, Mr. Logan? Anything happens to Alex, Ms. Taggert here is going to meet lethal force while resisting arrest."

"Cut it out, Ciara," Alex said. Still handcuffed, Meghan Taggert moved her elbow to press the control that lowered her own window—Ciara must have released that lock, too. "I'm not his girlfriend," Meghan said. "I want to be, but I'm not."

Kit blushed furiously. He reached out, though, and Alex saw him drop something into the backseat, next to Meghan. The rabbit's foot.

Ciara rolled the windows back up and locked the doors.

Kit took off walking at a rapid pace, and Alex followed, feeling strange wearing his lightweight hiking boots with his suit. Soon, though, he was glad to have them on—the ground was uneven. Logan had a strange way of pausing a little every few steps. Before long, Alex figured out that there were seven steps between each pause.

They avoided the gate, staying out of view from the school, and continued along the wrought-iron fence that fronted the entrance. When they reached a wooded area, Kit found a stick. He began making a quick sketch in the dirt.

Speaking softly as he drew a rough layout of the school, he said, "Sedgewick has been around for a long time. Some of it was built in the nineteen twenties, but most of the buildings are newer than that."

"I thought I saw signs of construction work when I was here earlier."

"You were on the campus?"

"No, just looked through the gates. There's a sign saying it's closed for renovations."

"That's strange." He thought for a moment. "I don't understand why he bought it. Everett always hated Sedgewick. He considered himself above it."

He pointed to a place near the center of the map.

"Here's the bell tower—the tallest building. You can see it from here if you look through the trees. It's in the center of campus. The tower and most of the buildings around it are made of fieldstone. When I was here, enrollment was declining. Only these four buildings were in use." He pointed out buildings close to the tower. "The others were locked up, but most of the boys broke into them at one time or another."

"Keeping their skills up."

"Or learning them. The old crooks train new crooks."

"Like prison."

"In many, many ways," Kit said.

Alex looked up at him.

"Not for me, really . . . I had been in worse situations. And I would have gone to any school as long as I could come home to my grandmother. Gabe and I were day students. Everett, Cameron, Frederick, and Morgan lived on campus."

"But their families lived in Malibu, didn't they? Or close by?"

Kit shrugged. "Their kids weren't in the way if they lived here, were they?"

Alex stared down at the sketch on the ground.

Kit added some buildings at some distance from the others. "These are the old stables. When it was a better school, they used to give riding lessons. No horse has been in any of those stalls for decades. There's a way into the property near there, a gate leading out onto an old trail. We'll go in that way—if you don't object? There are lots of trees and bushes between there and the campus. That will give us some cover, at least until we get to the baseball field." He drew a diamond. "That's out in the open, but if we can get past it, we can start working our way through the buildings while they're still watching for us to come in through the front gate."

"Sounds good—any chance that Everett knows of this back way in?"

"Probably. But my guess is that he'll stick to the central buildings. In school, he never wanted to go into the woods or to hike around. Cameron likes the outdoors, though, so we'll have to watch out for him."

"We're about to lose the last of the light. Can you find your way around this place in the dark?"

"Easily. And before long, if he stays indoors, Everett will probably turn on lights. We'll get a better idea of where he is. I think everything will depend on locating each of them before they see us." He paused. "I talked to your uncle. He says you're good with weapons, and that he taught you to . . . to move quietly. Moriarty taught me that, too. If we can take Cameron out of the picture, things will be easier. I'll do what I can to help bring him into your range."

After a moment, Alex said, "I only have my own weapon with me. And I don't think I can get Ciara to part with hers."

"I wouldn't want her to be without one. She needs to protect Meghan. It's better that you have the gun. I haven't been out to the range much since Spooky came to live with me. Moriarty says . . ." He gave Alex a quick, rueful smile. "Probably, your uncle told him—if you're going to use a gun for self-defense, you need to practice a lot, so that you can fire from any position, and not just in a booth at a firing range, because bad guys seldom stand around like paper targets."

"John verbatim," Alex agreed. "Moriarty taught you self-defense?"

"Yes, I learned a lot from him, and some things from . . . from my life before he found me." He looked away.

"From surviving."

"Yes. And of course, I'm really lucky."

He moved off again before Alex could ask him how anyone who was raised by a drug addict and a serial killer could consider himself lucky.

He closed the distance between them as the last of the light continued to fade. The moon would not be up for several hours, and here, in this small canyon, the sunlight was lost sooner. Kit slowed a little. Alex felt rather than saw the ground level out as they reached the old trail. When they came to the gate in the fence, instead of opening it, Kit crouched down, then bent close to the ground. When he stood again, he whispered to Alex, "Someone has been here already. The grass has been flattened by the gate."

"What do you recommend?"

"Let's listen."

They waited for what seemed an eternity to Alex before Kit climbed agilely over the gate without opening it. Alex did the same. He moved as quietly as possible, but he couldn't see three feet in front of him. He nearly bumped into Kit at one point. Kit took hold of Alex's left hand, put it on his shoulder, and began leading him in that way. Alex adjusted to the seven-step gait as they made their way to the edge of the woods that lay between the stables and the school buildings.

Kit came to a sudden halt. He stood very still. Alex began to feel the hairs on the back of his neck rise and unsnapped his holster. He let go of Kit. A sound came from somewhere up ahead—the snap of twigs.

Someone was moving through the woods.

Almost in the same instant, he heard someone moving behind them as well. Kit heard it, too. He put a hand on Alex's shoulder, and they both moved into a crouching position.

The man behind them was not far away now, and moving closer. If he was trying to move quietly, he wasn't succeeding. Suddenly, the one in front began to move quickly. Behind them, a flashlight came on, aimed toward the man in front, although it failed to reveal anyone. "FBI! Hold it right there!" the one with the flashlight shouted.

Alex knew the voice.

Kit took off running, into the trees. The beam of the flashlight followed him.

Alex stood. "Hamilton!"

But Hamilton was lifting his weapon to fire. Alex ran low and toward him. He dived and hit the FBI man's legs, knocking him over just after the gun went off. *Too late*, Alex thought miserably.

He had knocked the wind out of Hamilton, who had lost his weapon in the fall. Hamilton was looking up at Alex in complete shock.

"You son of a bitch!" Alex said. "Helping these assholes!"

Hamilton came to his feet. "Brandon, you stupid fuck—you just assaulted a federal agent."

"I've just started assaulting a federal agent," he said angrily.

In the next moment, bright light came filtering through the trees. Someone had turned on the baseball field lights. Alex flattened himself to the ground.

Hamilton frowned but stayed on his feet as he looked for his gun. Of course, thought Alex, Hamilton had no need to hide. A Sedgewick graduate, he must be Everett Corey's source of inside information. Any moment now, he'd point out Alex's location.

Hamilton found the gun and had just bent to retrieve it when a loud shot rang out. He made a grunting sound and fell.

Alex felt confused—why had Hamilton been shot? The answer occurred to him almost immediately: for the same reason Whitfield and Addison had been shot.

Alex listened, and not hearing any other sounds, moved on his belly to where the FBI man lay on his side. A large stain was spreading on Hamilton's shoulder and back. "Get out of here," Hamilton whispered.

"Save your breath for the jury," Alex whispered back. He loosened Hamilton's tie and pulled his jacket off, causing Hamilton to groan. He tore the shirt away from the wound. There was a small entry wound, a messy exit at the back, but it had missed Hamilton's heart, lungs, and spine. "You lucked out. If I can stop the bleeding, that is." He found two gauze pads in his first aid kit and applied pressure to the wounds. Hamilton groaned again.

"Keep quiet if you don't want your friends to finish what they started." He found some scissors and tape.

"Friends?" He clenched his teeth, fighting pain. "I'm not with them."

"Whatever you say."

"Explosives," Hamilton gritted out in a low voice. He closed his eyes.

Alex's hands stilled. "What explosives?"

"Maybe . . . timing device . . ." He was mumbling, drifting off.

"Where?" Alex said urgently. "Where?"

"Tower," Hamilton said, then passed out.

Alex did his best to stanch the bleeding. He heard someone moving through the woods, though, and decided to find better cover. He covered Hamilton's white shirt with the ruined dark jacket, both to keep him warmer and to make him less of a target. Alex crept as quietly as he could to heavier brush.

A tall figure clad in dark clothing cautiously emerged from the trees, a man carrying a rifle. He stood still, listening.

Cameron Burgess. He had grown taller and more muscular in the years since his father's death, Alex thought.

A sound came from Alex's right. Cameron turned quickly toward it, rifle raised. Alex took out his own weapon. But Cameron was staying near the trees, and at this distance, Alex wasn't going to chance a shot that would probably only reveal his own location.

Another sound, near the same place. Alex found a stone and threw it hard to his left.

Cameron spun on his heel and faced the place where it had landed.

The baseball field lights went out.

Cameron called out, "Everett?"

There was no answer.

Alex felt a rush of relief. Maybe Hamilton's shot missed Kit after all.

Cameron disappeared into the woods.

Alex followed carefully, doing his best both to keep track of the sounds of Cameron's movements and to avoid giving away his own position.

He could not proceed with any speed—in the darkness, without Kit to guide him, he was afraid of tripping over roots, or cracking his head on low-lying branches. But he wasn't going to use the flashlight and risk making a target of himself.

The sounds in front of him stopped. He waited.

Minutes passed. He thought of the explosives. He thought of Chase being held under Everett Corey's control. He made himself wait.

He heard a rustle of leaves and other sounds and was no longer sure that Cameron was alone. Was Kit nearby? Or had Everett overcome his dislike of the woods?

Suddenly there was a whiplike snap, a startled cry, the sound of what might have been a brief struggle, and then silence. A moment later, he saw light near the place where the sounds had been made. He heard a soft laugh.

He moved cautiously and quietly. He forced away thoughts of Hamilton's talk of explosives, and of the hostages and what might be happening to them.

One thing at a time, he told himself. *Get safely out of these woods.*

The light, he was certain, was nothing more than a lure. A flashlight, its beam pointing up through the tree branches. He considered ignoring it, but the sounds he had heard could only mean that someone was in trouble. Before long, he was near enough to see what the flashlight was illuminating: Kit, hanging upside down.

He appeared to have been caught in a snare, but someone had obviously set to work on him after that. His wrists were bound and dangled below his head—his fingertips were only a few inches above the ground. His ankles were bound together with a second length of rope, tied to the black one, which held him suspended. A piece of silver duct tape covered his mouth. His jaw was swollen, his forehead scraped and bleeding. His eyes were closed, but it seemed to Alex that he was holding them closed, almost as if he were meditating—or perhaps the light bothered him.

Alex looked for Cameron, but saw only darkness between the tree trunks. He listened but heard nothing. Kit opened his eyes, and Alex now wondered if he had been trying to adjust them to see something in the darkness. Alex waited for a chance to attract his attention, but he seemed to be looking up into the trees.

A sound came from above him, too late to provide real warning. Cameron dropped down from a tree branch, landing on Alex's back and shoulders, tackling him hard to the ground, knocking the wind out of him. The sound had given Alex time to tighten his grip on his gun, and he held on to it for dear life. Cameron's first objective would be to disarm him, he thought—then Alex felt the wire wrap painfully around his throat.

Immediately, he couldn't breathe. The wire cut into his windpipe. His ears rang, his vision began to dim. He tried to strike and claw at Cameron with his left hand. He tried to kick, to turn, to free his right arm. He tried to think, fighting his rising panic. He could feel Cameron's hot breath near his right ear. Cameron laughed. Alex switched his gun to his left hand and pulled the trigger.

Cameron give a cry of pain, but there was only an infinitesimal slackening of the garrote. Alex felt consciousness slipping from him. Cameron took Alex's right earlobe into his teeth and bit as he pulled sharply harder on the wire. One chance, Alex thought. He fired the gun into Cameron's face.

Cameron fell forward, further pinning Alex. The world went black.

5 0

He heard his own breathing, rapid and harsh, before he was aware of anything else. The wire, although still around his neck, was no longer cutting into his skin.

He didn't think he had been out for long. Cameron's body was still warm as it lay heavily over him. Alex felt a sticky dampness on his neck, but thought that was probably from the wound to his ear. He rolled Cameron off his back without strangling himself in the process. He managed it, then glanced at Kit, who was looking at him with relief. For a guy who was hanging upside down, Alex thought dizzily, he was remarkably calm.

Alex holstered his automatic, then unwrapped the garrote from his neck. He moved to his hands and knees, then sat up slowly. His throat and neck hurt like hell, but each breath made him feel stronger. He glanced at Cameron's ruined eye and lifeless face, the wound in his shoulder, then looked away. Alex felt his ear and was relieved to discover that most of it was still firmly attached.

"I'll get you down," he said to Kit in a low, rasping voice that didn't seem to be his. "Any traps between you and me?"

Kit shook his head.

Alex forced himself to search Cameron's body, and he found a knife. His strength returning now, he hurried to Kit. He saw that the ground was littered with the contents of Kit's pockets—*milagros* and the stone tortoise. He pulled the tape away as quickly but gently as possible. Kit took big gulps of air, then said, "Thanks."

Alex cut through the binding on his wrists.

"The light," Kit said.

"I need to see what I'm doing here. I don't want to drop you on your head." But he moved the flashlight so that it was no longer providing a beacon through the trees.

"Just cut me down," Kit said. "I can use my arms to help roll and break the fall."

But instead Alex also held on to him as he cut, so that Kit's weight didn't hit the ground all at once. They managed clumsily but without further damage. He handed Kit the knife and then used the flashlight to look for Cameron's rifle.

"I'm sorry," Kit said, cutting his ankles free, then rubbing his calves and ankles as circulation painfully returned to them. "I should have been more careful." Alex saw him pick up the stone tortoise.

"Could have happened to either of us. Are you going to be able to walk?"

"I'll be all right in a moment. I know we have to hurry. Everett will wonder where Cameron is. And he'll wonder why you haven't shown up yet." He paused and said, "I'm worried about your nephew. If Cameron was willing to kill you . . ."

Alex frowned. "I see your point. Why keep Chase alive if I'm dead, right?"

"Right."

He found the rifle and brought it to Kit, who had moved unsteadily to his feet. "You know how to use this, right?"

"Yes."

Alex turned off the flashlight. In the darkness, he said, "Ciara must have heard the shots. She's probably called for backup by now. So if you see someone from a SWAT team, lay the weapon down and let them handle whatever happens next."

Kit didn't answer.

"Kit—I know you're thinking about Spooky, but you won't do her any good if one of our snipers can't tell what team you're on."

"All right. Do you want the knife back?"

"No, you keep it."

"What about the FBI agent? Did Cameron kill him?"

"No—but he's wounded. Getting shot by his buddy Cameron seems to have wised him up some. One other thing—although I don't know if we should believe him. Hamilton told me there are explosives up in the bell tower."

"As long as we get Chase and Spooky out of here," Kit said, "Everett can blow up the whole school. Let's go."

• • •

The baseball field stayed dark. By the time they were able to move to the buildings, they saw lights on in the administration building and one of the classrooms. It was brighter here, but they tried to stay in the shadows.

Kit cautiously peered through a window into the classroom. He turned to signal to Alex that it was empty, and his eyes widened. Alex looked at himself in the light for the first time since coming from the woods. The front of his suit was covered with blood.

"Hamilton's and Cameron's," he whispered. "Not much of mine. Let's look in the other classrooms, too, though. Nothing says he'll have them in a room with a light on."

They were moving toward the next room when the school's public address system came on.

"Kit Logan and Alexander Brandon, report to the principal's office. You have visitors."

Kit and Alex froze.

"I repeat," Everett said, "Kit Logan and Alexander Brandon, report at once to the principal's office. Perhaps you'd like to hear from one of our visitors? Talk to them, my dear."

"Alex, I'm sorry." Ciara's voice, sounding strained. "We heard shots. We tried to sneak in, to find you. This asshole caught us."

They heard the sound of a blow and then a scream.

Alex paled. He watched Kit take out the little tortoise and roll it between his fingers.

"Christ almighty! This is no time to sit around playing with a toy."

"We shouldn't both go," Kit said.

There was another scream.

Kit seemed not to hear it.

"What the hell are you made of?" Alex asked angrily.

"Ice," Kit answered. "This is a trap, I think."

"You think. Heard a lot of screams, haven't you?"

Alex saw something that might have been disappointment briefly cross Kit's face.

"Yes," Kit said. "I've heard a lot of screams. Do what you want to do. I'm going to look for Spooky and Chase."

Alex pulled out his gun. "He wants to see you, you're coming with me."

"Bring me to him dead, then," Kit said. "Shoot me in the back." He began to run away.

Alex angrily lifted the gun to fire a shot over his head. But just as he started to squeeze the trigger, he heard J.D.'s voice in his mind, saying, *Don't get ex-*

cited. His hand trembled as he holstered the gun. He did what he could to calm himself.

Maybe Kit was right. He was undoubtedly walking into a trap. Maybe neither one of them should go. He could look for a phone, call a hostage negotiator, and a tactical team—

Another scream.

He didn't have time. He thought for a moment, then broke a window to let himself into one of the darkened classrooms. He used his flashlight and found what he was looking for—an intercom unit on the wall near the teacher's desk. He moved the switch to call the office and said, "This is Alex Brandon. Let the women go, and we can talk."

There was a long silence. He heard a door open and whirled as the lights came on. Everett Corey stood in the doorway, holding a gun to Ciara's head. He was wearing some sort of commando outfit. Ciara's hands were cuffed behind her back, and she looked as if she had been in a fight. Her upper lip was swollen on one side, and the skin of her face was scraped.

"I like my idea better," Everett said. "Drop your weapon and kick it across the floor. Take the Kevlar vest off, too."

He did as Everett asked.

Everett moved closer to Alex's gun. He was doing something with the handcuffs. Alex heard them released.

Alex did all he could to keep the smile off his face. Everett was underestimating Ciara.

"Pick it up, Ciara," Everett ordered.

She bent, picked up the gun, and aimed it at Alex.

"Should I shoot you now," she asked, "and see if Kit Logan comes running?"

5 1

He felt the color drain from his face. He couldn't hide his shock. But he pulled himself together and said, "Kit's dead."

"No!" she shouted, and kicked over a chair. "No!" Just as quickly, she calmed down. "I don't believe you."

"You've met up with Cameron," Everett said. "Look at his neck, Ciara."

Everett had called her by name twice now. Alex felt his stomach knot. There would be no backup, no SWAT team, no hostage negotiators. Just another hostage, unless he was convincing. Everything depended on that, and on Kit. "Kit wasn't so lucky," he said, letting his anger at Ciara find its way into his voice. He took a chance, and indicated the front of his suit. "I tried to stop the bleeding, but I was too late. At least I had the pleasure of evening the score."

Everett held his head to one side. "Cameron is dead?"

"I thought you'd be all broken up about it." So, he thought, Everett didn't know about Hamilton. Maybe Hamilton was telling the truth after all.

"Cameron and I had a bit of a falling-out," Everett said. "He told me he was going to deny me my long-awaited revenge, that he could set a trap for you and Kit in the woods that would be just as effective as my invention."

Invention? Alex looked at Ciara, but she only frowned at him.

"Obviously," Everett went on, "it was an inferior plan. Poor Cameron. Far too emotional when it came to hurting children. He was upset about what I've done to your nephew and—as I found out far too late—the *female* Kit adopted."

Alex's fists clenched, even as he fought a wave of nausea. *What I've done to your nephew* . . .

Everett laughed and said, "In any case, Cameron was intent on spoiling my fun. And I must say he did spoil it—most of it, anyway. But just in case you aren't telling the truth, I think we'll bring you along to the office. Handcuff him, Ciara—no, in front."

She had started to pull Alex's wrists behind him, and at this command, gave Everett a look of annoyance. But she did as he asked. Alex began to wonder why Everett had insisted on it.

"Take the daypack and any weapons from him," Everett said, "and give them to me. Be quick about it."

"Look here, Everett—" she began angrily.

He raised a brow. "Yes?"

She subsided and did as he asked.

"I take it your cell phone works fine?" Alex said as she searched his pockets.

"It was easy to put a dead battery in it after I had checked in with Everett," she said. "I would have asked for yours if you hadn't offered it."

"Hurry up," Everett said.

She shoved Alex forward, steering him toward the administration building.

"I'm just trying to figure out what I ever did to you," he said to her, unable to keep the rage from his voice.

She didn't answer.

He thought back to her reaction to his saying that Kit was dead. Her anger was toward Kit, then. But what could she have against Kit? That first night in Lakewood, she had obviously coaxed Alex into talking more about the similarities between the way Adrianos was left and the Naughton cases.

He suddenly recalled something she said on the day they visited Shay Wilder. She said it had been overkill when Kit attacked Naughton—and that she had read the files. But how could she have read the files on him? Those were sealed because Kit was a minor then, and there had never been an arrest. Those details had not been in the papers or in court records. She must have investigated Kit Logan on her own, at some earlier time.

He watched for an opportunity to escape, but they made sure he didn't have one. He hoped for a while that Kit might take a shot at one of them. But he saw no sign of Kit.

He was shoved into a room with a long counter in it. It was a typical school office. He could see a small infirmary through one door, a room with filing cabinets through another. Against one wall was a public address system. A microphone sat on a desk near it.

"I take it you provided all the screams?" he asked Ciara.

"I began to wonder if you heard them."

"I imagine everyone living up above this canyon heard them," he said. "Including the guards at Kit's house."

"He has a point," Everett said, glancing at his gold Rolex. He moved to a metal storage cabinet and locked up Alex's pack and weapons. "I'm not sure I should listen to any more of your ideas."

"Watch out, Ciara," Alex said. "Che Guevara Junior here has a rapidly shrinking number of partners—or haven't you noticed?"

"The old divide-and-conquer routine?" Ciara asked, pushing him toward a door marked PRINCIPAL.

The room was a large, carpeted one. Heavy curtains were drawn across the windows. Meghan Taggert sat bound and gagged in a chair turned to one corner.

"Alex, we'll have you sit here," Everett said, pulling out a second chair.

Ciara shoved him hard into it.

"Ciara," Everett said, turning Meghan around, "I know my darling resisted you, but did you have to strike her face?" Meghan's left cheek and eye were a little swollen, Alex saw. It would have taken more than one blow. However many had landed, it hadn't knocked the defiance out of her.

Everett caressed her cheek. She pulled as far away from him as her bonds would allow.

"Doesn't look as if you're satisfying him in bed, Ciara," Alex said. "But then, it doesn't look as if his new courtship is going all that well, either."

Everett smiled. "Things will go better now that Kit is dead."

Meghan shot a look of despair at Alex, then she seemed to notice the blood.

"I'm sorry," he said, meaning it.

She shook her head, but tears were welling up in her eyes.

"You know, you have a point, Meghan. I think I'll bring his body in here. It will give you closure. And then maybe you'll feel like telling me where your brother the loser is." Everett turned his attention back to Alex. "And for the record, Ciara and I have a strictly professional relationship."

"The story of her life," Alex said, and Ciara slapped him. He smiled. She struck him again, harder. That time he laughed. "This is obviously hurting you more than it does me."

She folded her arms, visibly resisting the urge to hit him again.

"Ciara owes much of her career as a detective to me," Everett said, as if nothing had happened. "Didn't you ever wonder how she solved so many cases?"

"Actually, Internal Affairs is investigating her," Alex lied. "She would have been fired long ago, but we wanted to catch those who were helping her. No one believed she was capable of that on her own."

"You're full of shit," Ciara said.

"He's envious," Everett said. "They all are. Do you know what we've done? The best law enforcement agencies in the country couldn't do what my small, select team could do. You see, Alex, your partner had an intelligent, privately operated, well-financed team on her side. Your underfunded lab with its six-month backlog? We could have answers in a week. I could hire men who could focus entirely on one case, while you had to take whatever came your way, whenever it came your way. And your stupid rules! When you're dealing with lawbreakers, what could be more ridiculous than worrying about rules? Why not level the playing field? Look what we've accomplished. Wiretapping? No problem. Electronic tracking devices? Not to worry. Need to inflict a little pain to get a guilty party to talk? We could do it. It worked perfectly."

"Not exactly perfect," Alex said. "You only caught nine out of ten."

"Oh, but one hundred percent of our goal—the truly guilty ones. It's really an incredible fluke that Gabe ended up on the Ten Most Wanted list. He was at that robbery, of course. So technically, he can be tried for murder. But anyone who believes Gabe Taggert could murder anyone, let alone a family with small children— Why do the police always take the easy way out?"

"One of his partners named him—" He broke off, seeing Everett's smile.

"Exactly. The whole thing went much bigger than we expected."

"Are you so deluded, you think none of this will catch up to you?" Alex said. "We were already looking at you and Cameron as suspects before you had my ex call me."

"She's a really fine fuck, by the way."

"If you don't mind leftovers," Alex said.

Everett laughed. Ciara made a sound of disgust and walked toward the door.

"Stay for a moment, Ciara," Everett said. "I'll need you to keep an eye on them while I check out his story about Kit."

Remembering what Kit had told him about Everett, Alex said, "The body is in the woods. Cameron's, too."

He saw Everett hesitate.

Ciara saw it, too. "Let me look for him."

"If you insist," Everett said, glancing at his watch again. "You'll have to hurry. And we'll need to make sure we aren't sending you into some sort of trap. There's a big switch that turns on the baseball field lights out there somewhere. Near one of the dugouts, I think."

Alex lowered his head to hide his reaction. He was sure Cameron had turned the lights on, after hearing Hamilton fire his gun. But when the lights had gone out again, he had assumed Everett had been the one to plunge the woods into darkness again. If it hadn't been Everett, was it Kit?

No, Kit wouldn't have been able to get to the switch to turn the lights off, and then back into the woods so quickly. But if it hadn't been Everett or Kit or Hamilton . . .

"He knows something," Ciara said, watching him.

"I know you've partnered up with a lunatic." He looked at Everett. "I told your old man to get help for you, but I guess he didn't listen."

"Don't try to pretend you had my best interests in mind," Everett said. "You wanted to destroy me then, but you learned that it wasn't so easy, didn't you? And in case you haven't noticed, the public doesn't think I'm so crazy. The public loves what we've done. We're heroes."

"Martyrs, most of you," Alex said. "There is that difference. Has he got another Bora waiting for you, Ciara? Who's going to take care of Laney when that happens? You sold your soul — and your sister — to have the highest clearance rate in Homicide?"

"You don't get it at all, Alex," she said angrily. "You never did. That's why people who should have been punished went free."

There was a sound in the outer office.

Ciara and Everett tensed. "Check it out," Everett ordered.

Alex saw the look of rebellion on Ciara's face, but she went out, leaving the door open. They heard her moving, opening and closing other doors.

When she came back she said, "No one inside."

Everett looked at Alex. "You know, Ciara, I think you're right. I think he lied about Kit Logan being dead."

"I'll look for him," Ciara said, and moved toward Alex. She pulled him to his feet.

"What are you doing?" Everett asked sharply.

"He's going to be my bait."

"You'd be better off using Meghan. If Kit Logan is alive, nothing will bring him more quickly to surrender than the threat of killing her. If he's dead, it will be good for her to see it for herself. Besides, I don't trust you, Ciara, dear. You might end up taking that badge of yours too seriously."

"You sure I won't just take off with your long-lost love?" she asked.

"You have no interest in her. But you do in Kit, and in Alex, here."

"What the hell do you have against Kit Logan?" Alex asked her.

She shoved him hard back into his chair. "Jerome Naughton—how many victims were there?"

"Eight."

"Wrong."

"We never found Serenity Logan's body, but we're sure—"

"Oh, I count her. But you're wrong."

"If you're telling me there may have been more, all the investigators agreed that was likely. Is this about some unknown victim of Naughton's?"

"No, I'm talking about known victims."

He was puzzled. She put the barrel of her gun to his temple. "Think, damn you!"

Alex's pulse raced, and his mouth went dry. He looked into her eyes and saw nothing but a desire to pull the trigger.

Everett must have seen it, too. "I'd ask you to remember that I have plans for him, Ciara. Besides, we may need a hostage to get out of here—especially after your screaming broadcast."

"How much time do we have?" she asked, her gaze not leaving Alex.

"A little more than an hour. So let's not waste precious moments. You'll have to spell it out for him, I'm afraid."

But Alex had kept watching her face and said, "The woman who lived."

"If you can call it that," Ciara said.

"Laney."

"He left her hanging there! Upside down. Do you know what happens when a person hangs upside down for a long time? It's really not good for you. You aren't designed for it—it's all wrong for your circulation. Pressure builds, your head swells, eventually your eyes are damaged, your throat swells up. It strains the joints you're hanging from, of course."

Alex lowered his gaze.

"No one can stay that way forever," Ciara said, "but in Laney's case, it was worse. Jerome Naughton had knocked her around—ultimately knocked her out cold—before he suspended her over that tub. So there was bruising, you see? A few places that were weakened by those blows. Normally, they probably wouldn't have done any long-term damage. But hanging upside down as long as she did? Before Kit Logan decided to let anyone know she was there?"

"Ciara—"

"You met her, Alex. There were nine victims. Nine. And you and everyone else who was impressed with Elizabeth Logan's money let the man who ruined my sister's mind and body get away with something worse than murder."

"I'm sorry Laney went through that, that she suffered as she did . . ."

"Like hell you are!" she shouted, her face twisted by her anger, her eyes wild and glistening with unshed tears.

"But Naughton was to blame, not Kit. Kit Logan wasn't a man," Alex said. "He was a boy. A frightened boy."

"I saw the pictures Naughton took. You saw them, too. Some of them even in graves—in graves holding dead women! The ones from when they were alive were worse. Those weren't the acts of a boy."

"You know what I hated about those photographs? The looks on the victims' faces."

"Exactly! Laney was so frightened . . ."

"So was Kit. You've lost count, too, Ciara. Two victims in each of those photos—not one. That kid hated every minute of it."

"Speaking of minutes," Everett said, "we're running out of them."

"Ciara, think!" Alex said. "What's going to happen to her now? You go through with this, you're no better than anyone who abandoned her that night. Who could love her as much as you do? Who'll take care of her?"

She lowered her gaze and said softly, "Did you think I would leave that to chance?"

He stared at her. "Ciara? Ciara . . . where is she?"

"It was peaceful," she said, wiping quickly at her eyes. "And painless. I made sure of that."

"My God." His next thought was that Ciara now had nothing to lose.

"Ciara met with us this morning," Everett said cheerfully, "so that she wouldn't have to stay in the house with her sister's body. And that turned out to be a good thing, because I needed her to keep an eye on your nephew. Cameron and I knew his parents would be bringing him home, but we were suddenly given an opportunity we couldn't pass up—Kit's little urchin was finally leaving that armed camp he calls home. So when you paged Ciara this morning, she was following a limo, not taking Laney to a doctor."

"You kidnapped Chase?" Alex asked her.

"No, but I would have, if necessary. You think I care about people who are important to you? You never cared about anyone who was important to me."

"I think it's about time we got things set up," Everett said. "There are two ropes hanging in that bell tower now, Detective Brandon. We've detached them from the bells, and tied them over two sturdy beams."

"We're going to hang you upside down in there," Ciara said. "You and Kit Logan, if he's still alive, and I hope to God he is. The bells will be silent, but before long, you'll hear a ringing in your ears, Alex. You'll feel your head pounding, and pressure on your eyes. In a matter of minutes, you'll be miserable. And it will get worse. You'll wish for death, Alex. You'll pray for it—just like Laney must have prayed for it."

"Ciara, don't say anything more," Everett admonished. "You'll spoil everything. Besides, we don't have much time left. Take Meghan with you—but don't strike her lovely face again."

"Okay—but you leave Alex to me."

"You get both Logan and Brandon? That hardly seems fair."

"You want to drag Miss America out into the woods? Fine with me."

He sighed. "Have it your way. But hurry. I'll take Brandon to the tower. We'll wait for you there."

Meghan stood straight and walked out with Ciara without showing any fear.

"Meghan's magnificent, isn't she?" Everett said. "I think we'll breed well."

"Don't count your chickens, as they say."

Everett smiled and said, "Speaking of offspring—would you like to say a final good-bye to your nephew? You are sure he's only your nephew, right?"

Alex hesitated, unsure of how to answer this to Chase's advantage.

"Ah, just a nephew, I see. Then I suppose you won't mind so much when you discover what's become of him. Stand up."

5 2

Everett hesitated when they reached the door of the bell tower.

"Now that's interesting," he said. "An unbarred door." He looked behind him—a little nervously, Alex thought.

He saw Alex watching him and smiled. "I recently made a little change to this door. You see the brackets that I welded on? They allow the door to be locked and barred on the outside. I have the lock with me, but I left the bar on—I'm sure of it. And of course, if you take that bar off and enter the building, you can't put the bar back in place, can you? At least, not while you're still inside."

Alex started to look over his shoulder, toward the rooftops of the buildings behind them, then suddenly looked forward again, as if he had belatedly realized he was giving a confederate's position away.

Everett quickly looked between Alex and the rooftops. He narrowed his gaze. "Unless you only want someone to *believe* you're still inside." He pulled the door open and stood aside. "All the same, I think I'll let you walk in first."

Alex stepped into the darkened tower. Everett moved in slowly behind him. Alex heard the click of a switch, and lights came on—one set of bright ones, illuminating part of the first floor, and along a wooden staircase railing, a long string of bare bulbs that went about three-quarters of the way up the tower. They stopped abruptly there. The railing enclosed a series of platforms and stairs. Here and there, small shedlike structures protruded onto the platforms.

A pair of thick ropes hung down the center of the tower. They ended about eight feet above the ground. A familiar rappelling rope hung between them, one end attached to a power winch, from where its length rose up into the tower and then back down, its end at the edge of an inner circle that was clear of sandbags. A short stepladder lay folded on the floor of the circle.

"The rappelling rope goes over a pulley," Everett said, his voice echoing. "The bell ropes are simply tied to a beam. As Ciara told you, there are no bells at the moment. You won't be able to raise an old-fashioned alarm." His voice echoed around them.

But Alex was staring at the sandbags, remembering what Hamilton said about explosives.

"Tamping," Everett said.

Alex felt himself break out in a cold sweat. Tamping was a way of directing the force of an explosion. With this many bags, he could only wonder at the size of the charge that must lay beneath them. He realized he was holding his breath, and slowly let it out.

Soft ticking sounds from one side of the tower drew his attention to a tall, almost L-shaped box made of a thick, clear material. It was attached to the wall, about four feet off the concrete floor. At first glance, it appeared to be the strange marriage of an oversize, tilted pinball machine and a grandfather clock.

At the top was a clock face. Beneath the clock was a clear, narrow cylinder filled with eight shiny metal balls about the size of billiard balls. The balls were stacked within the cylinder, one on top of the other.

At the end of the cylinder, and to its left, was a trough that sat at a slight angle, so that a ball entering it would roll onto a tilted strip. The strip opened on to nine channels, the channels also tilted down at a slight angle. Metal tabs could be seen at the end of each of these channels. They reminded Alex of the tabs that touch the ends of batteries in a battery-powered device. A ninth silver ball was in the first slot.

Alex saw then that there were thin metal gates at the tops of the channels. The gate above the channel holding the ball was closed. The gate for the channel next to it was the only one in an open position. The next ball to be released could fall only into that channel.

This whole platform of channels appeared to be supported from beneath by a thick pipe, but then he saw that it was not a stand but a conduit, and that it bent at the floor and continued toward the sandbags.

"Lovely, isn't it?" Everett said with pride. "I built it myself. But I see we really are running late."

To Alex's dismay, Everett blindfolded him. They were alone now, Alex thought. It might be best just to try to take him out. If he moved that close again . . .

"We're going to walk over these bags," Everett said. "The trick will be to do so without tripping a number of pressure-sensitive devices I have hidden beneath them. You understand, I'm sure, the need to move exactly as I guide you."

"Maybe I'll just set one off and send us both to meet our Maker. I think I'd come out better in the long run, don't you?"

"Really? I hope your nephew has led an equally pure life, then. I did a little remodeling near the top of the tower. Once my guests were installed in their suite, I had fun with an electric saw. They slept through it all, poor dears. I did consider turning them into morphine addicts, but I'm afraid I don't have the time for every form of revenge that occurs to me."

"Chase?" Alex called, lifting his face. He heard his voice echo, and silence. But then a distant, faint voice called back, "Uncle Alex?"

He felt his hopes rise.

There was another voice now, raised in sharp reprimand, and a brief argument. He heard it more clearly a moment later. "If you're really his uncle Alex, shut up, okay? He's too dizzy to stand out here. He'll fall and crack his head open again."

"Spooky?"

"You know Kit?"

Behind him, Everett suddenly screamed, "Put out that match, you idiot!"

Alex paled. "Yes. Spooky, honey, put the match out, okay?"

"Don't call me 'honey,' you macho asshole."

But apparently she blew the match out, because Everett sighed in relief. "I wish I had known she was a girl," he said.

"Who said that?" she asked. "Is he the one who called me an idiot?"

"The man who put you up there. Listen—there are explosives in here, so no more matches, okay, Spooky?"

She was quiet.

"Are you all right?" he asked.

"I want down from here. Where's Kit? Where's Meghan?"

Before he could answer, he heard the sound of a small chime. In the quiet that followed, he heard a click and the sound of a silver ball rolling. It seemed to him as loud as a gutter ball in a bowling alley. It came to a halt with a snap.

"Where the hell is that woman?" Everett said angrily. He jabbed Alex's back with the barrel of the gun. "We're wasting time. I simply wanted you to be aware of the risks." Alex felt a painful grip on his shoulder. "Now, Detective Brandon, step up onto the sandbag directly in front of you."

He continued to call directions, and Alex followed them, trying to memorize them. The nervousness in Everett's voice forced him to abandon any hope that there were no pressure-sensitive devices, that it was only a ruse. He could smell the sharp scent of Everett's sweat, feel the other man's palm dampening on his shoulder. Alex tried to rid himself of his own dread of tripping over the uneven surfaces of the bags by telling himself that he had a better sense of balance than most and that Everett wouldn't risk a fall. But the fear of setting off an explosion was never far away.

When he stepped down into the cleared section, Alex found that he was shaking with relief. He forced himself to breathe more evenly. Everett turned him around several times, like a child playing blind man's bluff. Then Everett removed the blindfold.

As Alex blinked up at him in surprise, Everett smiled.

"Take the end of the rappelling rope and sit down on the floor," Everett ordered. "Tie that around your ankles."

"How am I supposed to do that with my hands bound?" he asked.

"Don't take me for a fool. You can do it. Hurry."

He took hold of the rappelling rope and awkwardly sat down. This, he realized, was why Everett had insisted on his being handcuffed in front. As he tied the knots, he felt his hands trembling, his fingers growing clumsy and numb with fear. In the next instant, he again felt a surge of anger and bitterness overpowering that fear, raw fury at being made to do Everett's bidding. But he thought of Chase and Spooky, and kept himself in check. If he could delay long enough for Kit to come in through that door, or bring help . . .

When he had finished, Everett took something that looked like a television remote control and aimed it toward the winch. There was a click, and suddenly he felt a sharp pull on his ankles—the winch had been turned on.

He quickly lay flat on his back to avoid being yanked off balance, and felt the slow, inexorable pull of the rope as it began to lift him. His heart hammered.

Get a grip, he told himself, and felt himself calming. *You can get out of this. You will get out of this. Think.*

"I thought Ciara wanted you to wait for her to have all this fun," he said, as his hips began to feel the pull of the rope.

"She'll get her turn with Kit," Everett said absently. He was staring up at the staircase.

The rope went higher, and Alex's hips left the floor. Change fell out of his pockets, jangling as the coins struck the concrete floor below him. Then his spine and shoulders lifted, and with his blood already rushing to it, his head. His jacket fell around his shoulders and neck, covering his face and dropping pens and his PDA to the floor with a crack. The scent of dried blood on the jacket came to him with every breath. He had visions of being dropped onto the floor headfirst. *Let the rope hold. Let the knots hold. Let them hold.*

He felt as if he were on the rack, felt the pull of his weight on joints that weren't meant to sustain it in this direction for long. The rope pinched and abraded his skin, and his injured shoulder began to throb as his arms stretched beneath him. He gritted his teeth as he was pulled higher. The rope began to slowly twist and spin, he with it, in a motion that soon became dizzying.

He heard the winch stop.

Everett had to dodge him—Alex was swaying slowly like a human pendulum, and still spinning as well, about three feet above the sandbags. Alex's blood had already rushed to his head. He felt the strain on all his joints and was certain that his ankles were going to rip away from his feet. They burned from the pressure of the rope.

"What are you doing to him?" Spooky called.

"I'm okay," he called back. "Don't worry."

"Kit!" Spooky shouted frantically. "Kit!"

For a brief moment, Alex wondered if Kit and his rifle were inside the tower. But the echoes of her shouts faded into silence.

But her cries had distracted Everett, who lost track of Alex swinging near him.

"Look out!" Alex yelled.

Everett quickly ducked to avoid being hit. "God damn it! Don't!" he screamed.

"What the fuck do you think I can do about it?" Alex shouted, already swinging back toward him.

Everett ducked again and then quickly stood and tucked the gun into a holster at his hip. He planted his feet a little apart, grabbed onto one of the bell ropes, and as Alex came by this time, grabbed onto him. Alex felt the impact and Everett's loss of balance, felt the young man's strength as he used his grip on the other rope and Alex's body to both halt the sway and prevent himself from tumbling over. They tottered back and forth together for what seemed to Alex an eternity. When they finally came to a halt, he was so dizzy, the room still seemed to spin. He clamped down on an urge to vomit. Everett stepped away from him and looked into his reddened face.

"Have a headache yet? Maybe I should kick you in the face for almost knocking me over." He glanced up.

Alex lifted his head and saw a camera. The red recording indicator light was on. He thought of the videotape from Oaxaca.

Everett pulled a knife from his military-style belt. Alex felt himself go cold. Terrified of the style of torture he had seen inflicted on Everett's other victims, he considered trying to disarm Everett. Everett had been cautious until now, but he was now within range of Alex's hands, and Alex might be able to do it. But unless he killed Everett with one blow, Everett was likely to be able to recover a weapon, and Spooky and Chase would remain in danger. Or he might knock Everett onto one of the pressure devices. He prayed that Kit, who had been smart enough to see the trap, would somehow set them free before Everett blew them all to hell. Or before Everett decided to play surgeon with him.

Everett grabbed hold of Alex's jacket and cut it off of him in a few swift strokes. The knife was sharp. He did the same with his shirt. Alex tried to keep himself still, but when Everett grabbed hold of his belt, he brought his fists up hard toward Everett's groin.

Everett anticipated it just in time, shoving Alex away from him so that the blow landed on his thigh. Still, he doubled over in pain, his face twisted in anger.

"You stupid asshole!" he shouted as Alex began to swing wildly again. "You stupid fucking asshole!"

Alex closed his eyes. Even if he managed, as he had hoped, to grab onto Everett before he fell onto any of the sandbags, what good would it have done? If Everett took his time killing him, maybe that would allow Kit to get reinforcements here to save Spooky and Chase. The more he thought about it, the more likely it seemed that Kit would try to reach the former soldiers who guarded his house—genuine soldiers, not boys playing dress-up like Everett— to help them. He had to keep his head until then and not put Spooky and Chase at risk.

Everett grabbed him roughly and brought the swinging to a halt again. Alex tried to prepare himself for what was to come, to put himself mentally far away. He thought of his last climb, of conquering the hardest part of it, of clinging by his fingertips and nearly nonexistent toeholds. Then he heard a chime and the steady rolling of the next silver ball, and was back in the tower.

But instead of threatening him with the knife, Everett started to set up the stepladder, carefully placing it on marks that Alex could now see beneath him. Everett wiped his hands nervously and again glanced at his watch. He grabbed one of the bell ropes, then looked undecided. It occurred to Alex that he had not planned to be alone when he did this. "Cameron was the rock climber," he said.

Everett frowned, then climbed down, folded the ladder, and set it on the floor. He stood behind Alex and took hold of Alex's belt at the back, placed a booted foot on the chain of the handcuffs, and pressed down, so that Alex's already strained joints felt an even harder pull. His shoulders and elbows were on fire. Alex opened his mouth and exhaled hard, trying not to groan or make a sound that would distress Chase or Spooky. He heard the knife leave the sheaf again, and sweat began stinging his eyes. He felt the prick of the blade between his shoulders, a small, burning cut.

"A little deeper and you could spend the last hour of your life being paralyzed—you understand?" Everett said. "So don't go talking to me about what I can and cannot do. I can do what I want."

Alex felt a trickle of blood dampening the hair on the back of his head. He stayed silent.

Everett lifted his foot away and released his hold. He quickly made his way back over the sandbags. Alex tried but couldn't see the pattern of his steps.

Everett suddenly seemed distracted, as if he had heard a noise. He frowned and pulled the gun out again. He aimed it directly at Alex as he moved nearer to the door and opened it. He stood on the threshold, listening.

Alex heard the same sound Everett must have heard a moment before. Gunfire.

5 3

"Hold it," Ciara said.

Meghan stood still. She had heard it, too. A faint sound near the baseball dugout. Ciara had decided not to walk out into the open space between the baseball diamond and the woods until she searched among the buildings for any sign of Kit. They watched Everett take Alex into the bell tower, but otherwise hadn't seen or heard anything. Until now.

Kit, don't come any closer, Meghan thought.

Ciara waited and listened. She pushed Meghan ahead a little, then shouted, "Kit Logan!"

They heard another sound—this one just to their left. Ciara turned toward it, pointing the gun. Meghan launched herself at the other woman, knocking her over. The gun went off. Meghan landed sprawled over the upper half of Ciara's body—Ciara was pinned beneath her, her head beneath Meghan's shoulder, but she still had the gun. She was trying to point it back at Meghan but seemed to realize she wouldn't be able to get a clear shot.

Meghan, her hands still cuffed behind her, struggled to remain on top of Ciara, who began trying to roll over. If she did, Meghan knew, she'd be able to shoot the gun, and there wouldn't be much of anything she could do about it.

She heard a loud thud, the sound of someone jumping down from somewhere, and then there was another combatant adding his weight to hers and grabbing Ciara's gun hand. Meghan couldn't make out much in the darkness, but she knew it was a man. She saw him take hold of Ciara's wrist and try to peel her fingers away from the weapon with the other hand. *Not like that!* Meghan wanted to shout.

Ciara pushed hard, and Meghan felt herself rolling off. Ciara struggled to aim the gun at her despite being kicked by both Meghan and the man. Suddenly, Ciara was free of Meghan. Ciara launched herself toward her male attacker as Meghan kicked out again, her foot connecting hard with Ciara's knee, causing her to lose her balance.

The gun went off again.

She heard Ciara moan, then fall still.

"Meghan?"

Gabe. Meghan tried to make the loudest sound she could with the gag on.

"Sorry. Forgot you were gagged."

He pushed Ciara over, leaving the gun behind, and hurried to free Meghan from the gag.

"Gabe! Oh, Gabe — is she dead?"

He nodded.

"You're sure?"

He went back to the still form and felt for a pulse.

"Yes, she's dead. I guess I'm really in trouble now."

"No, no — get the handcuff key from her pants pocket. Hurry! We've got to help Kit and those kids."

"I thought they said Kit was dead."

"You heard that?"

He was searching for the key. He paused. "Meggie, is it true?"

"I don't know. I think Detective Brandon wanted Everett to think that, but I don't know if it's true." She swallowed hard. "I don't want it to be."

"Me neither."

"We have to try to find Spooky and Alex's nephew. Do you know where they're being held?"

"No. But Everett was doing something in the bell tower earlier, and after he took Cameron in there, they had a big argument."

"What were you doing in the office?"

He began searching the ground nearby. "Maybe the keys fell out of her pocket — oh, the office? I saw Everett and this one leave the building — sorry, Meggie — the door was closed, and I didn't know you were in there. I wanted to get into the infirmary. I was looking for a blanket and some bandages. There's a man Cameron shot — I took him to the stables after I tried to help Kit."

"What man? And what do you mean, tried to help Kit?"

"Got them!" He found a key ring and held it up in triumph. "Wait—there's another set, too."

"She has Alex's keys. We were supposed to wait in his car, but she drove me in here. Tell me about this man Cameron shot."

"Cameron was hunting Kit with a rifle," he said, moving behind her and releasing the lock. "He turned the lights on, and I came back here and turned them off—Kit can see better in the dark than a cat, Meggie. And he knows the woods. We used to hang out there to avoid Everett and Cameron and that group."

She rubbed at her wrists. "Are you okay?"

"Me? You're the one I'm worried about."

"I'm all right."

"The man who was shot—he's unconscious, but someone bandaged his wound—maybe Kit or Alex. I didn't want Everett to find him, because he's an FBI agent. And it's so weird—I think he used to go to school here."

She had started to search the ground for the gun, but at this she looked up. "What?"

"Yeah. His name is Hamilton. I think he was a senior when I was a freshman. Anyway, I don't like leaving him out there."

"We've got to look for Spooky and Alex's nephew," she repeated, finding and picking up the gun. "And we've got to try to help Alex." She paused and reached for a small, black object. Alex's cell phone.

"We should call nine-one-one," Gabe said.

She looked at him. "Oh, Gabe—"

"How can you even hesitate? It's not just about me, now, Meghan. If I get caught, I get caught. But I'll never forgive myself if anything happens to the others. And Agent Hamilton needs medical help."

She looked between him and the phone.

He made a sound of exasperation. "At least call Kit's guards."

She agreed to do this. She opened the phone up and saw that the display was cracked. Still, she tried to turn the phone on.

"Gabe—it's broken. Listen, let's look for them, and if we can't find them soon, we'll go back into the office and use the phone there to call for help."

She stood and looked down at Ciara.

"What she was saying about Kit—is that true?" Gabe asked.

"Some of it. Before killing those women, his stepfather sometimes forced him to . . . to pose holding them. And other things. He hated it."

She began hurrying toward the tower. He followed, but she heard him saying something softly to himself.

"What was that?"

"Just a part of a poem. I think I understand it better now."

"Jesus, Gabe, poetry? And by the way—have you forgotten everything we learned in self-defense?"

"I'm not the one who was handcuffed and gagged, was I?"

Suddenly they heard sounds coming from the tower—Everett's raised voice. They ducked between the classroom buildings.

5 4

At the same time Alex heard the shot, the door to one of the tower sheds opened, and Kit Logan stepped out onto a lower platform. He aimed the rifle at Everett's head.

"Drop the gun, Everett. Then get to work on disarming your contraption."

"Disarm it? I'm afraid that's not possible. As for the gun—"

He raised it toward Kit and fired as he hit the light switch, plunging them into darkness. Kit turned on a flashlight and ran down the stairs, but Everett had already slammed the door shut. Just as Kit reached it, they heard the bar fall into place, then the lock snap.

Kit pounded the door in frustration.

"So long, Kit!" Everett called through the door. "Sorry I couldn't stick around for the brief but sweet reunion."

Kit flattened his hand against the door. "Meghan . . ." Alex heard him say.

Kit moved back, and used the flashlight to find the light switch.

"Kit?" Alex said. "Were you hit?"

"He missed," he said in an unsteady voice.

"Thank God you didn't fire."

"And have a ricochet send us all to kingdom come? When he fired at me, I was sure we were going to end up in bits and pieces." He looked up. "Spooky? Are you and Chase okay?"

"We're okay. I did good, didn't I, Kit?"

He took a deep breath and seemed to refocus his attention. "You were wonderful. He never guessed."

Kit ran to the winch and used it to slowly lower Alex closer to the ground.

"Well," Spooky admitted, "I called your name. I'm sorry. I was scared."

"That's okay. We'll figure out a way to get you down soon," Kit said, already hurrying away from the winch, slinging the rifle onto his back. "First I have to help Alex."

"Kit, wait!" Alex yelled.

Kit had just stepped onto the sandbags and halted, looking at Alex in puzzlement. "I watched him twice," he said. "Besides, I'm good at this sort of thing."

He moved calmly until he reached the middle of the ring. There, he hesitated, as if undecided.

Alex found himself clenching his teeth.

Kit pulled the tortoise out of his pocket.

"Oh God—" Alex groaned. He bit back any further protest against having their fates decided by a stone tortoise. He saw Kit look up into the darkness above them, his lips moving silently, as if in prayer.

He looked back down, and with a look of determination, took another step.

Nothing happened.

They both exhaled loudly. Kit seemed more confident then, and within a few steps had reached Alex.

Ignoring the trickle of blood from the wound on his back that now dripped down his arms and from his fingertips, Alex called out, "Spooky? Is there a window in that room, or anywhere above it?"

"Yes. It's kind of long and skinny."

"Could Kit fit through it?"

"I think so."

"Try to break it out."

Kit was cutting him loose now, supporting his weight in much the same way he had supported Kit's in the woods. The relief to Alex was immediate—although there was still strain on his ankles, they were no longer bearing all his weight.

"I'm sorry I had to let him do this to you," Kit said, "but—"

"No, it was smart. I understand."

He knew that Kit didn't want to reveal his presence until he had some idea of what had become of Meghan. Neither of them said what Alex knew they both feared—that the gunshot they had all heard was Meghan's execution.

Just as Kit lowered him to the concrete, they heard a chime.

"Shit," Alex said.

5 5

Everett discovered Ciara's body near the baseball field. He felt relief. It wasn't merely that he hadn't much liked working with Ciara. For the last few minutes, he had been sure that Meghan was dead. He would prefer Meghan alive. He had plans for her.

He looked back at the tower, rising in the darkness. He could go back and spend more time tormenting Alex Brandon. But he hadn't especially enjoyed that. He missed having Cameron to appreciate it, but worse, the explosives were distracting. He felt rushed. That wasn't the way it should be. You had to be able to savor it.

He looked at his watch. Almost half the time gone.

He could look around in the dark for Meghan. She would be armed. She might be aiming a weapon at him right now.

He crouched down and moved closer to the buildings. Where would she be?

Everett looked toward the dark woods beyond the baseball field and suddenly realized he was alone.

Morgan. Frederick. Cameron. None of them could help him now. Not even Ciara.

The prospect of hunting in the dark seemed less and less appealing. In all likelihood, Meghan was going for help. His wonderful escape plans might come to naught. Should he take Alex Brandon as a hostage?

He glanced nervously at the tower. No. He had devised the timer, but Cameron had helped with the explosives. Everett, who was inexperienced with explosives, thought they might have overdone it. He could probably get Brandon out of there, but would they be far enough away when the tower blew up?

He began walking quickly toward the office. He decided he'd take a few precautions, then grab his keys and head for the driveway at the front of the school. One of the vans was parked there, packed with his luggage and all the false paperwork he would need. The jet was waiting.

At least after tonight, he would be able to stop riding around in vans. He longed to get back behind the wheel of his Testarossa, parked in the garage at the house, but that would have to wait, too.

He began walking faster. He thought of the stupid screams Ciara had broadcast over the loudspeaker. And there had been gunfire. The sheriff's department might already be on the way to investigate. After all, Kit's home, just at the top of the cliffs, had experienced soldiers patrolling outdoors, on every part of the grounds. They were probably calling 911 right now.

He suddenly remembered that Ciara had been carrying Alex Brandon's cell phone. Did Meghan have it now?

He began to run.

5 6

"How many of them are in there now?" Alex asked, looking toward the timer.

"Four. Almost half. But the time between each is decreasing."

His feet were completely numb, his legs useless, but he managed to move to a sitting position. Alex's legs and feet prickled with the burning needlelike sensation of returning circulation. As soon as he was able, he stood. "Let's get Chase and Spooky out of here."

"There's a huge gap between them and the next platform. I haven't been able to figure out how to get them down."

"We don't want to bring them down inside the tower," Alex said. "You and I need to go up. I think we can do it, even if I can't get out of these cuffs. If not, I'll have to try to teach you how to climb up to them."

He grabbed hold of one of the bell ropes. Seeing Kit's glance, he said, "We may need it."

Kit took hold of the other one. "A backup then. He planned to tie each of us to one of these?"

"Yes. The rappelling rope was just a way to get us in position."

They moved with urgency now and made their way back across the sand-bags, Alex following Kit's steps. Once on solid ground, they anchored the bell ropes to the stair rail. Alex ran to the winch and turned it on, reeling the rappelling rope in. He then hurriedly gathered the rope off the winch, making a coil.

Kit searched for something to use to break him out of the cuffs. He paused by the timer. He studied it briefly, looking for a way to disconnect it. "It will make connection after connection to complete the circuit," he said to Alex. "I can't think of a way to stop it. If I stop the clock itself, it may release all the balls at once and open all the gates to the connectors."

There was a loud banging at the door. They froze, then Kit readied the rifle. Then they heard Meghan's voice calling, "Alex? Alex, can you hear me? It's Meghan and Gabe."

"Meghan?" Kit called back, running to the door.

"Oh, God, Kit! We heard gunfire, and thought . . ."

"We thought the same thing. Listen—Everett has this whole place rigged with explosives. You've got to get out of here now. Gabe? Please, take her away from here, and I'll—"

"No way," Meghan said. "Everett just drove off—we've got to try to get you out of there."

Alex said, "Meghan, can you get Ciara's keys? I need to get out of these cuffs."

"I have them," Gabe called to them. There was a thin gap at the bottom of the door, and they saw the handcuff key come through it.

"Any way to bust the lock off this door, Gabe?" Kit asked as he picked it up.

"I'll try, but it doesn't look good."

Kit quickly freed Alex, who finished coiling the rappelling rope and placed it over his shoulder. As he worked he called to Meghan and Gabe, "Get my gear from the trunk of the car. Bring it to just below the broken window. And if you can find a phone, call nine one one. Tell them about the explosives. Use the loudspeaker system to yell to the neighbors if you have to."

They heard glass breaking, then a victory cry. "She did it!" Chase called. "She kicked it out!"

"Great!" Alex said, relieved to hear Chase's voice again. He was already on his way up the stairs, bringing the ends of the bell ropes and the rappelling rope with him. At the highest platform he could reach, he tested his weight on the nearer bell rope. It creaked but held. He looped and knotted it around the railing as Kit raced up to join him.

"Moriarty teach you how to climb a rope?" Alex asked.

"I don't know anything about rock climbing or equipment or knots," he said, "but I've climbed a rope in a gym, if that's what you mean. Moriarty showed me how to shimmy up one."

"Good. That's all you need to know," Alex said. Following Alex's instructions, Kit put the coiled rappelling rope around his shoulders. "You'll need to use it to pull yourself closer to the platform up there," Alex said. "You climb first. Yell when you're even with the platform. Go."

Kit stood on the railing. They heard another chime, another rolling ball, another snap.

"One thing at a time," Alex said, with a calm he wasn't feeling.

Kit took the nearer bell rope between his inner thighs, then wrapped it around his knee and calf and across the top of his boot. This created a brake, one that could be used to allow him to support himself without using his hands and arms if necessary. As quickly as possible, he shimmied up the rope, using mostly the power of his legs—squatting, resetting the brake point, straightening his legs, and beginning again at the next point on the rope.

Because the other end of the bell rope was tied to the center of a beam, the higher Kit climbed, the farther he moved away from the walls and closer to the center of the tower. He was just about even with the bottom of the platform Spooky watched from. It was darker up here.

"Kit!" Spooky yelled.

"We'll be out of here soon," he said, climbing a little higher. "Okay, Alex!" he yelled.

"Toss one end of the rappelling rope to Spooky. Have her wrap it around the rail, then pull yourself closer to her."

Spooky missed on the first try but caught it on the second.

"Wrap it as many times as you can," Kit said.

When she had done so, Kit called to Alex again, who helped to control the bell rope as Kit pulled himself along to her and finally climbed onto the platform.

"You made it!" she said.

"You think I would leave you up here? Where's Chase?"

Chase was already moving out toward him, his face and arms bruised and scraped.

"He's doing better now," Spooky said. Kit thought he looked confused. To his amazement, Spooky put an arm around Chase's waist. Chase put an arm across her shoulders, leaning on her for balance. "Where's my uncle Alex?"

Kit glanced down as he took the rappelling rope from his shoulders and said, "On his way up."

But suddenly, Kit heard a loud snapping noise. "Alex!"

Alex had heard it, too—the breaking of hemp. He reached for the second rope and caught hold of it just as the first one gave way. He slid several feet, unable to stop, the friction of the rough rope burning off the skin of his palms. Spooky screamed as he fell, and for terrifying seconds he envisioned becoming a human detonating device on the sandbags below. But he managed at last to wrap his legs around the rope, stopping his descent. Although the rope swung wildly with his sudden weight, he kept his grip on it. He repositioned his legs around it so that he was once again in climbing position, then forced himself to smile up at the group above him, who were looking at him with eyes wide with fear.

He heard another chime.

"I'm fine," he said, and prayed this rope would hold.

The burn in his raw palms was unrelenting as he gripped the rope, but he forced himself on and reached the level of the platform a second time. Kit had unwrapped the end of the rappelling rope from the rail and now tossed it to Alex. Alex caught it, and Kit worked with him, pulling him to the platform.

When he reached it, Chase held tightly to him. "It's going to be okay," Alex said. "We're all going to be okay. But we've got to hurry, all right? You sit next to Spooky, and I'll make a harness."

Spooky took Chase in hand and guided him to a place away from the edge. She sat next to him.

Alex leaned out of the narrow window. Meghan was below with the climbing bag. He lowered the rappelling rope, and Meghan tied the climbing bag to it. Alex pulled it up. He took out his harness, stepped into it, and quickly adjusted it to fit over his clothing. He tied a large loop into one end of the rope, making a simple adjustable sling. He attached a carabiner to his harness and an ATC—an "air traffic control" device, a belay brake that would allow him to control the speed of descent.

All the while, Alex was talking to the other three. He told them about leaning back with their knees slightly bent, keeping their legs almost perpendicular to the wall, their feet about shoulder width apart. He showed them how to hold the rope. "Use your feet against the wall, not your hands, and walk down it—don't bounce.

"I want you down there first to help on the ground," he said to Kit, knowing that Spooky and Chase would feel more confident if Kit led the way.

Alex placed the loop over Kit's head and shoulders, feeding Kit's arms through, so that it wrapped around his back just beneath his armpits. Alex checked to make sure the knot was close to Kit's chest, so that he wouldn't slip out. "Spooky and Chase, watch how Kit moves, okay?"

Kit squeezed through the window. Alex braced himself, then rapidly top belayed Kit down.

Meghan was below. "I couldn't make the calls," she said, as Kit came closer. "Everett cut the phone line and microphone line for the PA system."

"We're beyond that now," Kit said, reaching the ground and quickly freeing himself of the rope. He signaled to Alex that he was clear of it. He watched as Alex rapidly pulled it back up. "Where's Gabe?" he asked Meghan.

"Helping a wounded FBI agent."

Up in the tower, Alex heard another chime. Seven of the nine connections were in place. He told Spooky to go next. She looked mulish, but Alex, thinking of the loss of time, made it a sharp order. Chase watched as she was lowered. Alex found himself sweating again, thinking that it was taking too long. What if he had missed hearing one of the chimes? Maybe there were eight in place, and any moment now, the explosives would go off.

"She's doing okay," Chase said. "Kit has her!"

As Kit released Spooky from the rope, he turned to Meghan. "Take her out of here—please, Meghan! Go to the stables—run—get as far away as you can. You should be safe with Gabe."

"Promise you'll be right behind us."

"I promise."

Spooky opened her mouth to argue with the plan, then shut it and gave him a quick hug as she left with Meghan.

Alex pulled the rope up again.

"As fast as you can, Chase," Alex said.

"Sure."

Alex helped him secure the loop of rope beneath his arms, all the while afraid that he was asking too much of him in his present state. "Are you feeling dizzy?"

"No," Chase said, smiling at him. "I'm fine."

"Talk to me as you go, all right?"

Chase began the descent without trouble, calling as he went. It seemed he would manage after all. But when Chase was nearly to the base of the tower, Alex felt a change in the rope, and heard Chase's cry of pain even as the belay device locked under the sudden load. "Chase!"

"He'll be okay," Kit called back. "I think he's hurt his leg, though. Can you keep lowering him? I can almost reach him."

Alex slowly eased the rope out. He could feel the moment Kit had Chase, and hurried to look below. Kit had lifted Chase into a fireman's carry. Chase wasn't small, but Kit seemed to hold him easily.

"His ankle," Kit called up to him. "I think he's broken it. He passed out when he tried to put weight on it."

Another chime sounded below.

"Get him away from here!" Alex shouted. "Go, now!"

Alex heard the eighth ball snap into place.

"I don't want to leave you behind!" Kit shouted.

"I'll catch up. Kit—for God's sake, if anything happens to that boy—better one of us than all three. I'll make it. Just go!"

Kit hesitated a moment more, then hurried away.

Alex fumbled as he set up the harness and rope, his hands growing stiff, his fingers suddenly clumsy. He heard the final chime just as he reached the window, and knew he could not possibly make it down in time. Strangely, knowing that released him from his fear. He thought of Chase safe with Kit and leaned back to enjoy one last rappel.

Kit heard sirens as he ran across the baseball field. He was slowed by his burden, but began to hope they might make it clear of the explosion. Chase had passed in and out of consciousness, protesting mildly about being carried, but Kit ignored him and moved on. His chest felt tight, but he knew it was not from exertion or the weight of the teenager on his shoulders.

Just as he reached the edge of the woods, he heard the roar of the bomb going off. Its force knocked him off balance, and the ground shook beneath them. He moved to shield Chase as debris rained down on them in hard little pellets of stone and mortar. A cloud of dust rolled from where the tower had stood. The buildings nearest to the tower collapsed seconds later.

"Alex!" he screamed, but there was no answer. He stood and saw Meghan and Spooky coming toward him. "Take care of Chase," he called to them.

"Kit!" Meghan cried. "No—!"

But he had already turned back toward the cloud of dust that had once been stone.

He moved cautiously over the rubble. Fires were burning now, lighting his way, but the heat and smoke and stench were nearly unbearable.

He thought about the fact that he had been running without counting to seven. He told himself that didn't matter. But he didn't see Alex, and when he called Alex's name, there was no answer. Kit wondered, not for the first time, why he had been allowed to live.

There was still a fog of dust mixed with the smoke. It made his eyes dry. He coughed. As he moved closer to the tower, the air became worse. His nose and lungs hurt, as if he were breathing shards of glass. He coughed, then realized he hadn't, but had heard, faintly, someone else's cough. "Alex!" he yelled, but there was no answer—except the coughing. He crouched lower and followed the sound to the remains of one of the classroom buildings.

He heard a helicopter overhead now. It made it hard to hear anything else.

A bright light shone from it, though, on him, and on a figure slowing freeing itself from a pile of rubble—a ghost. The ghost was completely white, except for his blue eyes, which were squinting up at the helicopter's light. He coughed.

Alex.

Kit ran toward him, shouting, and then realized that a man who had been this much closer to an explosion wouldn't be able to hear a thing, at least not right away.

epilogue

The man who had once been known as Everett Corey awoke with a headache.

He tried to dispel the lingering effects of whatever he had to drink the night before, to make sense of the situation he found himself in. He saw a woman's navel come into view. It was a nice enough navel, he supposed, but she seemed to be upside down. It took him a little while to realize that, in fact, it was he who was upside down. That he was naked. That he was being held above the deck of a boat by a winch that was attached to ropes tied around his ankles. That his wrists, dangling uncomfortably below his head, were also bound. That there was a piece of duct tape across his mouth. There was something terribly familiar about it all.

"I think the roofies are finally wearing off," the woman said. She bent down so that he could see her face.

She was pretty, even upside down. Her hair was thick and wavy, an almost apricot-gold color. She had large green eyes. She was athletic-looking. He smiled at her, as best he could.

Alex Brandon and Moriarty stepped out of the hotel bar and into the island's afternoon heat. They began walking toward the harbor.

The hotel was favored by the most discriminating of American tourists. Everett Corey had not been a guest there, but a man matching his description was often found in its bar, buying drinks for those from his native country.

Wealthy American visitors to the island found him a helpful man of many interests, who asked nothing of them but news of home. In the few weeks he had been on the island, he had become a favorite of the staff—he was a man of style and charm—and a generous tipper.

Last night, the bartender told him, was the first time he had seen the gentleman drink too much. The bartender swore he did not serve many drinks to him, but perhaps he had been drinking before he came to the bar. He didn't behave obnoxiously. Everything was fine—he had left on the arm of a beautiful woman, a wealthy widow who was going to let him sleep it off on her yacht.

The bartender liked the newcomers, who were also generous and charming. He told them that the American gentleman was there almost every night—they should come back.

"You think he's given us the slip again?" Moriarty asked.

Alex shrugged. He looked up at the clear blue sky, felt the warm sun on his face.

Moriarty grinned. "Colorado getting too cold for you?"

"No regrets about moving there. By the way, I talked to John a little while ago."

"Let me guess. Emily and Chase were bickering. Rusty was barking, and John asked when the hell we were going to come back home."

Alex laughed. "That's about it. I could hear the fight in the background. Chase was calling Emily 'Spooky.'"

"Damn. She must have really ticked him off."

Alex felt contented with his new life, more contented than he had been in years. When the timing mechanism in the Sedgewick bell tower didn't immediately set off the explosion, he had been able to escape with not much more than a few cuts and bruises, and two cracked ribs.

He had wondered what malfunction had kept the bomb from going off immediately. Kit said, "I don't think it was a malfunction. It was intentional, I'm sure."

"Then why—?"

"For the same reason Cameron didn't kill you immediately with the garrote. If you enjoy the suffering of others, you don't grant your victims a quick death."

Alex stared at him as the implications became clear. "Everett planned for both of us to be hanging there, listening to the last ball fall into place, waiting in terror for the explosion."

"Yes."

•   •   •

Alex's recovery had given him time to think, and to consider a job offer from Kit.

He had sold the house in Manhattan Beach, and John had sold his in Long Beach. They had bought a place together in the Rocky Mountains—Kit and Moriarty each had homes nearby.

A few weeks after the night at Sedgewick, John had a long talk with Clarissa, and later, another with Miles. Alex didn't know what he had said to either of them, or if he had threatened Miles, but a decision had been made: Instead of sending him off to boarding school, Chase's parents would allow their son to come to Colorado to live with his uncles, where he'd be home schooled by a reputable, credentialed private tutor. Alex suspected, from hints John dropped now and then, that Clarissa had made it clear that she would leave Miles if he failed to agree to this arrangement.

Alex had talked to her a few times, but only about Chase. Still, he found it eased something in him to do so, allowed him to feel as if their past didn't have the bitter hold on him it once had.

They had all made it clear to Chase that he could return to California whenever he liked, for a visit or to stay. So far, he had remained in Colorado. Miles never called. Clarissa sometimes called when Miles wasn't home. Alex noticed that Emily was always a little kinder to Chase after he got one of those calls. Sometimes he thought she had picked up Kit's ability to read people.

Alex liked the work he was doing now. A man of Kit's fortune always had need of information and security, and Kit let Alex have a great deal of freedom in structuring his work life. And Alex now lived in a rock climber's paradise.

He traveled more. Some of his duties took him to California, so that when he missed it he could almost always find a reason to be there—but he never had to stay so long that the sorrow he sometimes felt in L.A. could overwhelm him.

Before coming to the South Pacific, he had gone to Southern California, to visit Gabe Taggert in the minimum security facility where he was serving a six-year sentence. Both the district attorney and the judge had been lenient, in part because an FBI agent and a recently retired sheriff's homicide detective had spoken of Gabe's heroic help in Malibu. In part it had been the incredible defense attorney Kit had paid for. It didn't hurt that Alex had helped to locate one Kevin Delacourt, the man who had done all the killing in the burglary gone bad, and proved that the only witnesses against Gabe had been on the payroll of Everett Corey. And to some degree, Alex thought, it was Gabe's genuine remorse. Judges and prosecutors didn't see that so often.

Agent David Hamilton testified that Gabe had returned to aid him, when he could have easily used the opportunity to run away. Hamilton felt sure he owed his life to him. While taking care of the agent, Gabe had discovered that Hamilton had a cell phone, used it to call for help, and stayed with him, despite knowing that he would be captured when that help arrived.

Far out at sea, under the heat of the sun, Everett Corey began to have vague recollections of the evening before. He had been feeling homesick, as usual, thinking of sneaking back into the U.S. This lovely young American woman had wandered into the place just then, a widow who invited him out to her yacht for a drink.

She had regaled him with crazy stories of her late husband, something about his parents being shot in Russia as spies, about his grandmother being a fortune-teller. He couldn't remember much else.

At that same moment, in the Colorado Rockies, while other members of the household were distracted, a yellow Lab began exploring the closet of his absent master. He found a leather dress shoe and stuck his nose down into it, verifying that its heady scent was that of his missing owner. Unable to get enough of this delight, he began gnawing it.

At that same moment, Mrs. Christopher Logan asked her husband to come out onto the lanai. He had just finished reading an e-mail from Alex. He shut the computer off and, taking a careful route that kept him away from the lines of grout in the marble tiled floor, reached his wife.

Meghan poured two glasses of champagne.

The woman on the yacht in the South Pacific stood up now and moved toward a winch. She operated it with the skill of someone who was at home on the sea and knew how to use all of the equipment on the vessel.

Everett was just over the water now. The boat was rocking gently, not under sail.

The woman lifted a bucket that seemed to have chum in it. She poured it over the side and waited patiently. Soon the water began to churn.

She took a small, sharp knife and began to prick his skin. To his horror, he bled profusely from these little wounds. He looked at the water beneath him. Single, long fins began to appear.

Terrified, he looked back at the woman. She calmly met his gaze.

"Give my *boyakina* my love," she said, and hit the switch that plunged him into the shark-infested water.

It was all over in a few minutes. She had wondered if she would feel horror or disgust. She felt relief.

She raised the sails and set a course for Hawaii. She would stop there before heading back to Malibu.

She poured a glass of champagne. She thought of her mother, at rest for almost a year now, finally free of suffering. She thought of her father, who—hearing the size of the fortune bequeathed to his daughter—had wanted to renew his relationship with her. She smiled, thinking of him waiting for a promised phone call. And waiting. And waiting. As she once had waited for his calls.

She thought of the Whitfields, who, thanks to her attorney, Mr. Blaine, had never had a chance of getting their hands on their son's money.

If she hadn't known how they had treated their son, she wouldn't have fought for it. She had never dreamed of riches, but getting the money had meant that after years of being the one who took care of others, she could do almost everything she wanted to do to take care of herself.

She couldn't say, knowing all she knew about Frederick now, that she admired her benefactor, but she had come to believe that they had met for a reason. She was the one who would not let him be forgotten, uncounted. She would remember him.

She could not deny that she remembered him fondly, or that even now, the memories of the pleasures of a single afternoon and evening made her smile. Something had happened then, something that nothing in the rest of his life or hers could diminish.

Even he had acknowledged that, she believed, with his note, and when law enforcement officials failed to find Everett Corey, she felt that she owed it to Frederick to seek revenge for Everett Corey's betrayal of him. It was not the killing on Mulholland that brought out this desire for vengeance. It was that Corey had taken what she had seen in Frederick that one evening and made the worst possible use of it. As far as she was concerned, Corey deserved to die as much for that as for any of the other misery he had inflicted on the world.

She unfolded the note that had been given to her by Mr. Blaine. The note Frederick had included with the will.

My One and Only Boyakina—

I told you I might surprise you, Vanessa. Drink a toast to me one day while you're sailing in the South Pacific. It makes me happy to imagine it.
  Thanks for making me less dangerous.

Yours always,
Frederick

P.S. If you are reading this, my mission didn't go so well. If you want to, feel free to use some of this money to hunt down the asshole who killed me. It makes me happy to imagine that, too.

"Be happy, Frederick," she said, and sipped the champagne, which had grown warm.

"What did you say the name was?" Moriarty asked the man at the boat fuel dock, who said he had refueled the young widow's yacht.

"The yacht was the *Boyakina*, sir."

"It left last night?" Alex asked.

"Yes. Please don't worry about her. The ship is seaworthy and well supplied, and she is an excellent sailor, sir. She won't have any trouble getting to New Zealand."

They thanked him and walked away.

"Auckland next?" Moriarty asked.

"A waste of time."

"You know something," Moriarty said.

"Yes. I know that we can go home now."

Moriarty studied him, then asked, "What's a *boyakina*?"

"It means 'lucky in love.' "

Moriarty laughed. "No wonder I don't know the word. Let's go back to the hotel and drink a toast to the skipper of the *Boyakina*, then."

In Maui, newlyweds Kit Logan and Meghan Taggert Logan tipped the edges of their glasses together.

"What are we drinking to?" Kit asked.

Meghan kissed him, then said, "Our luck."

acknowledgments

I have had the help and support of many generous individuals in the writing of *Nine*, but please don't blame any of those named below for my occasional inability to grasp explanations or follow instructions.

Major (Retired) John F. Mullins works as a writer and consultant when he is not training law enforcement groups or pursuing one of his many other interests. He served his country during the Vietnam War, running clandestine missions under the aegis of the Military Assistance Command–Vietnam Studies and Observations Group (MAC-V SOG). His Green Beret unit received the Presidential Unit Citation, and he is the recipient of the Silver Star, three Bronze Stars, the Purple Heart, and other awards, decorations, and badges too numerous to mention. John provided invaluable help with this book. His friendship, his wise counsel, and his sense of humor kept me going on those days when the Muse failed to show up for work.

Many thanks are due to members of the Los Angeles County Sheriff's Department for their help, most especially Barry A. J. Fisher, LASD Director of Scientific Services, who has also served as president of the American Academy of Forensic Sciences and the International Academy of Forensic Sciences, authored *Techniques of Crime Scene Investigation*, and otherwise worked tirelessly to promote a better understanding of the importance of science in crime scene investigations. Over years of talking about research questions and other matters, we've become friends, which has turned out to be a great job benefit for me.

I also thank other members of the department, including Sergeant Gil Carrillo, Homicide Detective Elizabeth Smith, and Sergeant Ken Davidson.

Other questions about police procedure were answered by John Pearsley, El Cajon Police Department; William Valles, who gave more than twenty years of service to the Long Beach Police Department before his recent retirement; and fellow writer Detective Paul Bishop, Los Angeles Police Department.

Much of what I know about dead bodies and what happens to the ones no one finds right away comes from talking to forensic anthropologists Paul Sledzik and Marilyn London. Dr. Ed Dohring has helped me to know more about what happens to the live ones, given certain injuries. Their friendship and support helps me get through every manuscript, and more. I also received help with medical matters in *Nine* from Dr. Douglas Lyle, whose generosity in answering such questions is well known by writers of crime fiction.

John Futch, Executive News Editor of the *Long Beach Press-Telegram*, never failed to provide answers to hastily e-mailed questions. Entomologist Dr. Sean O'Keefe of Morehead State University took the time to answer questions about some of Oaxaca's six-legged wildlife, and gave me good pointers about other places to look further into.

Rock climbers Chris Little and Steven Tu got me started with a helpful session about climbing, climbers, and gear, and recommended excellent reading as well as places to watch climbers. Fellow writer and rock climber Letha Albright went the extra distance—not only offering helpful, quick comments on several drafts of the book, but also by bringing her equipment to the Mayhem in the Midlands convention and demonstrating various knots and gear while we were there.

Questions about the world of true crime television programs were answered by television development executive Nancy Meyer; Justin Manask, manager with Renaissance; and video and film editor Chuck Montgomery, who has worked for ten seasons on *COPS*. I ask readers to please keep in mind that Ty Serault and *Crimesolvers USA* are totally fictional.

True friends Mary Jo Reutter and Jay Spothelfer didn't hesitate for a moment when I said, "Say, can I leave a dead body in your house?" But don't look for the house in Lakewood—it flew farther than Dorothy's place traveled to land on a witch.

The story told in *Nine* was better told thanks to the many hours of editorial work and the support given by Marysue Rucci. She's the insightful, dedicated champion writers dream of—an editor willing to help you take a chance on something new, smart enough to figure out what needs to change (and brave enough to tell you), and able to encourage you on those days when the manuscript's working title is *The *☾^@! Book*.

My deepest thanks also to Carolyn Reidy, David Rosenthal, Louise Burke, Victoria Meyer, Tara Parsons, and the incredible sales reps who work for Simon & Schuster and Pocket Books.

Many thanks to agents Philip Spitzer and Joel Gotler for their comments, support, and insights.

Sandra Cvar read the manuscript several times and gave me her Crow book, which caught my eye whenever I stared up at the bookshelves wondering what to write.

Being my friend or relative means there are long periods of time during which phone calls are cut short and one's invitations are answered with, "Sorry, I can't, I'm on a deadline." Thank you all for your patience. Especially my 'Buds—purple power rules.

Timothy, you are that center which holds me steady and true.

To you, and also to the descendants of the Moriarty Nine, my love.

about the author

Jan Burke is the recipient of the Edgar Award for Best Novel, the Agatha Award, the Macavity Award, the *Ellery Queen Mystery Magazine* Readers Award, and the *Romantic Times*'s Career Achievement Award for Contemporary Suspense. She lives in Southern California with her husband, Tim, and her dogs, Cappy and Britches. She is currently at work on her next novel.